Christmas
AT THE
CASTLE

Christmas

AT THE

CASTLE

Amanda   Joanna
McCABE   FULFORD

MILLS
BOON

Published in Great Britain 2015
by Mills & Boon, an imprint of Harlequin (UK) Limited,
Eton House, 18-24 Paradise Road, Richmond, Surrey, TW9 1SR

CHRISTMAS AT THE CASTLE © 2015 Harlequin Books S.A.

Tarnished Rose of the Court © 2012 Amanda McCabe
The Laird's Captive Wife © 2010 Joanna Fulford

ISBN: 978-0-263-91797-0

009-1115

Tarnished Rose
of the Court

AMANDA McCABE

To the Martini Club—Alicia Dean,
Christy Gronlund, Kathy Wheeler!
Thanks for the inspiration, and for always
keeping Friday nights fun…

Amanda McCabe wrote her first romance at the age of sixteen—a vast epic, starring all her friends as the characters, written secretly during algebra class. She's never since used algebra, but her books have been nominated for many awards, including the RITA®, RT Reviewers' Choice Award, the Booksellers Best, the National Readers' Choice Award and the Holt Medallion. She lives in Oklahoma with her husband, one dog and one cat.

Chapter One

Whitehall Palace, December 1564

It *was* him.

Suddenly dizzy, Celia Sutton reached out to steady herself against the panelled wall of Queen Elizabeth's presence chamber. The thick crowd had pressed in around her again, obscuring her view with a sea of jewelled velvet and embroidered satin. The nervous laughter and high-pitched chatter as they waited anxiously to petition the Queen sounded like a flock of birds in her ears, buzzing and formless.

She rubbed her hand over her eyes and looked again, standing on tiptoe to try and peer over the crowd. She could no longer see him. Not even that tiny glimpse of his tall figure by the door. The flash of his careless grin. He was gone.

Or maybe he had never been there at all. Maybe it had just been her imagination playing tricks on her. She had not been sleeping well—had spent too many late nights here at Queen Elizabeth's Christmas revels. She had too many worries, and it was wearing on her. That was all.

And yet—he had looked so *real*.

"It was not him," she whispered. John Brandon was gone. She had not seen him for over three years—three very long, hard years—and she would never see him again. What was more, she did not *want* to see him. It would only remind her of the foolish girl she'd once been, of her old weakness for his handsome face, and right now she needed all her strength.

She pushed herself away from the wall and took a deep breath, trying to stand perfectly still, to keep herself calm. The Queen would call for her soon, and she had to have all her wits about her when they met. Her entire life depended on it. She should look only to the future now, not to the past. Not to John Brandon.

But still that fleeting image lingered in her mind, that glimpse of his lean, muscled figure through the crowd and the pounding of her heart at the sight. Despite the roaring fire in the stone grates, the close press of the crowd, and her own fur-trimmed black and purple velvet gown, she shivered.

All around her were desperate faces—people who saw their last chance in catching the Queen's attention. Did she look like them? She feared it was so. What would John say if he could see her now? Would he even recognise her?

The door to the Queen's privy chamber opened and everyone's attention turned towards it in the hope their name would now be called. Hope sank down again when they saw it was only Anton Gustavson and Lord Langley, the last parties to be called to consult with Queen Elizabeth. The nervous chatter fluttered anew.

Celia froze when her gaze met Anton's. He was her long-lost Swedish cousin, recently arrived in England to lay his claim to their grandfather's estate at Briony Manor. That estate was Celia's last hope for a comfortable, independent life in which she did not have to answer to the whims of a cruel man any longer. But as she had watched Anton charm the Queen, and every other lady at Court, her hopes had slipped away. He would have the estate, and she would be thrown back to the dubious mercy of her late husband's family.

Anton gave her a wary nod, and she curtsied in answer. He was the only family she had left, yet she did not know him and could not trust him. That was one of the hard lessons John Brandon had once taught her—never to trust in appearances or emotions. Always to be cautious.

Anton's latest flirtation, the beautiful golden-blonde Rosamund Ramsay, came to his side and gently touched his arm. He smiled down at her, and they gazed into each other's eyes as if the crowded chamber, the whole world, had vanished but for the two of them.

A cold sadness washed over Celia at the sight. She had once looked at John like that, sure that he felt that incandescent connection too. But it had been false in the end.

She turned away from the sight of Anton and Rosamund and pretended to study the tapestry on the wall. But the vivid greens and reds of the silken threads blurred in her vision, and she saw only that long-ago summer day. The sun so bright and warm in a cloudless azure sky, the cool shadows under the ancient oak tree where she'd waited for him. Imagining his kisses, the embrace of his strong body…

But he had not come, even after he'd hinted at a future with her. The warm sun had melted away and there had been only the shadows.

It was not him, she told herself fiercely. He was not here. Not now.

The door swung open again, and this time it was the Queen's major-domo. A tense hush fell over the crowd.

Celia turned around to face him, wiping fiercely at her eyes. She hadn't cried in three years. She could not start now.

"Mistress Celia Sutton, Her Grace will see you now," the man announced.

Bitterly envious looks spun towards Celia, but she ignored them and slowly made her way forward. This was her chance. She couldn't let the memory of John Brandon distract her for even an instant. He had taken too much from her already.

Just inside the door a small looking glass hung on the wall, and she glimpsed her reflection there—the black cap on her smooth, tightly pinned dark hair, the high fur collar of her gown, the jet earrings in her ears. In mourning for a husband she could not truly mourn.

Her face looked chalk-white with worry, just like everyone else's in that room outside, but red streaked her cheekbones as if in memory of that long-ago summer's day. Her grey eyes glowed with unshed tears.

She forced them away, clasping her hands tightly before her waist as she followed the major-domo into the inner sanctum of the privy chamber. It was also crowded there, but the atmosphere was lighter, the conversation free of the strained quality outside. Ladies-in-waiting in their pale silks sat on cushions and low stools scattered over the floor and around the marble fireplace, whispering and laughing over their embroidery. Handsome young courtiers played cards in the corner, casting flirtatious glances at the ladies.

But the Queen's most favourite of all, Robert Dudley, was nowhere to be seen. Everyone said that after the alarming events of the Christmas season, the attempts on the Queen's life, he worked day and night to ensure the security of the palace. Nor was the Queen's chief secretary, Lord Burghley, who so rarely left her side, in evidence.

Queen Elizabeth sat by herself next to the window, a table covered with the scrolls of petitions beside her. The pale grey sunlight filtered through the thick glass, turning her red-gold hair into a fiery halo and making her fair ivory skin glow. She wore a splendourous robe of crimson velvet trimmed with white fur over a gold silk gown, rubies on her fingers and in her ears, and a band of pearls holding back her hair.

She looked every inch the young Sun Queen, but her dark eyes were shadowed and the set of her mouth was grim, as if the events of the last few days had taken their toll on her.

Celia had heard that those strange occurrences were not the Queen's only worries. Parties from Austria and Sweden were at Whitehall to press their marriage suits. Spain and France were constant threats. And the Queen's cousin to the north, Mary Queen of Scots, was always a thorn in Elizabeth's side.

It was almost enough to make Celia feel her own troubles were tiny in comparison! No one was trying to kill her *or* marry her.

"Mistress Sutton," Queen Elizabeth said. "You have had a long wait, I fear."

Celia curtsied low and made her way to the Queen's desk. Elizabeth tapped her long pale fingers on the papers, her rings sparkling. "I'm just grateful Your Grace has the time to meet with me."

Elizabeth waved her words away. "You may not be so grateful when you hear what I have to say, Mistress Sutton. Please sit."

A footman leaped forward with a stool, and Celia sank onto it gratefully. She had a terrible feeling this interview would not go as she so fervently wished. "Briony Manor, Your Grace?"

"Aye." Elizabeth held up a scroll. "It seems clear to us that your grandfather's wish was for the estate to go to Master Gustavson's mother and then to him. We feel we cannot go against this."

Celia felt that chill wash over her again—the cold of disappointment, of an anger she had to suppress. If she could not go to Briony, where *could* she go? What would be her home? "Yes, Your Grace."

"I am sorry," Elizabeth said, and there was a tinge of true regret in her voice. She even used "I" instead of the official "we". "When I was a girl, I had no true place of my own. No place where I could be assured of my own security. Everything I had was dependent on others—my father, my brother, my sister. Even my life depended on their whims."

Celia glanced at the Queen in surprise. Elizabeth so seldom spoke of the difficult past. Why would she now, and to Celia of all people? "Your Grace?"

"I know how you must feel, Mistress Sutton. We are alike in some ways, I think. And that is why I sense that I can ask a great favour of you."

Ask? Or demand? "I will do anything I can to serve Your Grace, of course."

Elizabeth tapped at the papers again. "You have heard the recent rumours surrounding my cousin Queen Mary, I am sure. She always seems of such acute interest to my courtiers."

"I—well, aye, Your Grace. I sometimes hear tales of Queen Mary. Is there a specific rumour you refer to?"

Elizabeth laughed. "Oh, yes, there *are* many. But I refer to the fact that she intends to marry again. They say she has hopes of a union equal to her first with the King of France. I hear she has her sights set on Don Carlos of Spain—King Phillip's son."

"I have heard such rumours as well, Your Grace," Celia said. She had also heard Don Carlos was a violent lunatic, but even a reputed great beauty like Queen Mary seemed willing to overlook that for the chance to be Queen of Spain.

Elizabeth suddenly slammed her fist down on the desk, sending an inkwell clattering to the floor. "That cannot be! My cousin cannot make such a powerful alliance. She is menace enough as it is. I have suggested she should marry an English nobleman. I must have someone I can trust in her Court."

"Your Grace?" Celia said in confusion. How could she assist in such a task?

Elizabeth lowered her voice to a whisper. "I have a plan, you see, Mistress Sutton. But I will need help to see it carried off."

"How can I help, Your Grace? I know of no candidates for Queen Mary's hand."

"Oh, I will take care of that, Mistress Sutton. I have the perfect candidate in mind—someone I can trust completely. I cannot say who just yet, but I promise you will know all you need to soon." The Queen sat back in her chair and reached for one of the papers on her desk. "In the meantime my cousin, the Countess of Lennox, who is Mary's cousin as well, petitions for her son Lord Darnley to be given a passport to visit his father who is now resident in Edinburgh."

Celia nodded. She knew well of the Countess's petition, as Lady Lennox had made certain indiscreet confidences to her in the last few days. Lady Lennox hoped that once Queen Mary met Lord Darnley, who was tall, blond and angelically handsome, she would marry him and make him King of Scotland. His own royal lineage would strengthen Mary's claim to be Elizabeth's heir.

Celia was not so sure such a plan could work, hinging as it did on Lord Darnley. Even she could see, from her brief time at Court, that he was a drunken braggart under his pretty exterior, and rather too fond of men.

"Yes, Your Grace," she said.

"It appears Lady Lennox has made a friend of you in these last few days."

"Lady Lennox has been welcoming to me. But she tells me little except that she misses her husband."

"I have been reluctant to let Lord Darnley travel north," Elizabeth said. "He seems the sort it is best to keep an eye on. But Lord Burghley counsels, and I concur, that we should allow him this passport now. He will depart for Scotland in a week's time."

"So soon, Your Grace?" Celia was surprised anyone could travel now. It was the coldest winter anyone could remember, with the Thames frozen through. Sensible people stayed home by their fires.

"I think time is imperative in this matter," the Queen said. "And Lord Darnley seems eager to go. I wish for you, Mistress Sutton, to be one of the travel party."

Celia tried not to gape at the Queen like a country lackwit. She had no idea what to say or even how to calm her jumbled thoughts. She—go to Scotland? "I fear I do not quite understand how I could help you in Edinburgh, Your Grace."

Elizabeth gave an impatient sigh. "You will serve Queen Mary as a lady-in-waiting—a gift from me. I need a lady's close eye on matters there, Mistress Sutton. Men are all very well for certain things, of course, and Burghley will have his spies in the party. But a woman sees things men are blind to—especially when it comes to other women. I need to know Mary's true thoughts concerning her possible marriage. And I need to know if she is…persuadable in that regard."

"And you believe I can do that?" Celia said carefully.

Elizabeth laughed. "I am sure you can. I have been watching you these last few days, Mistress Sutton, and I see how you notice everything around you. How you observe and listen. I need someone like that. Not a preening Court peacock who sees nothing but the cut of their own coat. It is vital that I know everything my cousin does right now. The security of our northern borders depends on her marital choice."

Celia nodded. She knew how unpredictable the Scottish Queen could be. Everyone knew that. And Celia did watch and listen; it was the only way for a woman alone to survive. She also knew how limited her own choices were. With no money or estate of her own, and no husband or family to lean on, she was dependent on the Queen's favour.

Better that than the cold charity of her in-laws.

"You would be rewarded for your efforts, of course," the Queen said. "As soon as Queen Mary's marriage is settled satisfactorily and you have returned to our Court you shall have a marriage of your own. The finest I can arrange, I promise you, Mistress Sutton. And then you will be settled for life."

Celia would rather have an estate of her own than another husband. In her experience husbands were useless things. But for now she would take what the Queen offered—and renegotiate later.

"What would be a—a satisfactory settlement?" she asked.

Elizabeth smiled and slid a folded letter from under the ledger on her desk to give to Celia. "This will tell you all you need to know, Mistress Sutton. I intend to propose my own marital candidate to Mary. When you have messages to send to me, you may give them to my own trusted contact and he will see they reach me quickly."

Celia tucked the letter into her velvet sleeve. "Contact, Your Grace?"

"Aye. You can meet him now." Elizabeth gestured to the major-domo, who bowed and disappeared through a door tucked into the panelling. He returned in only a moment, followed by a tall, lean man clad in fashionable black and tawny velvet and satin.

John Brandon. It *was* him she had seen before. He was no illusion. Celia half rose at the sight of him, and then fell back onto her stool. She felt cold all over again.

His eyes—those bright sky-blue eyes she had once loved so much—widened when they glimpsed her. For a fleeting instant she saw a flare of emotion in their depths. A hint of a smile touched his lips. But a veil quickly fell over those eyes, and she could read nothing there but fashionable boredom. He gave no signs of recognising her at all.

"Ah, Sir John, there you are," Queen Elizabeth said. She waved him forward, holding out her hand for him to bow over. He gave her an elaborate salute and a flirtatious grin that made her laugh.

"Your Grace outshines the sun itself," he said. "Even in the midst of the winter you send us warmth and light."

"Flatterer," the Queen said, laughing even harder.

Celia remembered that smile all too well, and how it also had made *her* laugh and blush whenever he turned it in her direction. Back then it had been half hidden in a close-cropped beard. Now he was clean-shaven, the sharp, elegant angles of his chiselled face revealed and the full force of that smile unleashed.

From the corner of her eye Celia saw some of the young ladies-in-waiting sigh and giggle. Yes, she remembered very well that feeling—that sense of melting under the heat of his smile. But that had been long ago, and she had learned the painful consequences of falling under John Brandon's spell.

"Sir John, this is Mistress Celia Sutton, who will also be journeying to Scotland," Queen Elizabeth said. She lowered her voice to whisper confidentially, "She will give you any messages to be dispatched directly to me. You must see that she stays safe in Edinburgh."

A frown flickered over John's face, as if he was not happy with the task. But he could not be any less happy than Celia. Her heart sank in appalled confusion. She would have to travel with *him*? Confide in *him*?

She had the wild impulse to leap from her seat, cry out that she refused the Queen's task and run from the room. But she forced herself to stay where she was, biting her lip until she tasted blood to keep from shouting. She could not refuse the Queen. There was nowhere for her to run.

John's frown vanished as quickly as Celia had glimpsed it. He bowed again and said, "I am Your Grace's servant in all things," he said.

Elizabeth leaned back in her chair with a smug little cat's smile. "Come now, Sir John. This is surely far from the most onerous task I have asked of you. Mistress Sutton is quite pretty, is she not? I'm sure spending time with her will not be so difficult on your long journey."

Celia froze at the Queen's teasing words. John's glance flickered over her with not much interest. "I fear that when Your Grace is near I can see nothing else," he said.

Elizabeth laughed. "Nevertheless, I expect the two of you will work together very well. Your mother was Scottish, was she not, Sir John?"

A muscle tightened along John's jaw. "Yes, Your Grace."

"She even lived at the Court of Queen Mary's mother, when Marie of Guise was Regent, I believe?" Elizabeth said carelessly, as if those years when the English and Scottish armies under Queen Marie de Guise had been at bitter war was a mere trifle. "So you should be able to assist Mistress Sutton in learning the ways of the Scottish Court. Perhaps you will even rediscover your own family there."

"I have no family but that of England, Your Grace," he said tightly.

Elizabeth waved this away and said, "You may both leave us now. You will have a great many tasks to prepare for your journey, and I must finish these petitions before tonight's banquet."

Celia rose slowly from her stool and curtsied, her legs trembling and unsteady. She still could not quite believe all that happened in this strange short meeting. Her worries of having no home or income had been whisked away, only to be replaced by the sudden reappearance of John Brandon and a journey to Scotland to spy on Queen Mary. Her head spun with it all.

She would have laughed if it was not so coldly serious.

John bowed to the Queen, and the major-domo came forward again to lead them away. He took them not to the crowded presence chamber but through a hidden door into a small, dimly lit closet. After the brightness of the privy chamber Celia could see nothing but the shadow of heavy tapestries on dark wood walls.

She rubbed her hand over her eyes and took a deep breath. When she looked again the servant was gone— and she was alone with John.

He watched her closely, his lean, muscled shoulders tense and his handsome face wiped of all expression.

"Hello, Celia," he said quietly. "It has been a long time, has it not?"

Chapter Two

Celia stared up at John in the shadows of the closet. The faint, hazy bars of light fell over his face, and she saw that the years had changed him just as they had her. He was leaner, harder, his eyes a wintry, icy blue as they studied her warily.

Once she had thought those eyes as warm as a summer sky, melting her heart, piercing all her defences. But now her heart was a stone, a heavy weight within her that was numb to all feeling. It was better this way. Feelings were deceptive, treacherous. Never to be trusted.

Especially when it came to this man.

Celia stepped back until she felt the hard wood panelling of the wall against her shoulders. He didn't move, yet his eyes never wavered from her face and it felt as if he followed her. It felt as if he pressed up against her in that dim, quiet light, his hard, hot body touching her as it once had. Demanding a response from her.

She twisted her hands into her skirts, struggling not to look away from him. Not to show her weakness.

"Aye, it *has* been a long while," she said, once she finally found her voice again.

The last time she'd seen him he had been kissing her beneath that tree, their secret meeting place. His body had held her against the rough wood of the trunk, just as she braced herself to the wall now. He had kissed her, his mouth and tongue claiming hers, demanding she give him all her response as he dragged her skirt up, baring her to his touch. There had been such a wild desperation between them that day, a need such as she had never known. He had made her dream of a romantic, glorious future with him.

And the next day he was gone. Vanished without a word.

"Yet not nearly long enough," she said coldly. "I thought never to see you again."

His glance swept down over her again, taking in her austere gown, her ringless fingers, the tight, smooth twist of her hair. For an instant another image flashed in her mind. John taking her hair down, freeing it from its pins and running his hands through its heavy length. Calling it a fairy queen's hair as he buried his face in it...

Those all-seeing blue eyes focused on her face again, narrowing as he watched her closely, as if seeking her thoughts. Once she had gifted him with all she was, given herself to him in every way.

She hoped she was no longer such a fool. She looked back at him with a steady, cool daring. Let him try to read her, play her again. The besotted, silly, giddy Celia he'd once known was gone. John had killed her—with the able assistance of her wretched husband and foolish brother.

"I've thought of you, Celia," he said.

She quickly scrambled to cover her surprise at his words. He had *thought* of her? Surely not. Unless it had been to chuckle at her naivety. The country girl who had fallen so easily for his charm, his dalliance to pass the time of rural exile.

Celia laughed. "I would have thought Court life would be far too busy for any idle nostalgia, John. So many tournaments to win, ladies to woo. I'm sure every moment is filled for a man of your…assets."

She let her gaze drift down over his body—the long, lean line of his legs in his tall leather boots, the snake-like hips and powerful shoulders. The years had not softened him one bit.

Her stare slid over the bulge in his breeches and she had to turn away. She remembered that part of him all too well…hot velvet over steel, sliding against her, inside of her.

"Aye," she said tightly. "You must be busy indeed."

Something seemed to crack in his iron control then. As fast as the strike of a hawk diving for its prey he seized her arms in his hard hands and held her against the wall. Those blue eyes she had thought so icy burned down at her in a white-hot blaze.

Celia could feel her own carefully built walls slipping and she struggled to hold onto them. Nay, this could not be happening! Five minutes in John's presence could not be destroying all she had built up to protect herself. She twisted away from him but he wouldn't let her go.

"Let me go!" she cried. His hands just tightened, holding her between the wall and his body. The heat of him, the vital, fiery *life* that had always been a part of him, wrapped around her like velvety unbreakable bonds. She remembered the tenderness, the need she had once felt with him.

"What has happened to you, Celia?" he said roughly.

"What do you mean?" she gasped.

She went very still and stared at the hard angle of his jaw above the high collar of his doublet. A muscle flexed there and his lips were pressed in an angry line. She imagined twisting her hands in that collar, tighter and tighter, until he let her go. Until she could hurt him as he had once hurt her.

"You look like the Celia I remember," he said. One hand slid slowly down her arm, rubbing her velvet sleeve over her skin until he touched her bare wrist. Something flared in his eyes as he felt the leap of her pulse, and he twined his fingers with hers.

Celia was too frozen to pull away. She felt like the hawk's prey in truth, mesmerised as he swooped closer and closer.

"You're even more beautiful than you were then," he said, his voice softer and deeper. "But your eyes are hard."

Celia jerked in his arms. "You mean I am not a foolish, gullible girl who can be lured by a man's pretty words? I have learned my lesson well since we last met, John, and I'm grateful for it."

He raised the hand he held to study her fingers. The pale skin and neat buffed nails. His thumb brushed over her bare ring finger. Celia tried to twist out of his caress, but despite his deceptive gentleness he held her fast.

"You aren't married?" he asked.

"Not any longer," she answered with a bitter laugh. "Thanks to God's mercy. And I intend never to be again."

He raised her hand, and to her shock pressed his mouth to the hollow of her palm. His lips were parted, and she could feel the moist heat of him moving slowly over her skin. It made her legs tremble, her whole treacherous body go weak, and she braced herself tighter against the wall.

That weakness, that rush of need she had thought she was finished with, made her angry. She made herself go stiff and unyielding, building her defensive walls up again stone by hard-won stone.

"I may have changed, John, but you certainly have not," she said coldly. "You still take what you want with no thought for anyone else. A conquering warrior who discards whatever no longer amuses you."

His mouth froze on her skin. Slowly he raised his head and his stare met hers. She almost gasped at the raw, elemental fury she saw in those depths. The blue had turned almost black, like the power of a summer storm.

"You know nothing of me," he whispered, and it was all the more forceful for its softness. "Nothing of what I have had to do in my life."

I know you left me! her mind cried out. Left her to the cruel hands of her husband, to a life where she had nowhere to turn for sanctuary. She bit down on her lip to keep from shouting the words aloud.

"I know I do not want to work with you on the Queen's business," she said.

"No more than I want to work with you," he answered. With one more hard glance down her body, he abruptly let her go and spun away from her. His back and shoulders were rigid as he raked his hands through his hair. "But the Queen has commanded it. Would you go against her orders?"

Celia braced her palms against the wall, trying to still the primitive urge to smooth the light brown waves of his hair where he had tousled them. "Of course I would not go against the Queen."

"Then to Edinburgh we go," he said.

He heaved in a deep breath, and Celia could practically see his armour lowered back into place. He shot her a humourless smile over his shoulder.

"I shall see you at the ball tonight, Celia."

She watched him leave the small closet, the door clicking shut behind him. She was surrounded by heavy silence, pressing in on her from every corner until she nearly screamed from it.

She let herself slide down the wall until she sat in the puddle of her skirts. Her head was pounding, and she let it drop down into her hands as she struggled to hold back the tears.

She had thought her life could become no worse, no more complicated. But she had been wrong. Sir John Brandon was the greatest, most terrible complication of all.

* * *

God's blood. Celia Sutton.

John shoved the pile of documents away so violently that many of them fluttered to the floor, and slumped back in his chair. It was of vital importance that he read all of them, that he knew exactly what he would be up against in Scotland, yet all he could see, all he could think about, was Celia.

Celia. Celia.

He raked his fingers hard through his hair, but she wouldn't be dislodged from his mind. Those cool grey eyes watching him in the shadows of that closet, sliding down his body as if she was remembering exactly what he was remembering himself.

The hot touch of bare skin to bare skin, mouths and hands exploring, tasting.

Her keening cries as he entered her, joined with her more deeply and truly than he ever had with anyone before. Or since.

But then her regard had changed in an instant, becoming hard and distant, cold as the frozen Thames outside his window. His Celia—the woman whose secret memory had sustained him for so long, despite everything—was gone.

Or maybe she was just hidden, buried behind those crossed swords he'd seen in this new, hard Celia's eyes. It was clear she had walled herself away from something, that her soul had been deeply wounded, and no matter what they had once been to each other she wouldn't let him reach her now. And she was quite right. One of those wounds on her soul had been placed there by him.

Once he had wanted her more than anything else in the world. She had awakened things in him he had thought he could never feel. He had even dared to dream of a future with her for one brief, bright moment. That connection was still there, after all these years. When he'd touched her it had been as if he could sense her thoughts, her fury, her passion. Hatred so close to lust he'd almost tasted it, because it had called out to the yearnings he felt just as strongly.

It had taken every ounce of his iron control not to push her to the floor, shove her skirts above her waist, raise her hips in his hands and drive his tongue into her. Taste her, feel her, until her walls fell and his Celia was with him again. The girl who had once made him smile.

He groaned as he felt the tightness in his codpiece, half-hard ever since he'd first touched her, lengthen. Just the memory of how she tasted, like summer honey, the way she would drive her fingers into his hair and pull him closer between her legs, had him aroused.

But if the murderous look in her eyes was any indication, memories were as close as he would ever get to *that* part of her again.

John pushed himself up from his chair and strode over to the window of his small chamber. He opened the casement to let the freezing wind rush over him, despite the fact that he had discarded his doublet and wore only a thin linen shirt. He needed the cold to remind him of his task, his duty. He had never failed in his service to the Queen. He couldn't fail now, no matter how much Celia distracted him.

He could see the river, a frozen silver ribbon as grey and icy as Celia's eyes. This Christmas season had been the coldest anyone could remember, so frigid the Thames had frozen solid and a frost fair was set up on the surface. It had warmed a bit in the quiet days after the Christmas revels, but chunks of ice still floated along the water and the people who dared to go outside were muffled in cloaks and scarves.

And he would have to travel to Scotland in the cold—and take Celia with him. Long days huddled together for heat, nights in secluded inns, bound together in danger and service to Queen Elizabeth. Surely there she would open to him? Surely there he could destroy all her shields, one by one, until his Celia was revealed to him again?

Nay! John cracked his palm down hard on the windowsill, splintering the cold brittle wood. This journey was meant to neutralise the constant threat of Queen Mary and her possible marriage alliances, not to be a chance for him to lose himself in Celia all over again. To dream of what he could never have. He had to remember that always.

Any chance he and Celia had ever had was long lost.

A knock sounded at the door.

"Enter!" John barked, louder than he'd intended. His temper was on edge and he had to rein it in.

But he hadn't completely concealed his anger when his friend Lord Marcus Stanville came into the room, caught a glimpse of John's face, and raised his dark golden brow.

"Perhaps I should come back another time," Marcus said. "If I don't want my nose bashed in by your fist."

John grinned reluctantly and shook his head. He sat back down in his chair and rubbed at the back of his neck. "The ladies of the Court would never forgive me if I ruined your pretty face."

Marcus gave an answering grin and shook back the long, tawny mane the ladies also loved. If they hadn't been friends since childhood, fostered in the same household after their parents died, John would surely hate the popinjay.

Yet he knew that the handsome face concealed a devious mind and a quick sword arm. They had saved each other's lives more than once.

"They *do* seem terribly fond of my visage just as it is," Marcus said, carelessly sprawling out in the other chair. "But a judiciously placed wound or two might elicit some sympathy in the heart of a certain lady..."

"Lady Felicity again?"

"Aye. She's a hard-hearted wench."

John laughed. "You just aren't accustomed to chasing. Usually women throw themselves under your feet for a mere smile."

Marcus gave a snort. "Says the man who has every woman in London lining up for his bed."

John scowled as he remembered Celia's grey eyes, cold as the winter sky when she looked at him. "Not every woman," he muttered.

"What? Never say a lady has refused Sir John Brandon! Have pigs been seen flying over London Bridge? Has Armageddon arrived?"

John threw a heavy book at Marcus's laughing head. Marcus merely ducked and tossed it right back.

"I never thought to see this day," Marcus said. "No wonder you looked so thunderstruck."

"Enjoy it while you can," John said. "For soon enough we will be on our way to bloody freezing Edinburgh."

Marcus grew sombre. "Aye, so we will. 'Tis not an assignment I relish, playing nursemaid to that drunken lordling lout Darnley. I wager the devil himself couldn't keep *him* out of trouble."

"I think there is more to this journey than that," John said.

Marcus sat forward in his chair, his hands braced on his knees. "You've talked to Burghley, then?"

"Not as yet, but I'm sure we will be summoned tomorrow."

"Will it be like our journey to Paris?"

John remembered Paris and what had happened there. The deceptions and danger. The sorrow over what had happened with Celia. "The Scottish Queen is always a thorn in Elizabeth's side."

"And will we have to pluck it out?"

"I fear so. One way or another." All while John dealt with his own thorn—one with the softest, palest skin beneath her barbs. "The Queen is sending someone else to Edinburgh as well."

Marcus groaned. "As well as Darnley and his cronies?"

"Aye. Mistress Celia Sutton." Even saying her name, feeling it on his tongue, twisted something deep inside him. Those tender feelings he had once had for her haunted him now.

"Celia Sutton?" Marcus said, his eyes widening. "She could freeze a man's balls off just with a look."

John gave a harsh laugh as he remembered the erection that had only just subsided. An almost painful hardness just from her look, her touch. The smell of her skin. "She is to be the Queen's own emissary—a representative to show Elizabeth's affections to her cousin."

"She might as well have sent a poisoned ring, then," Marcus scoffed. "Though there is something about Mistress Sutton that seems..."

His voice trailed away, and his eyes sharpened with speculation as he looked at John.

John held up his hand. "Do not even say it."

They had been friends so long that Marcus obviously saw the warning in John's face. He shrugged and pushed himself to his feet.

"Your passions are your own business, John," he said, "no matter how strange. Just as mine are. And now I must go and dress for the Queen's ball. I have little time left to woo Lady Felicity before we leave for hell."

Marcus strode from the room, leaving John alone to his brooding thoughts again. He looked back outside, to where the cold winter night was quickly closing in. Torches flickered along the banks of the river, the only light in the cloud-covered city.

It felt as if he was already in hell. He had been for

three years—ever since he'd betrayed Celia and thus lost her for ever. The only woman he could have dared to envisage a future with had been her.

Chapter Three

Celia stared at her reflection in the small looking glass as the maidservant brushed and plaited her hair before pinning it up in a tightly wound knot. She was even gladder now that the Queen had given her a rare, precious private chamber, away from anyone else's prying eyes and gossiping tongues. Anyone looking at her now would surely see the agitation in her eyes, the way she could not keep her hands still.

She twisted them harder in her lap, buried them in the fur trim of her robe. She had to go down to the ball soon, and there she would have to smile and talk as if nothing was amiss. She would have to listen and watch, to learn all she could about the hidden reasons for this sudden journey to Edinburgh. She had to be wary and cautious as always, careful of every step.

She closed her eyes, suddenly so weary. She had been cautious every day, every minute, for three years. Would the rest of her life be like this? She was very much afraid it would. Thomas Sutton was dead, but the taut wariness was still there. The certainty of pain.

In an unconscious gesture she rubbed at her shoulder. It was long healed, but sometimes she could vow she still felt it. She had fought so hard for control. She would not lose it now. Not because of *him*.

Behind her closed eyes she saw John Brandon's face, half in mysterious shadow as he held her to the wall, his blue eyes piercing through her like a touch, as if he saw past her careful armour to everything she kept hidden. His hands on her had roused so much within her— things she'd thought long-dead and buried, things she'd thought she could never feel again because her marriage had killed them in her.

One look from John scared her more than any of Thomas's blows ever could. Because Thomas had not known her, had never possessed her. Not really. She had always hidden her true self from him even as he'd tried to beat it from her. But John had once possessed all of her, everything she had to offer, and because of him it was gone now.

"Are you quite well, Mistress Sutton?" she heard the maid ask, bringing her back to the present moment.

Celia opened her eyes and gave the girl a polite smile. "Just a bit of a headache. It will soon pass."

"Shall I loosen your hair a bit, then? A style of loose curls here and here is quite fashionable."

Celia studied herself in the looking glass. Her hair was already dressed as it always was, the heavy black waves tightly plaited and pinned in a knot at the nape of her neck. Since it was a ball, a beaded black caul covered the knot, but that was its only decoration. It was all part of the armour.

"Nay, this will do," she said, slipping on her jet and pearl earrings. "I will dress now."

She eased out of her robe and let the maid help her into her gown: a bodice and overskirt of black velvet with a stomacher and petticoat of glossy purple brocade trimmed with jet beads. Her sleeves were also black, tied with purple ribbons. Even her shoes and the garters that bound her white silk stockings were black.

Thomas had been dead for many months. She could put aside mourning and wear colours again, the blues and greens she had once loved, but she liked the reminder of where she had been. Where she vowed never to be again. The half-world of mourning suited her.

Celia held up her arm for the maid to lace on the tight sleeves and pluck bits of the white chemise between the ribbons. As she stared at the fireplace she let herself drift away, just for a moment, and remember when she first met John.

She'd been just a silly girl then, who had never been to Court, never away from her family and their country gentry neighbours. John Brandon had been sent to stay with his uncle at a nearby estate, exiled from Court for some unknown scandal. He'd been meant to rusticate until he had learned his lesson and repented.

That dark hint of some roguish secret had made her cousins all afire with speculation even before they'd met him, and Celia had not been immune to it. She'd liked to sit by the fire of a winter evening and listen to romantic tales as much as any young lady, and a handsome rake from London seemed a perfect part of such stories. Then, when she had seen him at last, a glimpse across his uncle's hall at a banquet…

It had been as if the whole world tipped upside down and everything looked completely different. His eyes, his smile, the way he strode through the crowd right to her side and kissed her hand—she'd been dazzled.

Celia shook her head hard now as she remembered. *Foolish, foolish girl.*

And now foolish woman. For hadn't she almost melted all over again when he touched her today?

But the next time they met, touched, *she* would be the one in control. She had to be.

As soon as the maid had finished adjusting her gown she fastened a black feather fan and a silver pomander to the chain girdle at her waist. As she had no sword, they would have to do.

But when the maid turned away she bent and gathered up her skirts to tuck a small dagger in the sheath at her garter. She could not go down there completely unarmed.

As she made her way down the many staircases and along the twisting corridors of the palace the crowd grew thicker the closer she came to the great hall. After the nightly revels of Christmas Celia would have thought the courtiers would be weary of Queen Elizabeth's glittering displays, but there was a hum of excitement in the air, in the buzz of laughter and chatter around her as she was swept along.

She could hear music—the lively strains of a galliard—and the thunderous pattern of dancing feet. All around her was the rustle of fine satins, the flash of jewels, the smell of expensive perfumes, warm skin and wine. It all made her head spin, but she was caught in the tide now and could not get away. She was swept inexorably into the hall.

She slid her way through the crowd to a spot near one of the tapestry-hung walls, a little apart from all the frantic laughter, the jostling for position. She couldn't breathe when she was caught in the very midst of it all, buffeted by so many touches, so much desperate energy.

She took a goblet of wine from one of the servants in the Queen's livery and sipped at the rich red French wine as she studied the gathering. She prayed John would not be there, would not see her. She had barely recovered her hard-won composure after their last meeting. His body close to hers, his heat and scent in that dark closet…

Celia took a long gulp of the wine, and then another. She usually only drank small beer, slowly, always remembering what a monster drink had made of her husband. How it had destroyed her father after what had happened to her poor brother. But tonight she needed every fortification she could find.

As the wine warmed her blood she examined the company. The Queen led the dancing with her handsome Robert Dudley, who was now the Earl of Leicester, reputedly to make him of a stature worthy to be the Queen of Scots's consort. Queen Elizabeth's red-gold hair shimmered brighter than her gold brocade gown as she laughed and leaped, twirling higher and lighter than everyone else. The troubles of the last few weeks, and the troubles sure to come, seemed forgotten in the music and merriment.

Celia's gaze trailed over the Countess of Lennox, a great, large woman in black who stood near another wall and studied the revels with her lips pressed tightly together. She gave Celia a quick nod before turning to her son. Lord Darnley sulked and drank by her side, though even Celia knew he would not be there long. He could not stay away from his debauched pleasures for more than an hour.

He was handsome, Celia would admit that—very tall and lean, with golden hair and fine Tudor features. But, like his mother's, his mouth had a cruel cast that Celia recognised all too well. She didn't trust him, and she didn't know what game Queen Elizabeth played with him, Leicester and Mary.

She definitely did not know why *she* had to be involved in the messy quagmire. But beggars could not be choosers.

"Good evening to you, cousin." She heard a deep, quiet voice, lightly touched with a Scandinavian accent, behind her.

She turned to face the very man she had once blamed for that beggaring: her cousin Anton Gustavson. They had never known each other; his mother—her father's sister—had married a Swedish nobleman and disappeared to the frozen north before Celia was born. Then he'd appeared here at Court, with a party sent to woo the Queen on behalf of the Swedish King—and to claim a family estate Celia had hoped to have for her own. The last remnant of her family's lost fortune.

She had blamed Anton bitterly for this final disappointment. But now, as she looked into his wary dark eyes, she could no longer blame him. He sought his own redemption here in England, and perhaps he had found it with his new estate and his Lady Rosamund.

Celia still had to find hers.

"And good evening to you, too—cousin," she said. "Where is Lady Rosamund? Everyone says you two are quite inseparable of late."

"Not entirely so," Anton said. He gestured towards the dance floor, now a whirling stained-glass mosaic of brilliant jewels and silks. "She is dancing with Lord Marcus Stanville."

Celia saw that Rosamund did indeed dance with Lord Marcus, their two golden heads close together as he whirled her up into the air.

"Lord Marcus Stanville—one of the greatest flirts at Court," Celia said as she finished her wine and exchanged the empty goblet for a full one. "I'm surprised."

Anton laughed. "Rosamund is immune to his blandishments."

"But not to yours?"

He arched his dark brow at her. "Nay. Not to mine. We are soon to be married."

Celia swallowed hard on her sip of wine and carefully studied the dancers. A cold, hard knot pressed inside her, low and aching. Once she'd had the foolish hope she could marry someone she loved too.

"My felicitations to you, cousin," she said. "Surely you did not expect quite so much here when you left Sweden?"

"I had hoped to find family here," Anton said. "And you and I are all that is left. Can we not cry pax and be friends?"

Celia studied him over the silver rim of her goblet. Aye, he *was* her family. All she had. For an instant she thought she glimpsed a resemblance to her father in his eyes, and that hard knot inside her tightened. How she missed her family sometimes. She was so alone without them.

"Pax, cousin," she said, and slowly held out her hand to him.

Anton gave a relieved laugh and bowed over her hand. "You are most welcome at our home at any time, Celia."

Celia shook her head. "You needn't worry, Anton. I shall not be the dark fairy at the feast. The Queen is sending me on an errand, and I probably shan't be back for some time."

A frown flickered over his face. "What sort of errand?"

Celia opened her mouth to give some vague answer, but she stopped at a sudden sensation of heat on the back of her neck. She pressed her fingers over the spot, just below the tight twist of her hair, and shivered.

She glanced over her shoulder and met John Brandon's bright blue eyes staring right at her. Burning. His head tilted slightly to one side, as if he was considering her, as if she was a puzzle, then he moved towards her.

Celia reacted entirely on instinct. She shoved her empty goblet into Anton's hand and said, "Excuse me. I must go now."

"Celia, what...?" Anton said, his voice startled, but Celia was gone.

She only knew she had to run, to get away, before John could catch her and strip her soul bare with those eyes as he had come so close to doing earlier.

The hall was even more crowded and noisy than before, and Celia had to elbow her way past knots of people. She was a small woman, though, and slid past the worst of the crowds and into the corridor. She could still hear the high-pitched hum of voices, but it seemed muted and blurred, as sounds heard underwater. The air pressed in on her, hot and close.

Yet she could still vow she heard the soft, inexorable fall of his boots on the floor, coming closer.

"I am going mad," she whispered. She lifted the heavy hem of her skirts and hurried to the end of the corridor, where it turned onto another and then another. Whitehall was a great maze. It was quieter here, darker, the narrow, dim length lit at intervals by flickering torches set high in their sconces. She heard a soft giggle from behind one of the tapestries, a low male groan.

She didn't know which way to go, and that moment's hesitation cost her. She felt hard fingers close over her arm and spin her around.

She lost her footing and fell against a velvet-covered chest. Her hands automatically braced against that warm, solid wall and a diamond button pressed into her soft palm. It was John. She could smell him, knew his touch. The hawk had swooped down and caught its prey.

She forced herself to freeze, to go perfectly still and not panic and run again.

"Do you have an urgent appointment somewhere, Celia?" he asked quietly. "You certainly seem in a great hurry."

Celia tried carefully to move away from him, slide out of his hold on her arms, but it seemed she was not unobtrusive enough. His other arm came around her, a steel bar at her back.

She eased her hands down his chest, and that hold tightened and kept her where she was. Her head was tucked under his chin, and she could feel the strong, steady beat of his heart under her palm.

Her own heart was racing. She couldn't breathe too deeply because his scent was all around her. She closed her eyes and sought out the icy centre that had held her together all these years. The distance that had saved her. It was not there now. He had torn it away.

"I am tired," she said. "I merely sought to retire. There was no need to chase me down like this."

John gave a low, rough chuckle. "Usually when a woman runs like that she wants to be chased."

"Like a doomed deer on the Queen's hunt?" Celia choked out. She had been on such hunts, had seen Queen Elizabeth cut the fallen deer's heart out. Celia had thought she herself had no heart left to be ripped out. It seemed she was wrong. There was still one small, hidden part of it, bleeding, and he was dangerously close to touching it again.

John had surely chased scores of eager women since they had last met, and held them thus. Kissed them in the darkness until they happily bled for him too.

"I am not most women," she said, and tried once more to wrench out of his arms.

He only held her closer, until she felt her feet actually leave the floor. Lifting her in his arms, he carried her backwards until she felt the cold stone wall at her back, chilly through her brocade bodice.

Her eyes flew open to find he had carried her into a small window embrasure, where they were surrounded by darkness and silence.

"Nay," he said. "You, Celia Sutton, are quite unlike any other woman in all England." His voice held the strangest, most unreadable tone—bemused, angry.

"And you know all of them, I am sure," she muttered.

John laughed and eased her back another step. He braced his palms to the wall on either side of her head, holding her trapped by his body as he had earlier. "Your faith in my stamina is quite heartening, my fairy queen. But I have only had twenty-eight years on this earth. Alas, not long enough to find all the women out there."

Hearing his old name for her—*fairy queen*—once whispered in her ear as they embraced in a forest grove, snapped something inside Celia. He had no right to call her that. Not any longer.

Before she could think, her hand shot out and her fingers curled hard around his manhood.

He froze, and she heard the hiss of his indrawn breath. His eyes narrowed as he stared down at her, and the very air around them seemed to crackle with a new tension. This strange game, whatever it was, was shifting and changing.

The codpiece of his breeches was not a fashionably

elaborate one, and she could feel the outline of him through the fine velvet. He was already semi-erect, and as her fingers tightened he stirred and lengthened. Oh, yes, she did remember this—how he liked to be touched. Caressed. She felt her hard-won sense of control steal back over her.

She twisted her wrist to cradle the underside of his penis on her palm and slowly, slowly traced her way up. She remembered how it felt naked, hot satin over steel, the vein just there throbbing with his life force. She reached its base, and with another twist of her fingers she held his testicles.

"Is this what happens when you catch your prey, John?" she whispered. She stroked a soft caress, lightly scraping the edge of her thumbnail over him.

She could feel the burn of his eyes on her as he held himself rigid around her. For once *she* had caught *him* unbalanced. He didn't know which way she would jump. And neither did she. Not any longer. He did that to her.

She had acted on instinct, reaching out to bring her control back. But it seemed to be slipping even further away.

"Usually they get down on their knees to me and take me in their mouths about now," John said crudely.

One hand left the wall by her head and she felt his finger press lightly to her lower lip. He traced the soft skin there. The merest whisper of a touch.

Celia gasped, and he used that small movement to slide his finger into her mouth, over her tongue. She jerked her head back, but she could still taste him—salt and wine. She wished she could pull away from him and

snatch her dagger from its sheath on her thigh, plunge
it into his heart so he could not touch *her* heart again.

"That will never happen," she said.

"Nay? I think it will in my dreams tonight," John
answered. "But perhaps you want me on my knees to
you instead?"

Before she knew what he was doing, he'd deftly
twisted out of her grasp and arched his body back from
hers. The hand that had been at her mouth slid all the
way down to her skirts and drew up the heavy fabric
until her legs were bare. The white stockings glowed
in the darkness.

As Celia watched in frozen shock he fell to his knees
before her and let those skirts fall back over him. She
tried to kick him away, but his strong hands closed over
the soft, bare skin of her thighs above those stockings.
He caressed her there, on the tender inner curve of her
leg, and pressed her legs further apart.

Then she felt his hot breath soft on the vulnerable curve of her, light as a sigh, just before his tongue
plunged inside.

God's blood. Her eyes slammed shut and her palms
pressed hard to the wall at the trembling, burning
rush of sensation that shot through her body. Oh, dear
heaven, but she had forgotten how it felt when he did
that!

Just as she had remembered how he liked to be
touched, he remembered how she liked to be kissed
there. He licked up—one languorous stroke, then another—before flicking at that tiny, hidden spot with
the tip of his tongue. She felt herself contract at the

pleasure, felt a rush of moisture trickle onto her inner thigh, and he groaned.

How she wanted him. How she had missed him, missed *this*, the feeling of being so wondrously, vitally alive. It had been so long. She had been dead inside for so long...

For just an instant she let herself feel it, let him pleasure her. This was *John*. The only man who had ever touched her heart. But then his hand closed hard on her thigh, just above the dagger, stroking her there so tenderly. So deceptively—just like before.

Before he'd destroyed her.

With a ragged sob she jerked herself away from him. She pulled her skirts from above his head and sent him toppling to the floor. But she also lost her own balance, and fell heavily on her hip against the wall. She leaned onto the cold stone for support and tried not to cry. Not to feel.

But his heat was still around her, and the musky scent of their arousal, the heated swirl of her feelings for him. She had to escape from it all.

John found his balance on his knees again, lithe as a cat. In the shadows she saw the frown on his face, the darkness of his eyes. He started towards her. "Celia..." he began.

But she stopped him with the sole of her shoe planted on his chest. She knew he could easily sweep any of her barriers away, yet he stayed where he was, watching her. She dug the heel of her shoe in, just enough to hold him there as she had with his balls in her hand.

"Celia, what has happened to you?" he said quietly.

She gave a hoarse, humourless laugh. How could she even begin to answer such a question? She gave him a slight push with her foot, and when he sat back on his heels she lurched upright to her feet. She ducked out of the hidden embrasure, and this time when she ran he did not follow.

Curse it all! Every instinct within John shouted at him to run after Celia, to catch her in his arms and hold her to him until she broke open and gave him all she had. All those dark secrets in her eyes. He wanted to strip away her clothes until she was naked before him, every pale, beautiful inch of her, and drive into her.

But he was too angry, and she was too brittle and fragile. She would surely shatter if he pushed her too hard, and the way he was feeling now he could not hold back. He braced his palms against the cold stone floor and let his head drop down, his eyes close as he struggled for control.

It was that damnable nickname. *Fairy queen.* His fairy queen. He could see her as she had been that day, her midnight-black hair loose over her bare shoulders, her grey-sky eyes gleaming an otherworldly silver as she looked up at him. She'd lain on a grassy, sunny spot in the woods, the light dappled over her skin, and John had never seen anyone so beautiful and free, so much a part of the nature around them. A fairy queen who had cast her magical spell over him. His wild youth had been forgotten when he saw her—the first time he'd felt such a rush of tenderness, dreamed of what he couldn't have. All because of her.

There seemed nothing of the fairy left in her now. She seemed instead an ice queen, encased in snow. But when she'd touched his manhood, when he'd tasted her, his Celia had flashed behind her cold eyes.

And, z'wounds, but she tasted the same as he remembered—of honey and dew. She had become wet when he'd kissed her there, the silken folds of her contracting over his tongue. Not so frozen after all. Did she remember too?

But still so far away from him. He remembered the panic in her eyes when she shoved him away, the way those walls in her eyes had slammed up again. It hurt to know she was so wary of him, even as he knew he so richly deserved it.

It was good she had run, for he obviously had no control at all when it came to her. Had he not resolved that very afternoon to stay away from her? To forget their past? Not to hurt her again, and not to torture himself with what he could no longer have? Only hours later he'd been on his knees under her skirt.

John pushed himself to his feet and automatically reached down to adjust his codpiece. He felt again her slender fingers on him, caressing him just where it was calculated to drive him insane. Pleasure and pain all mixed up in a blurred tangle.

When he emerged into the corridor Celia was long gone. The music from the ball floated back to him, echoing off the walls, mocking him with its merriment. He could feel someone watching him, and spun around to find Marcus leaning against a marble pillar with his arms crossed over his chest. He arched his brow at John.

"*Are* your balls frozen off, then?" Marcus asked with a grin.

John shot him an obscene gesture and turned to stride away down the corridor. His friend's laughter followed him.

It was certainly going to be a long and wretched journey to Edinburgh. Or were they all headed into hell instead?

Chapter Four

"Is this all of it, Mistress Sutton?" the maidservant asked as she fastened shut the travel chest.

Celia glanced around the small chamber. All of her black garments and his meagre personal possessions had been packed and carried away, and the box containing her few jewels and Queen Elizabeth's documents was tucked under her arm. She had no more excuses to linger.

"Yes, I think that is all," she said. She glanced in the looking glass. She wore a plain black wool skirt and velvet doublet for travel. Her hair was pinned up and held by a net caul and tall-crowned hat. She looked calm enough, composed and quiet, but part of her wanted to hide under the bed and not face the inevitable.

The past few days had passed in a blur of meetings with the Queen and Lord Burghley to learn more of her tasks in Scotland. She was to befriend Queen Mary, who was said to chatter freely with her favourite maids, and try to gauge her marital inclinations and re-

port back to Elizabeth. To try and persuade Mary that
an English marriage of her cousin's choosing would be
best for her. To watch and listen, which Celia had become very good at. A wary nature was always cautious
of what would happen next.

But Elizabeth said Mary should wed Lord Leicester,
and Burghley said Darnley. Celia wasn't sure whom to
incline Queen Mary towards—if the Scottish Queen
could be "inclined" at all.

There had also been banquets and balls, tennis games
to watch, and garden strolls, which she had tiptoed into
as if they were the flames of hell. But the chief demon,
John Brandon, had never appeared there to torment her.
To draw her into quiet corners and reveal parts of her
she had long ago encased in ice and buried. To watch
her with those eyes of his that saw too much.

She wasn't sure if she was grateful or angry he'd
stayed away.

No doubt he has much to occupy him, she thought
as she jerked on her leather riding gauntlets. Like saying farewell to all his *amours*.

Lord Burghley had said John would be her conduit in
Scotland for any messages, so she knew she would have
to face him eventually. Face what he had made her feel.

Celia stared down at the black leather over her palm
and remembered the hard heat of him in her hand. The
power and, yes, the pleasure she had felt in that one instant as he grew hard for her. The way she'd longed to
pull away his clothes and feel him against her again.
Part of her in every way.

She convulsed her hand into a fist. Maybe if she had

crushed him, hurt him, she would be done with him now—as he had once been done with her.

But the feeling of his mouth on her, driving her to a mad frenzy, told her they were not done with each other. Not at all.

She spun around and snatched up her riding crop, cutting it through the air with a sharp whistle. She imagined it was John's tight backside under the leather's touch, but pushed away that thought when a disturbing spasm of desire caught at her. The less she thought of John Brandon and his handsome body and sweet words the better!

Celia hurried downstairs and out through the doors into the courtyard, where the travelling party was assembling. It was chaos, the long line of horses and carts struggling into place as servants loaded last-minute bundles and trunks.

Lord Darnley and his mother stood slightly apart from the others as Lady Lennox whispered intently into his ear. He nodded sulkily, his gaze straying to where his chosen companions played at dice on the steps. Though it was early in the day, and long hours of travel awaited them, they were all obviously inebriated.

Celia was thankful that at least her tasks did not include being nursemaid to *them*. She would just as soon they fell off their horses and froze in a snow bank somewhere.

She studied the rest of the people. Servants piling onto the carts and courtiers unlucky enough to be chosen for this journey finding their horses. Lady Allison Parker, another of Elizabeth's ladies sent to cozen

Queen Mary, was letting one of Darnley's friends lift her into her saddle. She laughed as she settled her bright green skirts around her, flirtatiously letting the poor lad glimpse her long legs as her red hair gleamed in the greyish light.

Celia had the feeling she and Lady Allison would *not* become bosom bows on this journey.

Then she saw John, the merest flash of his light brown hair from the corner of her eye, and she stiffened. Every sense suddenly seemed heightened, the wind colder on her skin, the light brighter in her eyes.

She half turned to find that he stood near the front of the procession, holding the reins of a restless jet-black horse. He softly stroked the horse's nose, crooning in its ear, but his eyes were on Celia, intently focused. His body was held very still, as if he waited to see what she would do. Which way she would jump.

Celia remembered her fantasy of her riding crop on his backside, and she felt a smile tug at her lips. Her gaze flickered down to his long legs encased in leather riding breeches and tall black boots.

When she looked back to his face some unspoken promise seemed to burn in his eyes. As if he could see her thoughts, her fantasies, and he was only waiting to get her alone to make them come true.

Celia spun away from him, only to find that Lord Marcus Stanville watched her from the doorway. She had seen him talking with John a few times. Obviously they were friends. Celia was inclined to like Lord Marcus, with his golden good looks and light-hearted demeanour, but she did not like the way he watched her now. Like John, it was almost as if he could see what she was thinking and it amused him.

"An excellent day for a journey, wouldn't you say so, Mistress Sutton?" he said.

"If one enjoys freezing off one's vital appendages, mayhap," she answered tartly. "I would prefer staying by a warm fire, but perhaps you have different inclinations, Lord Marcus?"

He laughed, and Celia sensed John watching them. To her shock, Lord Marcus took her hand and raised it to his lips.

"I hope I am as adventurous as the next man, Mistress Sutton," he said, "but I confess some of the finest adventures of all can be had by a fire. Still, we must all do the Queen's bidding."

"Indeed we must," Celia said. "Whether we like it or not."

"I admit I was not overly enthusiastic about this task at first," Lord Marcus said. "But with you and my friend Brandon along it's looking more promising than an afternoon at the theatre."

Before Celia could demand he tell her what that meant, he took her elbow in his clasp and led her towards a waiting horse. He lifted her into the saddle and grinned up at her.

"Let the games begin, Mistress Sutton," he said.

Celia glanced at John, where he still stood several paces ahead of her. He watched her and Marcus with narrowed eyes, and Celia was sure the games had begun long ago.

And she had the terrible certainty that she was losing.

* * *

Celia stared out at the passing landscape as her horse plodded along, and tried not to rub at her numb thigh. They had been riding for several hours now, and the cold and boredom had conspired to put her in a sort of dream state. There was nothing before or after this steady forward movement, only the moment she was in.

And it gave her far too much time to think.

She wrapped the reins loosely around her gloved hands and watched the bare grey trees on either side of the road. The wind moaned through the skeletal branches, almost like low voices carrying her back into the past.

She tried not to look back at where she knew John was riding, but she was always very aware of him there. In the quiet that had fallen since the cold had driven everyone into silence, she fancied she could almost hear him as he shifted in his saddle or spoke in a low voice to Marcus.

Celia shook her head. It was going to be a very long journey. She needed to keep her focus on the task that awaited her in Edinburgh. And on the reward Queen Elizabeth would give her if she performed the task well—a rich marriage where she would never have to beg for her bread again.

A rich marriage to some nameless, faceless stranger, which she could only pray would be better than her first. It was her only choice now. She had to survive, to keep fighting.

And when she looked at John she feared she would lose the will to fight. He had always made her want to surrender to pure emotion, from the first moment she'd seen him. A shiver passed through her as she remembered how he'd taken her hand that first day, how he'd smiled down at her as if he already knew her.

"Cold, Mistress Sutton?" she heard him say.

For an instant his voice made her think she had been hurtled back in time. She blinked and glanced up, to find that while she had been woolgathering he'd drawn his horse up next to hers. It was as if he could sense her vulnerable moments, the wretched man.

"Aye," she said. "It feels as if I've been in this saddle for a month."

A slight smile touched his lips, and his gaze swept down to where her legs lay against the saddle. The side pommel turned her towards him, her skirts draped over her legs, and she thought of how he had crawled beneath them at the ball. The touch of his hands and tongue…

Suddenly she was not cold at all. She looked away from him sharply, and to her fury she heard him give a low chuckle—as if he knew what she thought.

"We are almost to Harley Hall," he said. "We're to stop there for the night."

"Hmph. One night to get warm, and back out into the cold tomorrow. Is that kindness or cruelty?"

"To taunt us with a taste of what we can't have?"

Celia looked back at him, startled by the tension in his low voice. But his expression was entirely bland as he looked back at her.

"If it becomes too unbearable, Celia," he said, "you're welcome to ride pillion with me. I would gladly keep you warm."

Celia gave an unladylike snort and stared straight ahead. She couldn't keep the image of his words out of her head—herself perched before John on his saddle, his arms wrapped around her as he rested his chin on her shoulder, his breath warm against her ear.

She thought if she ignored him he would leave, perhaps go and flirt with Lady Allison, who kept giving him sidelong glances. Yet he stayed by Celia's side, riding along in silence for long moments.

"Do you live entirely at Court now?" she finally said, to break the silence and the thoughts in her head.

"Most of the time. Except when my estate requires my attention, which is not very often," he answered. "It is the only life I know. Why do you ask?"

"I have been at Court for many weeks now, and yet you only appeared that day I met with the Queen."

"So you had begun to think you could avoid seeing me again?"

Of course that was what she had thought. But she said nothing.

"Celia, surely you knew we would meet again one day?" he said. "Our world is too small to avoid each other for ever."

"I did think I would never see you again," she said. "I am a country mouse and you—well, after you left so abruptly I did not even know where you went. You could have sailed off to the land of the Chinamen or some such thing."

"I did not *want* to go," he said suddenly, fiercely.

Celia turned to him, startled. His eyes were icy blue as he stared back at her.

"I had no choice," he said.

"And neither did I," Celia answered. She had tried to wait for him, had believed he *would* return. But as days and then weeks had passed, with no word at all, she had seen the truth. He had left her. She was alone.

Suddenly it felt as if a knife's edge had passed along the old scar and it was as raw and painful as when it was fresh. She pressed her free hand against her aching, hollow stomach.

"After you left…after I had to marry…" After her brother and the destruction of her family. "I had to marry Thomas Sutton. His family had wanted an alliance for a long time, though mine was wary of them. But after what happened to my brother I had no choice in who to marry. We had to agree to the union."

"Tell me about your marriage, Celia," John said, and she could still hear that hoarse edge to his voice.

A tense stillness stretched between them.

It was hell. A hell she had only been released from when Sutton died. She had gone on her knees in thanksgiving at her deliverance. But she couldn't say that to John. She was already much too vulnerable to him.

She shrugged. "It was a marriage like any other, but blessedly short."

"Is he the reason you wanted to twist my manhood off when you had it in your hand?"

Celia gave a startled laugh. "I think you yourself would be reason enough for that, John Brandon. And that was not exactly what I wanted to do with it."

He looked at her from the corner of his eye, that half-smile touching his lips as if he too had a few ideas about ways she could make use of him.

"Have you never married, John?" she asked. But did she really want to know the answer? She hated the thought of him uniting his life with another woman.

"You know I have not. I haven't the temperament for it."

"Who does, really? It is merely a state we must endure—unless we are Queen Elizabeth and can make our own choice," Celia said wistfully.

"Yet you will let the Queen arrange a new marriage for you, despite what might have happened in your first?" John sounded almost angry. She could not fathom it—could not fathom him.

Celia shrugged again. "I have no choice. Briony Manor went to Anton, and I have little dower. I will endure."

"Celia..." His hand shot out and he covered her hand with his, holding tight when she tried to pull away. "Tell me what happened with Sutton. The truth."

"I owe you nothing!" she cried. "You have no right to demand anything of me, John. And I will thank you to let me go this instant!"

Her gaze flew to her riding crop, tucked in its loop on her saddle.

"You want to use that on me now, don't you, Celia?" he said roughly.

She jerked against his hand, but he held her fast. It was so infuriatingly easy for him to get her where he wanted her.

"It wouldn't be my hand twisting your balls this time," she whispered.

Lightning flared in his eyes. "I might let you try—if you told me about your husband. About what has happened to you since I saw you last."

The convoy suddenly ground to a stop, and Celia saw to her relief that the gates of Harley Hall, their stop for the evening, were just ahead.

John raised her hand to his lips and kissed the knuckles through the leather of her glove. His mouth was warm on her skin.

"This is not over, Celia," he said against her hand.

Celia pulled away from him at last. "Oh, John. This was over a long time ago…"

Chapter Five

Celia leaned her arms on the crenellated wall of Harley Hall's roof, high above the grand courtyard, and looked out into the night. It was very late—even Darnley and his cronies had stumbled off to bed after draining their generous host's wine stores. The house was silent, but Celia couldn't sleep.

She drew the folds of her long cloak closer around her and tilted back her head to stare up at the stars. They shimmered so brightly in the cold, like diamonds and pearls scattered across black velvet. When she was a child she'd used to lie on her back in the garden and look up at the sky just like this, and imagine she could leap up higher and higher and become part of them. Flying among the stars, letting their sparkle draw her in further and further until she was part of them.

But now she knew there was no escape from the claims of the world. Not among the stars. Not anywhere. There were only the hard, cold choices of the world they lived in. Marriages made for convenience; hearts that had to be protected.

Celia braced her hands hard on the stone wall until she felt the bite of it on her palms. Why couldn't John stay away from her? Why had he ridden next to her today, talking to her, watching her with those eyes as if he waited for something from her?

She had learned long ago that it was much better not to feel at all, to let herself be numb to everything around her. But every time she saw John he chipped away at that ice she'd put around her heart, carefully, relentlessly, until she could feel that terrible heat on her skin again.

She pressed her hands to her face, blocking out the night. Why was he here, suddenly in her life again, reminding her of the fool she had once been?

He had seen the way she'd wanted to reach for her riding crop today, guessed how she longed to lash out at him. To make him hurt as she once had. And that primitive emotion frightened her. It was far too much, too overwhelming.

Just let this journey be over soon, she thought.

Or let John disappear somewhere and cease to torment her.

As if to taunt her, the door to the roof suddenly opened, cracking into her solitude. Her hands dropped from her face and she stiffened.

It could be anyone, of course, but she knew it was not. It was him, John. She could feel it in every inch of her skin, could smell him. Some mischievous demon seemed intent on tormenting her tonight.

She carefully composed her face into its usual cool, calm lines that hid her thoughts, and glanced over her shoulder. She felt no surprise at all to see John there, leaning in the door frame with his arms crossed over his chest as he watched her.

Though the night was cold, he wore no cloak. The crimson velvet doublet he worn at dinner was carelessly unfastened, hanging open over a white shirt that was unlaced halfway down his chest. His hair was tousled, falling over his brow in soft brown waves.

Celia had to turn away from the sight of him before she devoured him with her eyes.

"I should have known you would find me here, John Brandon," she said as she stared out blindly into the night. "You do seem intent on tormenting me."

"I would have said *you* were the one doing the tormenting, Celia," he answered. "Though I would have been here much sooner if I'd known this was where you were hiding. I merely wanted to escape the cursed snoring of the other men in my chamber."

Celia smiled faintly at the disgruntled tone of his voice, glad he could not see it. "And I came here to escape Lady Allison's incessant prattling. The woman has an inordinate store of gossip."

"Then we can be quiet here together," John said.

She heard the soft fall of his boots on the flagstones as he approached the wall.

She stiffened, but he stayed a few feet away from her, leaning his arms on the low wall as she did and looking out into the darkness. Slowly Celia relaxed and listened to the soft rhythm of his breath.

He didn't look at her, but he said, "Your hair is down."

Celia shifted, and self-consciously touched the loose fall of her hair over her shoulder. "I didn't think I would see anyone here. The pins were giving me a headache."

"You confine it too tightly."

"I can hardly parade around with it hanging loose like a girl," she said with a laugh.

"But you don't have to torture it either," he said.

He shifted his body towards her and reached out to lay his fingertips lightly on her hair. He traced a strand all the way down to where it curled under at her elbow. He only touched her hair, but Celia could feel his heat on her collarbone, the soft curve of her breast, the angle of her ribs under her cloak.

She thought again of a predator tormenting its prey, freezing it with the glow of its eyes so it could not flee. Didn't even want to flee.

He slowly wrapped the hair around his wrist, holding her with him. "You have the most beautiful hair I've ever seen. It's like the night itself. I used to dream of it—of touching it, kissing it, wrapping it over my chest as you leant over me…"

Celia gasped at the jolt of heat that went through her at his words, at the flashing memory of how he had once done that. Drawn her hair around him as she'd straddled his hips and bent down to kiss him. A wave of the greatest tenderness swept over her. She tried to pull away, but his hand tightened.

"Tell me about your husband, Celia," he said, his voice soft and yet utterly unyielding.

His voice held her even more than his fingers in her hair.

"He doesn't matter now," she said, fighting to keep her own voice steady. Not to lean into him, wrap her arms around his shoulders. "He is dead."

"For how long?"

"Above a year now. There was a fever that swept through the neighbourhood. My parents died of it as well."

His hand slid up her hair, twisting it around his fingers, caressing it over his skin. His blue eyes glowed down at her in the night, as bright and unyielding as ice. Celia closed her eyes, and she felt his other arm slide around her waist above the cloak. He turned her so her back was against his chest. She wanted so much to give in to him again, not to be alone. To know only him.

"Were *you* not taken ill?" he asked.

Somehow behind her closed eyes, because she could not see him, with his hand soothing against her skin she felt strangely free. Her careful guard slipped just a bit.

"I was ill," she said, a frown fleeting across her brow as she remembered those terrible days. His touch brushed it away before sliding back to her waist. "I had the fever too, though I remember little of it. Only nightmares and that dry, burning heat, a thirst that could never be quenched. I do remember they wanted to cut off my hair, and I drove them away."

"Thank God for that," John muttered, and she thought she felt the press of his lips on her hair. "It would have been a terrible crime to lose this hair."

"I was the only one who caught the fever and lived."

"That is because you are the most stubborn person I have ever known. The devil himself could not drag you down to hell." He sounded so angry, so desperate—just as she felt.

Celia smiled bitterly. "He has tried."

John's hand pressed to her hair. "And when you awoke you found your husband was dead?"

"Aye."

"What did you do?"

To her shock, Celia found herself telling the truth. "I got on my knees in the chapel and thanked God, or the devil, or whoever had done it, for the merciful deliverance."

John's hands suddenly closed on her shoulders and spun her round to face him again. She opened her eyes and looked up to find raw fury on his face, with no polished cloak of civility to hide it. His hands were hard where they held her.

Celia tried to pull back, frightened, but his grasp immediately gentled and his face went blank. He slowly drew her closer, until she was cradled to his chest, and his palms slid over the back of his head to hold her there.

"Why did you marry him?" he asked tightly. "Surely your parents…?"

Celia shook her head fiercely even as she buried her face further into his chest, the soft linen of his shirt. She breathed in deeply of the scent of him, and curled her fingers into the loose fabric.

"I had no choice, and neither did my parents," she said. "After you—left…" She paused to draw a deep breath and her hands tightened into fists against him.

"You surely know what happened to my family then? Everyone knows."

His muscles tightened under her touch and he went very still. "Your brother?"

Aye, her brother. Poor, stupid William, caught up in matters far beyond his understanding. "He was a traitor. Part of a Catholic conspiracy to overthrow the new Queen." That had been the strange part—their family was not religious, beyond attending weekly services at the Protestant church, and her brother had never shown the slightest interest in such things. But he had chosen to go along with his equally foolish friends when they'd conceived a notion to replace Elizabeth with her cousin Mary on the throne, no matter what. And his choices had affected her life too.

"They were obviously quite incompetent at conspiracy," she went on, in the numb, quiet voice that held it all at a distance. "They were caught quite handily and justice was swift. He was dead within a fortnight. And even though my parents retained their estate the fines were crippling. When they died the estate was sold."

"That was why you were married to Sutton?"

Celia nodded against him. "The Suttons had long wanted certain lands from my family to extend their estate. So they got them. But they got me along with them. And an old name to go with their new money."

And she'd got two years of marriage with Thomas Sutton. Her punishment. Even on the eve of her ill-starred wedding she had looked for John, waited for him, prayed he would return. That there was a reason he had suddenly vanished, that he loved her and would come for her. Even after months of silence.

But of course he had not come back, and she had learned that one inexorable truth. She was alone in life. Even now, with his body wrapped around hers, she was alone.

Yet she could not resist one kiss to that bare, warm skin so close. She pressed her lips just over his heart, felt the powerful beat of it, tasted him.

Then she pushed him away and spun round to run for the door. She heard him take a stumbling step after her and she half feared, half hoped he would stop her, pull her back into his arms. But he let her go, and she tripped down the stairs and along the corridor until she found her borrowed chamber.

Lady Allison still slept, and Celia crawled unseen into her narrow bed and drew the blankets over her head. She couldn't stop shivering even as the woollen warmth closed around her.

Chapter Six

John stared ahead of him along the rutted, muddy road, where Celia rode with one of the other men, Lord Knowlton, who had begun to pay her attention. She nodded at something he was saying, a faint smile on her lips, but even from that distance John could see that her eyes were distracted, her fingers stiff on the reins.

Part of him was fiercely satisfied that she paid no attention to the man's flirtations. If she had laughed with Knowlton, let him kiss her hand, John would have had to drag the man from his saddle and hit him in the jaw. He felt as if he walked a sword's edge today, his temper barely in check.

Usually when that darkness came upon him he had to find a brawl or have a bout of rough, hot sex to appease it. Neither was an option today.

He glared at Celia and Lord Knowlton as she laughed at his coaxing words. A real laugh that sounded sharp and rusty, as if she had not laughed in a very long time.

John dug his fist into his thigh, his muscles taut with

the effort not to grab Celia and kiss her until she felt something again—felt *him*. He didn't know if his anger was because she laughed with someone else, or at himself for even caring.

Once he had cared for her far too much. She had slipped behind his defences before he'd even realised, with her black hair and her laughing smiles, her kisses and her passion that burned as hot and fierce as his own. Because of her he had nearly failed in his duty.

And because of what he had done she had been wounded and changed for ever. Every time he looked into her cold, flat eyes and remembered how they had once flashed and danced, every time she pushed him away, that guilt burned in his gut.

And he hated feeling guilty for the scars on someone's soul. Guilt was a burden he could not afford—not in his work. That work had once been his salvation. If he felt the pain of everyone caught in the Queen's justice he would be ruined.

But Celia was not just everyone, anyone. She was Celia. And he still cared far too much for her.

She reached up to rub at her shoulder, a small, unconscious gesture he had seen her make before when she'd thought no one watched. It wasn't a noticeable thing, but he saw her smile slip when she touched herself there.

Now he wanted to pull her from her horse—not to kiss her until she burned as he did, but to strip away her black doublet and see her bare shoulder. Soothe whatever ache she held there. He wanted to take away all her pain and make her life bright again, even as he knew he could not.

"God's teeth," he ground out, his fist tightening.

"Someone is in a foul mood today," Marcus said cheerfully as he drew his horse up next to John's.

"And someone is disgustingly cheerful for no reason," John answered.

"Temper, temper," Marcus said with a laugh. "I'm to meet with Lady Allison's pretty maid tonight. But I'd be happy to oblige you with a fight first, if me beating your pretty face would make you feel better."

"You obviously do not recall what happened the last time we fought."

"I certainly do. My eye was swollen shut for a week," Marcus said. He gave John a considering look. "But that time I was the one in a blind fury."

"I am not in a fury," John said. He glanced again at Celia, who was nodding at something Lord Knowlton said. She no longer rubbed at her shoulder, but she didn't smile either.

"If you say so," Marcus said. "Not that I blame you for being in a temper. A forced journey in the middle of winter could defeat even *my* good mood. And it looks as if the weather is going to get even worse."

John had been so caught up in Celia that he hadn't even noticed the bite of the wind around him, the frost on the muddy ruts of the road that slowed their progress to a crawl. He looked up at the sky to see that the clouds had grown thicker and darker. It was barely past midday, but already the light was being choked off. There was the distinct cold, clean smell of snow on the air.

"God's blood," John cursed. "We'll never make it to the next village by nightfall."

"We'll just have to ride harder, eh?" Marcus said. "At least I have a warm bed waiting at the end…"

The inn was crowded with travellers, all seeking shelter from the freezing rain that pounded down outside, but room was made for an important personage like Lord Darnley and his party. Celia was given a palette in a corner with Lady Allison, and then found herself hastily changed into dry clothes and put in a chair near the fire of the inn's great room for supper.

Celia sipped at a cup of spiced wine as she studied the crowded chamber. Lord Knowlton sat beside her, chatting with her of inconsequential Court gossip as they shared a trencher of beef stew. He had been very attentive on today's journey, staying close to her and entertaining her through the cold, tedious hours. He seemed nice—handsome enough, if older than her, and non-threatening with his kind brown eyes, his polite attentions and compliments.

Usually she stayed as far from men as she could, but she hardly noticed Lord Knowlton when he was right beside her. John Brandon, though—she always seemed keenly aware of where *he* was all the time, even though he had not come near her all day. He seemed to emit some kind of strange, lightning glow that drew her attention to him.

She turned her head slightly to find him again. He sat in a shadowed corner with Lord Marcus and two other men. Marcus had one of the tavern maids on his lap, the two of them laughing, but John didn't seem to see them at all. He stared down into his goblet with a brooding look on his face, as if he was far away from the raucous inn. She well remembered that look.

His fingers slowly tapped at the scarred tabletop, and Celia found her gaze drawn to that slow, rhythmic movement. He had beautiful hands, and long, elegant fingers that were so good at wielding a sword, soothing a fractious horse…

Pleasing a woman.

His stare snapped up from his hand to find her watching him. Some deep, heated anger simmered in those blue depths, and Celia felt her cheeks turn hot.

John had a façade of such elegance and charm, with his fine Court clothes, his handsome looks, his smile. But Celia knew that so much more lurked beneath—a storm of passion and volcanic fury. He could fight like a Southwark street thief—or make love with a force that burned away all else.

She remembered that part of him all too well now, as he watched her across the room, and it made her want to leap up from the table and run. She sensed that part of him was barely tethered tonight.

"…is that not so, Mistress Sutton?" Lord Knowlton asked.

The sound of her name made Celia turn away from John's stare, but she could still feel him studying her. Biding his time, waiting for something from her she couldn't even fathom.

"I beg your pardon, Lord Knowlton?" she said. "I fear I could not hear you."

He smiled, his brown eyes soft as he looked at her. "It *is* rather loud in here. I was merely asking if you planned to remain long at Queen Mary's Court after we have delivered our charge there."

He nodded towards Lord Darnley, who was dicing with his friends by the fire. The man's fine-boned, handsome face was already flushed with drink, his eyes glittering dangerously.

"If he can be safely delivered," she murmured. "It is a long way yet to Edinburgh."

Lord Knowlton laughed. "Hopefully there are enough of us to finish the job. If we can keep from freezing to death in the meantime. Do you look forward to our sojourn at Holyrood, Mistress Sutton?"

Celia laughed, relaxing under the admiration in Lord Knowlton's eyes. When was the last time a man had looked at her like that, in simple admiration that did not twist her up into knots? It was—nice. "I am not sure I look forward to it. Yet I do think it will be interesting."

"To say the least," he said with a smile, pouring her more ale. "They do say Queen Mary is a fascinating lady."

"And a beautiful one."

"Aye, that too. We shall see what her Court is like in comparison to her cousin's. What are you expecting of this sojourn, Mistress Sutton?"

They talked easily together for the rest of the evening, about Scotland and the situation they would find there, about their lives in England, drinking ale as the room became louder around them, the air hotter.

Celia suddenly felt tired. The voices around her were turning chaotic, and she shook her head when Lord Knowlton offered her more to drink.

"I think I should find my bed, Lord Knowlton," she said. "The hour grows late. But I am glad we had this chance to talk together again."

"As am I, Mistress Sutton. Very glad indeed." He raised her hand to his lips, and the look he gave her over their joined fingers was suddenly intense. His mouth opened on her bare skin.

A shiver of disquiet ran over Celia's back, her earlier quiet pleasure in his company dissipating. What had happened to change things? She couldn't fathom what he was thinking about her, and it made her think strangely of her dead husband.

She drew her hand out of his and edged away from him until she could stand up. "Goodnight, Lord Knowlton."

"Goodnight, Mistress Sutton."

Celia turned and hurried away from him, making her way through the crowd. She didn't like the atmosphere in the room now. She only wanted to find her bed and be alone for a time.

But her foot had barely touched the bottom of the staircase leading up to their lodgings when she heard a shout.

She whirled around just in time to see a massively burly man grab Lord Darnley by the front of his doublet and shove him to the wall. Darnley's cronies leaped on the man, tables flew as crockery shattered, and women screamed. The strange tension Celia had sensed snapped into a full-blown fight.

She hurried up the stairs to a point where she could see the fray but not be in danger. Her stomach lurched in fear at the violence, and she pressed her hand to her mouth.

She felt even sicker when she glimpsed John in the swirling melee, a tall figure throwing out his fist to catch a jaw, jabbing his elbow into a midsection, kicking with his booted foot to make a foe go down. There was a terrible grace to his movements, a power, and she wanted to scream his name. To dash into the fray and drag him to safety.

He seized the man who was pounding Darnley's face and threw him backwards. Darnley crawled away, but his attacker bellowed in rage and dived for John instead. John fended him off with a neat sidestep, and ducked under the man's raised arm to drive a fist into his belly.

He didn't see the other man behind him, who lashed out with a splintery log and hit John on his thigh. Blood bloomed on his leg and Celia screamed. Raw, heated emotion and fear overwhelmed her. She raced into the crowd, ducking around the brawlers even as the landlord and his henchmen came to break it up. She reached John just as Marcus did.

"John!" she cried, reaching for his arm as he reeled.

He pushed her away gently, bending to press his hand to the wound. "It is merely a scratch."

"Nonetheless, let's get you out of here," Marcus said, winding his arm around John's shoulders to haul him upright. "Before someone decides to ruin your pretty face. Mistress Sutton, if you would find us a chamber?"

Ignoring John's growled protests, Celia got the landlord's wife to show them to a small room where a fire was lit. Marcus followed her closely.

"Put him down here," Celia said, clearing a pile of mending from the bench by the fire.

Lord Marcus unceremoniously slid John from over his shoulder onto the bench, where John promptly let free a string of colourful curses.

Marcus merely grinned and stepped back. "Whatever she does to you, my friend, you deserve it for jumping into a brawl like that."

"I quite agree," Celia said. She knelt on the floor beside the bench, trying to ignore the hot, angry glare of his eyes as he watched her. That fear she'd felt for him when she'd seen him hit still hummed through her veins and made her tremble. "Why would you do that to save a looby like Darnley?"

"Because it is my task at the moment," he ground out. "If I had my way I would have left him to what he so richly deserves."

"But why?" Celia said. Slowly, cautiously, as if she feared the wolf might snap and bite, she peeled the torn breeches away from his wounded leg. "Why are you meant to be his protector?"

John hissed between his teeth, and his hands curled over the edge of the bench, but he did not pull away from her touch. "He has to get to Scotland in one piece somehow."

"I don't know why," Celia murmured. She delicately examined the bleeding gash on his leg while studiously *not* looking at the smooth, warm skin, the masculine roughness of the dark hair that curled there. "I think it would be no terrible loss if someone *did* remove him from the situation."

John and Marcus looked at each other over her head. "Unfortunately that is not our decision to make," Marcus said lightly.

"Not yet," John added.

Celia didn't really want to know what they meant by that. She didn't want to be involved in these secret matters of crown and families at all. She had enough to worry about on her own.

Such as ignoring what happened to her when she was close to John.

She almost sighed aloud in relief when a maidservant delivered her valise. Celia opened it and dug through the contents for the herbal salves and tinctures she had packed.

As she laid them out on the floor, Marcus said, "I will leave you to your task then, Mistress Sutton. I should make sure all is well out there now."

He bowed to her and turned on his heel to go, the door clicking shut behind him. For an instant Celia could hear sounds from the public room, cries and quarrels and the landlady demanding payment for the destruction. Then she was closed in firelight and flickering shadows, alone with John.

She bit her lip, trying to press down the nervous trembling inside her, and peeled the cloth back further.

The log had caught him halfway between the knee and the groin, leaving a long cut. The bleeding had mostly stopped, was clotting around the edges. She could smell the coppery tang of it, but blood no longer had the power to make her swoon. She had seen too much of it.

But the smell of John—that made her feel light-headed. Leather and wine, the faint whiff of spicy soap, the darkness of his skin and sweat. The musk of his manhood. It was heady, alluring. It made all the old memories of a time when they had been as close as two people could be return to her, so strong.

Celia sat back on her heels, away from the too vulnerable position of kneeling between his thighs, and reached into her valise for a clean rag. She soaked it with lavender water.

"There are splinters caught in the wound," she said. "I have to clean it before it can be bandaged."

His fists curled even tighter into the edge of the bench, and she saw the knuckles were bruised. He had certainly left his opponents in worse shape than he was. But it could have been so much worse. If the log had caught him higher...

"You're fortunate the wound is where it is," she said. She set her jaw in a determined line and leaned forward to dab at the raw edges of it with her cloth. His thigh tensed, but he said nothing. "A bit higher and all the Court ladies would be in mourning."

He laughed. "And would *you* have been disappointed, Celia?"

"Certainly not," she snapped. "I would have sung a hosanna—womankind safe again."

"I don't believe you."

He uncurled one hand from the bench and reached out. She felt his soft touch on a strand of hair that had fallen free in the tussle. He ran a caressing touch down its length.

Celia ground her jaw tighter, determined not to jerk away. Not to show how his touch made her so damnably weak. Made her remember things she should forget—like how she had once cared for him so very much.

"I'm sure you remember how many other delightful things there are to do," he whispered. "With hands and tongues…"

Celia pressed the cloth hard to his wound and he straightened up with a hiss. His hand fell from her hair.

"I need to finish this," she said quietly. "Unless you want it to fester until you lose the leg—among other things."

He chuckled and leaned back as he placed his palms flat behind him. "Do your worst, then, Celia. But I know you do remember."

He said nothing more as she finished cleaning and binding the wound. She tied off the ends of the bandage and sat back on her heels to look up at him.

A half-smile lingered on his lips as he watched her, his eyes dark, his skin gilded a molten gold in the firelight. His doublet hung open, his shirt half unlaced to reveal a chest damp with the sweat of the fight. He looked lazy, considering—like some Eastern king watching a slave who had been delivered to his feet.

Celia suddenly wanted to shatter his laziness, that look of casual possessiveness. She gave him a smile, and his own faded.

Slowly, deliberately, she leaned forward and rested her hand on his unwounded thigh. His whole body grew taut and wary. Celia held onto him and placed her parted lips on the skin left bare by the torn breeches. She moved her mouth over him, tasting him.

"Celia…" he said hoarsely.

She pressed her hand tighter on his leg and he went still. She closed her eyes and kissed her way higher, over the velvet fabric that lay tight over his upper thigh, until she could trail the tip of her tongue along the crease between leg and groin.

She could smell him there, the faint scent of sweat and musk she had once known meant he wanted her. He had left her, but he still wanted *this*, and the knowledge gave her a sudden surge of satisfaction. Of pleasure. At least she still had that. And now she wanted more, wanted to know all of him.

Her feelings surged inside her, so tangled and confused.

Her hand slid up his leg to just beneath his codpiece, cradling him in her fingers. He was already hard, but he grew even harder, longer. She found the vein on his underside beneath the cloth and slid her fingertips along it.

"Oh, aye," she whispered. "I remember all the things one can do with hands and mouths…"

She'd just barely touched her lips to the tip of him when she felt his fingers dive into her hair, tumbling the few pins that were left there free. He pulled her head back until she stared up into his eyes.

Those burning eyes that pierced right through her tore her careful defences down one by one and destroyed them until they were ashes around her.

"Celia, you drive me mad," he growled. Then his mouth drove down onto hers.

His tongue plunged inside, tasting her, claiming her—every part of her. She tried to draw back but he held her fast, his hand tight in her hair, his mouth sealed over hers.

She moaned and tried to push his tongue out with hers, but instead she found it twisting with his, tasting him return. He tasted dark and sweet, like wine and the night and John, and she wanted it. She wanted it with such raw longing it terrified her. She couldn't think, couldn't reason. He was all around her, all she knew.

His other arm came around her shoulders and drew her up until she sat on his lap, balanced on his un-wounded thigh. He never broke the desperate rhythm of the kiss, only drove deeper into her.

She wrapped her hands around his neck and felt the soft hair at his nape brush over her fingers. She ca-ressed him there, trying to learn the feel of his skin, the essence of him, all over again. John groaned, and untangled his hand from her hair to touch the base of her throat, pressing over her pulse.

He brushed aside the edges of her surcoat and traced his fingertips over the bare swell of her breasts above her bodice. His fingers were rough on that soft skin, and she wanted more. She arched her back with a soft moan into his mouth and his palm flattened over her breast.

One finger slid beneath the brocade and swept over her aching nipple once, twice, then harder, making her cry out. His thumb slid in with the finger and he pinched her between them.

Pleasure shot through her, and Celia accidentally fell

back on his lap. She kicked his wounded leg with her slipping foot and he gasped.

"Oh, hell!" she cried, tearing her mouth away from his. She pushed out of his arms and leaped to her feet.

He reached out for her, but she could see the fresh blood spotting his bandage.

It brought her coldly to her senses as nothing else could. He had held her captive in their own hidden world where there were only the senses, the way he made her feel. She couldn't stay there, no matter how much she wanted to. It had already destroyed her once.

"I—I will send someone in to finish tending to your wound," she stammered. John reached out for her, but she shook her head and spun round to run out of the room. She was always fleeing from him, from whatever terrible power lay between them, but it seemed it was all she could do.

Clutching her surcoat closed, she dashed through the near-empty great room and up the stairs. Past the sleeping bodies to the palette where Lady Allison already slumbered.

Trembling, Celia shed her clothes as best as she could and slid under the blankets in her chemise. She closed her eyes tightly, trying to find sleep, to forget John Brandon, even as her body still felt tingling with newly aroused life.

"Why, Mistress Sutton," she heard Lady Allison whisper, "you naughty thing."

Celia's eyes flew open and she peered at Allison over her shoulder. Allison grinned at her, as if they were conspirators.

"Is he as wonderfully skilled as they say?" Allison whispered.

Celia felt her cheeks grow warm. Ashamed of that ridiculous blush, she turned away and closed her eyes again as Lady Allison softly laughed.

Oh, aye, she thought bitterly. John Brandon was entirely too skilled for any woman's good.

Chapter Seven

John shifted in his saddle, trying not to wince as his bandaged leg brushed the hard leather. It had been some time since he had indulged in a tavern brawl, despite his reputation for wildness, and he felt every bit of the violence in his bruised muscles and the healing gash on his leg.

But it was worth every ache just to remember how Celia had cared for him, bandaging his wound, kneeling between his knees. Kissing him so passionately, so wildly, as if he was all that mattered to her.

Just as he had felt when his lips touched her, tasted her. Nothing else existed. Nothing had ever come between them.

That had been last night. Everything was always different in the cold light of day.

And a damnably cold day it was. Snow had set in soon after their hasty midday meal of bread and cheese—great fat flakes that melted on his cloak and drifted into white piles at the side of the road. The wind felt like needles as it swept around them. Even Lord Darnley, his pretty face bruised and sulky after last night, has subsided into the silence of endurance.

John looked to where Celia rode in one of the carts, lodged between the meagre shelter of two travel trunks. The hood of her black cloak was drawn over her hair, and he could see only the curve of one pale cheek. The long, thick lashes that cast shadows over her cheekbone as she stared down at the book in her gloved hands.

She hadn't turned a page in fully fifteen minutes. John knew because he had been watching her the whole time. Yet she was not asleep. Her shoulders and slim back were too stiff and straight.

She never looked his way, never indicated by the slightest gesture that she knew he was there. Her walls were back up, her drawbridge slammed closed to him. It would be best for both of them if he just let it stay closed. Old scars did not need to be ripped open all over again.

Yet still that desire burned deep inside him to see her eyes free of that caution, that icy chill, to see *his* Celia again. To make her admit she had never ceased to be his.

But she was *not* his. She never had been. It had all been a terrible mistake. He couldn't let her touch his heart as she once had—until he'd found out her brother was one of the conspirators he had come to the countryside to catch. Too late, for by then he had already fallen for Celia.

"You look as if last night's fight was merely a prelude to what you'd like to do today," he heard Marcus say as his friend's horse fell into step beside him. "You look furious."

"Then shouldn't you best stay away from me?" John growled.

"I'm not that easily frightened," Marcus answered carelessly. "If you need to beat on someone that badly, Darnley is over there. But I don't think that would help."

"Of course it wouldn't. The Queen would have my hide if I damaged her pretty pawn."

"I mean I don't think violence will ease you. When were you last with a woman?"

John slanted a hard warning look at his friend. "Marcus…"

"That long, eh? No wonder you're so fierce."

Aye, John thought, it had been a while since he tupped a woman. Since before he'd seen Celia again. Now it seemed when he looked at another woman, talked to her, saw her smile of invitation, it stirred nothing at all within him. It was not enough.

"Lady Allison is always up for a lark, you know," Marcus said, as if heedless of the turmoil within John. "Or Mistress Andrews. She is meant to be Darnley's *inamorata* right now, but she's bound to be bored waiting around for him to get it up. Or the next town is sure to have a decent brothel—"

"I don't need you to play pimp for me, Marcus," John interrupted.

"Of course you don't. Women fall at your feet everywhere you go. You hardly have to seek them out. But you need *something* to free you from whatever demon has you in its clutches."

John grimly shook his head. "Just leave, Marcus."

"So you can go on brooding? Nay, we have been friends for too long. I know this journey is hellish, but there is something more. What is it?" Marcus's tone had become suddenly serious. He and John had known each other for too long—through their wild youths and into this dangerous work.

John's stare unconsciously went to Celia, where she sat in the cart. Lord Knowlton was with her now, and she smiled at whatever he'd said to her, just as she had when the man had sat with her in the tavern last night. She seemed to like him too much.

His hands tightened into fists on the reins.

"Ah," Marcus said softly. "I see."

John tore his eyes away from Celia to glare at Marcus. "What do you see?"

"Every time the two of you are together I would vow you are about to murder each other or strip each other's clothes off—or both."

A wave of despair rolled over John, hard and cold. All his years of careful subterfuge and one moment with Celia pulled all the lies and façades away. He was being such a fool. "Am I so obvious?"

"Only to me, as I would be to you. To everyone else you are still the rakish, careless Sir John Brandon. But I have never seen you like this with a woman. What is she to you?"

John glanced around to see that they had fallen slightly behind the others and no one was near. They were all too occupied in their own cold misery to pay attention to anyone else.

"A few years ago, when I was in the country on a task, we had a—dalliance," he said.

Marcus gave a low whistle. "And I take it matters did not end well?"

Considering he had betrayed her brother and his friends to their death, nay, it had not ended well, and he had left Celia—and his heart—behind. And he had never forgotten her since. "Nay," he said shortly.

"But you still want the lady?"

John said nothing, and finally Marcus laughed. "Then I think we can look forward to many more brawls on this journey. Unless you make love to Mistress Sutton again, get past those icy walls of hers and rid her from your system."

"Do you really think she would let me in her bed again, knowing all she does now?" John said bitterly.

Marcus said nothing in reply, and they rode on in heavy silence.

"Halt!"

Celia glanced up from the book she held in her hands to see the head of Lord Darnley's guard blocking the procession on the road. She had not been reading at all, merely staring at the book as she felt John stare at her. As last night's kiss flashed through her mind over and over.

Something had shifted between them in that kiss, something she sensed was profound even as she could not decipher what it was. What a hold on her he still had.

She was glad of any distraction. She put the book back in her saddlebag and slid off the cart, holding onto the wooden slats as the legs she had tucked under her cramped. Everyone else had come to a halt as well, looking relieved to stop. The day had only grown more bitterly cold, the snow falling thickly.

"The bridge across the river ahead is out," the guard said. "We can either turn back and make camp, or go downstream to the next bridge and continue to the next manor."

Either way, they were surely in for more cold. Celia sagged back against the cart as she watched the guards consult with Darnley and his men. It looked as if they would be here for a time. Celia turned and made her way through the milling crowd, away from the noise, until she found a silent spot on the sloped icy banks of the river. She wrapped her arms around herself and stood there very still, watching the freezing water rush past below her.

Surely this journey would never end? She would never be free of John, of seeing him every day and re-membering. Remembering the foolish girl she had once been, how much she had wanted him. How much she *still* wanted him, curse it all.

She heard a soft footfall crunch on the frosty ground behind her, heard a breath, and she knew without turn-ing who it was. She always felt when John was near.

"You seem to enjoy spending time with Lord Knowl-ton," he said roughly.

Celia almost laughed. Was that *jealousy* in his tone? Surely not. That was too ridiculous. He was always sur-rounded by women. "He is charming."

John gave a half-snort, half-laugh. "Of course he is. He wants to tup you."

"He is a gentleman!" Celia protested, trying to dismiss the feeling of disquiet she had felt with Knowlton.

"So am I," John said solemnly.

Celia shook her head. She turned to look at John and found he wore a fierce scowl on his face, his hands curled into fists. Because she had been talking with Knowlton? He had no right to care. Should *not* care. And she should not be feeling as she did either. As if her whole being was wound so tightly she might burst.

"John, you are the very furthest thing from a gentleman there could be," she said.

"God's teeth, Celia, don't push me away like this any more!" he suddenly shouted.

He moved so fast she couldn't back away, lunging forward to seize her arm and pull her towards him.

"Tell me what you're feeling. Tell me how I make you feel."

How he made her feel? Anger and pain as she had never known, everything she had locked inside her for so long, rose up in her like the fiery force of a volcano. It exploded from her, and she lunged forward to slap John across the face. "You left me!" she cried, all the pain of years ago flooding out of her. "Tell me why you did that? Tell me how you felt then. Tell me…" She slapped out at him again as he instinctively stepped back.

In her blindness, she caught him low on the jaw with the flat of her hand. It wasn't a hard blow, but he was caught by surprise and fell back a step. She reached out to hit him again, and he caught her wrist in his hand.

His fingers tightened on the slender bones there and she sobbed as she struggled to break free.

The flash of fury in his eyes, of some pain that answered her own, made her sob again.

"You have no right to question me, John Brandon," she cried raggedly. "You have no right to say anything to me at all. You left me. You have no part in my life!"

"Celia…" he began, his voice tight as if he too was on the brink of an explosion. As if he held himself tightly leashed.

"Nay! I survive however I can now. And you— you…"

His fingers closed even harder on her wrist, a manacle she couldn't escape from, and he reeled her closer. She tried to dig her boots into the frozen mud, but he was stronger.

His stare was so glittering, so intense. No one had ever looked at her like that before—as if he *knew* her, was part of her. Yet he wasn't. Hadn't been in so long. She had been alone.

She wanted only to leave him, to run and hide, to be free at last of whatever hold he had on her. She twisted her body hard as it touched his, trying to wrench away. But she overbalanced on her uncertain feet and fell heavily to the side.

Her hand was pulled from John's at last, yet she couldn't right herself. She felt herself toppling to the ground.

"Celia!" she heard him shout.

As she fell heavily onto the ice her leg caught on a fallen branch and she rolled forward. She had only a dizzy glimpse of him, of the raw horror on his face, of the flat grey sky above her, and then she was tumbling down the steep riverbank. Faster and faster.

She tried to catch at the ground, at anything she could find, but it slid out of her grasp. Her head struck something and bright stars whirled around her. Her whole body seemed to go numb.

Yet she felt it when she tumbled into the water. The icy-cold waves closed over her head, and it felt like a thousand daggers plunging into her skin. She tried to scream at the agony, and water rushed into her mouth.

Celia did know how to swim, and she struggled to push past the pain and fight her way to the surface. Her heavy skirts and boots grew sodden, weighing her down. She kicked hard against them and managed to break upwards and gulp in a precious breath. But the river wasn't finished with her yet. It caught at her again, pulling her down.

And suddenly she only wanted to *live*. When her brother had died, when she'd been with Thomas, she had never really wanted to die. But merely surviving, putting one day behind her and then the next, had been all she could do. Otherwise the pain and anger would overwhelm her.

But now, with her whole body numb and the rushing river carrying her away, she wanted life again. Music and colour and sunshine. She wanted to see John—to slap him properly, to find out once and for all what had really happened when he left her. Or to kiss him as she once had, with nothing held back.

That was her last thought as she was sucked under the water again. The precious air was cut off.

Suddenly a hard arm caught her around her waist and jerked her up towards the light.

She gasped and let her head fall back onto a naked shoulder as she was drawn towards the shore. It seemed so very far away, yet she wasn't scared now. Somehow she knew it was John who held her, and that he wouldn't let her go. He wouldn't let the river have her.

He reached the bank and hauled her up its slippery length under his arm. Celia couldn't stop shivering, couldn't think. When they reached the top, he laid her on the ground and pulled up her skirt, to draw her own dagger from its sheath at her thigh.

He cut away her sodden doublet and the stays beneath in smooth, quick strokes and spun her onto her stomach, his legs straddling her hips. The flat of his hand hit her hard between the shoulderblades once, twice, until she expelled the water that choked her lungs.

She sobbed out all her fear and relief, and through her tears she felt him pull her back into his arms. He wrapped his body all around her, all his heat and strength. He pressed his lips hard to her cheek, and to her shock she felt his own tears on her skin.

"God's teeth, Celia," he growled. "I thought you were dead. I thought…"

"You saved me," she sobbed through her chattering teeth. "You—you could have drowned."

"I won't let you go," he said. "Not without me."

Celia heard a shot and the pounding of running feet on the icy mud.

"John!" Lord Marcus said, and for once there was no lightness at all in his voice. "What happened? Are you hurt?"

"She fell into the river," John answered. He still held onto her.

"Oh, sweet God, Mistress Sutton, but you will surely freeze to death!" Lady Allison cried.

Celia heard the swish of fabric and a warm, fur-lined cloak covered her icy skin.

She was drawn away from John even as she tried to hold onto him. "Nay," she cried.

But darkness closed in on her, born of the cold and shock, and she fainted into its weighty oblivion.

Chapter Eight

"Shh. Be still. Rest now." John slowly smoothed the cool, damp cloth over Celia's brow and whispered to her until she settled back in the bed. She still frowned, and her hands were curled tightly against the sheets as if she fought demons in her sleep. But she quieted.

John sat back in his chair by the bed and ran the cloth over her shoulders and along her arms. It had been three days since she'd tumbled into the icy river—three days that they'd been alone in the small hunting lodge tucked into the woods. The chills and fever that had come upon her seemed to be subsiding, but sometimes he feared that was his own wishful thinking. His own fear of losing her all over again—for ever this time.

He balanced her hand on his palm and studied the delicate pale fingers. She had survived the fever that killed her parents and husband because her delicacy hid a fierce spirit. He had told her she was the most stubborn person he had ever seen, and she was. She would survive this. He would make certain of it. He would use all his strength to pull her back to him.

Once he had dared to begin to think of a future with someone else, with Celia. Could he afford to think of that now? What could he offer her? She was in this place now because of him. He never wanted to hurt her again.

"I should never have quarrelled with you that day, Celia," he whispered. He should have known she would fight like the warrior she was, his fairy queen with claws. But he wasn't willing to let her hurt herself.

He laid her hand back on the sheets at her side and went on bathing her skin. She felt cooler to his touch now. Most of the heat on her bare arms was from the fire he had built up in the grate. She wore a chemise with the sleeves cut away, a bandage wrapped above the elbow, where the physic had bled her before the others moved on with their journey. Her hair fell over one shoulder in an untidy black braid.

John slowly smoothed the cloth up her arm and over her collarbone. He saw again the shoulder that had had him so furious when he first undressed her.

It had obviously been damaged, wrenched out of its socket and then reset improperly, so that it stood out crookedly under her smooth white skin. Pale scar tissue lay in a pattern over it. There were also faint marks on her back and buttocks, thin white scars that had not been there when they'd made love three years ago.

Her bitterness and distance, her hatred of her husband and gratitude for his death, made terrible sense now. If the man hadn't already been dead John would have killed him with his own hands, in a slow, terrible way involving red-hot pokers and dull daggers.

But torturing Thomas Sutton wouldn't bring his Celia back. How could he do that?

"You have to fight to live now, my fairy queen," he said fiercely. "Fight so you can go on hating me." Go on punishing him. He deserved no less. Yet he could never bear it if Celia died. She would take with her every dream he'd ever had of a better life than the one he led.

"Fight, damn you!" he shouted.

"Oh, John, do leave me alone," she murmured hoarsely. "I cannot sleep with so much noise."

John's eyes shot to her face. Her eyes were open and clear, not glassy from the fever, and she watched him as if she actually saw him, not some nightmare hallucination.

"Celia, you're awake!" he said, and a new happiness pushed away the fear and fierceness. He carefully took her hand in his, reassured when her fingers weakly squeezed his.

"Am I?" she said. She carefully shifted on the bed, frowning. "I feel as if I've been drawn and quartered. Where are we?"

"At one of the Queen's hunting boxes. Luckily one of Darnley's cohorts remembered it was nearby."

"Nearby what?" She looked terribly confused, so young and vulnerable.

"Do you not remember?" John asked.

"I remember riding in the cold. It was snowing…" Her eyes widened. "I fell into the water! I wanted you to tell me…something."

John shook his head. "And you caught a feverish chill. We've been here three days."

"Three days?" Her gaze darted quickly around the chamber: the large bed, the faded tapestries on the walls, the fire. The freezing rain that lashed at the mullioned window. "Alone?"

"Don't worry, Celia," John said with a teasing grin. He suddenly wanted to burst out laughing like a fool, to shout with exultation. She was awake! He could face anything if she would only stay alive, stay with him. "I am not in the habit of ravishing unconscious females."

"But you came in after me. How are you not ill?"

"I was not in the water as long as you. And we can't both be ill."

She glanced down at her body under the sheet, at the bandage and the basin of cool water. "You have been taking care of me?"

"The others had to continue on their journey if they were to make it to Holyrood when expected. And that cursed Darnley was fearful of contagion."

"It would serve him right," Celia muttered. She shifted on the bed. "I'm so thirsty."

"Here, take some wine. The doctor said it would strengthen your blood, but you haven't been able to keep it down." John slid onto the mattress beside her and eased his arm around her shoulder to help her sit up against his shoulder. She shivered, and he frowned as he felt how thin she was under the chemise.

Celia was too slender anyway, much thinner than she'd been three years ago. Until they were able to travel and catch up to the others John would see to it that she ate, that she grew strong again. A heated, tender rush flowed over him as he looked at her.

He held up a goblet of fine, rich red wine to her lips and she drank deeply. When it was gone, he eased her back down to the pillows and tucked the blankets around her.

"Could you take some broth?" he asked.

She shook her head. "I feel so tired."

"Then just sleep now. You will feel stronger in the morning."

He started to leave the bed, but her hand reached out to grasp his arm.

"Stay with me?" she whispered.

He looked down into her eyes, now the pale grey of a winter's day. She looked back. Steady, calm. Beseeching.

Oh, how he wanted to stay with her. To hold her close in his arms and feel her breath, her heartbeat, the very life of her. Even as he knew he should stay away from her, not hurt her any more, he couldn't stay away.

He lay slowly down on the bed beside her and she turned onto her side, her back to his chest. John wrapped his arms around her waist and felt her relax with a sigh. She was with him now, in this moment. That was all that mattered for now. All that had ever really mattered.

"Thank you," she breathed, and sank down into healing sleep.

But John stayed awake all night, cradling her against him and remembering all he had lost when he'd lost her. Did he dare hope to get it back?

* * *

Celia slowly drifted up from her soft, dark sleep, becoming aware of the world around her again. It had been a good sleep, not the plague of nightmares like before, and her body didn't ache and burn. She could feel a soft pillow under her cheek, clean linen sheets around her shoulders, the brush of a fire's warmth on her face.

Everything felt so quiet and peaceful. Safe. When had she ever felt safe? She couldn't even remember. Had she died and gone to heaven, then? She slid deeper into the warm cocoon of the bedclothes—and then she truly remembered where she was. Who was with her.

John. He had pulled her from the river, had nursed her here, just the two of them alone. It felt so strange to be here with him, it felt—right. Yet she had been so angry with him. She was utterly confused.

Slowly, carefully, Celia raised her head from the pillow and opened her eyes to look around. She had vague memories of John holding her as she fell asleep, lying on the bed with her. He wasn't there now, she was alone on the wide feather mattress, but she could see the imprint of his head on the pillow beside her.

Holding the sheet against her, she sat up. She realised she wore only a chemise with the sleeves cut away, one arm bandaged. Had she done that? Undressed herself, torn away her sleeves? Nay, it had to have been him. And that meant he had seen her bare shoulder.

Celia rubbed at the bump there and wondered what he'd thought of it. Well, he had his own secrets and she had hers. Nothing could change that, not even the most fervent wishes. She had to remember that, even when she felt so overwhelmed with tenderness for him.

But where was he now?

She eased back the blankets and carefully slid off the edge of the bed. Her legs trembled they were so weak, but she held onto the carved bedpost until the dizziness passed and she could stand. She saw his doublet tossed over a chair, and picked it up to wrap around her shoulders. It smelled of him, of that lemon soap he used, leather and John.

It made her shiver all over again.

She carefully made her way to the window, her bare feet cold on the uncovered wood planks of the floor. The diamond-shaped panes of glass were covered in frost, and she scrubbed away a small spot to peer outside.

Snow still fell, a silent white blanket that covered the ground and iced the trees, obscuring the whole world in cold and silence. They were at a hunting box, John had said, and everyone else had ridden on ahead. How long would they be here together?

She heard the chamber door open, and glanced over her shoulder to see John standing there in his shirt-sleeves, a tray in his hands. A frown darkened his face, and he dropped the tray onto the table to stride across the room to her.

Celia instinctively backed away, but the window was behind her and she could only go one step before he was upon her. He caught her up in his arms, holding her high against his chest, and turned towards the bed.

"You foolish woman," he said roughly. "What are you doing out of bed?"

Celia tried to kick, to push him away, yet that damnable weakness still pulled at her limbs. "I'm not ill now! I wanted to see what was outside."

"I can tell you what's out there. Snow and more snow." He deposited her in the middle of the bed and climbed up beside her to hold her there when she tried to scramble away. "You've had a terrible chill, and you'll catch it again wandering about in bare feet."

"Then where are my boots?" she asked, to cover what she really wanted to say. She wanted to demand to know why he had left her three years ago, what he felt now—what he was making her feel. But she dared not.

"Your trunk is here. You can have your boots when I tell you you can. Until then you'll stay right here."

"Villainous bully," Celia muttered. She slumped back on the pillows.

John grinned at her, that mischievous smile that brought out the dimple in his unshaven cheek and made such odd, disturbing things happen inside her. She felt so ridiculously young and vulnerable again.

"You remembered," he said. "If it takes bullying to keep you here until you are completely well, then I'm prepared to do it. Don't make me tie you to the bedpost."

Celia narrowed her eyes as she studied the new, hard light on his face. She couldn't tell if he was joking or not. She had a sudden vision of herself bound to the bedpost, naked, and John kneeling between her legs with that expression of intent determination on his face…

She rolled away from him, her face feeling embarrassingly warm.

"You would not," she whispered.

"Why don't you try me and see, fairy queen?" he said.

When she crossed her arms over her chest, he laughed. He drew her feet onto his lap and started to rub them gently, bringing heat into her frozen toes.

Celia slowly relaxed under his soothing touch. She let herself lean back into the pillows and closed her eyes. His gentle touch moved in slow, soothing circles over her ankles and her calves, tracing a light pattern over her skin that felt delicious.

She knew she should pull away from his touch, hold herself back from him, but she was so tired, so horribly weak. It felt too good to feel his touch, not to be alone just for a moment. To remember all the good things about when they had first met.

"You said we are at a hunting box of the Queen's?" she asked.

"Aye, though not one that's been used since her father's day, I would wager. This is the only chamber that has any furniture. Everything else is covered with dust."

"But there is food?" she said, remembering the tray he brought in.

"They left us provisions. There is broth and bread there, and I'm going to make sure you eat every bite."

"You *are* a terrible bully, Sir John." But she smiled as she said it. She could feel her whole body relaxing under his touch.

"Of course I am. A man has to be to get the best of a minx like you."

Celia rubbed her toes over his thigh, feeling the shift of his powerful muscles under the leather breeches. "Just wait until I have my strength back."

She felt him bend down, and his lips touched the inside of her ankle. The tip of his tongue flicked over the sensitive skin there, then was gone.

"I'm shaking with anticipation of that day, Celia," he said quietly. "But come and have your supper now. Or you will never have that fiery spirit again."

After she had taken as much of the broth as she could, and hastily washed in a basin of warmed water, John tucked her under the blankets again and blew out the candles. Once the chamber was dark, with nothing but the flickering shadows from the fire in the grate, he climbed back onto the bed beside her.

She felt him hesitate, felt the tension of his body, but then he drew her against him again, her back to his chest and his arm light over her hip. His palm flattened on her abdomen, and to her surprise she followed her instinct and traced her fingertips over the bare, hair-roughened skin of his forearm.

He went very still, his body taut against hers, yet he didn't draw away. Celia closed her eyes and just let herself feel him under her fingers, his chest curved around her protectively. The ice pattering at the window, the crackle of the fire, seemed to enclose them in their own little world. Their own special moment. The anger had drained away, and there was only the warm tenderness of old memories she hadn't let herself think about for so long. It was one moment out of real time.

Maybe that feeling of deceptive security was what made her open her mouth and ask, "Where did you go? When you left your uncle's house in the country?"

His hand tightened, and she closed her fingers over

his arm to keep him from moving away. She didn't want to lose the good feelings with him. Not just yet.

"I went to Paris," he said brusquely.

"Paris?" She wasn't quite sure what answer she'd expected, but it hadn't been that. He'd gone to France? So very far away? To get away from her, from their flirtation that had burned so out of control? Was that why he had left so suddenly?

And what had he found in Paris?

"I was given a position in the ambassador's household," he said.

"How long were you there?"

"Above two years," he answered.

Two years—at the most sophisticated, licentious Court in Europe. No wonder he had forgotten his country dalliance. Celia turned her face into the pillow and tried to force away the old pain that was trying so hard to rise up in her again. She didn't want that again. Not yet.

"I was told I had to return to London for a new task," he said. "But I had other work to perform on the journey."

Celia gave a laugh. "Perhaps you would have stayed in France if you'd known the *task* was minding Lord Darnley and the Scottish Queen."

John laughed too, and his warm breath stirred the loose hair at her temple over her skin. It made her shiver despite the warm room, and that tenderness she had always felt towards him returned. So dangerous.

"Perhaps I would have. But then perhaps I would

have returned much sooner if I'd known you were here, Celia."

He brushed aside her hair and kissed her just beside her ear. At the touch of his lips she closed her eyes tightly, and thoughts of French ladies and what John might have done with them flew out of her mind. Only this moment mattered.

John kissed her cheek, and the corner of her mouth. The tip of his tongue touched her, but when she opened her mouth to make him kiss her properly, he drew back.

His arm tightened around her and pulled her closer against his chest. He tucked his legs along hers, their bodies perfectly aligned. She could feel his erection on her backside, but he just pressed his mouth to her ear and whispered to her.

"Sleep now, Celia," he said. "You need your strength. Especially if you still think you can give me that whipping you promised."

Celia laughed and closed her eyes. She *was* tired. Her whole body was sore from fighting off her illness. Yet she feared that when she slept her dreams would be filled with images of John, stripped naked and stretched out on his stomach across the bed as he waited for her pleasure, his blue eyes aglow with tenderness…

John held Celia against him closely as she slept, listening to the soft, even sound of her breath, feeling the movement of her, the wondrous life of her. For a few moments there, in the depths of her fever, he had feared to lose her. He had already lost her once. He wasn't sure he could bear it again—not when death was such a great severing and he'd never been able to make things right for her again.

And all he wanted to do now was make things right for Celia, as he should have done so long ago. If only he knew how.

Celia sighed in her sleep and curled into him, trusting him in her dreams as she could not when awake. He smoothed tendrils of her dark hair back from her brow and thought of the first time he'd seen her. It was a moment he had never been expecting—a moment like something in a sonnet or a madrigal—something he would have scoffed at before he knew Celia.

His youth had been a mostly wasted one, his years at Cambridge a tangle of drink and women and brawls, until one particularly vivid fight had caught his uncle's attention and he'd been forced to find a new direction in his life. Forced to take the chance to redeem himself by serving the Queen. He'd been sent to the country to ferret out the participants in a rumuored Catholic plot to unseat Elizabeth and put Queen Mary on the throne—the sort of plot that came up like weeds every year and had to be chopped down. It had seemed a simple enough task. An easy way to get back in his family's good graces and make a name for himself with Elizabeth.

But then he'd seen Celia standing across the room at a banquet, dressed in a simple white gown and with her hair loose over her shoulders in midnight-coloured waves. It had seemed as if all the light in the chamber gathered only on her, on her shy smile, the pale, serene cast of her face. Everything had gone so still in that moment.

Everything had changed, and he had never forgotten it. He had always liked women—their voices, their laughter, their soft, perfumed bodies. He'd liked them too much to think of settling with only one, but Celia was different. She'd made him imagine a new life, new ways of thinking and being. Until it all had exploded—as he'd known it would from that first moment.

Yet he still couldn't stay away from her. It seemed he never could.

Celia sighed again, and a frown drifted over her brow as if she saw something in her dreams that disturbed her.

"Shh," John whispered, and she settled in his arms. In her sleep she trusted him.

And in that moment, in the silent, cold darkness of the night, enveloped in their own small world of firelight and snow, they were together. He held her safe. He only wanted to make that moment last.

Chapter Nine

When Celia woke again, she could tell it was day by the pale grey light beyond her closed eyes. Yet she didn't quite want to relinquish her dreams. Not yet. She wanted to hold onto that fantasy world, and to those fleeting moments when she and John were not enemies.

She slowly stretched against the rumpled sheets and realised most of the ache was gone. She only felt a new, fresh energy flowing through her, the brush of warm air over her bare arms.

She turned her head on the pillow and opened her eyes to find herself alone on the bed. No snow fell outside the window; there was just that hard grey light.

She pushed herself up against the pillows and saw that John sat by the fire, frowning down at some papers in his hand. A basin and a length of towelling lay on the table beside him, and he looked as if he had just washed. He wore no shirt, and the damp ends of his hair slowly trailed crystal drops of water over his naked shoulders and chest. That light golden skin glowed with the water and the firelight, as if he was an idol in some pagan temple.

She watched avidly as one drop traced a path through the light scattering of brown hair on his chest, arrowing down to the fastening of his leather breeches. For a moment she indulged in the fantasy that it was *her hand* touching him there, teasing him until that ridged abdomen tightened and…

He glanced up and caught her staring. A roguish grin curved his lips, as if he knew exactly what she was thinking. She felt her cheeks turn hot, and she sank back down to the bed so he couldn't see that she blushed like a silly, innocent girl. She remembered so well that old feeling with him.

"So you're awake at last," he said. "Did you sleep well?"

"Aye, thank you," Celia managed to answer. "I feel much recovered."

She heard the papers he held flutter to the table, and the tread of his bare feet on the wood floor as he walked purposefully towards the bed.

She felt his knee press into the mattress and tried to draw the sheet over her head. His fingers curled over the edge of the fabric and pulled it away as he knelt over her. She found herself staring up into his glowing blue eyes as he smiled down at her. He seemed in a strangely good mood.

"I'm glad to hear you're feeling better, Celia," he said, still smiling. "Perhaps you're wanting your breakfast now? You looked hungry enough just then."

"I…"

Before she could say anything else, his mouth swooped down over hers. Open, hot, hungry, as if he wanted to devour her. It awakened something deep inside of her, that seed of longing and need that only John had ever created. He had caused such pain and anger in her life, but such wondrous things too. Emotions and sensations she had never dreamed could exist.

He still did. And when he kissed her he swept her away on a river of fire.

She opened her lips and drew his tongue in over hers. His taste filled her mouth and she moaned. Oh, yes—she did remember this, so very well. And it made her feel just as it once had.

John's arms came hard around her and dragged her closer to his naked chest. As they kissed, deeper, hungrier, their tongues entwining, thrusting, she laid her hands flat on his shoulders and felt the damp heat of him against her palms. John groaned deep in his throat, his hands fisting in the cloth of her chemise as if he would rip it from her.

Emboldened, Celia slid her caress lower, slowly, savouring the way he felt against her. He was just as she remembered—just as he was in her fevered dreams of the past—only even better. Stronger, harder, hotter. *This* was what she needed. This was what would close her past with him, let her put it all aside. To have him as he was now, as she was now, and know that was all there was. Free of the past, with only the feelings of this one moment to think of.

She traced her fingertips over his flat nipples and felt them pebble under her touch. She scraped the edge of her thumbnail over one and he growled. She pressed slightly harder, hard enough to give just the slightest edge of pain, but he didn't shove her away or slap her as her husband would have. His skin rippled, but he went on kissing her.

She slid her touch lower, feeling every inch of his torso, every bit of his skin. He felt like hot satin stretched taut over hard muscle, and the light whorls of hair tickled her palms. She dipped the tip of her smallest finger into his navel before she moved even lower to the band of his breeches.

Suddenly her boldness fled. She could feel his erection, rock-hard against her wrist.

"Curse it, Celia, don't stop now," he whispered as his mouth left hers. He pressed hot, open-mouthed kisses to her jaw, the soft curve of her throat. He nibbled at her there, drawing the skin between his teeth to nip lightly at her.

Celia gasped and let her head fall back as her hand convulsed against his waist. Her heart was pounding as if it would burst, and she could feel that his was too as his body pressed closer to hers.

His mouth opened on the pulse that beat at the base of her neck, that vulnerable hollow so sensitive to sensation. He licked at it, swirling the tip of his tongue there before he closed his teeth on it.

"John!" she cried, her head arching back even more until the braid of her hair lashed at his arm. She felt him tug the binding free and her hair fell loose over her shoulders. He didn't raise his head. His open mouth swept over her collarbone, the little hollows just at her shoulders, until he could nip at the soft upper swell of her breast. The edge of his teeth scraped over that skin too, and Celia's fist closed on the band of his breeches until he gave a rough laugh.

"You still like that, then?" he whispered.

"And do *you* still like this?" She moved her hand lower, until she covered the hard bulge behind the leather fabric. She slid her fingers down its length, not as hard as when she'd touched him at the Queen's banquet, but slower, caressing softly until he groaned.

She pressed her thumb to that spot on the underside she knew he liked, that had once driven him to such fierce need. He seemed to grow even harder.

Suddenly he pulled her chemise over her head, tearing her hand from him. She knelt in front of him, her body naked for him as it had not been in so long. For an instant the heat of passion faded and she remembered she was not as she'd been then. She was thinner, her breasts smaller. And there was her shoulder. She wanted him to remember her as she once had been, not as she was now.

She tried to turn away, to draw her hair over that shoulder, but his hands were already on her again. He turned her back into his arms, his head lowering to her breast.

"So beautiful," he muttered. "You are so damnably beautiful, Celia."

And when he looked at her, touched her, she could almost feel beautiful again, as she once had with him. As his mouth closed over her nipple her head fell back and her eyes closed. She felt the soft brush of her hair on her back, and the heat of his lips on her aching breast.

He suckled hard, drawing her deep into his mouth. She bit her lip to keep from crying out at the way it made her feel. Her body, which had felt so frozen and numb for so long, roared back to burning life again.

He covered her other breast with his palm, his fingers spread wide to cradle her, caress her. One fingertip brushed over that engorged nipple and a cry burst free from her lips. She felt him smile against her, just before his teeth bit down lightly and he pinched her other nipple.

She reached desperately between their bodies to unfasten his breeches and push them down over his lean hips. His penis sprang free against her abdomen, rock-hard and hot. As she touched it, naked in her hand at last, it jerked and he groaned. His teeth tightened on her nipple before he arched his head back.

Celia looked into his eyes and they were burning and dark, the blue almost swallowed in black lust. She bent to kiss the side of his neck, to bite at him as he had with her. He tasted salty and sweet under her lips, of that night essence that was only John. It was intoxicating, dizzying.

As she kissed him she ran her palm down his manhood to its swollen tip. There was a drop of moisture there, and she caught it on her finger to spread it upward again, slow, steady. *Aye*—she remembered this so very well.

John's hands suddenly closed on her backside, his fingers digging into the soft skin as he dragged her even closer. Her hand dropped away from him and he slowly pressed the tip of his penis against the soft nest of damp curls between her thighs. He moved up and down, lightly teasing at her swollen cleft.

"John..." she whispered against his neck.

"So wet—so hot," he growled. He pulled her flush against his hips, and then suddenly pushed her back to the bed. He came down on top of her, his hips between her spread legs, his lips claiming hers in a wild, desperate kiss.

Celia wrapped her legs around his waist and instinctively arched up into him. He was so large, so strong and—and overwhelming. She was completely surrounded by him, by his heat and power. Suddenly she couldn't breathe.

She tore her lips from his kiss and tilted her head back to try and gulp in a breath. Her hands dug into his shoulders as if she would push him away.

But he seemed to sense something was wrong, that the icy hand of fear was creeping over her, reminding her of the horror that was her marriage bed. His hands slid around her waist, and in one deft twist he lay on his back on the bed and she was on top of him. Her legs lay to either side of his hips as she straddled him.

She stared down at him in dizzy astonishment. The air suddenly seemed clearer around her, the fear dissipating like clouds after a storm. She wasn't held down, overpowered. She was free, yet still tethered to John by the light touch of his hands at her waist, the look in his eyes. He watched her with an almost feral gleam in those eyes, as if he was so hungry he could devour her now in one bite, yet there was tenderness there too, so deep and reassuring. His face was set in taut lines of fierce control.

Yet he made no move. It was as if he knew what she needed now: to be in control of what was happening. Celia swallowed hard. She had never been in this position before, never looked at a man in this way. It was—quite nice.

Very nice indeed, she thought as she braced her palms flat on John's chest. She slid them down, down, a slow, hard glide on his skin. He felt so tense under her touch, as if he waited for her, held himself tightly leashed to let her touch him as she would.

It made her want him even more.

She shook her hair back and smiled down at him. A muscle flexed in his jaw and his eyes never wavered from her. She gently moved his hands from her waist and held them to the bed as she leaned down and laid her open mouth on his chest. His hands jerked but he didn't push her away.

She tasted him with the tip of her tongue, and moved to swirl it lightly over his flat, brown nipple. It hardened under her kiss, and she could hear the harsh hiss of his breath.

She nipped her teeth over the arc of his ribs.

"I always remember this, John," she whispered. "Even when I hated you, when I cursed your name, I would remember this late at night. Your taste. Your smell. The way your skin felt on mine. It was as if I could still taste you on my tongue. You must be a sorcerer, to hold my dreams so enchanted by what you would do to me."

She licked at the indentation along his hip, that enticing masculine line of muscle that dipped towards his manhood. She exhaled a sigh over the base of his penis, and sat up again.

"You're the witch," he ground out as he stared deep into her eyes, not letting her go. "No one has ever made me feel like you did, Celia, from the first moment I saw you."

Celia shook her head. She didn't want to know he had thought of her. Not now. She wanted to remember how it had once been. She only wanted *this*, them together, now.

"Sometimes when I dreamed of you at night, John, I ached so much. I had to do this." She closed her eyes and laid her hand lightly between her breasts. Slowly, slowly, she traced her touch down her body, over her abdomen, until her hand lay over the place that was so wet for him she ached with it all over again. *He* had taught her to do this, and she remembered how the sight of her hand there affected him. How it made him explode.

She slid one fingertip between her folds, and that was all it took.

"Hell, Celia!" he shouted, and his control snapped.

Her eyes flew open as his hands seized her hips. But he did not drag her under him to drive into her. He drew her body up along his until his mouth closed over her womanhood. She knelt over his face as his tongue plunged deep into her.

Celia screamed, and grabbed onto the carved wood

of the bed as his mouth claimed every intimate part of her. His fingers dug hard into her buttocks as he kissed her, licked her, tasted her so deeply. She was no longer in control, but she didn't care. She only wanted his mouth, his hands on her. Claiming her. Making her remember—and forget.

His tongue flicked on that tiny knot high inside her, and she moaned. One of his hands let go of her and slid around her hip, until he could drive one long finger inside of her, just below that talented tongue. He moved it in and out, pressing, sliding, until she cried out wordlessly.

"John," she moaned.

"Let go, my fairy queen," he whispered against her. "I have you with me. You're safe."

And strangely she did feel safe, as she never had before. Another finger slid into her, and she felt pressure building low in her belly. Oh, sweet saints, but she had not felt like this in such a long time! Sex had come to mean only pain and humiliation, but now she remembered what it could be, what it had been—with John. Only John. That heat built and built, expanding inside of her until she couldn't breathe. Her whole body was suffused with golden light.

"Let go!" he said, and his tongue pressed hard to that knot as his fingers curled inside her.

And she did let go. She shattered, that pressure exploding like a bonfire within her. She screamed again, her hands clutching at the bed to keep her from falling into the abyss below.

But John wasn't finished with her. He lifted her trembling body off his mouth and pushed himself up to half-sit against the headboard. He drew her down until she straddled his hips again, her open, wet womanhood spread over the tip of his penis.

"Ride me, Celia," he said hoarsely. "I am yours."

She braced her hands on his slick, sweaty shoulders and tried to focus her pleasure-dazed mind. She stared down at him, at the way his lips glistened with her own essence, the way his eyes were so dark and wild with lust. She could smell herself on him, the scent of the two of them blended, and it made her want him all over again. Need him.

And she wanted him to need her just as much. To remember how they had once been together.

She raised herself slightly, until she felt his swollen tip at her opening, and then she held tightly to his shoulders and slid down. Lower, lower, until he was all the way inside of her, their hips pressed together.

His eyes suddenly went blurry, and his head fell back as his hands closed on her waist.

"Ah, curse it, Celia," he groaned. "You're so tight—so perfect. I can't..."

She raised up again and sank back down, over and over, until she found her rhythm. His hips arched up to meet her. They moved together, harder, faster. Until she felt her climax building up all over again.

Her body fell back and she braced her hands on his thighs as he thrust up into her. She closed her eyes and saw whirling stars in the darkness, blue and green and white, exploding around her until she cried out his name.

"Celia!" he shouted, amid a flood of incoherent curses as his whole body went rigid. She felt him go still inside her, the hot rush of him against her as he too let go and soared free.

She let herself fall to the bed, her legs unable to hold her up any longer. She trembled as she felt a heavy, hot languor steal over her, a boneless exhaustion as she had never known before. The beamed ceiling spun above her as she tried to catch her breath.

John crawled up to collapse beside her. They didn't touch, but she could feel the heat of his sweat-damp body close to hers, could hear the rough rush of his breath.

She rolled her head to look at him. His eyes were closed as he kicked his breeches away, his hair falling damply over his brow. She gently brushed it back, and he caught her hand in his to kiss her palm.

She sighed and closed her eyes, feeling the way he pressed her hand flat to his chest and held her there. She felt the brush of cold air over her heated skin. The fire had died away in the grate, but she didn't care. She was too tired and replete to care about anything but John's hand on hers.

"You still talk filthy in bed, John Brandon," she whispered teasingly. "Where did you learn those words? In Paris?"

He gave a drowsy chuckle. "And you still remember everything that drives me insane. Did you really touch yourself when you thought of me?"

Celia smiled. "A lady must keep her secrets, John," she said. And then she let herself tumble down into a deep, dreamless sleep.

Chapter Ten

☘

A lady must keep her secrets.

John heard Celia's words in his mind as he watched her sleeping in the bed they had shared. Cool grey light moved over her bare skin as she lay on her stomach, her arms around her pillow and her black hair spilling over the rumpled sheets. The coverings were low on her hips, leaving her slender, supple back bare to tempt him.

And, God's teeth, but he was tempted. His muscles were coiled to send him striding across the chamber, to grab the sheets and tear them away until she was naked for him again.

Until she opened for him again, let him in, let him see every part of her, body and soul. Until she cried his name and needed him, as he needed her in that moment.

He braced his fists on the table and let his head drop between his shoulders, shutting out the sight of her. Shutting out the temptation. It had always been that way with Celia, even when they'd first met. She had been innocent then, more vulnerable, but there had always been that sharp intelligence behind her cool grey eyes. That edge to her words, that unwillingness to suffer fools.

That desire as she looked at him, that passion that matched his own and drove him higher and hotter.

The memory of her had haunted him for years, until he'd become sure he made her into something she had never really been. An elusive fairy queen who'd never existed except in his mind, his dreams.

But earlier she had shown him she was every bit all he'd once thought her, and so much more. He had never wanted anything or anyone as he wanted her. When she'd taken him inside her, her body over his, her eyes burning with raw need, he had gone mad with it. With *her*. He'd dared to begin to think he *could* make it different at long last.

She had been his again, only his. No rational thought, only feeling—primitive, ferocious feeling.

But now he wished with all his might that she would run from him. Push him away and flee so far they could never see each other again. When they came together it was as elemental as that storm outside, and as lethal. They would destroy each other even as they couldn't stay apart.

Secrets. Aye, she had been so very right about that. So many secrets lay between them. How could he ever make it right?

He opened his eyes and reached out for the papers scattered across the table. Marcus had sent them via messenger while Celia slept yesterday, and they were updates on their travels. It seemed all was not well there, and Marcus needed John to rejoin them soon. Something was amiss among Darnley's cohorts. Something besides drink and fights.

More secrets.

John heard a soft sound from the bed, and looked up to see that Celia was stirring awake. She slowly stretched against the sheets, the fabric easing lower until he could see the vulnerable hollow of her back. Just one of the soft, sweet spots he had so recently kissed. He snapped his too-eager stare up from her bare skin to her face, turned in profile on the pillow.

A smile touched her lips, and she looked so young then. So happy and innocent that he almost went to her. Almost climbed beside her on the bed and kissed her, damning the consequences.

Then she seemed to come fully awake and remember. The smile faded into a small frown and her eyes opened.

Celia rolled onto her back—and caught him staring at her. She gasped and sat up straight on the bed, yanking the sheet up to cover her nakedness. John pushed down the sharp sense of disappointment and gave her a humourless smile.

"Good day to you, Celia," he said.

The tip of her tongue touched her lips—a tiny, nervous gesture that sent a bolt of pure fire straight to his groin. She shook her tangled fall of hair back from her shoulders and lifted her chin in a gesture he had become too familiar with by now. Her armour was closing around her again. He had to decipher how to tear it away.

"So it is true," she said softly.

"You can pretend it was all a dream if you like,"

he answered, keeping his voice cool and calm even as his heart ached. He did not want her to think it was a dream! He wanted her to remember every second, every touch and kiss, as vividly as he did. To want him as he had always wanted her.

"I'm not as good at pretending as I once was," she said, just as calmly.

"Just as you like. You don't have to cower there under the bedclothes. I'm not a starving wolf, set to devour you as soon as you move."

"Nay, the wolf is sated for now. And I do not cower," she snapped. Then softer, as if she spoke to herself, "Not any more."

Her words made him look at her damaged shoulder and think of the fear that had flashed in her eyes when he'd pinned her to the bed. The fear that had only eased when he'd rolled her on top of him. He longed to go to her, to snatch her up in his arms and hold her against him until she knew only him. Only remembered him.

But he had not been able to protect her from her villain of a husband. He had to protect her now.

He made himself stay where he was, his fists braced to the table as he watched her reach for her crumpled chemise on the floor and pull it over her head. He had the briefest glimpse of her bare breasts before she was covered again.

She walked to the table where he stood and reached for the pitcher of ale set there. She didn't look at him as she poured out a gobletful and sipped at it. He tried not to stare hungrily at the soft movement of her throat as she swallowed, at her slender fingers wrapped around the goblet. Tried not to remember what she had done with them.

"What are those?" she asked, gesturing with the goblet at the papers.

"Messages from Marcus," he said, forcing his attention back to the documents. "It seems there is trouble."

Celia gave a little snort of a laugh and took a deep sip of the ale. "Now, why am I not surprised to hear that? Is our presence required?"

"Soon, I think. When you are strong enough to travel. I don't want you to become ill again."

She shrugged and turned away to refill her goblet. "It was only a chill. I am perfectly able to travel. Today, if needs be."

"Celia…" That fierce protectiveness rose up in him again.

"I said I can travel! I want to go," she snapped.

The words she left unspoken hung in the air, and John knew what she meant—she did not want to stay there with him. It was what she should feel, and yet he was angry. He wanted to change her mind.

"I should send for a litter for you," he said, pushing himself back from the table. From her.

"That would take too long, and you know it," she said. "I can ride."

"Nay, Celia."

She spun back to face him, her eyes sparkling. "Do you doubt my strength after earlier this morning?"

He crossed his arms over his chest, his jaw set in a hard line as they stared at each other. The very air seemed to crackle around them.

She turned away first, her shoulders slumped. "Just see to the horses," she said, her voice small and quiet. "I will get dressed."

He did not want to leave her—not like this, with so much still between them. So much that could not be said. But her very stillness held him away. She looked as if she would crack if he touched her. He could bide his time. He had learned patience in the last few years.

"Aye," he said, and strode towards the door. He let it close softly behind him even as every instinct in him urged him to drive his fist into the wall.

Or to grab her, slam his mouth down on hers as he stripped away her chemise and repeated what they had done earlier.

Celia stabbed the pins into her upswept hair as she stared at her reflection in the window. Even in the fractured wavy glass she looked pale and gaunt, ghost-like. Haunted.

She twisted her hair harder, glad of the sting on her scalp as it distracted her and brought her back to her task. She hadn't been herself earlier this morning. Now she had to find herself again.

She glanced over her shoulder at the rumpled empty bed. Earlier, in those tangled sheets, she had been wild and free. Everything she had held so tightly in check for so long had flown free. All because of John. His touch, his kiss—they had always unleashed something in her she didn't understand. And earlier the pleasure of that wildness had been unfathomable.

Now she wanted to scream with the anger and sadness of losing it all over again. When she'd woken up from delicious dreams and seen the distant, wary look in his eyes, the cool lack of expression on his face, she'd longed to fly at him. Slap his face, scratch at his golden skin until he reacted to her. Showed her something, anything, that told her he had been affected by their lovemaking. That, despite everything, he wanted her still.

She'd managed to hold herself still, to match his distance with a chill of her own. She had become quite good at hiding her thoughts and emotions. Sometimes not reacting, keeping herself apart, had been all that saved her.

And now, in the cold daylight, she saw that he was right to stay away. Perhaps their swiving had been inevitable—something that still lay between them from the past. Their bodies still knew each other, no matter what their minds said.

But it *was* the past. This was the present, and a gulf wider than the English Channel lay between them.

She finished pinning up her hair and turned from her reflection to put the final touches to her dress. Some of her clothes had been left for her, and she put on her warmest quilted petticoat and wool skirt, a high-necked black wool and velvet doublet. She wedged her feet into her riding boots and reached for her hat and gloves. She was ready to ride into any battle now.

She hurried out of the chamber where so much had happened and down the stairs, as if she could flee John and what he had made her feel there at the same time. But he waited for her in the cold, empty foyer.

He was also dressed to ride, in brown leather and

wool, his hair brushed back from his face. She let her eyes linger on those strands, thinking of how they'd felt as they slid through her fingers, as she'd used them to pull him down to her.

She turned sharply away to jerk on her gloves.

"You still wear mourning," he said, his voice flat.

"I can't afford new Court clothes," she answered. "My black was the last thing I could get from my husband's cheese-paring family. I couldn't let it go to waste. Are we ready to depart, then?"

John frowned as if he wanted to say something else, but he merely nodded. He swung open the door and a blast of cold wind curled around her.

"Let us go, then," he said.

Chapter Eleven

Celia reined in her horse at the crest of the hill to catch her breath after the hard gallop. She tossed a smile over her shoulder at John as he drew up beside her. Her uncertainties of before had been lost in the exhilaration of the ride, the sheer joy of still being alive.

"I do believe I was the victor," she said.

"So you were," he answered with a grin. "This time."

"I will outrun you again, John Brandon. And again and again."

"I wouldn't be so confident if I were you, my lady. Perhaps I allowed you to win out of gallantry."

Celia laughed. "Certainly you did not. The great Sir John, victor in all his endeavours, bested by a woman? You would never want word of that to spread. It would quite ruin your reputation."

"I don't see anyone here to witness my loss, do you? I would say my good name at Court is safe."

Celia glanced around as he gestured with his riding crop at the landscape below. She still smiled as she surveyed the frozen fields, bisected by grey stone walls. It felt good to laugh and tease with John again, to feel at least a bit at ease in his presence.

In the days since they'd left the hunting lodge they had ridden in silence, saying only the little that was necessary as they'd travelled hard over the mostly deserted roads. At night they'd stopped at quiet inns to gulp down a hasty meal and fall into bed—alone. She noticed he always slept at a careful distance from her, close enough to protect her in a strange place, but far enough that there was no contact at all.

He would take her hand to help her from the saddle, would ask her how she fared, make sure she had enough wine or blankets, but that was all.

Celia was happy to be quiet with him, to keep her distance. She thought too much about him as it was. The bare, wintry landscape they passed offered little distraction from memories of what had happened between them in that bed. The feel of his hands on her bare skin, his mouth and tongue on her, his hoarse moans and curses as they rode each other. She saw the look in his eyes as he watched her. It was all still there, vivid and painful—sweet in her mind.

She glanced at him from the corner of her eye. He was absently patting his horse's neck as he surveyed the land around them, a small frown on his lips. He looked as if his own thoughts were a hundred miles away, and against her better judgement she found she desperately wanted to know what they were. What he kept hidden deep inside himself.

But she feared that if she caught a glimpse of John,

the real John, she would have to share the real Celia in return. That she could not do.

"So this is Scotland," she said. "It looks scarcely different from England."

Or rather scarcely different from the England they had seen in the last few days. Harsh, austere, forbidding northern England, so different from the softness of southern England, the noise and commotion of London. The place seemed like a separate world from all she had ever really known. It was silent and grey-green all around.

Yet she liked it. The very harshness seemed beautiful to her, seemed to respond to something hard and cold and wild inside her.

"Aye, this is Scotland," John said. "What do you think of it so far?"

Celia looked around her again and drew in a deep breath. She even liked the air here, clean and diamond-clear, smelling of frost, green, and the faint tang of a peat fire.

"I like it very much," she said. "I like the loneliness of it."

John gave her a strange look, and she thought she saw a flash of surprise in his eyes. "I doubt there will be any time for loneliness once we reach Edinburgh."

"I dare say there won't. If Queen Mary's Court is anything like her cousin's, there won't be a moment of silence."

"They say she is trying to bring elements of her French life to the Scottish Court," John said. "Dancing, cards, masquerades, hunts. I doubt that pleases Knox and his Puritan cohorts. They thought never to see their French Catholic queen again."

That must certainly be true. Surely they'd thought that with Mary in France Scotland was theirs to run as they wanted. The country's religion, alliances and culture in their hands. Until suddenly she'd returned, with her own ways of doing things.

"Has there been trouble?" Celia asked quietly.

"Nothing serious as yet. Mary has proved strangely popular with her subjects since she returned from Paris—except for the men who thought *they* ruled Scotland and dictated its religion and allies. Threats, stones thrown at courtiers' carriages, ugly pamphlets railing against female rulers. But there will be more to come. That seems inevitable."

"Is that what Lord Marcus's message said?"

John shifted in his saddle. "Knox and Queen Elizabeth aren't the only ones who want to control Queen Mary. She still has her French attendants with her, who have their own ideas of what she should do."

"Not to mention the Spanish," Celia murmured. It was so nice to be able to talk to John like this again, to share her ideas and hear his, to know what he thought of their strange situation. "To have a Catholic ally right on Elizabeth's northern border could only be a boon to them. Is the marriage of Queen Mary to Don Carlos still a possibility?"

"A distant one, perhaps, or Mary would have snapped it up by now. She wouldn't dally with the likes of Darnley if she had the Spanish heir."

"And one of these parties is not causing trouble in Edinburgh."

John suddenly gave her a rakish grin. "Celia, where a crown is at stake there is always trouble. We must make more of it for our opponents than they do for us."

Was that how he lived his life, then? Made trouble for others before they could do it to him? Before she could say anything to him, he tugged at his reins and took off down the hill.

"We need to find a place to stop for the night," he called to her, his words caught on the wind.

Celia dashed after him. The cold wind kept them from saying any more as they galloped over the fields and found the road again. The narrow track was muddy and rutted, clotted with fallen branches, but they made good time. Dusk was falling when they finally stopped in front of a pair of gates that stood ajar.

They were of an elaborate design of twisted wrought iron, surmounted by a family crest, but they were being eaten away by rust. Beyond the gates she glimpsed an overgrown trail winding away between towering trees.

John stared up at the crest with an unreadable look on his face.

"Are we stopping here?" Celia asked quietly.

He was silent for a long moment. So long she thought he might not answer. That he had forgotten she was even there.

Finally he said, "Why not? It's growing dark, and it's still a fair ride into the village."

He led his horse through the gap in the gates and Celia followed. As they made their way slowly down

the path she felt as if she had stepped into a troubadour's song of enchanted forests and ghosts. It seemed
even quieter here than on the hill, perfectly silent, as if
even the wind dared not brush through the bare, skeletal trees.

She could see that once this had been a grand park,
laid out for pleasure rides and pretty vistas, but now
it was all a tangle. She glimpsed a half-frozen lake in
the distance, with a pale stone folly crumbling on the
shore. The gathering evening mist only made it more
mysterious.

Celia shivered.

"Are you cold?" John asked. "We will soon be there,
and we can build a fire."

"I'm quite well," she said, even as that chill danced
up her spine again.

They turned at a twist in the path, and Celia saw a
house rise up before them. It was a surprisingly fine
manor of faded red brick and dark wood latticework
that had once been painted. The small windows stared
down, blank and dark.

Above the door was another chipped stone crest.

"How did you know this place was here?" Celia
asked as John swung down from his horse and came
round to help her dismount. "Have you been here before?"

"Nay, but I heard about it as a child," he said. When
he lowered her to her feet he didn't immediately release
her, as he had been doing, but kept his arm around her
waist. He held her with him as he studied the house

with narrowed eyes. "This was my mother's family's house," he said.

"Your mother?" Celia gasped in surprise. Then she remembered John's mother had been Scottish—one of the reasons Queen Elizabeth had given for sending him here. But John had never spoken of her before. "Where are they, then?"

"All dead. They died even before I was born. After my mother was sent to England to serve one of Henry's many queens. Since my parents died when I was six, it is mine now." He kicked at a fallen chunk of brick on the ground. "For all the good it does me."

Celia blinked as she looked up at him. She had seen John angry, cold, passionate, but never like this. So very distant. It made her shiver again, and his arm tightened around her.

"Come, you should be inside," he said.

Celia nodded. She didn't want to go inside. This place seemed haunted in truth. But it was dark now, and there was nowhere else to go.

John pushed the door open with his foot and led her inside.

She had thought the hunting lodge was quiet and desolate, but it was nothing to this place. Everything in the foyer was so still she could hear the wind whistling outside, creeping through the walls. The floor was warped and cracked, the balustrade of the staircase broken. From somewhere up in the ceiling she thought she could hear the rustle of birds.

She rubbed at her arms through her sleeves and followed John into what had once been the great hall.

There was a large fireplace at one end, and a few broken bits of furniture littered on the floor. He found an almost intact stool and set it by the empty fireplace.

"Sit down and rest," he said. "I'll try to make a fire so we can stay somewhat comfortable tonight. We should catch up to the others by tomorrow."

Tomorrow. Their time together was ending so very soon. The reality of their lives, their two separate lives, grew closer with every moment. She should be eager to leave John behind, to move towards the future. Work for Queen Elizabeth; a new marriage. The past gone.

But instead she only felt colder. Hollow inside. She had been closer to John than she had ever been to another person, no matter how deceptive those feelings had been in the end. Yet she craved it again—that warmth she sometimes glimpsed in his eyes.

She had put him out of her life once. Surely she could do it again?

She wrapped her arms around her waist as she watched him use the remnants of the wooden furniture to build a fire. The flames were slow to grow at first, until they grabbed onto the dry, brittle wood and crackled to life. Celia slowly felt herself grow warmer, steadier, calmer. They were here together now. That had to be enough.

Once the fire was well lit, John brought in their saddlebags and made a quick meal of hard biscuits, dried beef and wine. It was full dark outside when quiet fell between them, broken only by the snap of the fire and the wind outside.

Celia saw the way he rolled his head between his

shoulders and rubbed wearily at his neck. Something softened deep inside of her, and before she knew what she was doing she reached out to touch his arm. She couldn't stop herself. His back tightened, and he gave her a wary glance over his shoulder.

"Lean against me for a while," she said softly. "Let me rub your shoulders. You used to like it when I did that after a day's hunting."

For a moment she thought he would refuse. Would stride from the room and leave her alone. But then he leaned against her legs and let his head fall back to her knees, heavy through her skirts.

She sat on the stool while he was on the floor, so her hands floated naturally to his shoulders. His doublet was unfastened, and she eased it down his arms. He wrapped his arms around her calves as she kneaded at his hard shoulder muscles. His skin was warm and smooth through his shirt.

She pressed her thumbs into the tense knots of his back. "This must have been a grand house once," she said as she felt him slowly relax against her.

"My mother always said it was, when she told me stories when I was a child." John's voice sounded deep and distant, as if her touch carried him far away. "There were grand banquets here. Especially at Christmas. Dancing and music, minstrels' tales here by this very fire. Queen Marie of Guise was even invited here one year."

Celia studied the hall around them, seeing it not as it was now but the way it had been. Could be. The floors polished and gleaming, tapestries on the walls, delicacies piled high on silver plates atop carved sideboards. Musicians playing a pavane in the gallery above as the brightly dressed guests danced.

"It's a shame the house isn't ready to receive Queen Marie's daughter, then," Celia said.

"Who knows if my mother's tales were true?" said John as he leaned back into her hands. "This place might have been a ruin for decades before she was born. She just liked to make Scotland sound like a romantic dream. Z'wounds, Celia, but that feels good! I should keep you close to me after tournaments. You would banish any wound with a touch."

Celia smiled, but she didn't want to dwell on how good his words felt. How much she would love to see him ride in a tournament, her favour tied to his lance. "You remember your mother, then?" she said.

"Some things. She had brown hair, and wore a rose-water scent. She liked to sit by my cot at night and tell me tales in her Scots accent. Sometimes I wonder if I merely imagined all that."

"What happened to your parents?"

John gave his head a hard shake, as if to clear it of old dreams. "Like yours, they died of a fever. I was a mere child."

"I'm so sorry," Celia whispered, and smoothed her palm gently over his shoulder. His skin rippled under her touch. She had not known that, like her, he was alone in the world. To be so young a child…

"My uncle was my only family left then, and he was fighting in France," John said coolly, as if he discussed the weather outside. "So I was given to the Court of

Wards. I met Marcus when we were fostered in the same household, and together we made our own family of sorts."

"And you have never seen your mother's home before."

"Nay." He looked up at her with a wry grin. "Not much of a legacy, is it?"

Celia looked around the hall again. "'Tis more than I have. It could be made habitable again."

A frown flickered over his face. "But I am the servant of Queen Elizabeth. I could be no Scotsman."

Silence fell between them, and Celia smoothed her fingertips over the nape of his neck. A strange and most unwelcome tenderness washed over her.

"You must be tired, Celia," John said, drawing away from her touch.

She blinked away the last tendrils of that quiet, yearning dream and watched as he spread out their cloaks and blankets from the saddlebags to make a makeshift bed by the fire.

"Aye," she whispered. She did feel tired, bone-deep weary, and so very cold.

"Then lie down beside me and sleep for a time. Let me keep you warm." John held out his hand to her, but Celia hesitated. A smile touched the corner of his lips. "I vow I will not ravish you tonight, Celia. Just stay with me."

Celia smiled back, and tried to push away a twinge of disappointment at not being ravished again. She took his hand and let him draw her down beside him on the blankets. She lay on her side, facing the fire, and he curled his body around her, his knees tucked behind hers and his arm around her waist. She felt his warm breath on the back of her neck.

She closed her eyes and tried to give in to the exhaustion that tugged at her, but sleep would not come. It felt far too good to be wrapped in John's arms—too safe, too right. It seemed even more intimate than their passionate lovemaking.

She wanted to turn in his arms, kiss his hard, hot mouth and lose herself in his body again. She wanted that mindless lust, that forgetfulness of need.

She understood physical need. She could even somewhat control it, use it.

But the longings of her heart, unleashed by his tenderness, were tearing her apart.

John braced his hands on the cracked windowsill and stared out into the black, frost-tinged night. Celia slept in the room behind him, tossing fitfully in her dreams for a moment before she settled again with a sigh. He wished he could join her in the oblivion of sleep, hold her in his arms and find peace, at least for the night. Celia had once brought him such a peace as he had never known before.

But tonight they were in his family's home, a place he had thought never to see except in his mother's tales, and it made him feel restless in ways he had not expected. He shouldn't have brought Celia here, but there had been little choice. He'd had to find her a place to rest, to take care of her, and this was the nearest house he knew of.

John turned to study the bare, dusty chamber, so full of crooked shadows and the shifting light from the fire. In the night, it looked almost as it might once have been, the cracked plaster and warped floors hidden. The crackle of the flames might have been the ghosts of old laughter.

Once this had been a home, a place for a family. He had never known such a thing, having been orphaned so young and tossed upon the world alone. He had known only that, only looking out for himself, and for a time it had been enough. Until Celia. But the thought that he could have more had been only an illusion in the end. Much like this house in the firelight.

He crossed his arms over his chest and studied Celia where she lay sleeping, still and calm now, her face sculpted by the light. Her arm was flung out, her fingers curled as if she reached out for something elusive.

Nay, he should not have brought her here. She and this house only made him feel things he should not. He couldn't dream of her again. Couldn't hurt her again.

Celia stirred a bit, her hand closing on the blankets. "John," she murmured.

"I am here," he answered. He moved across the room and lay down beside her, even as he knew he should stay away. Something always drew him back to her, some dark force he couldn't understand. He drew her into his arms and she curled against his chest, soft and vulnerable as she so seldom was when awake.

John pressed a soft kiss to her hair and inhaled deeply of her perfume, as if he could memorise the scent and hold it with him always. "I am here," he said again. "Sleep now."

Celia smiled and fell back into her dreams. But John could not follow her. He lay awake until dawn, holding her there in that house of ghosts.

Chapter Twelve

Edinburgh at last.

Celia stretched her aching shoulders as she rode with John through the city gates and along the narrow, winding lanes of the city. She felt as if she had been years and years on this journey, not just weeks. So much had happened since she'd left London. She hardly felt the same person she'd been before.

But now she was here, the journey behind her and an unknown precarious future ahead. Her days alone with John were at an end.

She glanced at him where he rode just ahead of her and to her side, sheltering her from the worst of the crowd. She should be happy that they wouldn't be thrown together any longer. Happy that he could no longer chip away at her defences, remind her of how she had once felt about him, opened herself to him. He could no longer tempt her.

She tore her gaze away from his muscled shoulders and studied the city around her as he led her onward.

After weeks of travelling the winter-silent countryside the sounds and smells of a busy town felt like an assault to the senses. Shouts and cries, laughter, and the rhymes of food sellers bombarded her ears. The mingled scents of smoke from hundreds of chimneys, fried meat pies, chamber pots and too many people in too small a space were raw and pungent.

John suddenly reached back for her horse's bridle and tugged her out of the way as one of those pots had its contents hurled down onto the cobbled street from a window far above. It ran down to the sloped channel down the middle of the street along with all the other rubbish of city life.

Celia looked up from under her hat brim. The streets here seemed even narrower than those of London, the houses packed even closer together. Everything seemed coated in a layer of grey soot and grime, with snow in slushy drifts beneath windows and in the gutter. The rooftops nearly touched above the street, blocking out what little daylight there was.

Celia looked ahead again, and found John watching her. Ever since they had left his family's house he had been quiet, his face wiped clean of any expression. He was calmly efficient, solicitous of her comfort—and cold. For an instant she thought she saw something flicker deep in his eyes, but then it was gone.

"Are you well, Celia?" he asked quietly.

"Of course. I've dodged chamber pots before in my life."

"We'll be to the palace soon."

"Very good. Though I dare say if Whitehall is anything to go by it won't be much cleaner."

A small smile touched his lips before he turned away. "Hopefully it will at least be warmer."

They left the city's most crowded centre streets and climbed higher up the steep lanes to a more open, airy section of the larger houses. She could see the rugged crags that rose up above the town, blank and austere against the cold sky, and the silent grey-green bulk of Arthur's Seat, a long-dormant volcano. It still looked ominous to Celia, as if it just waited to swallow up the whole land again.

At last they came to the arches of a gatehouse and passed through them to the forecourt of Holyrood Palace itself.

Celia recognised it well from the descriptions she had read. Squat and low, it was built of honey-coloured stone around a quadrangle, rising only two storeys in the front and three at the sides.

It looked surprisingly modern and comfortable. Celia had read that the old palace had been damaged by King Henry's campaign of "Rough Wooing" many years ago, when he'd tried to negotiate a marriage between his son and the infant Queen Mary by warfare and invasion. Instead Marie of Guise had sent her daughter to France, to be betrothed to the Dauphin, and fought on until Henry was persuaded to look elsewhere for a match. Holyrood had been rebuilt in a more modern style, with towers, large windows to let in the light, and battlemented parapets.

There were graceful towers to either side of the

entrance, surmounted by the royal arms of Scotland carved over the door. Queen Mary's standards fluttered from the parapets, the arms of Scotland, France and England emblazoned on them.

Celia followed John over the iron drawbridge and along a wide gravelled drive, around a silent fountain towards the palace. She could hear voices floating from a hidden garden somewhere, laughter and music, growls from the menagerie, but she could not see anyone. The rolling lawn to either side of the drive was deserted, and only guards in the Queen's livery could be seen outside the doors and along the towers.

But as they drew to a halt the doors opened and a woman ran down the front steps. Celia recognised Lady Allison's red hair, and stiffened when the woman gave John a brilliant, flirtatious smile.

"Here you are at last!" Allison cried. "Both of you. Marcus said you would probably arrive today and that I should watch for you."

Celia struggled not to frown as John smiled back at Allison. It was nothing to *her* if he flirted with every lady at Queen Mary's Court! That was his reputation in London—why would it be different here?

Because she had seen another part of him at the hunting lodge and in his family's house, when they had both let their façades drop for an instant. She'd seen that he struggled with something dark and hidden in his heart. She longed to know what it was, but at the same time it frightened her. Fascinated her.

Yet this man before her now looked as if he hid nothing more dire than a need for mischief of the sort found amid a royal Court—sex, sport, drink. He still grinned as he swung down from his horse and came round to lift Celia from her saddle. He held onto her for a moment as she swayed on numb legs.

His gloved hands were hard and warm against her waist, and she had to hold herself stiffly rigid to keep from clinging to him. To keep from wrapping her arms around his neck and burying her head in his chest. Begging him to take her away from here and back to the hunting lodge.

Instead she pulled herself out of his touch and stepped back. His smile dimmed, his eyes narrowing as he looked down at her. Then he too stepped away and turned to Lady Allison. He took her outstretched hand and kissed it as she laughed up at him.

Celia twisted her riding crop between her fingers.

"How is everyone here, Allison?" he asked.

Allison giggled. "I'm sure we will be much merrier now that you are here! But Queen Mary is not at Holyrood, I fear. She and most of her courtiers are off on a hunting expedition. Lord Darnley has gone to meet her at Wemyss Castle. They should return within a few days."

"I hope he has not gone unattended," John said darkly.

"Nay, certainly not! He would vanish into the village alehouse and not be found for months," said Allison. "Most of his friends are with him, with Marcus to keep them steady. That's why he left me to look out for you. And now you two must be so tired. Mistress Sutton—if you care to come with me I can show you to your lodgings and send for some food. I know John here can look after himself quite well!"

"Thank you, Lady Allison," Celia murmured. She followed Allison through the doors, forcing herself not to look back at John. To leave him behind.

Allison led Celia into the dim palace and along a narrow corridor. John vanished behind them. The halls were deserted and cold.

"Certain people have been missing you very much," Allison said as they climbed up a winding staircase.

Celia laughed. "I can't imagine who."

Allison shot her a sly smile over her shoulder. "Can you not? Why, Lord Knowlton has been asking after you every day."

"Has he?" Celia asked in surprise. She certainly did remember their conversations, his admiring glances— the way John had been strangely jealous of him. Her stomach gave a nervous twinge.

Allison laughed. "Aye, he has. I'm sure he will be very happy to see you tonight. And I vow he won't be the only one…"

John took a long drink from his goblet of strong ale, closing his eyes as its rough heat slid down his throat. But there was no forgetfulness in the drink tonight. There was nothing but Celia.

He leaned his arms on the stone parapet of the palace tower and stared up into the night sky. The stars were blanketed with thick clouds, and snow had started to fall again, cold and damp. It was late—long past the hour when everyone had stumbled off to find a bed. John had no hope of sleep, so he prowled the battlements.

He thought of Celia, of how she had smiled and laughed with one of the courtiers left at Holyrood over supper. Smiled—when she would not smile at *him* at all now. It had twisted at something deep inside of him, something he had thought long dead, and it had made him angry. Angry and full of a dark longing.

"You do not deserve her smiles," he muttered to himself. He deserved nothing from her. And yet he wanted so much. Dared to hope for so much.

John took another drink of the ale and wiped at his mouth with the back of his hand. All his life he had been alone, had needed nothing and no one. His parents had died when he was so young he could scarce remember them, and he had made his own way since. His work for the Crown had filled a purpose within him, the yearning to do something great for something more important than himself.

Yet always that hollowness had been there, that hole in his heart. Until he'd seen Celia for the very first time, so beautiful with her shining black hair and her smile— the smile she'd turned on *him*. For the first time that emptiness had vanished.

Until he'd lost her.

"Never again," he vowed.

Suddenly a door flew open somewhere below his tower and amber-coloured torchlight spilled out into the night, along with the sound of laughter. John leaned over the wall to see Allison and one of her swains, along with a few others, dash along a pathway as the snow drifted over them.

And behind them was a slender figure wrapped in a black cloak. She paused to glance over her shoulder and her hood fell away, revealing Celia's pale profile. She glanced up and saw him watching her.

For the merest flash of an instant the loud voices faded, the night grew still, and there was only Celia and him. Her lips parted, and John could vow he felt the touch of her mouth on his.

But someone touched her arm and she turned away, the delicate moment shattered. John saw it was the young courtier she'd sat with at supper. Celia smiled at him and let him lead her away.

"God's teeth," John growled, and drained the last of his ale. He would find no rest tonight.

Chapter Thirteen

"The Queen is approaching!"

Celia looked up from the book in her hands as the page's shout echoed down the corridor. Across from her, Lady Allison put down her embroidery with a smile.

"At last," Allison said. "Now we'll have some excitement."

They hurried out of the small sitting room and joined the flood of people rushing towards the doors. Celia heard the blast of trumpets from somewhere up in the ramparts, announcing that Queen Mary was returned at last to Holyrood. The days of waiting were at an end.

Outside in the forecourt snow was falling in earnest—fat, wet white flakes that piled into cold banks along the walls. Even though it was only afternoon, the sky was a dark grey, throwing everything into shadows.

The servants and courtiers lined the steps, watching as the gates swung open. Celia smoothed her hair, tightly pinned under her black cap, and twitched her fur-trimmed surcoat into place over her gown. She felt nervous as she watched those gates slowly move inward. She hated being uncertain about anything, unsure of her control. She knew Queen Elizabeth's Court, but Scotland was very different from London.

As she folded her hands at her waist she thought she felt the sudden heavy heat of someone watching her, the tingle of it at the back of her neck. And she knew, with a terrible certainty, exactly who it was.

She didn't want to look behind her, didn't want to see him. She had been avoiding him ever since they'd met on the battlements, tried to focus on what she had to do here so she could go back to England. But all her efforts couldn't keep him out of her dreams at night.

She dared a glance over her shoulder and saw him standing in the doorway, his arms crossed over his chest as he watched her closely. He wore his Court clothes again, fine velvets in emerald green and black, with emerald buttons and gold embroidery. A pearl drop dangled from his ear, and his light brown hair was brushed back from his face in sleek waves. He almost seemed a stranger after the man she'd become accustomed to on the road. That intimacy and tenderness she had dared imagine with him.

A lady's hand, soft and white, slid over his arm, and John turned away from Celia. She saw it was Lady Allison who touched him, and John bent his head down to her as she whispered in her ear.

Celia spun away from the sight and focused her attention on the riders making their way closer up the drive. She could still hear John's laugh, low and rough, flirtatiously amused, and her fingers twisted tighter together.

No more, she thought fiercely. She couldn't be distracted by John Brandon any longer.

The lead rider bore Queen Mary's standard, and behind him rode a flock of courtiers. When Queen Elizabeth rode out on a hunt she and her people were a blur of bright colours, feathers and jewels, but Queen Mary was still in mourning for her late husband, the French King. He had been dead since 1561, but still everyone wore greys and dark purples, which made them seem part of the wintry sky.

Yet the sombre colours could not conceal the expensive fabrics, the stylish French fashions. In the surroundings of rough Scotland they exuded sophistication and elegance.

Queen Mary rode in their midst on a white palfrey. She wore black and white, glossy satin and soft velvet, a plumed hat set at a rakish angle on her high-piled auburn hair. Celia could tell she was the Queen because she seemed to tower over everyone around her, the tallest woman Celia had ever seen.

The only one in the party even taller was the man who rode beside her, Lord Darnley. He and Mary laughed together as they rode, their horses drawn close.

When everyone came to a halt at the foot of the steps, Darnley leaped from his saddle and lifted the Queen to her feet, spinning her about with a laugh. Mary laughed in return, and didn't move away when he held onto her waist a moment too long.

Very interesting, Celia thought as she watched them.

Had Queen Mary made her decision already, so very easily? Were Don Carlos, Lord Leicester and some unknown French candidate gone from the competition?

What would Queen Elizabeth think of that?

Queen Mary lifted her hem and hurried lightly up the steps, a smile lingering on her lips. Darnley and the others followed her, but she stopped to speak to the major-domo who waited for her.

To Celia's surprise, the Queen's golden-brown eyes turned to *her*, and Mary's smile widened.

"Ah, at last! My dearest cousin's emissary has arrived." She swept over to take Celia's hand in hers and Celia dipped a startled curtsy.

"Y-Your Grace," she murmured.

"We heard of your terrible accident," the Queen went on, still holding Celia's hand. She spoke English perfectly, but the words were touched with a French accent. Her smile turned concerned. "Have you completely recovered, Madame Sutton?"

Celia could see why Queen Mary was so renowned for her great charm, why it was said every man she met was wildly in love with her. She had the gift of focusing every bit of her attention onto whomever she spoke to, as if they were all she cared about.

"I am quite well now, Your Grace, and eager to be of service to you if I can," Celia said.

"And I am so happy you are here! You must tell me every, everything about my cousin Elizabeth and her Court. I do long to meet her myself, but for now I shall be content with your excellent report!" Her warm-sherry eyes swept over the crowd. "And which man is your rescuer? I am eager to meet him as well."

John stepped forward from the group and swept her a low, gallant bow. "Your Grace, I am Sir John Brandon."

Mary laughed—a soft, musical sound. "Ah, yes, we have heard all about *you, monsieur*. My ladies will certainly be eager to meet you."

As she allowed John to kiss her gloved hand she gestured with her other hand to the women who clustered behind her. "These are my dearest Marys, who have been with since we were children. Mary Seton, Mary Livingston, Mary Beaton and Mary Fleming. And this is Lady Helen McKerrigan, who will look after *you*, Madame Sutton, so you can come to know my Court as well as my cousin's."

Queen Mary laughed once more before she went on, "But she will not look after *you*, Sir John. She has a terribly jealous husband, and I will have no fighting among my people."

John gave the Queen an audacious wink. "Thank you for the warning, Your Grace."

"As if you listen to warnings, *monsieur*. I have seen your sort many times before." Queen Mary laughed again, and held out her hand to Darnley, who slid his arm beneath her fingers. "And now I am cold and must rest. I shall talk with you both more at the banquet tonight."

The Queen swept inside, followed by her courtiers. John gave Celia a long glance, but to her relief he too returned to the palace. Lord Knowlton walked past and gave her a bow and a warm smile. Celia remembered what Allison had said about him, that he admired her, and she felt her cheeks warm at the thought.

"Mistress Sutton?" a soft voice said.

Celia turned to see the lady the Queen had introduced as Lady Helen McKerrigan, she with the jealous husband. She was a petite, pretty redhead, dressed in lilac-coloured velvet and a jewel-embroidered white cap—the sort of sophisticated beauty Celia usually mistrusted.

But Helen's smile was friendly and open. "I am Lady Helen McKerrigan. We've all heard the tale of your near-drowning, I fear! I am very glad to see you have recovered."

Celia almost groaned aloud. She was supposed to be quiet and unobtrusive, to observe everyone around her. How could she do that if she was an object of gossip? "I fear I was merely being clumsy. It was no dramatic tale, Lady Helen."

"Nay?" Helen's auburn brow arched. "Not even your rescue by the oh, so handsome Sir John Brandon? All the ladies here are half in love with him already."

"Are *you*?" Celia said, sharper than she intended.

Helen laughed. "Not me. Did you not hear of my jealous husband?" She took Celia's arm and led her back indoors. "Now, let me show you to your new chamber. Queen Mary has ordered you to be moved to a larger one all to yourself. And I want to hear all about your great adventures…"

Queen Mary's great hall was not as large as the one at Whitehall but it was quite as grand, with a coffered ceiling and a parquet floor scattered with sweet-smelling rushes. Elaborately worked tapestries hung on the walls, and silver and gold plates gleamed on the sideboards, a glowing cave of treasure. Small dogs in jewelled collars dashed about and yapped underfoot.

Celia followed Lady Helen through the open doors into the midst of the gathered crowd as everyone found their places at the long tables lining the sides of the narrow room. English and French words mingled in the air, the Scots' accents even heavier next to the musical Parisian cadences. It was easy to tell Queen Mary's French coterie from her native courtiers as well. The Scots were more colourfully dressed, louder, flashier.

Celia had heard that Mary tried to recreate her life in France here as much as she could, with music and dancing, theatricals, intimate card games. But her Scots nobles were too impatient for that, too rough, too set in their own ways after her long absence.

Celia could see evidence of that dichotomy all around her. Did the Queen think her powerful charm could bring them all together, hold her kingdom firm in her grasp?

Perhaps it could at that, Celia thought as she stood with Lady Helen and watched Queen Mary sweep into the hall. She had never seen a woman quite like her before. It was not merely Mary's height and beauty, her elegant clothes and royal bearing. It was something in her smile, in the great confidence that seemed a bone-deep part of her.

Mary had practically been born a queen, taking her throne mere weeks after her birth. Unlike Queen Elizabeth, who had a powerful charisma of her own, she had never had to fight for her place in the world. That certainty showed in her every gesture, her every easy smile. She owned the world around her and it showed.

Celia wondered with a pang what that would feel like. Not to rule a kingdom, but to be sure of one's place, not to have to fight and scrape for every inch. Not to be constantly on guard. Really to belong.

She curtsied as the Queen swept past and studied Mary's tall figure from under her lashes. She had her hand on Darnley's arm again, their heads bent close together as they talked, and Celia saw that even Darnley seemed to be not the same with her. The sulky cruelty was gone from his handsome face, and it made him even better looking. Younger, lighter.

Mary's face glowed as she smiled at him.

"I wonder who would prevail if Queen Mary ever did meet face to face with Queen Elizabeth?" Celia heard someone whisper beside her.

She glanced over to see Lord Knowlton watching her, a half-smile on his face.

"I am not sure," she answered slowly. Lord Knowlton also looked different here in the amber torchlight— older, more serious. Harder. "But I think I would very much like to witness it."

His smile widened. "Queen Mary thinks she could charm even her prickly cousin and they would be amiable neighbours for ever after."

Celia watched the Queen sit down on her dais, Darnley beside her. "I think that might require a bit more than charm."

"A miracle, mayhap?"

Mary gestured for everyone to be seated, and Celia let Lord Knowlton lead her to a place at one of the tables, their shining lengths laid with the finest silver plates and gilded baskets of white bread interspersed with elaborate salt cellars and ewers of wine. Pages rushed past, laden with serving trays of fragrant delicacies.

"I am most happy to see you looking so well again, Mistress Sutton," Lord Knowlton said as he slid a choice morsel of spiced chicken onto her trencher.

"Thank you, Lord Knowlton. I am happy to feel well again." Celia took a sip of her mulled wine and carefully studied the crowd around her, listening to the chorus of their loud voices and laughter, examining their faces.

None of them was John. She didn't see him anywhere in the hall, and slowly she let herself relax and enjoy the fare spread lavishly before them, and Lord Knowlton's conversation. He really was an interesting man, and knew a great deal about music and poetry as well as vast amounts of amusing Court gossip. Which lady had had a romance with which lord, who had come to blows over the Queen's favours, which Frenchman hated which Scot and vice versa. All fascinating and useful.

Celia even found herself laughing at some of his light flirtations. He did not make her emotions boil up inside her as John did, did not make her feel angry and frightened and full of dark desire. He was merely amusing, kind. She could not imagine why once he had disquieted her.

Perhaps Queen Elizabeth would find someone like *him* for her to marry.

When the meal finally came to a close Celia was still smiling, chatting easily with Lord Knowlton, and with Lady Helen and her devilishly handsome husband. Servants moved the tables away to make room for dancing as the musicians began tuning their lutes and viols in the gallery above.

"Mistress Sutton, I hope that you will favour me with a pavane," Lord Knowlton said with a bow.

Celia laughed and shook her head. "I fear I have not danced in a very long time. I do not know the latest steps."

And suddenly she recalled exactly when she'd had her last dance—with John Brandon, the night before he'd vanished from her life. It had been a slow Italian passamiento, his hands holding her hard and close as their bodies slid together. He had not smiled as he'd looked down at her in the turns, only stared deeply into her eyes as if to memorise her face. Know her thoughts. She had not yet been betrothed to Sutton then, and had dared to dream the romantic dreams of a young, romantic girl.

She pushed the memory away, buried it deeply with all the others. If only they would cease to work their way free! Cease to make her hope again.

"I do not dance now," she said.

"Then perhaps you will sit with me for a while," Lord Knowlton said. "I find I am loth to lose your company so soon, Mistress Sutton."

Celia made herself smile at him. It felt so unnatural

on her lips, where before it seemed almost easy again. Damn John Brandon anyway. Hadn't he already taken enough? Hadn't she given him enough?

"Only if you will tell me more of those delicious tales you have heard in Edinburgh," she said. "Tell me of the Queen's pet poet over there. They say he is quite in love with her."

As she allowed Lord Knowlton to lead her to one of the benches near the wall she half listened to his voice and tried to summon back the easiness she had felt as they ate together. She nodded and laughed at all the right places, and watched the dancers as they swirled past in the intricate patterns of the dance.

Queen Mary was a graceful dancer, and had an obvious pleasure in the exercise which spread over everyone else. There was much laughter as the men lifted and twirled their partners, skirts flying in a dark, rich pattern. It made Celia wish she could bring herself to dance again. That she could be the girl she had once been, a girl who revelled in music and movement, the feel of a man's arms around her.

One man's arms.

The line of dancers shifted for a moment, and she suddenly saw John standing across the room, as if her memories had summoned him there. For one second it felt as if the years fell away and she saw him for the first time. Her throat tightened, and she felt the pounding of her pulse under the high, tight collar of her gown.

She sat up straighter as his stare focused on her. She couldn't look away, and it seemed that neither could he. His jaw tightened, a muscle flexing in his cheek, and she felt just as she had that very first day. When she'd seen him across a room and something had tightened inside her, pulling her to him. She hadn't been able to explain it then, and she assuredly could not explain it now.

Nor did she want it. She looked away, and when her gaze flickered back to him he was smiling down at a pretty redhead beside him. One of Queen Mary's Marys, who laughed up into his eyes and laid her hand on his arm. He let himself be led away by her, and they vanished into the crowd.

Celia slumped back on her seat, as if the band that held her to John had suddenly been released.

"Are you quite well, Mistress Sutton?" Lord Knowlton asked, his voice concerned. "You look pale."

She shook her head. "I am well, Lord Knowlton. Merely tired, I think. Perhaps I am not entirely recovered from the journey."

"Then let me fetch you some wine."

"Nay, I thank you. I think perhaps I should retire. Queen Mary looks as if she may dance until dawn, and I know I shall fade before then."

Lord Knowlton gently touched her arm. "Shall I escort you?"

His touch made her feel so warm, pleasant—not overwhelmed with desire and need for more. Aye, he would make a fine match for her. If she could summon up more enthusiasm for the notion of marrying again.

"I can find my chamber now, Lord Knowlton," she said. "I would hate for you to miss the dancing. I shall see you tomorrow?"

"Certainly, Mistress Sutton." He kissed her fingertips and let her go with a regretful smile. "Have a good rest."

Celia made her way back through the crowd, which had become noisier and warmer as the night went on. The music was faster, the press of bodies closer. She needed air.

She was almost to the doors when someone caught her hand. She spun around in a sudden panic, ready to slap them with her free hand.

Only to be brought to a skidding halt by John's blue eyes looking straight into hers.

"Going so very soon?" he asked.

Chapter Fourteen

〜〜〜〜

Celia wanted to pull her arm free, turn her back on him and those eyes that saw too much. She wanted to push him away, slap him, force him out of her mind. But she just went very still and gazed back at him. "I am tired. I don't feel like dancing tonight."

"Ah, Celia, but I fear our work is never done. Come, dance with me. There are matters we must discuss."

She glanced over his shoulder, through the doorway to the dancers. The hall seemed even more crowded now, a thick press of people all the way to the far walls. The music was faster, louder.

"I don't remember dancing being a requirement of this task," she said.

"Oh, many things are required of you now, Celia," he answered, with an infuriatingly charming grin. "Come now. One dance. I promise I will not let you fall."

Too late for that, Celia thought wryly as he held out his hand to her. But she was meant to keep a watch over Queen Mary, and that wouldn't be accomplished by running away. Nor could she keep running from John. There was no place far enough away where she could forget him.

She slid her hand into his, and his fingers closed over hers. She felt the heat of his touch, the slight roughness from where he gripped a sword or a jousting lance. His smile widened, and he drew her with him back into the hall.

The last dance had ended, and couples were taking their places for the next as the musicians warmed up for a volta. Queen Mary still led the dance with Lord Darnley, and she seemed not tired at all. A brilliant smile lit her beautiful face, and she clapped her hands together to summon everyone else into the form for the dance.

Celia often forgot how young the Queen actually was: only twenty-two—Celia's own age. A lifetime of being queen had bestowed upon Mary a regal confidence that belied her years, but now, with the pleasure of the dance, she looked young and happy. Whereas Celia felt a hundred years old.

Until John touched her waist and drew her closer to his body. His smile faded as he watched her, his eyes narrowing. His hand tightened, and she felt the press of him through the satin of her bodice, as if he touched her naked skin. His fingers slid around to the small of her back.

Celia licked at her dry lips, and his stare flickered to that small movement. "I haven't danced for a long time," she whispered. "I'm not sure I remember the steps."

"Just follow me and I'll show you the way," he

said. "I'm sure you remember far more than you think you do."

She did. She remembered dancing this same dance with him, laughing merrily as he swung her in the air and drew her close.

The music started, the lively strains washing over her just as they had back then. How she had once loved to dance! How she had revelled in the movement and sound, the energy of the other couples around her. And she had never had another partner like John, never danced with someone else who moved as he did, all lithe, graceful power. They'd danced together then, and did so now, as if their bodies knew each other, moved naturally in perfect unison.

Just the same way their bodies had sex. As if they had always been together, with a warm, delicious intimacy and need. A belonging.

John's hand on her back flexed and he led her into the figures of the dance, smoothly guiding her steps. One, two, sway, turn, leap. She did remember how it went now. She went up on her toes as he spun her under his raised arm, and her feet seemed to tingle with happiness at dancing again.

How many things she had forgotten in life. How many things John was bringing back to her. As she jumped lightly from one foot to the other and turned against him she actually laughed. She lost herself in the moment, the music and movement and his touch, and for a few precious moments it was all she knew. All she wanted.

But all too soon it ended.

She curtsied low as the music spun to a stop, and John bowed. When she looked up he smiled at her.

"You see, Celia," he whispered. "You do still know how to dance."

Only with you, she thought. He was the only one who could ever make her feel like that.

Suddenly his gaze went over her head and sharpened. His hand tightened on hers as he drew her up beside him. Celia glanced back to see Marcus standing in the doorway. Marcus gave a small nod.

"Come with me," John said roughly.

"Where are we going?" she demanded.

"You always ask so many questions," he muttered. "Can you never just trust me?"

Celia feared she was beginning to trust him again too much, and that realisation frightened her to her core. She could not trust John Brandon again, could not open herself to him. The first time had nearly broken her, and her heart had never entirely mended. One blow would surely shatter it beyond redemption.

"Nay," she said. "I cannot."

Still holding onto her hand, he slid a long glance down her body—a look she could swear she felt on her bare skin.

"Are you wearing your dagger?" he asked.

Celia nodded.

"Then if I prove untrustworthy, if I break the trust you give me, pull it out and use it on me," he said. "That should keep me in line."

Celia doubted anything at all could stop him from what he wanted to do. But she followed him out of the crowded hall and into the corridor where Marcus waited. He leaned against the panelled wall, his arms loosely crossed over his chest and a small smile on his face. He looked the image of a lazy, careless courtier, but Celia saw his sharp glance take in her hand in John's.

"News?" John asked.

Marcus shrugged. "Of a sort. Come with me." He led them up a staircase, past couples deep in quiet conversation, and down a narrow corridor to a small closet. The open window let in a cold breeze, flakes of snow, and the only light in the chamber was the silver glow of the moon. It fell on two chairs and an empty fireplace.

"We aren't alone here in Scotland," Marcus said.

"Of course not," John answered. "All of Europe has a stake in Queen Mary's marital plans."

"But I think now one of them may be ready to take action."

Marcus outlined all he had discovered—all the factions aligning against Queen Elizabeth here at Mary's deceptively bright Court. The French Guise family, who didn't want to lose Mary and her royal French connections, the Spanish, who wanted control of Elizabeth's northern neighbour, and Mary herself—so unpredictable.

And the unknown agents who worked for one or all of them.

Celia's head began to ache. She could scarcely fathom what she had found herself embroiled in. And it grew late.

"Let me escort you to your chamber," John said, as if he sensed that she grew weary.

She barely heard Marcus as he made his excuse and left the room, the door sliding shut silently behind him.

Celia felt the light touch of John's hand on her back, just over the lacings of her bodice. She gave him a smile over her shoulder, and prayed she looked far cooler and steadier than she felt. She needed all her wits about her now.

"I do know the way there," she said.

"The hour is very late," he answered. He didn't smile in return, merely watched her, that hand very still on her back.

"I don't think our foes would attack me in the very halls of Queen Mary's palace," Celia said. "I am merely a simple lady-in-waiting, no threat to their plans."

He did smile at that, his mouth flicking up at the corner as that dimple flashed in his cheek. "You were never a simple anything, Celia. But there are drunken men roaming free here, and I don't entirely trust your skill with that dagger."

"Oh, do you not?" Celia whispered. Something about his too-smug tone, the hot touch of his hand on her back, awakened a spirit of mischief in her that had slumbered for too long. She slowly turned, sliding her body against his until she stood pressed to his chest. She slid her palms flat on his abdomen, tracing the hard ridges of his muscles under the brocade doublet. He tensed beneath her touch, and she could see the fire catch in his eyes as he looked down at her.

"Perhaps you would care for a demonstration of

my—skill," she said, and she barely recognised her own voice because it was so low and soft. He made her feel that way, so full of passion and need.

John's arm closed around her back, pulling her up hard against him. "Celia…"

She grasped the slippery, rich fabric of his doublet in her fists and slid it up until she could ease her fingers beneath it and up over his chest. She could feel every hard inch of his body under his thin linen shirt. He felt so strong, so solid under her touch, as if he really could keep her safe. As if she could curl up in his strength and forget the rest of the world for ever.

But who would protect her from him? She had always had more to fear from him than anything else.

And she was so tired of fear. Of always feeling cautious, as if she always walked on a knife's edge of disaster and pain. She drew her hands out from his doublet and flattened them over his heart to push him back against the wall. His other arm came around her waist to trap her to his chest like iron chains. But she wasn't running. Not yet.

She wound her arms around his neck and buried her fingers in the hair that curled over his collar. John drew her up until she was on tiptoe, leaning into him until every inch of their bodies were pressed together.

His erection throbbed against her belly through her skirts, iron-hard. Celia moaned softly and closed her eyes. Her head fell back.

"God's wounds, Celia, but what you do to me," he whispered roughly.

"What *do* I do to you?" she said. Did she drive him

to madness? Drive him out of himself? For that was what he did to her. Had always done to her.

He lowered his head and she felt his lips at her temple, his warm breath stirring her hair, brushing over her skin.

"I don't know if I should kiss you," he muttered, "or tie you to my bed and give you a sound spanking."

Celia gave a startled laugh—and then trembled at the erotic vision his words created in her mind. Herself, bound to John's bed, naked, available to all his desires. She could never trust anyone enough for such games again, never be so helpless, but it was an alluring fantasy.

"I think perhaps we should try both," she said, twisting his hair around her fingers. She gave a sharp tug and pulled his head up. "But I would prefer *you* tied to *my* bed, John Brandon."

"We shall see about that, fairy queen," he growled. Suddenly his mouth slammed down over hers, hard and open, taking what he wanted from her with no quarter given.

Not that Celia wanted to surrender. Not with her own desire rising up within her as if it would obliterate all else. She wanted John, yes, but she didn't want him to obliterate her. To shatter her heart again. She didn't want to be that naive girl any more.

She wanted John as the woman she was now, a woman who knew how cold and desolate the world was and craved the heat of him to drive it all away for a moment. To fall into that warm intimacy that closed around them when they were alone together.

She opened her mouth to his kiss and met the thrust of his tongue with her own, twining with his, tasting him. He tasted like the most wondrous of forbidden nectar, wine and herbs and his own dark essence. She wanted more and more of that.

And he wanted more too. She could feel it in every tense muscle of his body, every hungry thrust of his tongue against hers. She drew harder on his hair as if she could bring him closer, closer, meld him into her. Get drunk on him.

He growled deep in his throat, the primitive, animal sound of it echoing through her body. He pulled her up, up, until he could shove her skirts back and wrap her legs around his waist. Celia braced her arms on his shoulders and tightened her thighs on his hips. Her skirts were tossed up between them, and she felt his penis pressed to her spread pelvis with only the velvet of his breeches between them. She arched into him and he moaned.

Celia laughed, filled with a bright joy that he wanted her, that she could pleasure him. That he was ever so briefly in her power, as he always held her in his. She pressed her legs closer to his hips until he could feel the outline of her dagger, encased in its sheath above her stocking.

"La, John, but I do think you're right," she whispered against his neck. "There *are* men waiting to accost poor ladies-in-waiting in these very corridors. Whatever should I do?"

"Get on your knees and take me into your mouth?" he suggested hopefully.

Celia shook her head and laughed. "Use my dagger on it, mayhap?"

"Witch." He groaned. "You are no fairy queen—'tis obvious now you carry evil magic with you."

Celia pressed her parted lips to his neck, just beneath the hard arch of his jaw. She slid her mouth down the strong, bronzed column, lightly scraping her teeth over the damp skin until she could lick at the pulse pounding at its base. He tasted of salt and wine, of that masculine essence, of John.

She tugged open the jewelled buttons of his doublet and slid the edges apart until she could see a vee of his chest under the loosened shirt lacings. Smooth golden skin overlaid with a rough sprinkling of dark hair.

She nuzzled him there, kissing his skin as she inhaled deeply of his essence. "Then teach me to use it only for good, John."

He groaned, a sound of agonised pleasure deep in his chest, and claimed her mouth again. A hard, desperate kiss, a claiming of lips and tongue that sought to seize something deeper, more profound from her. Celia let her head fall back to her shoulders and surrendered to the emotions that raced through her.

Then she heard a sound, a stumbling footfall outside, a soft laugh that echoed down the corridor. It was quickly silent again, but Celia suddenly knew where they were. What they were doing—what *she* was doing.

She dragged her mouth from John's and sucked in a deep breath of air. She opened her eyes to find him staring down at her, his own eyes dark with desire. She glimpsed a flash of anger deep in their depths.

Anger? She was surely the one who should feel that towards him, this man she should distrust with every fibre of her being and yet who kept drawing her in to him. Closer and closer, until she feared she would fall back into him all over again.

She unwound her legs from his waist and jumped to her feet, so desperate to get away that she stumbled. His hands tightened on her arms, holding her steady.

"Come to my chamber with me now, Celia," he whispered in her ear.

His fingers slid up her arm to her bare shoulder, caressing the skin there until she shivered.

So tempting. She could see how it would be in her mind, the two of them entwined on his bed, skin to skin. But the emotions that went with it were far more frightening.

She shook her head and stumbled back a step from him. His hands fell away from her.

"Not tonight," she said.

"Celia…"

She shook her head again, and spun around to hurry away as fast as her shaking legs could take her. Once she was not with him, once she could take a deep breath that did not smell of him, she'd feel stronger.

He called her a fairy queen, a witch, yet he was the one with a magical spell. He cast it over every woman who came near him, drawing them to him with his smile, his raw aura of power and sensuality. She was no different. Her body knew him, wanted him.

She had to learn to be stronger than her treacherous body. Her heart.

Celia turned onto the narrow corridor that led to her small chamber. It was dark, the only light one torch that glowed in its sconce at the far end. A cold draught raced along the stone floors and she hurried her steps. She wanted to be safely in her chamber, alone.

A soft sound brought her to a halt. She stood poised on tiptoe, every sense alert. She had dismissed John and Marcus's warnings about enemies, since she was too insignificant in this game of queens to be in any danger, but she suddenly felt on edge. This was a strange night, and Holyrood was a strange place. Surely anything could happen.

She grasped her skirts in one hand, ready to draw them up and pull out her dagger. Carefully, she backed towards the wall and glanced around her, holding her breath.

She let out a sigh when she saw the source of that sound. Marcus and Allison stood entwined in the embrasure of a doorway, kissing. Her hands were pushing his doublet off his shoulders as his delved into her bodice. Their bright hair, golden and red, gleamed in the torchlight.

Celia bit her lip to keep from laughing. Perhaps there had been a potion in the wine tonight—one that turned anyone who drank of it lustful.

Marcus reached behind Allison to open the door, and they fell together into the chamber. Celia was alone again. And she wasted no time in finding her own room and locking the door behind her. She had had enough of the enchantments of the night.

Chapter Fifteen

Celia half-listened to Mary Fleming, one of Queen Mary's Marys, as she sang a French ballad and softly played the lute. She was accompanied by giggles and whispered conversations, the rustle of silken skirts and the brush of needle and thread against cloth. It was such a feminine scene: Queen Mary's ladies all gathered around her in her chamber during a long, cold afternoon. A scene fragrant with French perfumes and powders, the rose oil in the burners set in the corners, the sweetness from platters of honey cakes.

But Celia's thoughts lingered far away, on a very masculine object. What did he do today? Was he angry she had left him so dissatisfied last night? She hadn't been able to read the swirl of emotions in his eyes.

She stabbed her needle hard into the cloth she held. She did not care what he did, what he thought. Not now, in the harsh light of day.

She really did not. She did *not*. Only she knew she did—far too much.

"Ouch!" She gasped as her needle caught the tip of her finger. As she raised it to her lips to soothe the sting she saw Lady Allison watching her. Allison gave her a little smile and looked back to her own work.

Celia saw that she had sewn the edges of the sleeve she worked on together and would now have to unpick them. She glanced over at Queen Mary, who sat by the window with her embroidery frame, her little dogs gathered around her footstool. Unlike Celia, the Queen obviously enjoyed her needlework and was very skilled at it. She moved the gold thread slowly in and out, humming along with the song, a smile playing over her lips.

Celia had been surprised to receive a summons from the Queen that morning to join her ladies in the Queen's apartments. She had been sure it would take longer to work her way into Mary's company, her trust. But the Scottish Queen seemed to have none of Queen Elizabeth's caution. She was all open, friendly smiles, greeting Celia as she arrived, asking her questions about England and her English cousin, making sure she met all the ladies.

But there had as yet been no talk at all about Mary's marital intentions.

Celia lowered the mangled sleeve to her lap and examined the chamber around her. It was not the grand, opulent space she would have expected, this chamber high up in one of the towers. It was reached only by a narrow spiral staircase, and had a low ceiling of compartmented panels, covered with the entwined initials of Mary's parents, King James and Marie of Guise. Despite the large windows, looking out on the nearby abbey, and the large fireplace filled with bright flames, the room felt small and dark.

Celia glanced through one open doorway to the outer chamber, where the Queen's guards waited, and then through another, half-closed door into a tiny, octagonal supper room. Behind her was the Queen's bed, a massive, carved edifice hung with red curtains. It all felt very intimate and small.

Surely not what Mary had been used to in France.

"They say the Queen's chief adviser Lord Maitland is in love with her," Allison suddenly whispered to Celia.

Celia glanced up, startled. "In love with the Queen? That's not surprising—every man seems to be."

Allison laughed. "Mayhap not *every* man. But Maitland is also in love with Mary Fleming, despite the fact that he is at least twenty years older than her. They say the Queen is planning a lavish wedding for them."

"Is she?" Celia murmured.

"Don't you remember, Mistress Sutton? The Queen's Marys vowed never to wed until *she* did. If one of them is soon to marry…"

Celia looked sharply to the Queen, who was laughing at her dogs' gambols. "Who?"

"Who do you think?" Allison whispered with a giggle.

Suddenly Mary clapped her hands, drawing everyone's attention to her. "It is such a dull, grey day," she said merrily, in her musical French accent. "I think we need to liven things up a bit."

Mary Fleming clapped her hands in answer. "Your Grace! Do you mean…?"

"I do," the Queen said happily. "It has been much too long, *n'est-ce pas*?"

All the Queen's French ladies laughed. Celia watched them uncertainly.

"Mistress Sutton, Lady Allison—perhaps you would join us?" Queen Mary called. "I'm sure you would enjoy it very much."

Celia could not help but wonder how she found herself in such predicaments when she tried to live so cautiously.

On the other hand, perhaps she had had enough of caution. Sometimes freedom was so much more enjoyable. She had never felt quite like this before.

Celia caught a glimpse of herself reflected in an icy puddle on the street as she followed Queen Mary and a few of her ladies through the shadowy lanes. She hardly recognised herself. She wore a pair of velvet breeches and tall boots, with a man's velvet and wool doublet and a short cloak, all in green embroidered with gold. Her hair was pinned up tightly and covered with a plumed cap she had tugged low on her brow. With her slender figure she could pass for a young man, if no one looked too closely.

She looked like her brother, as she remembered him when he was alive. Slim and dark-haired.

But she did not want to think of her brother and what had happened to him in the end, of his stupidity. Not today, when she actually felt the hum of excitement in her blood, the warmth of dangerous life. The only other time she had felt that of late had been in bed with John.

Or in the corridor, with her legs around his waist...

She pushed away the heated memory of the night before, losing herself in John's kiss, and hurried after the Queen. Queen Mary was also dressed in men's clothes, rich crimson and black, and with her tall figure she was far more convincing as a male than Celia. She held the arm of Mary Fleming, who wore her own gown and cloak, and the two of them laughed together as if they were in a conspiracy.

And so they were. So they all were now.

Celia glanced at Lady Helen McKerrigan, who walked beside her. Helen also wore men's garments, but she moved in them more easily than Celia. She looked as if she had done this before. With the Queen— or perhaps as a game with her handsome, broodingly dark husband?

Celia wondered what John would think of her in these clothes. Would his eyes darken, as they always did when he was aroused? Would he reach for her, his hard fingers sliding into her breeches, his blue eyes burning with emotion...

Stop it! she told herself sternly. She needed to cease this at once. Such thoughts were too dangerous.

"Does Queen Mary do this often?" she whispered to Helen.

Helen smiled. "Not as often as she would like, I think. But sometimes, when life at Holyrood becomes too serious for her. It's never easy living between her Scots courtiers and her French friends."

Celia nodded. She had certainly seen the great tension between the two factions, the way Queen Mary trod carefully between the two. "And no one recognises her?"

Helen laughed. "No one says anything to her, at least. She wanders where she will on these days. I think she hopes to hear unguarded gossip in the streets and taverns."

"And does she hear such things?"

A clutch of Puritan clergymen in their stark black garments appeared on the front steps of a chapel as Queen Mary passed by, laughing merrily. Their grey faces were pinched with disapproval, and one made a gesture after her.

"Sometimes she hears more than she would care to," Helen murmured. "The Queen was gone from Scotland for a very long time. Some don't care for a French Catholic monarch."

They hurried after Mary as she turned down a narrow lane. The cobbles were cracked and broken under their feet, the humid smell of rotting food and human waste sharper. Celia pulled out a scented handkerchief and walked faster.

"But we should speak of more pleasant matters!" Helen said, taking Celia's arm as they walked. "What is happening with you and that handsome Sir John?"

Celia gave her a startled glance, suddenly filled with uncertainty. Was it all so obvious that now she was an object of gossip? "What do you mean?"

Helen laughed. "I have seen how he looks at you. It's quite delicious. How could any woman resist?"

"Aren't you married, Lady Helen?" Celia said, remembering Helen's handsome husband and the way he always watched his wife with such love in his eyes.

Helen just laughed louder, drawing glances from passers-by. "Very much so, and my husband keeps me very happy indeed. But I can still look, can I not? And I fear I am a terrible romantic. My husband teases me about it. He says I want life to be like a troubadour's ballad."

"Sometimes life is far too much like a ballad," Celia murmured, remembering the feelings that swept over her whenever she was near John.

"Is it?"

"I prefer matters to be more peaceful."

"But that is so dull!" Helen protested. "Who wants peace when a man like Sir John looks at you as if he wants to eat you up right then and there?"

Celia laughed. "Does he?" She had to admit the thought of John looking at her like that, of being devoured by him, was not entirely unpleasant.

"Yes. Right then and there." Helen's hand tightened on Celia's arm and she drew her closer. "Such intensity from a man can be frightening, I know. I tried to run from my husband at first as well. But surely not to give in to those feelings, not to live fully, is worse?"

Celia shook her head. "You don't understand. I gave in once. It did not end well."

Helen gave her a long, searching look. "And ending can change. It did for me and my James."

"It cannot for me," Celia said firmly. But her emotions were far more confused.

Helen looked as if she wanted to say more, but Queen

Mary suddenly veered off through an open doorway and they had to follow. There was no time for more conversation.

Helen's words lingered with Celia. Better to give in to feelings, to live fully. Once Celia would have completely agreed with her—until her feelings had crushed her. Now...

Now she didn't know how she felt. Not really. She wanted John, but did she dare to trust him? Trust the way he was making her feel again?

Queen Mary had led them into a tavern, a cheap, dark place with scarred tables and a sticky, warped wooden floor. A fire smoked in the grate, and the smell of ale and stewed onions was thick in the air. It was crowded even at that hour, with a rough group who seemed deep in their cups. Any talk here was low-pitched, and stares followed them as they passed.

Celia rested her gloved hand on the hilt of the short sword at her waist, ready to draw it at the slightest hint of trouble.

Mary seemed to notice nothing. She strode confidently through the room to an empty table in the corner. She waved them all to sit down around her and called for ale as she drew Celia to the chair right next to hers.

"My dear Madame Sutton," Mary whispered, in that confiding voice that drew so many people to her. "You must tell me more about Lord Darnley."

Celia looked at the Queen in shock. "I—me, Your Grace? I have never spoken to him."

Mary smiled. "But you live at my cousin's Court.

And you were on this long journey here, yes? I know you watch people, see things."

Celia took a quick gulp of her ale. She hardly knew what to say. She could scarcely tell this queen, this woman with her wide, glowing amber eyes, the truth. Not until she was sure of what Queen Elizabeth would want.

"They say he is exceedingly handsome, Your Grace," she said carefully.

Mary laughed—a silvery sound that made everyone around them laugh too. "I do see that, Madame Sutton! Very well. But what of his affections? Are they engaged?"

Celia was saved by a burst of song, too loud to talk over, and Mary turned to clap along to the tune. Celia looked away as well, but she knew it was only a short reprieve. Mary would ask her again, and she would have to know what to say.

Suddenly a hidden door opened across the room and shadowy figures appeared there. Still laughing at the bawdy song, Celia turned to study the newcomers over the edge of her tankard.

She froze before she could take a sip. *John* was standing there, staring right back at her with those blazing blue eyes. She carefully lowered the ale back to the table before she could spill any.

Marcus appeared at John's shoulder as several men she did not recognise slipped past and out of the tavern. John spoke quietly to Marcus, his gaze never leaving her. She found she was caught by that stare and couldn't turn away.

What was he doing here? A meeting at such a tavern surely seemed to bode ill. Was he in some conspiracy she knew nothing about? She had had quite enough of conspiracies of late.

He came towards her slowly, deliberately, dodging around the crowded tables. He still watched her, his eyes narrowed.

"Sir John! Lord Marcus!" Queen Mary cried brightly. "Come and join us. We were just teaching our English friends some Parisian songs."

"Such a surprise to see you all here," Marcus said, as smoothly as if finding a queen dressed like a man in a rough tavern happened all the time. "And a charming surprise at that. You've brightened a very dull day."

"You look as if your days are never dull, Lord Marcus," Mary Fleming teased. "Do you know any good songs?"

"I just might know one or two," he said, sliding onto the seat by Mary Fleming and wrapping his arm around her shoulders. "None as fine as yours, though."

John took the chair next to Celia when Lady Helen obligingly slid down. Celia watched him warily as he removed the tankard from her suddenly cold fingers and raised it to his mouth. With a flick of his wrist he turned it and drank from the spot where her lips had been. The smooth muscles of his neck above the open collar of his doublet shifted as he swallowed, and Celia had to look away.

"Do *you* know any French songs from your time in Paris?" she said.

"None I would teach to you."

"Oh? Why is that? Because I have such a wretched voice?"

"Because they are all naughty, Celia, and I don't think I could take hearing you say those words with your pretty mouth," he said roughly, and drank deeply again. "You have me too lustful as it is."

Celia was surprised he would admit it. *She* would never give *him* that power, even though she seemed to burst into desire every time they touched. She caught a glimpse of Lady Helen from the corner of her eye, and Helen grinned at her.

Celia almost laughed aloud. Maybe it was the clothes she wore, the ale she was drinking, but she felt a sudden surge of some strange power wash through her. She did not feel quite like herself.

She reached for the ale and took a long gulp. "Words like swive? Or tup? Or maybe…" She whispered a word in his ear she had never said aloud.

John growled low in his throat. "Celia…"

She put down the tankard and slowly eased her hand down below the concealment of the table. She felt his thigh beneath her fingertips, his lean muscles bunching and shifting under her teasing touch. She trailed her fingers up slowly, slowly, the wool of his breeches a soft friction on her skin.

Just as she brushed his codpiece he seized her wrist and held her away. But he didn't put her hand back on the table, merely held it there, a mere inch from his manhood. She could feel its hardness, his desire, could see that need in his eyes.

"What game do you play, Celia?" he demanded, his voice low.

"The Queen commanded me to accompany her today," Celia said, flexing her fingers. "I could hardly refuse."

"I don't mean appearing here in these clothes," he answered. His bright blue stare swept over her slowly, taking in every inch of her body in the form-fitting clothes until it felt as if he caressed her. "Though you do look tempting. I want to—"

"Sir John!" Queen Mary suddenly called. "Lord Marcus tells us you do know some songs. Teach us one now."

John gave Celia one more long look—a hard glance that promised their conversation was not nearly over. Then he turned to smile at Mary, pressing his body against Celia's shoulder.

"Of course," he said. "Your wish is my command. What is your pleasure tonight? A comic song? One of adventure? Or one of romance?"

Mary sighed. "Oh, romance! I do love a love song the very best. What is life without love?"

Chapter Sixteen

John followed Celia closely as they made their way back through the streets of Edinburgh to the palace. Night was gathering around them now, shadows seeping down over the steep roofs and flowing over the wet cobblestones. Queen Mary was laughing with her friends, all of them a bit unsteady on their feet after an afternoon of tavern ale and bawdy songs.

Celia and John brought up the end of the group, and she was quiet, thoughtful, as if she wasn't really there in the winter streets. She so often seemed somewhere else, somewhere deep in her own mind, her own sadness, where he couldn't reach her. Couldn't know her, possess her. Not as he feared he wanted to. He wanted so many things from Celia, wanted to give her so much.

He wrapped his fist over the hilt of his sword to keep from caressing her firm, high backside so enticingly outlined in those breeches. He became aroused just watching her, smelling her perfume. He always wanted her. Sex had always been so easy for them—

explosive, undeniable. But the sex had also led to so much more, to tenderness and need.

It had been everything else that drove them apart.

Celia glanced over her shoulder at him, and her eyes widened when she saw the desire that must be blazing in his eyes. A slow pink blush spread across her cheeks, making him want her even more. He wanted to seize her around the waist, push her up against the wall and feel her legs wrap around him, her mouth open under his...

A smile quirked her lips and she reached back to secretly brush her hand over his clenched fist. It was a soft, fleeting touch, a secret smile, and it made something clench deep in his chest. Something warm and tender that he remembered so well with her, only felt with her.

A burst of laughter from up ahead drew her attention away, and she turned from him. Without those cool grey eyes searching his face that tight feeling eased and he sucked in a deep breath. But he stayed close to her as she hurried to catch up to the others.

"Ah, but Sir John must remember the Elysee gardens, since he was so lately in Paris!" Queen Mary cried. "Where are you, Sir John? Come and talk with us!"

"I am here, Your Grace," he answered.

"You must tell them how lovely the gardens are. I want to recreate their pathways and groves here at Holyrood, to remind me of Paris," the Queen said. "If only I could see it again—"

Suddenly the night was shattered by a deafening blast. Up ahead the dark sky lit up red and orange, with flames that shot high above the rooftops. Screams and cries broke out. John barely glimpsed Marcus shoving Queen Mary to the wall before he himself grabbed Celia up in his arms and arched his body over hers to protect her from the sparks that showered down.

She trembled in his arms, her hands curling hard into his doublet as she clung to him. "What is it?" she gasped.

"I don't know," he said, feeling only the primitive drive to protect her, keep her safe. "We need to get to the palace. Now."

Holding her under his arm, he ran behind the others until they burst out of the maze of streets and found the gates of Holyrood. The Queen's guards were already gathered there, halberds at the ready. There was barely a glimpse of a building ablaze somewhere in the city below.

The Queen, looking pale and startled but composed, was borne into the palace.

John tried to set Celia on her feet, to steady her, but she still held onto him.

"What was that?" she whispered. "It all happened so very fast…"

"Shh, you're safe now," he answered. He kissed her hair, her cheek, felt the warmth of her under his lips, the precious life of her—life that was very fragile. He held her now, kept her safe with him. But for how much longer?

"I do not feel safe," she said, her voice unsteady, breathless. "I never feel safe. Not since—since…"

Since her brother's death. The death John had helped hasten. He held her even closer.

"John," he heard Marcus say softly. John looked over Celia's head to see his friend's grim face, his gesture towards the doors.

"Celia, I must go now—find out what has happened," John whispered in her ear. "Go and see to the Queen. I will find you later."

He kissed her once more and gently set her away from him. She nodded. Her face was white and strained, her eyes bright, but she did not cry. He had never seen her cry.

She hurried to the stairs, and John watched her go until she was out of his sight and gone from him.

Chapter Seventeen

Celia slowly paced to the end of her small bedchamber and back again, one deliberate step after another. It was very late, and the whole palace seemed silent and still even after the clamor of the afternoon. The Queen had insisted on dancing again, pretending nothing had happened, but now even she had retired.

Celia knew she should go to bed as well. There was to be a hunt in the morning and they would ride out early. But she knew that even if she lay on the bed, crawled beneath the inviting blankets and closed her eyes, she would not sleep.

John had not been at supper, had not appeared for the dancing. She hadn't seen him since he'd left her by the doors.

She closed her eyes and drew her fur-trimmed robe closer around her as she tried to force away the worry and uncertainty. She could still feel the way his arms had closed around her as the sky exploded, the way he'd shielded her with his body and she'd felt his heart thunder in his chest. The way she trusted him to keep her safe.

Trusted him.

But who would keep *him* safe now, wherever he had gone? Would he vanish from her again? Would she be left to mend her heart all over again? Because she feared her feelings now were stronger than they ever had been before.

Celia shuddered and clutched tighter to the folds of her robe. She wanted to run away from him, as far and as fast as she could. Yet even stronger was the urge to run *to* him, to touch him again and know he was there, alive and real and hers.

Only he was not hers. He never had been.

A quiet knock suddenly sounded at her door, and Celia gasped at the sound. She whirled around, reaching for her dagger where it lay on the table. The noise breaking the heavy silence had pulled her senses taut.

"Wh-what is it?" she called.

"'Tis me, Celia. For pity's sake let me in."

Her fingers convulsed on the dagger's cold hilt. *John.* It was John, here, right when her longing for him was too great. She wanted to send him away; she wanted to throw open the door and catch him in her arms.

She carefully set the dagger back down and took a deep breath before she crossed the floor to unbolt the door.

He stood there in his shirtsleeves, his arms braced on the door frame. He smelled faintly of smoke, and she glimpsed a dark smudge on his bristled cheek. His eyes were hooded, veiled as he stared down at her.

"What has happened?" Celia whispered.

In answer, he closed his arms hard around her and lifted her into the room. He kicked the door closed behind him, and her single candle flickered and went out, enclosing them in darkness.

"John…" she said, but her words died in her throat as his mouth came down over hers. His tongue pressed roughly past her lips, hungry, desperate.

Celia felt an answering need swell inside her, driving out everything else but him. But the thought that she could have lost him for ever drove her on. She felt his hands hungrily push her robe back from her shoulders and onto the floor, felt his fingers tear at the lacings of her chemise and strip the last thin layer of cloth from her body, leaving her naked. She didn't care, didn't want to shield herself from him. She only wanted his touch on her, everywhere.

One of his hands drove into her hair, angling her head for his kiss, while the other swept in a hard caress down her back to the curve of her backside. His fingers dug into the soft skin as he dragged her closer to his body.

She went up on her toes and wound her arms around his neck, cradling his head as she opened her mouth wider to his tongue. He groaned against her, and she felt his erection grow even harder against her bare stomach through his breeches. She arched into it.

John's hand slid to her thigh and lifted her up higher, until her legs wrapped around his hips. She held close, lost in a sizzling haze of sensation, of his touch, his kiss, his body wrapped around hers.

His hand tightened on her leg, and one of his long fingers touched her between her legs, pressing into her damp folds. She cried out at the bolt of pleasure and her head tilted back.

He used his hand in her hair to draw her back even further, leaving her neck vulnerable to his seeking mouth. It slid, open and wet, down her throat until he closed his teeth hard on the soft curve just above her shoulder.

"John!" she cried.

"Do you want me, Celia?" he whispered against her skin.

The tip of his tongue licked at the sting of his bite and a tremble swept through her with the longing.

"Tell me you want me as much as I want you."

Want him? Whatever she was feeling now, whatever was making her damaged heart crack wide open, it went far beyond mere want. It went into sheer need, tenderness she could not fathom.

"I do want you," she said. His mouth slid lower and closed over her aching nipple, sucking it deep. "God's blood, but I want you!"

He backed her up until he could lie her on the bed, amid the soft velvet blankets. As he stepped back her legs slid from his hips, and she almost cried out at the chill of loss. But he merely stripped away his own clothes, ripping them off and tossing them away before catching her up in his arms again.

Their mouths clashed in a heated kiss, and the very air around her seemed to turn warm and heavy, as before a storm. That storm raged inside her, violent and powerful as everything she had locked away and suppressed for three long years broke free and threatened to drown her. She held onto John and let herself go under, let herself feel again at long last.

He pulled his mouth from hers, making her moan with the loss, but he did not leave her. His hands held onto her hips, so tight she felt almost bruised, yet she didn't care. She needed that hardness, that edge of pain and passion that told her he was with her, they were alive together. And soon he would be inside her, making him hers even if only for the night.

They knelt facing each other in the middle of the bed. He let go of her for an instant to untie the bed curtains, enclosing them in their own tiny world with red velvet, shutting away everything but the two of them. Then he reached for her again and slid her close to his naked chest.

Celia laid her palms over the curve of his shoulders. "So beautiful," she whispered. That smooth, damp skin over his lean muscles, so perfect but for a white scar arcing over his ribs, a crescent on his hip. She let her hands slide slowly, slowly down his chest, feeling every inch of him, every taut shift and ripple of his skin. He held her lightly by her hips, letting her explore him.

The light whorls of hair sprinkled across his chest tickled her skin and made her smile. The smile faded as her fingertips slid over the flat discs of his nipples. Her nail scraped over one and it went taut as he groaned. His head fell back, his eyes closed, and she felt his penis jerk where it was pressed to her abdomen.

She lowered her head and took that pebbled nipple

into her mouth, sucking, biting as he held onto her. She could feel the heavy beat of his heart on her lips, the ragged rhythm of his breath. His hands convulsed on her hips. She let her fingers trace down his chest lower, lower, over his ridged stomach to the arrow of hair from his navel to his manhood, the hard line of his hips.

Her open mouth followed the path of her touch, licking, caressing, tasting him. As she bit at the arc of his hip she let her hand flutter over his penis. It was hot satin stretched taut over rigid steel, the veins etched on it pulsating with his need. His need for *her*, for what she was doing to him now, and that realisation flooded her with a powerful pleasure.

She pressed her lips to his taut stomach as she ran her hand down the length of him and up again to its base. She caressed that spot just behind that she knew he liked.

"Celia!" he shouted. He drove his hand into her hair again and pressed her against him.

She smiled and trailed her mouth lower, until she could slip the tip of him between her lips. He tasted sweet and musky, his skin burning as she slowly took him deeper. When her husband had made her do this it had made her feel so ashamed, ill. But now, with John, with her own choice, it made her feel so very different. So in control. She could give *him* pleasure in return for what he gave her, and it felt glorious.

"Celia," he said, his voice no more than a rough growl. His hand slid through her hair and she ran her tongue over him. His hips twitched but he didn't push himself deeper.

She slid her hands around to his tight buttocks and held him to her as she caressed that warm skin, the curve at the small of his back. His hips thrust against her.

Suddenly he caught her shoulders and pushed her back from him. Celia tilted her head to look up at him, and in the red shadows of their bed his face looked harsh, carved into hard lines with lustful need.

"I can't bear it any more, Celia," he said, and pulled her up to kiss her. There was no seductive art to his kiss now, only hunger and a raw lust that called out to her own desire.

She wrapped her arms around him as they fell back onto the bed. John rolled her beneath him, his hips between her spread thighs as he kissed her jaw, the soft, vulnerable spot beneath her ear. He bit down on the curve of her neck, and she cried out as she arched against him. The pain and pleasure sparkled through her.

He trailed his open-mouthed kiss lower, tasting her with his tongue until he captured her aching nipple between his lips and suckled her, rolling her between his teeth.

"John, John," she cried. She cradled his head in her hands, holding him against her. Her whole body felt so *alive*, burning with need for him and what he was doing to her. What only he could do to her.

His hand drove between her thighs and traced her wet seam before he dipped one finger inside her, pressing deep. His palm rotated over that tiny spot of pure sensation, moving over her as he slid in another finger.

He plunged deeper, harder, just the way she needed right now.

He always seemed to know just what she needed, what she wanted, as if he could see into her very heart.

She shook away that disturbing thought, that knowledge that he could know her as no one else ever could, and just let herself feel. Let herself be with him.

But he seemed to sense that instant of disquiet. His hand slid away from her and he held onto her waist as he rolled beneath her and held her on top of him, strong and steady.

He turned her away from him, astride his hips, and traced his touch down the length of her back over her buttocks.

"Ride me, Celia," he commanded.

She laughed at the heady rush of his words and rested her hands behind her on his thighs as she raised herself up and slowly lowered onto his erect penis, one inch at a time. She let him slide deeper, deeper, until he was fully inside her, joined to her. She closed her eyes and let her head drop back as she revelled in the sensation of being filled by him. Part of him.

He wound the ends of her hair around his wrist and thrust his hips up beneath her.

She let her need take her over and moved on top of him faster, harder, until they were moving as one. She felt that hot pressure build from where he touched her, slid against her. It expanded inside her, up and up, until it exploded.

She cried out her pleasure, her back arching like a taut bowstring over his body.

"Celia!" he shouted, and she felt him go still and rigid beneath her, felt the heat of his release inside of her.

The energy drained slowly out of her, leaving her weak and shivering. She collapsed beside him to the bed and listened to the harsh, unsteady rhythm of his breath.

He reached for her and drew her to his side as he covered them both with the bedclothes. In the darkness behind the curtains she knew only the soft touch of his hand in her hair, the sound of his body shifting on the pillows. Her own thoughts were a confused jumble in her tired mind.

She rolled onto her side and let him cradle her against him as she closed her eyes. She needed to rest—just for a moment...

Celia slowly swam up from beneath her hazy dreams, becoming aware of the world around her again. She fought against waking up as her dream had been a sweet one of lying in a warm summer meadow as John kissed her. The sun had streamed down over her in the vision, hot and golden, melting away the long winter, and she had been laughing with John, happy in his arms, lazy and content.

Now she could feel the cold again, the draughts of the old castle pressing against the bed curtains. She blinked her eyes open to find herself lying on her side, surrounded by darkness, the blankets drawn up over her breasts.

And John's mouth on her bare shoulder.

His arm was heavy over her waist, drawing her back

against him. His lips were lazy, slowly exploring her skin, but the sensation that kiss evoked in her was not contentment.

He awoke a restlessness in her, a need that she could feel in the sudden dampness between her legs. He had brought her such pleasure in the night, moments when all thoughts and worries flew away and she could be free. Now sanity was trying to return, to remind her of who they were and all that had happened, but his kiss drove them away again.

"You're awake, Celia," he murmured. "I can feel it." He swept her hair over her shoulder and pressed his mouth to the vulnerable nape of her neck.

She slid herself closer to him and felt the unmistakable proof of his desire, hard against her backside. "So are you."

John laughed roughly. "I have been for some time. But I wanted to hold you in my arms while you slept."

"Why?" she asked, a ridiculous hope blooming deep in her heart.

"Because there are no daggers or sharp words while you dream. You were actually smiling. What did you see there?"

"A world with no snow," she answered.

"And no games of queens and thrones?"

"That would be too much to ask for." Celia laid her hand on the arm over her waist and slowly trailed her fingertips over his warm skin. She felt the soft brush of his hair, the strength of his muscles. She remembered how he had snatched her up in his arms and held her safe amidst the explosion. How she had felt safe with him even in the midst of chaos.

"Did you and Marcus discover what happened today?" she asked.

For an instant he grew tense against her, before drawing her closer and relaxing again. "It was nothing. Merely a young hothead of a Puritan, a disciple of Queen Mary's great enemy Knox. He thought an abandoned building at the edge of the city was being readied to be made into a Catholic chapel so he set it afire. Unfortunately barrels of whisky were stored there for a tavern down the street and the place exploded."

"Was it really going to be a chapel?"

"Certainly not. The only Catholic chapel left in Scotland, aside from secret ones, is the Queen's own, here at Holyrood. She has declared that Protestantism will remain the faith of Scotland even as she follows her own faith privately."

"Was the man captured?"

"Aye. But there are plenty to take his place."

Celia trailed her fingers along his arm again, thinking of all the trouble, all the evil that lurked in the world. The grave danger of coming into the orbit of princes. Her poor brother had learned that lesson all too well, and here she was in Scotland, surrounded by things she only half understood.

"And will the Queen marry soon?" she asked.

"Almost certainly. She is not the sort of woman who can be long without a man."

"Darnley?"

"Aye."

"But why?" Celia asked. "He is the veriest knave. And she is a queen."

"A queen with few options. There are few eligible princes of her rank in Europe, and her pride won't let her wed a subject."

"Queen Elizabeth has offered Leicester."

John laughed. "Mary is a woman of pride—a great deal of it. She won't take her cousin's man."

"So that leaves Darnley." Celia had never thought she could pity a queen—not in her own impoverished, homeless state. And yet she found she did. She pitied Mary and Elizabeth both, trapped by their lives. They would never know a feeling like she had with John, and even when she knew she should not feel that way she could not let it go.

"Mary does not see Darnley as we do," John said.

"Does she not?"

"Nay." He wound a long strand of her hair around his wrist, running it between his fingers. "I have learned a great deal about people in my life, Celia. How to read them, how to guess what they will do next."

"About women?" She knew he could read women all too easily, their secret needs and desires.

He gave a humourless laugh. "Aye, about women. Though some are harder to understand than others." His arm tightened around her. "Some I can't fathom at all."

"And Queen Mary?"

"Even though she grew up at the French Court, a viper pit if there ever was one, she is terrible at prevarication. She wears her heart on her sleeve, her emotions at the surface. She is very impulsive. And she is lonely. She has been a widow for a long time."

"And Darnley is handsome," Celia said. But she knew too well what happened when a woman looked beyond a handsome face.

"He is, and charming when he wants to be. And, as Mary's cousin, he is nearly as close to the English throne as she is. It is all she can see now. The surface." He released her hair and smoothed it over her shoulder. "But after she weds him she will soon come to regret it. He will not be a strong consort for her."

Aye, Celia no longer envied queens at all. And she was suddenly weary of them and their labyrinthine doings. She only wanted John right now, and the way he made her feel. She rolled over to face John and sat up on the bed, letting the blanket fall to her waist.

"What about me, John?" she said. "What can you read about me?"

He reached out to wrap his fingers over the curve of her hip and drew her closer to him. "You, Celia—you drive me mad," he muttered. He pressed his open mouth to her belly, just below her navel. "I want to know you, to see you, but you keep slipping away from me."

Celia wove her fingers through his tousled hair and held him against her. Her head fell back and she closed her eyes as she let the pleasure of his kiss wash over her. Perhaps she did understand something of what drove Queen Mary onward to disaster—she missed *this*, this sensual haze created only by a lover's caress. The heat of a kiss, another person nearby in the darkness. A

man and a woman and the mystery of what happened
between them.

His fingers tightened on her buttocks and he drew
her closer to his mouth. He dipped the tip of his tongue
into her navel and traced it lower over her abdomen in
a hot, sinuous pattern. It was a slow, careful touch, as
if he branded her skin with his tongue and marked her
for ever.

Behind her closed eyes she felt him slide lower on
the bed, until his mouth was over her womanhood. He
laid her down flat on the pillows and parted her legs.
He blew a soft breath over her and she gasped at the
ripple of sensation. She ached for more, but he merely
touched his mouth lightly to her damp opening.

"John…" she whispered brokenly.

Then his tongue slid over her, licked her slowly up
and down before he plunged into her. He tasted her
deeply. His fingertips caressed that tiny spot just above
and pleasure overwhelmed her. She arched up into his
mouth, holding onto his hair as he kissed her *there*,
deeper and deeper.

He took her leg and draped it over his shoulder, so
he could slide even deeper between her legs. Somehow
it felt even more intimate than when they coupled, as
if he could see into her soul, become part of her. And
she did not even care. She wanted him there, in every
part of her. Needed him there.

He pinched lightly at that spot and speared his tongue
into her hard, making her cry out as a climax built in
her core. It broke over her, and John groaned against
her, making the feeling even more intense.

As she floated back to earth he kissed her once more, softly, and rose up on his knees between her legs. She saw him smile in the shadows, saw him raise his fingers to his mouth as he tasted her again on his skin.

Lust and emotion spasmed deep inside her all over again.

"So sweet," he said, and leaned down to bury his face in the side of her neck, in the tangle of hair that fell over her shoulder. He just held her there, inhaled the scent of her hair as if he would draw her into him.

Celia felt a terrible longing envelop her, and she wrapped her arms around his back. His skin was damp, sleek, and he shifted under her touch.

"Celia, Celia," he whispered into her hair.

Just her name, over and over.

It made her want to weep. Never to let him go.

He sat up and drew her with him until she straddled his lap, her legs spread over him. She felt his erect manhood slide against her, and wanted him all over again. She raised herself up on her knees and reached down to guide him into place, so she could slowly lower herself onto him.

He groaned and thrust his hips up until he was fully inside her, their hips pressed together, her legs wrapped tight around his waist. She let her head fall forward onto his shoulder, and it felt as if they were one being.

He drew back and thrust up again, a long, slow slide. She could feel every inch of him move against her, inside her. She rose up as he drew back, and then down, finding their rhythm together again. Even their breath, their heartbeats, matched.

He growled, and his hands closed tightly on her waist as they moved faster, rougher. He thrust up into her hard, his hips grinding against hers, circling.

"John," she gasped. Her nails dug into his shoulders as she matched him thrust for thrust. Her breasts slid over his chest, their legs tangled together, and she couldn't breathe, couldn't think, could only move. Could only slide her body over his as he thrust against that one pleasurable spot over and over.

"John!" she cried as she flew apart all over again.

He threw his head back, the veins in his neck taut, his eyes closed as he pushed into her one more time. "Celia," he moaned.

Her name had never sounded quite like that before.

They sank down to the bed, arms and legs still entwined. John drew her down on top of him, her body stretched out over his as her head rested on his shoulder. His hand moved slowly through her hair, a gentle caress over and over, soothing her pounding heart.

She couldn't say anything. She had no words any longer. She could only hold onto him as she spiralled ever downward.

Chapter Eighteen

Celia had to hold her hand over her mouth to keep from laughing as she trailed behind the others from the church after the lengthy—and loud—service. Darnley felt he had to attend John Knox's Protestant services to establish his religious allegiances in Scotland, and Celia and the others went to keep an eye on him. She wished she could have stayed at Holyrood, or was back at Whitehall with Elizabeth's clergymen's short, simple sermons. Knox had railed against the "horrors" of female rule until Celia had feared she would collapse in giggles. Poor Queen Mary—she would surely soon wish she had stayed in France.

She was so deep in her own thoughts she didn't realise anyone had moved to walk beside her until she felt a gentle touch on her arm. She looked up, startled, to see Lord Knowlton smiling at her.

"It makes one miss Queen Elizabeth's less devout clergymen, does it not?" he said.

Celia laughed. "Her services *are* rather shorter, that is true. Knox is slightly terrifying."

"Who will win this battle, do you think? Knox or Queen Mary?"

"They are both strong-willed. I would not care to make a wager. And hopefully by the time matters come to a head between them we will be gone from here."

Lord Knowlton gave her a long, searching glance, studying her so closely she had to turn away. She had not spent all that much time in his company, but she had enjoyed his easy conversation. Being with him was simple—nothing like John.

Yet today Lord Knowlton's regard felt somehow different. He looked as if he wanted to discover something from her, about her. Everyone here said one thing and thought something very different. She had done the same thing for so long, always hiding, also cautious.

She was tired of it all.

She hurried her steps to catch up with the others, and Lord Knowlton stayed at her side.

"So you are eager to return to England?" he asked. "You do not care for Scotland?"

"Scotland is most interesting. I've enjoyed my time here," Celia answered carefully. "But, yes, I will be happy to return to England."

"And what will you do when you're there again?" Lord Knowlton said. "Will you remain in Queen Elizabeth's service? Or perhaps return to your family?"

What *would* she do in England? Celia had been trying not to think of that, to push away the future while she concentrated on her work here. Her brief time with John. But Knowlton's words made her realise how fast the future was bearing down on her.

"I have no family," she said. "So I will stay at Court for the time being."

"Perhaps you would prefer a household of your own?" he said quietly.

Celia looked at him, surprised by his words. "I would, but such things are not so easy to find, I fear."

He nodded. "I have been a widower for many years, Mistress Sutton, and it is a lonely life. But very soon I will have a great deal to offer a wife, if all goes as I hope."

"That is—very good. I am happy for you, Lord Knowlton," Celia murmured, not sure what to say. He had never spoken thus to her before, and she was bewildered.

Did he intend *her* for his wife? And what would happen to ensure his fortune? Did he also work for Elizabeth?

"Perhaps I may speak to you again on the subject when we return to London?" he said.

Celia simply nodded, and Lord Knowlton smiled at her as they kept walking. "Tell me, Mistress Sutton," he said. "What are your impressions of Queen Mary's Court? I am very curious…"

Celia was tired and puzzled as she made her way towards her chamber, weary of the effort of smiling and laughing with the Queen's ladies when all she wanted to do was find somewhere quiet to think. She had much to consider. The two Queens, Lord Knowlton, John—it was all too much.

At last she reached the door of her chamber and

pushed it open—only to find she was not to be alone after all. John lounged on her bed, leaning back lazily on the bolsters as he studied a stack of papers beside him. As she closed the door behind her, he looked up at her with a roguish grin.

Celia suddenly wished with all her might that he would *not* smile at her like that, would not confuse her even more, torment her with all she had once longed for and couldn't have. But truly he was not the one who did the tormenting. It was her own heart, her own feelings.

"I wondered when you would be returning," he said. "Do you feel properly pious now?"

"I feel it was quite unfair that you managed to stay here while the rest of us had to listen to the sermons of hellfire," Celia grumbled.

She put her gloves and prayer book down on the table and unpinned her veiled cap from her hair. As she smoothed the windblown strands she caught a glimpse of John in the looking glass. He'd braced his hands behind his head and leaned back as he watched her with hooded eyes. His doublet was open and his shirt clung to his chest and shoulders, reminding her of what he looked like naked. What they had done to each other last night in that very bed.

What she suddenly wanted to do again.

She licked her dry lips with the tip of her tongue and his stare sharpened. He sat up straight and watched her as she unfastened her surcoat and let it drop from her shoulders. She slowly untied the high frilled collar of the chemise that rose above the low, square bodice of her black velvet gown and parted the fabric.

"And did you learn anything enlightening today?" John asked, his eyes never wavering from her.

"Oh, a great deal." Celia tugged the pins from her hair and let the heavy dark mass fall over her shoulders as she took up her brush. "Lord Darnley is very good at counterfeiting piety when he wishes. And Knox practically froths at the mouth with hatred for women rulers. I fear Queen Mary would have done better to stay in France."

She drew the brush slowly through her hair, closing her eyes. She heard him leave the bed and move to stand behind her. The heat of his body wrapped all around her, drawing her closer to him.

He took the brush from her fingers and his hands slid slowly, caressingly, through the fall of her hair as he drew it back over her shoulders. She hardly dared breathe as she felt him ease the bristles through her hair.

"Anything else you observed?" he whispered in her ear.

"I think Lord Knowlton is going to propose to me," she blurted out.

The brush ceased moving and John tensed behind her, but only for an instant. Then the slow, gentle motions resumed. "Hardly surprising. Many men surely want to marry you, Celia."

But not you, she thought sadly. "He also said something rather odd about how soon he would be in a position to offer much to a wife."

"What do you think he meant by that?"

Celia shrugged. "That soon his fortune will increase, I suppose. They do say his present estate is rather modest. Perhaps Queen Elizabeth has promised to reward him, as she has with us. Or perhaps…" A thought suddenly struck her.

"Perhaps what?"

"It is silly. Lord Knowlton is the quietest, most mild-mannered gentleman I have ever met, and seems as devoted as any courtier to Queen Elizabeth. Yet Lord Burghley did say we would have to face French and Spanish spies who all have their own ideas of Queen Mary's marital plans."

She felt foolish even as she said it. Lord Knowlton? A foreign spy? But she had to think of such things. Suspect everyone.

Not that she could think much at all when John touched her like that.

"It sounds as if we should keep a closer eye on Lord Knowlton," John said. "And what will you say to his proposal?"

"He has to make one first," Celia murmured. "But I will have to marry someone, and he seems as good a choice as any. I doubt he is anything like my first husband."

"Should you not consider other offers first?"

She gave a bitter laugh. "Which offers would those be?"

He didn't answer. He dropped the brush and she felt him gather the length of her hair in his hands as he drew the slippery mass to his face and inhaled deeply. Celia let her head fall back until it rested on his shoulder, and he kissed her, open-mouthed and hungry, on her neck.

She reached up to thread her fingers through his hair, letting the short silken strands drift over her skin as he tasted her. His teeth nipped at her, and she gasped.

"Celia," he groaned, resting his forehead on her shoulder. "I've missed you so much, thought of you so much in all these years. Beautiful Celia…"

His words made her heart pound in her breast, as if it was coming alive within her after being frozen. Had he really thought of her as she had him? She felt such hope, but also fear. What did that mean for the past—and for the future?

She slowly turned in his arms and stepped back to look up at him. She laid her hands lightly on his shoulders and studied his eyes. He went very still under her touch, and his eyes were dark and full of stark pain. She had never seen him like that, and it made her tremble.

But she forced herself to keep watching him, staring into his eyes. Once she had hated him for making her love him and then leaving her. When she looked at him now she could see he was not the same impulsive, roguish young man who had swept away her foolish, girlish heart. He had seen things—things she could not fathom and which she longed to know. She wanted to know *him*, as he was now, every part of him.

She reached up and traced her fingertips over his face. She felt the sharply curved lines of his cheekbones and jaw, his knife-blade nose, the sweep of his brow. His eyes closed under her touch, and she drifted a caress over his lips. They parted and he caught her finger between his teeth and sucked it.

"John," Celia whispered. She went up on tiptoe and kissed his cheek. "John."

"I am here, Celia," he answered. He swept her up into his arms and carried her with him to the waiting bed.

She fell back onto the pillows and raised herself on her elbows to watch him. He looked back at her, his eyes hooded as he slid her shoes off her feet. His palms moved slowly up the back of her legs, pulling her skirts out of his way as he went.

He bent his head and kissed the sensitive spot behind her knee, his open mouth hot through her silk stocking. Celia let her head fall back and closed her eyes to let the feelings wash over her. She wanted to feel every touch, every kiss, every breath.

John loosened the ribbon garter and eased her stocking down and off before reaching for her other leg and doing the same there. As the white silk rolled down his mouth followed, a fiery trail over her skin. He licked over the arch of her foot and rose up between her legs to reach for the ties of her skirt.

Celia arched her hips to let him strip away her clothes. Every part of her he bared he kissed, slowly, reverently, as if he worshipped every curve of her body. It was achingly tender, and she wanted to cry from what it did to her. It was as if her heart was cracking all over again and letting him slip inside.

When she lay before him naked, he stood beside the bed to strip away his own clothes, his doublet and shirt tossed to the floor as his gaze never left her. She sat up and reached for the fastening of his breeches, unable to wait a moment longer to see him.

She peeled them away from his lean hips, down his thighs, until his erection sprang free. She caressed with her thumb that spot he loved until he pushed her away.

"Celia," he groaned.

Watching him, looking deeply into his eyes, she lay back down on the bed and opened her legs to him, welcoming him to come atop her and love her however he chose. Giving herself to him.

He seemed to see exactly what she was telling him. His nostrils flared and fire kindled deep in his eyes. She nodded, and he lowered his body slowly against hers, until she could wrap her legs around his hips and draw him to her. He slid along her, skin to skin, heartbeat to heartbeat, until his lips met hers in a soft, searching kiss.

Celia moaned at the touch of his mouth, at the way his tongue tasted the seam of her lips before sliding over hers, twining with hers. She *had* to touch him. She dug her fingers into his back, feeling the sweat-damp heat of his skin, the shifting and tensing of his muscles. They had come together so many times before, coupled as if compelled to each other, but in this moment she felt as if they were truly together.

One moment they were two people, two beings, then with a twist of his hips he slid inside her and they became one. He pressed forward until he was fully seated, his pubic bone pressed to hers, deeper than ever before. And then he rested against her, letting her feel their bodies together, feel him truly touching her.

"John, please…" she whispered, even though she

had no idea what she begged for. She just needed more, needed *him*.

And then he drew back, slow and steady, until he almost pulled out of her. When she cried out he thrust forward, harder, rougher, only to draw back again.

Celia grasped his taut backside and dug her fingers in tight, urging him forward, silently asking for him to make her his. To show her he was hers, if only for now. He braced his hands on the bed to either side of her and thrust hard. She heard his breath, heavy and intoxicating in her ear as he kissed her, and she couldn't breathe at all.

She closed her eyes and tilted her head back as she opened herself to him. She let him take her, hard and hungry, and felt her heart pound inside her breast as she reached for her climax.

"Wait for me, Celia," he growled. "Come with me."

"Yes," she panted. "Yes."

His movements grew faster, all rhythm gone to leave only hunger. Celia cried out as pleasure burst inside her, and he shouted her name as his back arched. She opened her eyes to see his features contorted with raw pleasure, the muscles in his arms taut.

And then he collapsed to the bed beside her, his hand on her hip. She had never felt anything like the peace that descended on her like a silvery cloud. She curled into his side, against his chest, and he pressed a kiss to her hair.

She couldn't say anything. She could hardly even

breathe. She could only slide into sleep again, held in John's arms. She never slept as deeply as when she was safe with him.

Chapter Nineteen

John smoothed his hand softly down Celia's bare back and over her scarred shoulder as he watched her sleep. Her skin felt so soft under his touch. Soft and slender—so vulnerable.

He slid his touch down her arm to take her hand, and thought how those delicate fingers held everything he was within their grasp.

She shifted against him, sighing in her dreams, and he lay down beside her again with his arm around her waist. Her hair drifted over his bare chest in a black cloud, and he buried his nose in the satin strands to inhale her perfume.

Their mission was drawing to a close and his time with Celia was slipping away. John closed his eyes on a spasm of pain deep in his heart. Something had moved inside him when he took Celia today. Nay—he had been changing ever since he saw her again that day at Whitehall. For so long she had lived in his mind as a memory, a dream, a beautiful and passionate young woman who had brightened his life for all too short a moment, given him hope for a different sort of life. He had seen so much that was violent, ugly and full of greed, and Celia was soft and as brilliant as the sun. Not sweet—never that—but even her tart tongue made him laugh. Made him live again, want to live again.

He had repaid all she'd given him with pain and trouble. Yet still he cherished every memory of their time together.

Celia now was so much more than he remembered. More beautiful, more brave. And when she'd lain back on the bed and held out her arms to him, surrendering to him, his soul had broken wide open and everything he was had flown free. She'd set him free.

And now he only wanted to keep her for ever, to make her his, even as he knew that could never be for them. Celia would never belong to anyone again—especially not him.

Not once he told her of his part in what had happened to her brother. He would have to tell her, he owed her no less now, and he would have to make amends for what he had done to all the people he had hurt in his service to the Queen. Part of his penance would be to lose Celia for ever, and then he would be only the hard, cynical shell he had always been without her.

But not yet. Not today. Today he still had her.

He slid down on the bed and moved the fall of her hair to kiss her shoulder. He wanted to heal those scars, to take away all the pain of her past. Her body undulated against him and she gasped as he kissed a hot, open-mouthed path down her back. He licked at the hollow just above the curve of her buttocks. His fingers caressed her softness there and she whispered his name.

"I am here," he answered. His fingertips brushed against the soft cheeks and she hissed.

John smiled against her skin and rolled her onto her back. He rested his chin on her stomach and looked up at her to find she stared at him with stormy grey eyes. Her pale cheeks were flushed with desire.

"Did I wake you, my fairy queen?" he said. "A thousand apologies."

"You aren't sorry at all," she answered. She slowly drew up her leg, brushing against his erection. He grew even harder at the merest touch of her skin. "Someone obviously seeks amusement."

"I watched you while you slept," he said, pressing soft kisses over her hip, her tight stomach, around her navel. "You looked so beautiful while you were dreaming."

Celia stretched her arms above her head, her whole body laid out for him. She closed her eyes and arched her back, sensual as a cat. "I was dreaming of you."

"Of me? And what exactly was I doing?" He bit at her hip, making her gasp again, and slid lower to kiss the inside of her thigh, just above her knee.

"Oh—something much like this, I think. Only a wee bit higher."

"Ah. Like here, mayhap?" He traced his tongue in a light pattern over the seam between her thigh and hip. Her legs fell further apart and he felt her fingers twine in his hair as she drew him closer.

"Or—here?" he whispered, and blew out a soft breath over her damp pink folds.

Celia moaned and her fingers clenched in his hair. "Aye, there!"

"You drive me mad, Celia," he groaned, tasting her sweet essence with the tip of his tongue. He needed her so much, felt so much. "The more I have of you the more I need you."

"I know, I know. Oh, John, I—"

Her words were broken off at the abrupt sound of a knock at the door. John reared up on his knees and automatically reached for the dagger under his pillow. Celia had gone perfectly still beneath him.

"John?" he heard Marcus call, as he knocked again. "I have to talk to you now. I know you are there."

John bit back a filthy curse and let go of the dagger. His friend had always had wretched timing. Even now his body ached and vibrated with lust, at the smell of Celia's arousal on his skin, her gasp in his ears.

But he also knew Marcus would not have come here if it was not vital. He would be off with Lady Allison or one of his many other women. John looked down at Celia, who stared back at him with wide eyes. She nodded and pushed herself up on the pillows, drawing the bedclothes over her nakedness.

John tore himself away from her and leaped from the bed. He scooped up his clothes, tossing her the shirt as he slid into his breeches. He drew the curtains around the bed before opening the door.

"What?" he growled.

Marcus's face was etched with concern, but as he

glanced over John's shoulder at the shrouded bed he grinned.

"I thought you might have been making a jest about seeking out Mistress Sutton," Marcus said. "Yet here you truly are."

John seized his friend by the shoulder and pulled him into the room. "What has happened?"

"And it had best be something very important, Lord Marcus," Celia called from the bed.

Marcus's grin widened. "Indeed it is. But I could be persuaded to delay my news if I did not know that my friend never shares."

John almost hit Marcus, but then he heard Celia laugh. She yanked the curtains aside, and he turned to see she knelt at the end of the bed. His shirt fell almost to her knees, covering her body even better than her satin gowns in folds of soft voluminous linen. Yet her black hair tumbled free down her back and her cheeks were pink, and he found he wanted no one else to see her like this. Ever.

Marcus was quite right. He did not share. Especially not Celia. He had no claim on her. Not really. But he wanted to. He wanted her to belong only to him.

He covered his emotions by tossing her the surcoat she had left on the floor. As she draped it over her shoulders he leaned against the bedpost and crossed his arms over his chest, glaring at Marcus.

"I don't care to share either," Celia said, far too calm for his taste. "And we are rather occupied at the moment. What has happened?"

"I was rather *occupied* myself," Marcus answered. "But I thought you should hear this."

"What is it?" John said.

"We have known all along that despite her strange infatuation with Darnley Queen Mary has been reluctant to make an English marriage. Now Allison has discovered someone is in the pay of Mary's Guise uncles and has been pouring out persuasions to accept *their* candidate instead—a certain Comte de Mornay. And Mornay has no love at all for the English. He would destroy any alliance, any chance of peace between the Queens."

"And there would be war with Scotland again," John muttered. "Even bloodier than under Marie of Guise."

"Who is this traitor?" Celia asked. "And how did Lady Allison find out?"

"She has become friendly with a certain Monsieur d'Alblay," Marcus said. "And that gentleman is not smart enough to guard his secret papers as he should. Allison is adept at reading codes. As for the Englishman taking French coin—it is Lord Knowlton."

"What?" Celia cried.

John swung towards her to see the flash of shock on her face, and he remembered that the man wanted to marry her. It made a spark of some dark emotion catch inside of him, thinking of her as another man's wife. "You are surprised about your suitor?"

"He did hint to me that he would soon be much wealthier," she whispered, as if to herself. "So he could take a wife."

Another spasm of anger passed through John's body. "And he wanted you."

"He admires you, Mistress Sutton?" Marcus said. He looked at Celia with a speculative glint in his eyes. "Perhaps he would talk to you frankly? Confess?"

"Nay!" John nearly shouted. "She will not be involved in this." She would not put herself in any more danger. He would not allow it. He would keep her safe.

Celia slid from the bed and came to his side. Her hand was soft on his arm. "I *am* involved, John. That is why I was sent here by Queen Elizabeth—to help protect her interests here. I confess I understand little of our true purpose here, and I have not done much to be assistance. It's obvious that Lady Allison is far more useful. But I *can* meet with Lord Knowlton. If I hint that his feelings are returned perhaps he will tell me more of the French plans."

"An excellent idea, Mistress Sutton," Marcus said. "It would make that part of our task much easier."

John nearly drove his fist into his friend's face. "Nay, it is no idea at all. You should stay away from Knowlton, Celia."

"He cannot hurt me here," she argued. "I won't let myself be entirely alone with him. I merely want to discover what he is doing in return for his newfound wealth."

"And we will stay near her, John," Marcus said. "No lady has ever been harmed in our care."

John stared down into Celia's grey eyes. She looked so calm, so cool and composed. Once she had been deeply hurt by him—more than once. He could not do that again. Not when he had vowed to keep her safe. Even from himself.

But her hand tightened on his arm. "I promised the Queen," she whispered. "And she will only help me if I help her. This task is small enough."

He remembered what the Queen had promised Celia in return for the task—a rich marriage, a secure future. All the things his own actions had stolen from her.

He glanced at Marcus, who watched them warily. If John did not agree to Celia doing this he knew she would just go with Marcus and do it anyway, without him knowing or being able to protect her. He looked back to Celia. She was cool-headed, calm. He knew she would keep her wits about her.

And talking, questioning—it was far less than he had done on missions in the past. He and Marcus would watch over her.

"No talking to him without us being near, even if it's in hiding," he said roughly. "And not until you are ready."

Celia nodded. "Of course."

"Excellent!" Marcus said with a grin. "Shall we meet tomorrow, then, on the ramparts? I will just leave you now to resume your—occupations."

He slid out of the door, and John and Celia were alone in the silence again. They merely stared at each other for a long moment and he tried to read her thoughts in her eyes. He could see nothing until the grey went smoky and a slow smile curved her lips.

She stepped back from him and let the surcoat fall from her shoulders. Never looking away from him, she reached for the hem of the shirt she wore and slid it over her head. She shook back her hair and stood before him naked, the light glowing on her skin, the rosy tips of her breasts pebbled.

All anger and worry fled as his stare avidly took her in, and all knowledge of the truth he would soon have to tell her. All he could see, all he knew, was her. Celia. Within reach of his arms. This had always been easy between them—perfect, fiery and full of delicious forgetfulness.

He reached out and wrapped his hands hard around her waist to drag her up against his body. He buried his face in the curve of her neck, smelling her, tasting her. His Celia. *His.* She would always be that, even when she hated him again. Even when she was gone from him.

"We still have the night ahead of us," she whispered, her fingers twisting in his hair. "However will we fill it?"

John growled in answer, and lifted her in his arms to carry her back to the bed. Her laughter echoed like the sweetest music in his ears.

Chapter Twenty

Celia slowly paced to the end of the lane, keeping close to the stone wall, and turned to walk back the other way. She hadn't expected to feel so nervous. After all, this was what she had come to Edinburgh to do—to deceive, discover. Yet her hands felt icy cold even in her gloves.

She drew her cloak hood closer over her head and tried not to glance at the doorway where John and Marcus, along with a young apprentice of Marcus's named Nathan, were meant to be hiding. The street was narrow and shadowed, quiet. So quiet she thought she could hear the snowflakes drifting to the ground. She felt so terribly alone.

She turned and walked slowly back to the end of the lane. She was meant to meet with Lord Knowlton under the apothecary's sign there, but what if he did not come? What if she failed before she even began?

Nay, she could not fail. She would have nowhere to go then.

"Mistress Sutton," she heard Lord Knowlton call.

She spun around to see that he had appeared at the end of the lane. He was also wrapped in a cloak against the cold, and for an instant there on the deserted, snow-dusted lane he looked ominous. Like a crow in a church-yard.

But he smiled as he reached her side and took her hand in his, even as his eyes flashed with a puzzled look. "I was surprised to receive your message," he said as he kissed her hand.

Celia shivered at his touch. Not with delight, as when John kissed her, but with something that felt strange, wrong. A surreal sort of haze seemed to come over her mind, as if she was not there at all.

"Not an unpleasant surprise, I hope?" she said. She managed to give him a smile.

He smiled back, but still that something flashed in his eyes. He tucked her hand in his arm and led her over to stand by the wall. "Not at all. You must know I've wanted to speak with you alone, without the distrac-tions of the palace."

"Have you really, Lord Knowlton?"

"I had hoped my words to you when last we met were not too subtle," he said, still holding onto her hand, "and did not frighten you away. I have admired you greatly ever since we met."

"That is very kind of you. I have not been accus-tomed to admiration since my husband died."

"Do you miss being married as I do?"

Not at all. She had loathed being married, and some-thing about that glint in Knowlton's eyes, the touch of his hand on hers, told her she would not enjoy it much with him either. But she had learned one thing in her marriage, and that was to conceal her true feelings at all cost.

She smiled and leaned into him, letting him feel her body against his. "Very much. It is lonely for a single woman in the world."

"Lonely for a man as well." His eyes heated as he looked down at her, took in her loose hair around her face, her parted lips. "I have had no one since my wife died."

"No one at all? A titled gentleman in the Queen's favour such as you?"

He shook his head, and raised one finger to trace the line of her jaw. She forced herself to stay still under his touch. "I have very specific tastes, Mistress Sutton. Celia. I want someone beautiful, sophisticated, but also a challenge. Someone not easy to conquer."

"Co-conquer?" Celia stuttered. She had not quite expected that from him. The kind, mild man she had enjoyed chatting with seemed to have vanished now that they were alone.

"You always seem so distant, Celia. So cool and composed." His palm traced down over the line of her throat, nudging her cloak out of the way so the leather of his glove was against her bare skin. "I have longed to know what you hide beneath all that disdain," he whispered. "To be the only one who can uncover your secrets."

Celia shook her head and fell back a step. His arm swept around her waist and brought her up against him. "I have no secrets."

"Oh, but I think you do. We all do."

"Do *you* have secrets, Lord Knowlton?"

"Of course I do. And they are why I can now take care of you as you deserve, lovely Celia. I can take you away from England to somewhere secret and safe, just the two of us, where we can share all our secrets."

Celia drew in a deep breath and forced herself to relax in his arms. Was this it, then? Was it really this easy to make someone confess?

"I will not live here in Scotland," she said.

He laughed. "Here, in this godforsaken place? Certainly not. Once my work is done we will live in a much more hospitable land. One where your beauty will be appreciated as it should be."

"Your work?" she said. Did she sound too eager?

His gaze narrowed on her and his arms tightened around her. "I cannot give away my secrets for free, my dear. I'll need something from you in return."

"I told you. I have no secrets to share. And I must be sure that whoever I marry will be able to care for me."

"You need have no doubts about *that* if we decide we suit." He lowered his head to press a soft kiss on her brow. "Show me that we will suit, Celia. That you are what I have been working for, waiting for."

"How?" she gasped as his parted lips trailed over her cheekbone. His kiss was hot, dry, seeking. It made her stomach seize in a painful knot.

"Kiss me," he demanded. He pulled her up on her toes and her mouth with his. His tongue forced her lips apart and pressed deep inside.

Celia screamed in her mind, over and over, as that

terrible trapped feeling she had always had with her husband closed over her. Black ice seemed to trickle over her body, freezing her, holding her fast so she could not move.

"You *are* a cold wench, aren't you?" he growled as his lips finally, blessedly, left hers. He nipped at her neck. "But we will soon change that."

Celia closed her eyes tightly and tried to pretend she was not really there. That she merely watched the scene from a distance, as at the playhouse. That was what she had done in her marriage. That distance was sometimes all that had kept her sane.

"I cannot marry a man who can't take care of me," she said again. "If you have Queen Elizabeth's favour…"

"Queen Elizabeth?" Lord Knowlton said bitterly. "She is nothing. England is nothing. The power in this world lies with France and Spain, and one day they will crush Elizabeth like the bastard upstart she is."

His harsh outburst shocked Celia after his earlier caution. She stared up at him, at his face that was so contorted she could hardly recognise it. "That—that is treason."

"It is merely the truth, as all wise men know." He suddenly tightened his arm around her waist and swung her hard to the wall, trapping her there with his body. "And if *you* are wise you will come with me before it is too late."

"To Spain?" she whispered.

"Spain?" He laughed. "There is no merriment in Spain. We will go to France, you and I, as soon as Queen Mary does what her Guise uncles wish. Despite

her foolish infatuation with Darnley she will soon remember where her true advantages lie."

At last the truth Celia sought. She closed her eyes
and tried to think. He had confessed, or as good as. It
would be enough for Elizabeth and Lord Burghley. Yet
he still had Celia trapped.

"You are allied with the French, then?" she said.
"They will give you the fortune that will let you marry
where you will?"

Immediately she knew she had pressed too far. His
body stiffened against hers. "Why do you want those
words, Celia?" he asked calmly. "I have already offered
you all you need."

Celia shook her head. "My husband lied to me. I cannot bear that again…"

"And did you lie to him?" His lips pressed hard to
the side of her neck, making her shudder. "Are you
lying to me now?"

"Nay!" she cried. Suddenly one of his gloved hands
was clapped over her mouth, strangling her words, her
breath. Holding her to the wall with his body, he reached
his other hand down to grasp the hem of her skirt and
drag it up over her leg.

Celia felt the cold wind on her skin, the hard trap of
his body on hers, and wanted to scream.

"Show me what a good wife you will be, Celia," he
said against her ear, and his hand swept over her thigh.

And then in an instant he was torn away from her.
Her breath flooded back into her lungs, painful and
cold, and she shook so hard she could scarcely stand.
She braced herself against the wall, and through the

filmy haze of tears she saw John throw Knowlton down into the street.

John had the man down on his stomach, his knee on Knowlton's back as he twisted his arm behind him. Celia had never seen John look like that before, his handsome face contorted with rage, with primitive fury. All his elegant sophistication was stripped away, leaving a killer in its place.

As she pressed herself back to the wall, watching in horror, John and Knowlton fought like dogs in the middle of the street, first one man and then the other down, until blood and sweat flew in the air. She almost screamed when Knowlton threw John to the ground, but John turned the tables yet again and had his opponent beaten down.

But when John staggered to his feet and started to turn away Knowlton suddenly snatched a hidden blade from inside his boot and lunged forward to drive it into John's side. John staggered back, staring down at the blood that had appeared on his torn doublet.

"John!" Celia cried.

He glanced at her for only an instant, then whirled around and drove his own blade into Knowlton's chest, twisting it until the man fell to the ground again, perfectly still, and the fight was over as quickly and violently as it had begun.

Celia ran to catch John's arm as he started slowly to fall, struggling to hold him up, to will her own life into him. To beg him silently not to leave her.

Suddenly Marcus was there. "Get John back to the palace," he said.

His firm touch on her arm seemed to be all that held her tethered to reality as she looked down at John's blood.

"Nathan will help you. I will take care of—that."

He nudged Knowlton's body with his boot, and Celia shivered.

"What if—? Did anyone see?" she whispered.

"If they did, they will know well enough to keep it to themselves," Marcus said roughly. "Go now. See to John."

Celia nodded. As the other man slid John's limp arm over his shoulder and drew him to his feet, she went to his other side and wrapped her hand over his waist. She could feel his breath dragging painfully in and out of his body, and she was glad for it because it meant he still lived. He was still with her.

"Celia, I am sorry…" he gasped.

She shook her head. "No talking, John. Save your strength now or we will never get you to the palace."

She glanced back over her shoulder as they carried John to the end of the lane, but Marcus, his assistant and Knowlton's body were already gone. The night was quiet again, as if the whole violent scene had never happened at all.

Except for the coppery tang of blood and steel in the air.

Celia shivered and turned away.

He couldn't reach her.

A thick, silvery mist swirled around him, concealing everything but the tantalising glimpse of Celia just ahead of him. Her black hair fell loose over her shoulders, and her smile was enticing as she called out to him. She held her hand to him, but when John reached for her she laughed and spun away.

"Celia!" he shouted, and the word echoed back at him, mocking him. A terrible desperation swept over him. He *had* to find her, grab her in his arms and know she was real. That she was his again and he could never lose her.

But she was gone. He ran through the mist, calling her name. He could hear her laughter, hear her whisper, "I am here, John. Right here," but he couldn't see her.

And then even her laughter was gone, and he knew with a horrible certainty that he had lost her. He was alone again, and he could never find his way free of that.

"John," she said again. "John!"

He spun towards the sound of her voice, hope rushing through him again. Foolish hope when he had thought he knew better than to allow such a thing. But there was no teasing laughter to her voice now, no enticement. Only fear and tears.

Nay, that could not be. Celia never cried.

John forced his gritty, heavy eyes to open and found himself staring up at a green canopy. There was no cold mist, only the warmth and smoke of a fire, the feeling of soft sheets against his bare skin.

And a cool hand on his arm, the summery smell of a woman's perfume. Celia's perfume.

He turned his head to see that she sat on the edge of the bed, staring down at him with her grey eyes. They were dark with concern, and they really did shimmer with the bright sheen of tears.

"Oh, praise God, you are awake," she said. "I feared you would open your wound with all that fierce thrashing about."

"Am I awake?" he said, and found his throat was dry. His body ached, the wound on his side was throbbing, but he would bear any pain if she would just stay there beside him.

"I hope so. You were feverish, but you feel cooler to the touch now." Her hand gently curled over his cheek and she smiled down at him. "Your eyes are clearer. I think you will recover."

John covered her hand with his, holding her with him. He turned his face and kissed her palm as he closed his eyes to inhale the sweet scent of her skin. "Because you were here with me. You brought me back."

"This has become a terrible habit of ours," Celia said. She raised her other hand to smooth back his hair, her touch light and gentle. "Nursing each other through wounds. You must take better care of yourself in the future."

John had to grin. "Why should I, when this is the result? You sitting at my bedside, not arguing with me, not flaying me with that sharp tongue of yours."

Celia pressed a fleeting kiss to his brow and drew away from him, leaving him without her touch. "That is not all I will flay you with if you do this again." She reached for a goblet on the table and held it to his lips. "Drink this."

John took her wrist between his fingers. "Not poisoned, is it?"

Celia snorted. "I wouldn't have worked so hard to heal you only to do away with you now. It is merely healing herbs in wine. Queen Mary herself sent her finest stock of French wine for you."

"Queen Mary?" John drank deeply, draining the goblet before he lay back on the pillows. The wine seemed to restore him so she could think clearly again.

"Aye. She is quite distraught that an emissary of her 'dear cousin' would be treated thus in her own city." Celia laid aside the goblet and moved to sit on a stool by the bed. John saw she wore one of her black gowns, but it was rumpled, as if she had sat there in it for a long while. Black tendrils escaped from the braided knot of her hair. "She has sent home Lord Knowlton's French contact and written to Queen Elizabeth with her apologies."

"How long have I been here, then?" he asked.

"Only two days—three as it is nearly nightfall now. Queen Mary moves quickly when she wishes to." A small smile touched Celia's lips. "She also cries a great deal."

"And has she made up her mind to marry?"

Celia shrugged. "I doubt a French alliance of any sort now. She says only that she finds Queen Elizabeth's advice to marry an Englishman very sound. And she was dancing with Lord Darnley again last night."

"You saw them?"

"Nay, I was here, nursing a hot-headed rogue through

a nightmare. Lady Allison told me. She is much sharper of wit than I would have guessed."

John winced. "It is what makes a good intelligencer. The ability to hide one's true self, to be whatever one needs to be at the moment."

"And you are a good intelligencer, are you not, John?" she said quietly.

He looked at her. Her tears were gone, her cool, pale mask back in place. It made him want to grab her and hold her hard, until his Celia came back from behind that mask. "Until I lose my head and find myself wounded, aye," he said.

Celia nodded. "How did you come to this work?"

John's eyes narrowed as he studied her face, her hands folded in her lap. What did she know? What did he dare tell her now? And yet he could not hide from her any longer. He cared about her far too much, owed her too much.

A wave of weariness washed over him, and he closed his eyes and let his head fall back. What was in those cursed herbs? He couldn't tell her everything right now—not when he didn't have the strength to make her understand, make her forgive him for his long-ago betrayal.

"I was a wild young man—aimless, angry. I wanted only to fight, craved violence, but there were no wars to fight then, where I could utilise my energy. It came out in tavern brawls, brothels, trouble of all sorts."

Celia nodded. "You were sent to the country?"

"After a spell in Bridewell, after a friend of mine killed a man in a brawl I was involved in, my uncle de-

cided I needed a quiet place to contemplate my sins."
That was true. He didn't add that Lord Burghley had
given him the chance to redeem himself by breaking a
conspiracy against the Queen, and that his reward for
succeeding had been more and heavier tasks. Matters
that had kept him away from her for too long, things
he'd had to protect her from.

"But there I just committed more sins," he said bitterly.

"Was I your sin?" Celia asked. "But I wanted what
happened—wanted you. I have never felt like that before, from the first moment I saw you."

"Nor had I. You were—are—unlike anyone I have
ever known. I knew then that I should stop, that I should
stay away from you, but I could not." He still could not.
Something about her kept drawing him back to her,
over and over again.

"I am glad you did not," Celia said quietly, firmly.
"What happened between us sustained me through everything that happened after."

John's heart gave a spasm of pain, a raw ache at the
hurt he had caused her. That he had caused himself
when he'd had to leave her. "Celia…" he said tightly,
knowing he had to tell her everything. Had to make it
right somehow.

But the chamber door opened and the hand John
had started to hold out to Celia fell back to the bed.
Lady Allison stood there, her shrewd gaze sweeping
between them. She set the tray she held down on the
table and smiled.

"I have brought you some supper, Sir John, and come

to relieve you of nursing duty for a time, Celia," Allison said. "You must be very tired."

Celia nodded wearily. "Thank you, Lady Allison. I *am* tired." She rose from her chair, watching John as he stared back at her. He would read nothing in her eyes now. "I will be back in a few hours."

John stared after her until the door closed behind her. He could still smell her perfume in the air. He heard the rustle of Allison's silk skirts as she settled herself in the chair, and turned to see her knowing smile.

"Well," she said, "who would have thought such a simple-seeming task could cause such trouble? You look wretched, John."

"What a charming flatterer you are, Allison," he said, closing his eyes. "A veritable silvery-sweet tongue."

She laughed. "Your friend Marcus seems to like it well enough. But, alas, the two of you will be going back to England soon, while I must stay here and mind Queen Mary. So dull for me."

John's eyes opened. "Going back to England?"

"Aye, Queen Elizabeth's orders arrived by messenger today. You are urgently needed in London—though I think you must travel at a rather slower pace at the moment."

"And Celia?"

Allison shrugged. "You will have to ask her, I think." She drew a small book from the pouch tied at her waist and settled back to read. "You should rest now. I fear there is still much more work to come."

Chapter Twenty-One

"Will you be happy to go home?" Lady Allison asked Celia as they strolled through the Queen's private garden at Holyrood.

"Home?" Celia said. She wrapped her cloak closer against the cold day and watched Queen Mary and her ladies as they gambolled with their little dogs amid the trees. She had no home to go back to; she could hardly remember what a home felt like at all. A place that was hers, where she belonged. She had been a prisoner or a guest for too long.

Only when she was in John's bed, wrapped in his arms, did she feel she was meant to be there. And it felt too good, too frightening.

She realised Allison was looking at her quizzically. She had been silent for too long. She smiled and said, "I will be happy to see England again."

Allison laughed. "You don't care for Scotland?"

"It is a strange place. A rough one." Celia studied the craggy face of King Arthur's Seat rising beyond the palace. She remembered John's crumbling family home. "But beautiful in its own way. I'm glad to have seen it."

"But also glad to leave it behind, I think?"

"Perhaps." Scotland had been a dream, Celia thought, a moment out of her real life when she had found John again, had come alive again when she had thought herself dead inside. How could she regret that, even if the dream-time had to end? She could not be sorry.

Yet she felt so fragile inside, as if she was barely held together. One cold wind would shatter everything.

"I'm not sure what waits for me back in England," Celia said. "But I must face it soon. I cannot stop time."

"Perhaps you could do more services like this for Queen Elizabeth," Allison said quietly. "It has its own rewards."

Celia looked at her, still unused to seeing such a solemn look on Allison's pretty face. She couldn't fathom how she'd missed it before, how she had failed to peer behind the façade.

It made her frown, wondering what else she had missed.

"Have you been doing such work for a long time, Lady Allison?" she asked.

Allison shrugged, and the hood of her cloak shifted from her red hair. "I was the daughter of an earl who was sadly impecunious. When I was fourteen he married me off to a much older man."

In those simple words—the tale of so many young ladies—Celia could hear a vast amount of pain. Had she not experienced that herself? "Were you married very long?"

Allison shrugged. "A few years. I learned many useful things from my husband. He was—demanding in the bedchamber, even though he could not often become aroused. When he died I found myself without money again."

"So you worked for the Queen?"

"Aye. Lord Burghley saw what I could do and gave me a task to prove myself. Then another and another. I do well for myself, and serve England as well."

Celia stopped at the end of the pathway, listening to Queen Mary's laughter, the shrill barking of the dogs. She could only think of John, of all her old foolish hopes. Hopes she had dared to resurrect even as she knew better.

"Do you never want anything else?" Celia asked.

"Such as what?" Allison said with a small smile. "I have no wish to marry again. Especially to another man who is not my own choice. I am content."

And Celia envied her that. To have work she was good at, a purpose. To serve something important, larger than herself, and be free to do it. It was what John did.

"I was wrong about Lord Knowlton," Celia said. "I never suspected him. How can I do what you do when I can't read people?"

"You learn that," Allison said. "Once you know a few things people can be shockingly transparent. Most people." She laughed. "I could never understand *you*, Mistress Sutton."

Celia had to laugh in return. "I cannot understand myself at times. But how did you learn to do this?"

Allison's face softened. "Marcus helped me when we first met. He and John have been doing this work longer than I have."

"And do you often work together?" Celia asked, pushing away a small pang of jealousy. It seemed it was Marcus Allison had the soft spot for, not John. Even so...

"With Marcus, aye. Not so often with John. But we were all in Paris together for a time, working to discover a traitor in the embassy there. There are always those ready to take French coin, just as Knowlton was. It was a dangerous time."

"But you all survived?" Celia whispered, afraid that might not always be the case. Her hands were suddenly cold, her brain numb at the thought.

"Aye, we watched each other's backs. John had just finished with the Drayton conspiracy when he was sent to Paris, and I don't know what happened to him but he was fiercely looking for a fight. Even the French could not stand against him."

Celia froze. Arthur Drayton was the name of her brother's friend—the one who had embroiled him in his traitorous scheme. Surely she had heard Allison wrong? Surely—? Nay, it could not be. It could not! She wouldn't let it be. And yet she feared it *was* the truth— the truth that had always been staring her in the face even as she denied it.

Clutching at her cloak with numb hands, she spun towards Allison. "What did he do before he went to Paris?" she whispered.

Allison frowned, as if she was disquieted by what

she saw in Celia's face. "Lord Burghley knew there was some sort of trouble brewing, and that John's uncle lived nearby. He was sent to ferret out the traitors there. Once he did that he was sent immediately to France. You have turned very pale, Mistress Sutton. Are you ill?"

Celia shook her head. She felt as if she had been turned into a block of ice. Her face, her skin, her heart were so cold, and thoughts raced through her head.

Of *course* John had not really been sent to the country to atone for some scandal. He had come to trap her poor, foolish brother and his friends in their silly game of conspiracy. William had never had a chance against a cool, deceitful predator like John Brandon. And neither had she.

She had fallen into his bed like a ripe plum. But at least then she had been a naive girl who could not know better, who had never encountered anyone like him before. Now she was a woman, a widow, who knew she should guard her heart. But she had gone to him again, opened herself to him again.

She was a doubly damned fool. And she could feel her heart cracking inside her and falling into a thousand shards of doubt.

"I must go inside now," she said tightly.

"I will go with you," Allison said, but Celia shook her head.

"You stay with the Queen," Celia managed to say. "I am well. I only need to rest for a while."

And to kill John Brandon. But even if he was gone from her life, gone from the world, she would never be able to banish the hollow pain inside of her. The pain had been diminished for a time, while she lay in John's arms, but now it was back, a steel vice on her soul.

She had the terrible certainty it would never be gone again.

She turned and walked away. She forced herself to move slowly, to make her steps measured even as she wanted to run. She still walked slowly when she reached the palace, climbed the stairs past the courtiers who swept past her laughing and stood whispering in niches. They were all a blur to her.

Her mind felt quiet, hazy, as if time had ceased to have all meaning. She felt nothing at all. The pain had gone too deep. If only she could go on feeling thus the rest of her life.

As she turned onto the quiet corridor lined with closed chamber doors she reached up to unfasten her cloak. She didn't notice as it dropped to her feet. Her eyes were on the door to John's chamber, the innocent-looking wood that concealed the mouth to hell.

She pushed it open without knocking and stood frozen on the threshold. John was packing books and papers in a valise, wearing a loose shirt over his bandage, his hair tousled. He looked so beautiful, so much like the John she had loved, that her heart gave a painful squeeze within her.

But that John had never existed except in her own foolish mind, Celia reminded herself. *This* John was a hardened intelligencer, a liar. He had destroyed her brother, her family, her whole life.

Yet she loved him still, and that only made her hate him more.

He glanced up, and a smile spread across his face at the sight of her. His eyes lit up a brighter blue than any summer sky.

"Celia," he said. "What do you do today?"

The sound of her name on his lips made the ice that encased her crack violently. Flames of utter fury roared through her—fury at him for making everything between them a lie, at herself for wanting to believe him. She lunged towards him and caught his cheek with her nails. The long scratch on his golden skin stoked her anger higher, and she slapped him with the flat of her palm.

Caught by surprise, he fell back a step and she slapped him again. With a scream, she tried to strike once more, but he was ready for her. Her fury gave her an abnormal strength, yet he was still much stronger. He caught her wrist, his fingers like steel manacles, and swept her arm behind her back as he spun her round, her back to his chest. His other arm banded around her waist.

"How could you?" she cried, and to her horror felt hot tears spill down her cheeks. She kicked back at him, twisting against his arms, but her skirts tangled around her legs and bound her in place. "I hate you."

"Hush," John growled against her ear. He easily evaded her strikes, holding her bound against him. "Hush now, Celia."

"You killed him," she sobbed. "And I let you. I let you deceive me because of my foolish lust for you, and he died because of it."

John's body went rigid against hers. "You know."

A tiny, foolish part of her had actually hoped he would deny it. That part died at those quiet words, and Celia went limp in his arms. The angry fire burned away, leaving her cold again. So cold.

She slumped in John's arms and let her tears fall. They had been held back for so long. "So it is true. You were sent to find the traitors, break their conspiracy."

"Aye," he said roughly. She felt him lower his head and press his face to her hair. His breath was harsh against her. "That was why I went there. It seemed a simple enough task. But I never expected you, what you would do to me."

Celia closed her eyes and sniffed back the last of her tears. She turned her damp cheek into his shoulder, but the familiar smell of him made her heart twist again. "Did you use me for information? Suspect me?"

He gave a bitter laugh. "If you remember, Celia, we seldom had time to talk at all. You never told me anything. They gave themselves away easily enough."

"But then why...?"

"Why did I take you? Because I *had* to. I knew it was wrong, foolish, but I had to have you. No woman has ever made me feel as you do, Celia, so wild, insane with need for you. My fairy queen." His tone was rough, strained, as if he held back a flood of emotion.

Celia gave a ragged sob. Her whole body felt weak, empty. "Do not call me that."

"I am sorry, Celia." He was silent for a long moment, their breath the only sound in the room. "Have you done with beating me now?"

"For the moment," she said. She felt too weak and sad

even to lift her arms. There was nothing but the numbness. Remorse that she had let herself trust in him again against everything. She was a fool, a fool.

John carefully lifted her in his arms and laid her on her back on the bed. She closed her eyes and turned her head away, achingly aware that he stood over her, watching her intently. At last she heard him walk away and sit down on the stool where she had sat for so many hours while he was wounded.

"I was going to tell you," he said.

"When?"

"Soon. Or perhaps long years from now, when you were too old and weak to attack me like that. But I did know that after everything we had been through you deserved the truth."

Celia still could not open her eyes, could not look at him. "Why did you not say before…?" Before she'd made love with him again. Opened her heart to him again.

She heard the rasp of his hand rubbing over his bristled jaw. "Because I was weak and selfish. I wanted this time with you. Needed it."

"There are dozens of other women who would happily warm your bed. Why toy with me again?"

"God's blood, Celia, but it is not like that with us and you know it," he cursed. "I know it was wrong of me, but I had to have you again and I would have done anything to get you."

Celia wanted to cry again, to sob out all her hurt and confusion, but she simply had no tears left. She had nothing left at all.

She slowly pushed herself up until she sat at the edge of the bed. John didn't move, but he watched her as closely as a hawk watched a mouse, as if he could read her and know what she would do next.

But he couldn't know. She didn't even know herself. She wanted to demand he tell her why he had done this to her again, what it was about her that set her up for hurt like this. But she did not want to give him the satisfaction of knowing what she felt.

"Well, then, you had me, John," she said. "And I had you. But no more. Never again. I have nothing more to give anyone."

"Celia, I beg you—" he began, but she held up her hand to stop him.

"I need to be alone now," she said. "Please don't follow me."

She slid off the bed and moved towards the door on trembling legs. John moved to help her, but at the touch of his hand she flinched away and took a step back.

"Celia, this is not over," he insisted.

"Not now," she whispered. "Please, not now. If you care even one tiny bit for me, John, you will let me go now. I might shatter if you touch me." She could not connect with him again. She did not trust herself any longer.

She felt the tension in his body, the urge he had to grab her in his arms again, yet he made no move towards her. Celia wrapped her arms around herself tightly and moved to the door. She felt cold and fragile, and very, very old.

Once the door had closed behind her she ran. She

scooped up her cloak and kept running until she was alone in her chamber. She collapsed to the floor, her hands over her face, and wished the terrible ache would go away. That she could just be numb again for ever.

But she feared the hurt would never, ever be gone.

John smashed his fist down onto the table, scattering papers everywhere. Pain drove up his arm but he didn't even notice it. All he could see was Celia's face as she turned away from him. So pale and still, with eyes that were void of any light. Dead.

And *he* was the one who had done that to her. To Celia, the woman he loved.

"I love her," he whispered, and the truth of those words was like a bolt of burning lightning, illuminating what had been hidden in darkness for him for too long. What he had hidden from himself.

He loved Celia, and he had lost her. Because of his own actions, his past, he had hurt her far worse than her hell-damned husband ever had.

"God's teeth!" John shouted, and swept the table clean with a vicious swipe of his arm.

He had to go to her, make things right for her again. He would give her anything, *be* anything, if she would just trust him again as she had when she took his body over hers.

Full of violent desperation, John swung towards the door and flung it open, intent on finding Celia. But Marcus stood on the threshold, blocking the doorway. His friend's face, usually so full of humour and mischief, was solemn. He shoved John back into the room and slid inside, slamming the door behind them. He crossed his arms over his chest and blocked the exit.

"Whatever this is, Marcus, I have no time for it now," John growled. "Get out of my way."

Marcus shook his head. "So you can go to Celia Sutton?"

John froze, his hands curled into tight fists. "Aye."

"What is between the two of you?" Marcus demanded. "I thought she was merely some kind of challenge to you, an unattainable lady for you to try and seduce. But now your quarrels are the talk of the palace."

"She was never *merely* anything to me," John admitted.

"Then what? Why are you running after her now, with that violent look in your eyes? I have seen that look before, right at the moment you ride into a tournament."

Violent? Aye, he did feel violent. As if he could grab Celia and hold her fast between his body and the wall and force her to listen. To understand, to forgive. Even if he knew her forgiveness was impossible now. He would do anything to get her back, but that would only drive her further away.

John slumped down onto the stool and ran his hands through his hair. "I knew her before…years ago."

Marcus relaxed his stance, but still stood by the door. "And you had a youthful affair that ended badly? One you renewed here in Scotland?"

"Aye, something of the sort," John muttered. "Do you remember the Drayton conspiracy?"

"Of course. You more than proved your worth on that one."

"Her brother was one of the men involved, but I did not know he was until after I had made love to Celia. He was executed and her family ruined."

"Curse it," Marcus breathed. "And she did not know before?"

"Not until today. I was going to tell her, but she found out somewhere else. Now she despises me."

"Then that is why…"

"Why what?"

"Allison told me Queen Mary has arranged an escort back to London for Mistress Sutton and they are to leave at dawn tomorrow."

"She is going already?" John burst out. "Then I must see her now!"

"Nay, John, that would not be a good idea! She needs time to think," Marcus protested.

John shoved him out of the way and tore open the door. He ran hard through the corridors, seeking her chamber. Her door was locked, but he could hear the murmur of soft voices inside.

"Celia!" he shouted as he pounded his fist on the door. He drew startled glances from passing courtiers, but he did not care. All he knew was that she was leaving, and time grew so very short.

"Celia, I know you are in there," he said, resting his forehead on the door. "Please, just listen to me for a moment."

There was a long silence, then the sound of a bar being drawn back. The door opened a small amount and Celia peered out at him. Her hair was drawn back tightly again, and she wore solemn, unrelieved black.

Her eyes still held that flat, stone-grey deadness.

"John, please," she said softly, tonelessly, "there is no more to say."

There was everything in the world to say, John thought as he stared down at her. She was right before him, and yet she was as unreadable as if oceans were between them. All he could say, all he could feel, was, "I am sorry."

"Sorry for what? You were doing your task. I merely got in your way." She sounded so bitter as she looked away from him, her whole body stiff and still. "It will not happen again."

"Because you are going back to England without me?"

"Queen Mary has agreed to provide an escort. Queen Elizabeth will want an account of what happened here. You will not have me to burden you any longer."

"Burden me?" John could not hold himself back any longer. He caught her hand in his, holding it fast. Her skin was cold and she did not draw away. But neither did she yield, and he had to restrain that primitive urge to push her down, hold her until she gave in and admitted what they were to each other.

"Celia, tell me how to set this right," he demanded. "Tell me how to prove to you I have changed!"

She shook her head. "You do not have to prove anything to me, John. Please, I am tired. Let me go."

"Nay, Celia. Not until you let me tell you all that happened."

"I know what happened! It doesn't matter now. Nothing matters." She wrenched herself free and slammed the door.

John pounded his forehead on the wood that lay between them and rested his clenched fists against it to keep from pounding the barrier down and claiming Celia as his own. It wouldn't work now, he knew that well—not when that coldness was upon her. He had to cool his temper, wait and plan.

Celia *would* be his again. There was no way either of them could be without the other now. She simply did not know it yet.

Chapter Twenty-Two

Celia stared down into the rushing water of the river far below where she stood on the edge of the bluff. The water was a cool grey-blue, dotted with lacy chunks of ice, and she remembered all too well how it had felt when she'd fallen in and it had closed around her. How it had felt when John pulled her out of the cold depths and saved her life.

She closed her eyes and shivered. But it wasn't the bite of the wind. It was the memories that made her feel so cold on this journey home. It had been days since she'd left John and started to make the long trip back to England, and she had thought she could leave him behind. Forget him and how she had given her heart to him—again.

But the images bombarded her at night in her dreams, and during the long, cold days. Images of John's face as he made love to her, his stark intensity as they moved together. His smile as they danced, his fierce protectiveness as he shielded her from the blast. So many memories, overlaying those of that past, so much deeper and richer than the wild moments of their youth.

So much more hurtful now, when she felt as if she had glimpsed John's true soul and let him see hers.

Celia turned away from the river and walked along the bank as she listened to the echo of her escorts' conversation as they rested for the midday meal. She hadn't been able to eat or be still since they'd left Edinburgh. She kept turning John's words over in her mind as she tried so hard to make sense of the past and the future. To make sense of him and how he made her feel.

As she walked now, the sound of the rushing river in her ears, she made herself remember her brother. William had been older than her but had always seemed younger, in the way he'd been so easily seized with strange passions and ideas. He had been her parents' darling, their heir, their hope for fading fortunes, but even they had seemed to realise he could be as changeable as mercury.

When the Queen's men had come to their house and arrested him for his part in his friends' conspiracy, Celia had been shocked and grieved, but there had been little surprise. It had seemed the sort of wild fancy he would have. But it had cost him his life and her parents the last of their fortune. And it had been John who had found William out. The man she had begun to love with all the fire of her young heart.

The man she had begun to love again with all her wounded soul.

Celia shook her head hard, as if she could rid herself of her troubled thoughts and emotions, but they clung stubbornly. The fury she'd felt when she had first found out about the true nature of John's work had burned itself out in the cold, solitary days since. Her rational knowledge of how the world really worked had begun to come back again. Her brother had gone against the Queen's law in his foolishness and would have inevitably been caught. John had had no choice in what he'd done.

But he *had* left her. That she could not understand. She needed to hear it from his own lips, needed to know if she had meant anything to him. And she had things she had to tell him as well.

It was time to lay the past to rest and move into the future.

Celia turned and strode back to camp, sure now of what she had to do.

Chapter Twenty-Three

⤜⤛◦⤚⤝

She was back where it had all begun, as if nothing had happened at all.

Celia looked around the crowded presence chamber at Whitehall and remembered when she'd stood there all those weeks ago, watched those same people waiting, whispering, desperate for Queen Elizabeth's attention. It looked the same, sounded the same, and yet it was not the same at all. Things *had* happened, and she had changed profoundly.

But she was still alone.

She rubbed at her arms through her purple satin sleeves as if she was chilled, even though the close-packed bodies and the roaring fire created a humid heat against the freezing rain outside. She stayed in her shadowed corner and ignored the curious stares around her. She could hardly see them anyway.

She just saw John, the last time she'd glimpsed his face before she had closed the door on him. That final glimpse had haunted her on the long journey back to

England—that image of anger and passion and something she couldn't even recognise on his handsome features. His voice demanding she listen to him.

A swift glimpse of his family's house on her journey—the place where they had stayed together, held
each other, talked—had almost torn out what little was
left of her heart. She had glimpsed John's past there,
what had driven him to do what he did now. She had
seen what might have been a home.

But she could not have listened to him after that—
not when she was so raw, so furious. She wasn't sure if
she could ever listen. He had betrayed her not once but
twice, and she in her infatuation had let him.

The journey had given her time to be quiet and think,
to start to mend her heart again, but she was still so very
confused. She needed to talk to him, to make sense of
everything that swirled in her mind and heart.

Celia studied the crowded chamber, the swirl of fine
velvets and silks, the taut voices and brittle laughter.
She saw in her mind all that happened—John, Queen
Mary and Lord Darnley, Holyrood, Marcus and Allison—had it been real? Or had it been a dream, and this
room the only reality?

"Mistress Sutton?" she heard someone say behind
her, and she snapped out of her daydream to turn and
see one of the Queen's pages.

"Yes?" she said.

"Her Grace will see you now."

Celia followed the man through the crowd and past
the guards at the doorway. Just as at that first meeting, she was taken through a series of chambers into

the inner sanctum of the Queen's own room, where the page bowed and departed and Celia was left alone with Elizabeth.

They were truly alone now. There were no ladies on the scattered cushions and stools, no Lord Burghley hovering. The household was soon to move to another palace, and there were open crates and cases around the room. The Queen sat at the table by the window, a quill in her long fingers and papers scattered before her. She wore stark black and white today, her red-gold hair pinned atop her head with pearl combs.

Elizabeth glanced up and smiled. "Ah, Mistress Sutton. You have returned to us."

Celia sank into a curtsy. "I have, Your Grace."

"Are you happy to be back in England?"

Happy? Celia wasn't sure she understood that word now, not for a long time. "Very much."

Elizabeth gestured to her, jewelled rings sparkling in the firelight. "Then come, sit here with me, and tell me about Scotland. You trapped a villain, so I understand."

"I played a very small role in that indeed," Celia answered as she lowered herself onto a stool across from the Queen.

It was John who had fought Lord Knowlton, John who had been wounded, who'd killed the man. John who had done so many things to change her life.

"That is not what I have heard." Elizabeth sat back in her chair and tilted her head as she studied Celia thoughtfully. Her careful solemnity in that moment was a contrast to her cousin's merry laughter. "You helped rid us of a traitor in the pay of the French. We owe you our thanks."

Celia swallowed. "Yet I fear I failed you in your request."

"Concerning my dearest cousin's marital intentions?" Elizabeth said. She tapped her fingers on the table. "Aye, I did hear she is quite infatuated with Lord Darnley. She is nursing him through a bout of the measles even as we speak. But you did not fail me, Mistress Sutton. You helped me a great deal."

Confused, Celia shook her head. "But Your Grace…"

"Do you think me foolish, Mistress Sutton?"

"Not at all, Your Grace!"

Elizabeth laughed. "Good. Growing up, I had to learn to read people very closely, to learn their real fears and desires. To know what they were going to do even before they did it. It was the only way to stay alive at times. I sense you have lived in much the same way, Mistress Sutton."

Celia could only nod. Her entire life had felt that way until John.

"Aye. You also know that sometimes we must make our hearts cold, deny what we want in order to do our duty. My cousin has been a queen since she was born. She does not understand these things. She doesn't know what it feels like to lose everything. I knew she would never marry Lord Leicester, or I would never have offered him to her."

"Oh," Celia breathed. A slow understanding dawned in her mind, a realisation of how clever Queen Elizabeth had been. How she had moved them all in her game—even Lord Burghley and Darnley.

"You see, Mistress Sutton? I couldn't allow Mary to ally herself with France or Spain again. It is too perilous. Nor could I give her my Robin. She would not have appreciated him. And he would be too strong a consort. Darnley, on the other hand…"

"Is a cruel, drunken knave," Celia whispered.

"But a handsome one, charming when he wants to be, and from a family almost as close to the throne as Mary's. He could maintain a façade long enough to draw in a woman desperate to be married again. Once the crown matrimonial is on his golden head…"

"Disasters will likely ensue," Celia said. "Very clever, Your Grace."

"Thank you, Mistress Sutton. But you spent much time at my cousin's Court. Do you think my little scheme will work?"

Celia thought of Mary's hand on Darnley's arm, the way she'd laughed with him as they danced. The loneliness in her eyes that Celia understood too well. "Very probably. Queen Mary seems ripe for romance."

"Then you did serve me well." Elizabeth rose from her chair and went to the window. She pushed it open to let in the cold breeze, staring out at the garden below, and Celia saw a quick spasm of pain pass over her pale face before her queenly mask fell into place again.

"I can't help but envy my cousin in one respect, Mistress Sutton," she said softly.

Celia laughed. "Having Darnley as a husband?" She could not imagine such a thing.

Elizabeth laughed too, and gestured for Celia to join her at the window. "Nay, never that. I would never choose so poorly. Only that she *can* choose—that she can be married and have someone beside her. A throne can be a cold place alone—as can life."

Celia peered past the Queen's shoulder to the garden. A man walked there, tall and broad-shouldered in a green velvet doublet, his black hair covered by a plumed cap. Lord Leicester. He also looked alone as he strode down the path. Elizabeth watched him, her fingers clutching the window frame.

"You have been married, Mistress Sutton," she said. "Do you miss it?"

"Nay, Your Grace," Celia answered honestly. She did not miss being married to Thomas Sutton at all.

"Yet you would accept a marriage as a reward for your service to me?"

Celia shrugged, wishing she could push away that old longing for a home, a place to belong. "I have no home, Your Grace. I need a place to be."

"Yet we don't need marriage for that." Elizabeth slanted a speculative look at Celia. "How did you fare on the journey with John Brandon?"

The sound of John's name, so unexpected and sudden, seemed to hit Celia in her soul. She didn't know what to say, and stared down at the garden. "Sir John?"

"He is handsome, is he not? Half my ladies are in love with him. Yet he won't let any of them near—not really. When you two met here…" Elizabeth shook her head. "I *see* people, Mistress Sutton, as I told you. I know things they don't even know themselves. But you may leave now. I will consider your reward."

"Thank you, Your Grace." Celia bobbed an unsteady curtsy and made her way out of the chamber.

Such a strange conversation. She scarcely knew what to make of it. Did the Queen know what had happened with her and John? How could she, when Celia hardly knew what had really happened herself?

She walked slowly up the stairs, nodding at greetings, feeling numb and removed from the scene around her. She didn't know where she was going until she found herself at the door of her chamber.

She pushed it open and stepped over the threshold—only to find John sitting on the edge of her bed.

He watched her as she slowly closed the door behind her, not smiling, his blue eyes glowing.

"Good day, Celia," he said. "I trust you had a fruitful meeting with the Queen."

Chapter Twenty-Four

"So you have returned to England," she said slowly. Her eyes greedily took him in—every detail, every inch of him. She had thought of him every day on the long journey home, had gone over every word they had shared, all the touches and kisses. Now he was here, with her again, she didn't know what to say.

She wanted to run to him, throw her arms around him and feel that he was really there with her again.

Yet he was not *with* her. The short distance between the bed and the door might as well be the distance between Edinburgh and London.

"I left soon after you did and rode hard the whole distance," he said.

She could see the marks of a fast journey on his face, the harsh lines and dark circles under his eyes that spoke of weariness. His hair looked damp, as if he had just washed it, pushed back from his face to reveal the austere, elegant lines of his features. His doublet was a fine Court garment of crimson velvet, but was only half fastened.

"Such haste," she murmured.

"I had to see you again," he said.

His own stare roved hungrily over her face, as if he had missed seeing her. Had he truly missed her? Thought of her when they were apart?

The thought, the longing, made something raw crack inside Celia again. She wrapped her arms around herself tightly as if she could hold it in. Could contain all the emotions that threatened to burst free when she thought of all that had happened in Scotland.

"I wanted to run after you—to run your horse to ground and pull you into my arms until you listened to me," he continued harshly, staring into her eyes. "To *make* you understand."

Celia couldn't bear the look in his eyes, so hungry and hard, for another moment. She shifted away. "Why did you not?" she asked as she went to peer out of the window. She couldn't even see the half-frozen river below through the haze in her eyes.

"I wanted to. Every primitive instinct in me told me to!" he said ruefully. "But Marcus held me back. He said you needed time to be calm, to think about all that had happened, and that I needed to think as well. He was right."

Celia gave a choked laugh. "For miles after Edinburgh I half wanted, half feared to hear you coming after me."

"What would you have done if I had?"

"I do not know. Hit you. Screamed at you. So Marcus was quite right to urge caution."

She heard a soft rustle as he rose from the bed, the

fall of his booted steps on the floor as he crossed the room to stand behind her. He was so close she could feel the heat of his body wrap around her, his breath on the nape of her neck. She trembled and closed her eyes.

"Do you want to scream at me now, Celia?" he said quietly. "Do you hate me?"

She thought she felt the light touch of his finger on her hair, but when she let her head fall back it was gone. Nay, she did not hate him. Perhaps for one moment, in that searing hurt when she had found out what he had done, she'd hated him. Now she knew what kind of world he lived in, what he had to do to survive. Now her feelings were so much more complex, so tangled.

"Did you use me back then, John? To find out information about what my brother and his friends were planning?" she demanded. That question had haunted her for days. "Was that all I was to you? Tell me the truth."

"Never, Celia," he said firmly.

His hands closed on her shoulders and spun her round to face him. His eyes burned with a pale blue fire, and she feared she would fall into them and be consumed. Lost.

"I knew you had nothing to do with your brother's actions. I only…"

"Only *what*? Tell me! I need to know."

John shook his head. "I tried to stay away from you, but I could not. Every time I tried you would draw me back to you with just a kiss, a smile. I had never felt anything like it before. It was like an irresistible force."

"An irresistible force," Celia whispered. "Aye, it was

the same for me. I *needed* you. You were all I could see."
And she feared she still needed him. Would always need
him despite everything.

"I never wanted to hurt you," he said softly.

"My brother's actions were foolish and he paid for
them," she said. "You could not have stopped him. Nor
could you have betrayed the Queen because of him. I do
see that now." Because of her own actions in Scotland
she saw the world so much more clearly.

"Before I went to Paris I came back to find you," he
said hoarsely, his hands tight on her shoulders. "I knew
I should not, but I couldn't stay away. I wanted to beg
you to come with me."

Celia gasped, and shook her head as if she would
deny his words, the hurt and hope of them. "But you
did not! I never saw you again until that moment here
at Whitehall."

"It was your wedding day." There was a world of
pain in his voice she had never heard from John before.
It made her want to cry, to weep at what was once lost.
What she still wanted despite everything.

"I saw you from a distance on your way to the
church, in a blue gown with flowers in your hair," he
said. "I did not know the truth of Thomas Sutton then.
If I had I would have snatched you from the road, forced
you to go away with me no matter the consequences.
But then I thought you were better off without me."

"Better off without you?" Celia cried. She pressed
her hand to her mouth to hold back the ragged sobs. "I
missed you so desperately for three years, John! Ached

with the loss of you, the fear of what had happened to you."

"I ached for *you*, Celia. Thought of you every day. But I imagined you safe with your family, a home of your own. Content with your life after the terrible things I had done. If I had known—God's blood, Celia." He pulled her against him, one hand cradling her head to his shoulder as he held her fast. "Can you ever forgive me for all I have done?"

Celia pressed her face into the soft linen of his shirt and breathed in deeply. Tears ached behind her eyes, but she couldn't let them free. Not yet. "Do you love me, John?"

"I love you so deeply, Celia, so fiercely that I know I can never be free of it. I am yours."

With that she cried, letting the tears fall down her face even as she laughed. Her heart, so closely locked and guarded for so long, cracked open and hope and joy flew into the world. She was free.

She tilted back her head to smile up at him, and he framed her face in his hands as he hungrily took in every part of her. Tears and exultation both. Everything she was.

"As I am yours, John. I love you," she said. "I will forgive you everything, for ever, if you will only promise never to leave me again."

"I could never leave you, Celia," he said. "You are trapped with me for ever now, come what may."

For ever. Celia had never heard sweeter words. She went up on her toes as John's lips claimed hers, hard, hungry, and in that kiss she tasted what the words love and for ever truly meant. The past was gone, the pain banished, and all they had now was each other.

He was hers and she was his. For ever.

Epilogue

Scotland, One Year Later

"Lady Brandon! Whatever are you doing up there?"

Celia turned around at the maidservant's shriek, the corner of the tapestry she was holding up clutched in her hand. The table she stood on was hard and smooth under her stockinged feet, and felt perfectly solid. "I'm trying to see what this would look like here, of course, Mairie. It has just arrived from London, and I think this wall is the place for it."

"Then you should have called for me, or for one of the pages. Sir John would be so angry if he saw you standing up there in your condition."

"I'm being very careful, I promise," Celia said calmly. She laid her hand over the small bump under her satin skirt, as yet still almost undetectable. But in a few months there would be the music of a baby's cries in these corridors and chambers that were finally coming to life again after all these years.

Celia let Mairie help her down from the table to the flagstone floor, and as she smoothed her skirts she studied the hall around her. It was very different from when she had first seen it, the night John had brought her there to shelter her from the storm and told her of his family's history.

When Queen Elizabeth had sent John back to Scotland after their marriage, as part of her delegation to Queen Mary's Court, Celia had despaired of making it a real home. Now the rooms were cleaned and refurbished, filled with fine furniture and colourful tapestries, and painted cloths, new glass in the windows, and warm rugs on the floors to keep the Scottish chill away. But the very best thing to keep the cold away was surely the hours she spent with her husband in the cocooned, sensual privacy of their curtained bed. There John kept her warm every night with his caresses, his wondrous kisses, the words of his love she had lived without for so long.

"Here, my lady, let me hang the tapestry for you," Mairie said. "You should sit by the fire for a while. You mustn't get too tired."

"I'm not tired at all," Celia said, blushing at her thoughts. But she let Mairie take the heavy cloth from her.

As she watched the maid clamber up onto the table there was a sudden commotion in the entrance hall, the boom of voices and the clatter of spurs.

"Sir John is home!" Celia cried. She spun round and dashed out of the room, her skirts clutched in her hands, even as Mairie called after her with a warning not to run. John had been to Edinburgh for many days, and Celia had begun to think he would never return.

But now he stood there in their home again, the cold wind sweeping around him from the open doors, his hair tousled and his black velvet and leather clothes creased from the hard ride home. He looked weary from his journey, but a brilliant smile touched his lips when he saw her and he opened his arms. Celia ran into them, holding onto him as if he was the most precious treasure in all the world.

"My fairy queen," he said roughly, lifting her from her feet as he buried his face in her hair. "How I have missed you."

"As I've missed you," Celia said. "Welcome home, husband."

And as he kissed her she knew they had truly both found their home, their hearts' deepest desire, at long last. Together.

* * * * *

Author's Note

~~~~~~~~~~~~~

When I wrote my book *The Winter Queen*—the story of Anton Gustavson and Rosamund Ramsay—I was very intrigued by Anton's cousin Celia Sutton. She seemed so unhappy, so haunted, and I wanted to know why! I wanted to know what had happened to her, and what it would take to make her believe in love again.

I so enjoyed spending time with her and her gorgeous hero in this story. I also enjoyed researching the story's setting and learning more about Mary Queen of Scots. I knew quite a bit about her late life in English captivity, but not much about her early days back in Scotland after years in France. It was fascinating to read about this time in her very complex and tragic life, but very hard not to shout warnings at her not to marry Darnley!

Her life does indeed slide into disaster after her marriage, just as Queen Elizabeth predicts. For a detailed look at the events surrounding her marriage and its violent unraveling I like Alison Weir's *Mary Queen of Scots and the Murder of Lord Darnley*.

Celia and John's part in the tale is fiction, of course, but much of what happens to them and the people they meet is part of history. Mary and Darnley, Elizabeth and Burghley—and their disagreements over Mary's marriage—Mary's four Marys, the terrible weather on Darnley's journey to Scotland, Mary's efforts to recreate a French Court in the rougher environs of Scotland, her religious feud with John Knox, even her excursions out into the city dressed in men's clothes, are all things I enjoyed incorporating into the story. It also seemed like the perfect backdrop for Celia and John's tumultuous romance!

If you'd like to read more about this period, there are many, many sources on Mary Queen of Scots. Here are just a few I enjoyed:

—John Guy, *The True Life of Mary Stewart, Queen of Scotland* (2004)

—GW Bernard, ed., *Power and Politics in Tudor England* (2000)

—J. Keith Cheetham, *On the Trail of Mary Queen of Scots* (1999)

—Roderick Graham, *The Life of Mary Queen of Scots: An Accidental Tragedy* (2009)

—Antonia Fraser, *Mary Queen of Scots* (1969)

—G. Donaldson, *All the Queen's Men: Power and Politics in Mary Stewart's Scotland* (1983)

—M. Swain, *The Needlework of Mary Queen of Scots* (1986)

—Jane Dunn, *Elizabeth and Mary: Cousins, Rivals, Queens* (2003)

—Caroline Bingham, *Darnley: A Life of Henry Stuart, Lord Darnley, Consort of Mary Queen of Scots* (1995)

—James Mackay, *In My End is My Beginning: A Life of Mary Queen of Scots* (1999)

—Alison Plowden, *Elizabeth Tudor and Mary Stewart: Two Queens in One Isle* (1984)

—S. Haynes, ed. *State Papers of William Cecil, Lord Burghley*

—JS Richardson, *The Abbey and Palace of Holyroodhouse* (1978)

Plus the guidebook to Holyrood, now available at the palace—the photos were invaluable!

The Laird's
Captive Wife

JOANNA FULFORD

Joanna Fulford is a compulsive scribbler, with a passion for literature and history, both of which she has studied to postgraduate level. Other countries and cultures have always exerted a fascination and she has travelled widely, living and working abroad for many years. However, her roots are in England, and are now firmly established in the Peak District, where she lives with her husband, Brian. When not pressing a hot keyboard, she likes to be out on the hills, either walking or on horseback. However, these days equestrian activity is confined to sedate hacking rather than riding at high speed towards solid obstacles.

For Helen,
who shared so many childhood adventures

Prologue

The Scottish laird rested a moment on his sword, letting his gaze range the length of the defile where his men were now searching the bodies of the slain. Though the ambush had been successful the exhilaration of the fight was underlain by frustration as he realised the one he sought was not there. Surveying the scene now, his dark gaze hardened. Before he left he would find out what he wanted to know. Not all the men lying here were dead.

As the laird's shadow fell across him, the wounded Norman mercenary glanced up quickly, taking in the naked sword and the uncompromising expression of the man who held it. Then he spat. The Scot's gaze never wavered.

'Where's Fitzurse?'

The Norman returned him a cold stare but made no reply. A moment later the point of a blade was pressed against his throat.

'I'll ask you just once more,' said the quiet voice. 'Where is he?'

'We're dead men anyway. Why should I tell you?'

'Tell me and you can take your chance with the kites and the ravens. Refuse and I'll cut your throat and ask someone else.'

The man swallowed. 'Fitzurse rides north with the rest of his force.'

'Where?'

'Durham.'

'You're certain of this?'

'We're in his pay.'

'Paid to destroy everything for miles around?'

'Aye, for sixty miles around. On King William's orders.'

Recalling the devastation he had seen on the journey north, the laird felt his gorge rise. Once upon a time, in a past life, French society had been dear to his heart. At fourteen the world had been new and green, a place full of exciting possibilities of which France had been one. At the time it had seemed like a dream come true, a welcome chance to escape the cheerless confines of Dark Mount and his father's enmity. Back then the castle at Vaucourt had been the warm centre of his universe; the military training it afforded the highest peak of achievement. At Vaucourt he had grown to manhood. At Vaucourt he had first met Eloise…

That recollection inspired others less welcome. All the dead faces he had seen in the past days blurred and merged until he saw just one, the one that had been all to him. Time dulled the pain of loss but it did nothing to extinguish anger—or hatred. Both burned brighter for being cold.

'Why are you so anxious to find Fitzurse anyway?'

The prisoner's voice drew the laird back to the present. 'That's my business,' he replied.

'Suit yourself. It's nothing to me.' The other paused. 'I doubt if Fitzurse will care either.'

'Oh, he'll care all right when *I* catch up to him.'

'And who are *you* exactly?'

'My name is Iain McAlpin.'

The Norman's eyes widened slightly in recognition and with it the first flicker of fear.

'I have heard of you, my lord.'

'You're like to hear more, assuming I let you live of course.'

The other licked dry lips. 'I've told you what you wanted to know.'

'You can have your life, you Norman scum. I'll not soil my sword with you.' With that the laird sheathed the blade and walked away.

He headed back to the edge of the path where his men were wait-ing with the loot taken from the Normans.

'Well?' he asked.

His lieutenant shook his head. 'Not a lot, my lord. We found only copper coin and a little silver. Hardly worth their effort to get it.'

'Loot is only their secondary aim, Dougal. The first is revenge for the death of an earl.'

'De Comyn was a fool.'

'True, but he was also William's chosen man and Northumbria will pay the blood price.'

He had found out early in life about the abuses of power, first at his father's hands and later from other men. They were lessons well learned. Only when you were strong and feared could you protect yourself and others. His reputation might have come too late to help Eloise, but it now served well to protect all those for whom he was responsible.

Dougal eyed him quizzically.

'What now, my lord?'

'Tell the men to mount up. We ride for Durham.'

The other lowered his voice. 'Is that wise?'

'Wise? Aye, if I am to find Fitzurse.'

'Have a care, my lord. The man has the king's favour.'

'That will not save him,' replied the laird. 'I have waited eight years for the chance to get him within my sword's length.'

'Aye, and you have just cause to seek him out. I know that if any man does.'

'And your point is?'

Undaunted by that hawk-like stare his companion met and held it. 'I'm only asking if Durham is the right place to meet him. The area is like to be swarming with William's men. Fitzurse will be well protected.'

'Not well enough to save him from me.'

'Cut the bastard's throat with my blessing, but what of your mission and your oath to Malcolm?'

'Both will be honoured. He'll get the intelligence he seeks at the appointed place and time.' Retrieving the reins of a dapple grey stallion, the laird swung easily into the high saddle. 'But come what may I shall have my revenge.'

Chapter One

'Keep your guard high, Ashlynn. Like this.' Ban held his own sword aloft in demonstration. 'That's it. Now let's try those moves again.'

Nothing loath Ashlynn closed in to attack, trying to remember everything her brother had taught her over these last weeks, her whole attention focused on the two blades. The clash of metal rang in the frosty air. Ban parried dextrously and for a moment or two she had the satisfaction of seeing him forced back several paces.

'Ha! Take that!'

He returned the grin. 'You grow cocky, little sister.'

Ashlynn redoubled her efforts, laying on with a will, and saw him give ground again. Exultant she laughed. Laughter turned to a yelp as a blow beneath the hilt sent the blade flying out of her grasp and he tripped her neatly, sending her sprawling on her back, his sword point coming to rest against her throat.

'Do you yield?'

She sighed. 'I yield…*again*.'

'Don't be disheartened.' He put up his blade and extended a hand, pulling her to her feet. 'That was much better.'

'Not good enough.'

'It takes time, Ash, and you've made real progress.'

His praise heightened the flush of colour in her cheeks. At nineteen Ban was a year her senior and had already established his fighting credentials, his career having been founded at Stamford Bridge and Hastings three years earlier.

'Progress of a kind,' she replied. 'Yet I think my skills would not long withstand those of a seasoned mercenary.'

'God send you never need to put them to the test.'

'God send none of us does.' She shot him a shrewd glance. 'And yet you think it may come to that, don't you?'

'William will not suffer resistance lightly.'

She knew the words for truth. In recent days the manor at Heslingfield had seen a steady stream of people fleeing north from Durham ahead of the approaching army. None would willingly stay to face the Conqueror's wrath, knowing it would be terrible indeed, for the slaying of the Earl of Northumbria would be avenged with interest.

'De Comyn should have listened to Bishop Aegelwine. If he had he might be living still. Commandeering men's homes and womenfolk was never going to win him friends.'

It was an understatement and they both knew it. What had followed the arrival of the new Earl of Northumbria was an orgy of violence and cruelty. Provoked beyond endurance, the people of Durham had risen up in the night and slain the hated invaders, almost to a man. The streets of the city had run with blood. De Comyn had been burned alive when the mob set fire to the house where he and some of his men tried to make their last stand. Of the original force of seven hundred Norman soldiers only two had lived to tell the tale.

Ban shook his head in disgust. 'The Normans are arrogant brutes and heed none when their minds are set on blood and conquest.'

'William will find the city empty when he comes.'

'Then his wrath will fall elsewhere.'

It was the reason he had begun to teach his sister the rudiments of swordsmanship. Women were vulnerable in these unsettled times, even those possessed of courage and spirit.

'Surely he would not punish the innocent, Ban?'

'A man like William won't bother with such distinctions. Why, he even burned his own men at York.'

'He could not have intended it. No commander in his right mind would destroy his own troops. 'Twas only that the fire burned out of control.'

'He seemed to find it an acceptable level of loss all the same. The man holds life cheap.'

She shivered, feeling the cold for the first time. By tacit consent they sheathed the swords and retrieved their cloaks from the foot of a tall oak. Then they began to retrace their steps towards the manor. Beneath their feet the snow, already ankle deep, scrunched with each step. It had come early this year and above them a lowering sky gave promise of more.

As they left the shelter of the trees they paused,

seeing movement on the road in the distance. Roused from her thoughts, Ashlynn saw a small group of people heading that way.

'More fugitives from Durham, would you say?'

Her brother nodded. 'Aye, most likely.'

The bitter weather must surely have rendered any journey unthinkable that was not undertaken from strictest necessity. It was a measure of their desperation that the people came anyway. As they drew closer she could see they numbered a dozen in all, men, women and children, their frightened faces pinched with cold. A few pitiful bundles contained all that they had been able to carry when they fled the city. Ashlynn's compassion woke and, exchanging a swift glance with her brother, she saw the same thought reflected in his expression.

'I'll take them to the kitchen house,' she said. 'They'll need hot food before continuing their journey.'

'No, I'll go. You'd best change your clothes before Father sees you.'

Ashlynn nodded, knowing very well that he was right. She watched for a moment as he went to meet the refugees and then hurried off towards the women's bower. She had only just reached her chamber when a servant arrived with a message.

'Your father desires your presence, my lady.'

Ashlynn grimaced, more than ever aware of her unorthodox appearance. Having dismissed the servant, she swiftly divested herself of leggings and tunic, and dressed again in her blue wool gown. Pausing only to tidy her hair and throw a mantle over her shoulders against the chill she made her way to the hall.

Lord Cyneric had been sitting in his accustomed

chair by the fire but hearing her step he looked up, his shrewd blue gaze appraising, surveying her in silence. Then he inclined his head.

'Sit down, Ashlynn.'

Obediently she took the offered chair opposite and waited, wondering what this meant. For a moment or two he said nothing, his weathered face thoughtful. Almost it was as though he were seeking the right words. His expression was more sombre than usual and for the first time she felt the vague stirrings of unease. Had he found out about the sword practices with Ban? Was she about to be rebuked again for unladylike behaviour? Would her brother get into trouble too? It wouldn't be the first time, of course. As long as she could remember, their escapades had landed them deep in the mire. Her mind, following that track, was quite unprepared for what came next.

'It is time you were married, Ashlynn.'

For a moment she was rendered speechless and could only stare at him.

'We live in dangerous times,' Cyneric continued. 'For your own protection you must have a husband, and one well able to defend you.'

She swallowed hard. 'But I am under your protection, my lord.'

'It may not be enough. The situation is dangerous and getting worse.' He paused. 'I would see you safely settled. Heaven knows you've had suitors enough. Yet at eight and ten you are unmarried still.'

Her face grew hot. It was true. By rights she should have been married long since. 'I never met a man I liked well enough.'

'You have had plenty of time to choose, but you have not done so. Now the circumstances force me to choose for you.'

Her heart lurched. 'My lord?'

'The Thane of Burford has asked me for your hand several times already and—'

'Burford!'

The name brought her out of her chair. In her mind's eye she could see the man for they had met several times during the celebratory gatherings for Yule and Beltane. Older than her by ten years he was of average height with a stocky frame and, like many Saxons, his colouring was fair. He was unfailingly attentive and courteous yet nothing about that homely, bearded face attracted her in the least.

Her father fixed her with a piercing gaze. 'He is much smitten with you, Ashlynn, and it's my belief he will make you a good husband.'

She shook her head. 'I do not love him, my lord.'

'It is not necessary to love your future partner in life, only to respect him. The rest will come later when you know him better.' He paused. 'You are a pretty wench, enough to twist any man around your little finger if you wished to.'

Ashlynn took a deep breath, fighting panic. 'I don't want to twist Athelstan round my little finger. I don't want to get to know him better!'

She had only ever behaved towards him with the requisite good manners though his interest in her had been clear from the first. She had never encouraged it knowing she could not return the sentiment. The thought of receiving much closer attentions from him was inconceivable.

'Ashlynn, listen to me—'

'No! I am not some chattel to be handed over thus.'

'I would not give you lightly to any man. Athelstan is worthy and he has been most constant in his affection for you. He will treat you well.'

'I will not agree to this.'

'My word is given. You will be married at Yule.'

The blue eyes widened. Yule was only a few weeks away. 'No!'

Lord Cyneric's jaw tightened but he held his temper in check. 'There is no time to be lost. Burford's lands lie further off some five days' ride, and he has at his command a large force of men under arms. He will protect you.'

'But I—'

'No more argument, Ashlynn. You will marry him and there's an end. This year our accustomed Yuletide feast will be to celebrate your wedding. Afterwards you will leave with your new husband.'

'My lord, please…'

'Enough. I am the head of this household and I shall be obeyed.'

If the tone had not been enough to convince her of the futility of further argument one look at that implacable expression was. Ashlynn turned on her heel and ran from the room, ignoring the exclamation that would have demanded her return. Half-blinded by angry tears she had no real idea of where she was going, only of a need to be alone for a while. In the event, her precipitate flight brought her to the stables and she slipped inside, pausing a moment on the threshold to look around. Mercifully the place was devoid of human company. Dashing the tears away with a shaking hand she made her way along the stalls until she came to Steorra's. The chestnut mare heard her step and turned to look, whickering softly in recognition and presenting the white star on her forehead for which she was named. Ashlynn stroked the velvet muzzle for a moment or two. Then she buried her face in the horse's mane and wept.

It was late when she returned to the hall. The evening meal was preparing though in truth she had little appetite for it. A group of people was gathered near the fire, among them her father and brothers. Ethelred was deep in conversation with his parent but Ban saw her come in and smiled. Then the smile faded a little and his eyes narrowed, taking in her altered appearance, for although she had sluiced her face with cold water before rejoining the company, her eyes were still suspiciously pink-rimmed, her face unwontedly pale. However, one warning glance held him silent and he merely watched as she turned away, extending her hands towards the blaze.

Letting the conversation wash around her Ashlynn kept her gaze on the fire, though in truth she saw nothing. All she could think of just then was being tied for life to a man she did not love, and being taken from her home and everything that was familiar to live in a distant place among strangers. Her father used the excuse of the troubled times but both of them knew it was more than that. Whenever he looked at her he saw her mother, the beloved wife he had lost just days after Ashlynn's birth. Though he tried to hide his resentment afterwards he had never quite succeeded. With this marriage she would be gone and the reminders with her.

In due course they took their places at table but Ashlynn's appetite had deserted her and she ate little. Around her the conversation continued, still very much focused on the political threat that hung like a pall over all their lives.

'Will Heslingfield remain safe from the Conqueror's anger?' said Gytha.

Her sister-in-law's voice penetrated Ashlynn's consciousness and she glanced up, her attention caught in spite of her sombre mood.

'We have done nothing to provoke it,' Ban replied. The tone was even enough but Ashlynn detected the criticism beneath. Her brother had been much in favour of the rebellion and their father's refusal to allow his kin any involvement had rankled with him. Lord Cyneric threw him a shrewd glance.

'Be thankful for it.' He frowned. 'All the same we shall be ready to defend ourselves if the need arises.'

'Against an army?' replied Ethelred.

'William will hold the city and use it as a base to consolidate his position as he has with York. Besides, the weather is on our side too. He will seek winter quarters for his men. We may perhaps see forays for food and supplies but little more, I think. We shall be secure enough until the spring.'

'If William finds none to punish within the city he will look elsewhere. Heslingfield may not be as safe as you think, my lord.'

Lord Cyneric frowned but he did not immediately reply, pondering his son's words. Though they did not always see eye to eye on every issue, Ashlynn knew her elder brother's opinion carried weight with their father.

At three and twenty Ethelred had much of the look of his parent, being tall and well made and with the tawny hair and blue eyes that were a family characteristic.

'He is right, my lord.' Ban threw his brother a swift glance. 'It may not be safe to stay.'

'The women should be moved to a place of safety,' Ethelred went on, 'though heaven knows those are precious few these days.'

'We shall consider Gytha's situation in due course,' their father replied. 'Ashlynn is to marry Burford at Yuletide. Her future safety is assured.'

The news fell like a thunderbolt and for several seconds there followed a deep silence in which all eyes went from Cyneric to his daughter. Ashlynn felt her face grow warm as resentment rose like a tide.

'Ashlynn to wed Burford?' said Ban. 'Since when?'

She could hear disbelief in his tone. The same incredulity was registered in his face.

'Since this morning,' she replied.

He threw her a penetrating look. 'I didn't know you cared for him.'

'Why should she not?' replied Ethelred. 'He is a worthy man in every way.' He smiled at his sister. 'Congratulations. I wish you happy, Ashlynn.'

As the others hastened to add their felicitations Ashlynn bit her tongue forcing back the angry denial that would otherwise have burst from her. Inside, her heart felt like lead.

'You will be safe enough with Burford,' Ethelred continued. 'Would I could say the same about Gytha. The only way to go is north and the border country is dangerous enough.'

'Aye,' said Ban, 'and always will be while men like Black Iain of Glengarron ride unchecked.'

''Tis said he's a friend of Malcolm Canmore, so he's not likely to be checked, is he? Besides, the man commands a small army and raids with impunity deep into English territory. No doubt the rogue will use the current situation to his further advantage. If William is busy hereabouts he'll not be able to see off the Scots as well.'

'Black Iain or no Black Iain 'tis a risk plenty of folk are prepared to take.'

'Belike he would not bother with refugees anyway. They are too poor to tempt him.'

'Let's hope so for all those wretched souls fleeing the Norman wrath,' Ethelred replied. 'He has been known to seize much more than gold and cattle. The tales of his deeds are legion.'

Lord Cyneric snorted. 'Tales grow with the telling. The man would have to be at least ninety just to have had the time to carry out all the exploits attributed to him.'

'Even if only half are true his reputation has been well earned, and I would not have my wife fall into his clutches.' Ethelred threw another thoughtful glance at the two women. 'But may not Gytha go with Ashlynn after Yule? I am sure that Burford would readily offer her his protection too, until such time as the situation becomes clearer.'

Ashlynn's heart thumped. With every passing moment it seemed that this loathed marriage was becoming more real.

'The idea has much merit,' replied Cyneric. 'I will speak to Burford on the matter as soon as may be.'

Gytha's brown eyes revealed her anxiety more than

words. The prospect of a lengthy journey in the depths
of winter, with a young child to boot, did not appeal.
Ashlynn could well understand it. However, she also
knew that Gytha would do whatever was necessary to
protect her son.

She was fond of her sister-in-law whose pretty
plumpness and placid nature were enhanced by her gentleness. Sometimes she wished she could be more like
her; wished she had the same sweet patience and
outward serenity. Ashlynn promised herself that one
day she too would comport herself with the same
ladylike demeanour and good humour for Gytha surely
was the model of a perfect wife. She loved Ethelred and
her child and put their needs above her own with a
degree of selflessness that Ashlynn wondered if she
could ever emulate. For a start her tongue was too ready
with quip or argument to admit of her ever being so
completely under a man's thumb. Yet Gytha did not
seem to mind. Ethelred's every word was law to her,
even on those occasions when, in Ashlynn's view, she
would have done better to hit him rather than humour
him. Yet Ethelred was a good husband in his way and
the marriage was a success.

Ashlynn's hands clenched in her lap. She accepted
that she must marry one day and have a husband and
family of her own. But not like this, she thought, not like
this. Had she still been free to choose, the man she
married would be very different from either Athelstan
or her brother. Both had their good qualities: they were
steady and hard-working and honest; kind enough too
in their way, but they lacked vital passion somehow,
passion and fire. And something more that was harder

to define: a certain dangerous edge that should set the pulse and heart racing. Ashlynn acknowledged to herself that she had never met such a man. Now she never would.

Sleep proved elusive that night. Her mind was racing with thoughts of the Norman retribution and of her proposed marriage. Unless something happened to change her father's mind, then in a matter of weeks she would be Athelstan's wife. The duties of the role were familiar to her: she had been tutored in them since childhood. It was not the thought of running his household that filled her with foreboding. Visualising her future husband, she swallowed hard. How was it that the good qualities he undoubtedly possessed could not render him any more attractive?

The new day dawned without bringing her any closer to an answer. Wanting to be alone Ashlynn avoided the hall and made her way to the stables. There she told the groom to saddle Steorra. Five minutes later he led the horse out.

'Do you wish to be accompanied, my lady?'

'No, Oswin, I'll ride alone today.'

He held her stirrup and watched her mount. She smiled her thanks and headed the chestnut away from the buildings, following the path across the fields towards the wood about a league distant. She kept the pace gentle for the ground was hard and the snow tended to ball in the mare's hoofs causing her to stumble. However, when they reached the wood the covering was less and they made better progress. Despite a warm gown and thick cloak Ashlynn could feel the aching cold in her hands and feet and face, felt it parch her throat and lungs with each breath. Above her grey clouds massed against the blue. More snow was certainly on its way.

She continued on to the edge of the trees as planned, intending to ride a wide loop around the wood before turning home. It was good to be alone for a while. The quiet countryside and fresh air were soothing, but nothing could detract from the fact that Yule was fast approaching. Ordinarily she would have looked forward to the celebrations. Heslingfield was renowned for its hospitality and the season was associated in her mind with joy and laughter and good fellowship. This year it would all be very different. Her throat tightened. Unwilling to think about it until she had to, Ashlynn nudged the horse with her heels. At once the mare broke into a canter. The swifter pace and the rushing air blew away some of the gloom and Ashlynn found herself smiling again in spite of everything.

She had almost reached the road before she saw the clouds of thick dark smoke rising into the sky. The wind brought with it the smell of burning. Ashlynn's smile faded and she reined the horse in, staring at the billowing plume with a deepening sense of disquiet. Her mind turned over the possibility of a hearth fire but rejected it; the smoke was too high and too dense. She also knew it originated in the direction of Heslingfield. Instinct told her to get back there and soon.

Pushing Steorra to a swifter pace she rode for a mile or so before drawing rein again. The feeling of uneasiness intensified for the smell of burning was much stronger now. Moving forward with more caution she came to the top of the rise above the manor and looked down on a sight of horror: Heslingfield was ablaze, hall, barn, stable and byre sending great tongues of flame shooting skyward. Above the sound of the fire could be heard the dying screams of trapped animals. All around human forms lay crumpled on snow reddened with blood and trampled by the hooves of many horses. Ashlynn could only stare in disbelief, her face ashen, while fear closed like an icy fist around her heart. Then she screamed.

'Nooooo!' The word echoed across the winter landscape in a protracted and desperate cry of denial. Then she was spurring forward, her mount plunging down the slope towards the burning manor.

The roar of the fire was much louder now and the acrid stench of burning choked the air. The mare slid to a stop on her haunches, wild eyed with fear from the din and the hideous oily reek. Ashlynn could feel the heat of the flames on her face, see the sprawled bodies. Tears of rage and grief stung her eyes. By the shattered gate lay her father's mangled form and near it Ethelred. Ban was nowhere to be seen but all around lay many others, retainers and servants, men, women and children, their eyes staring in sightless terror. None had been spared. Of Gytha and her child there was no sign either. Ashlynn looked around wildly and her horrified gaze came to rest at last on the burning hall and the women's bower, and in a final leap of understanding she knew where they were. The image splintered in her tears as, leaning down the side of the horse, she vomited repeatedly until her stomach was empty.

Then, turning the animal's head she guided it away from the scene of devastation, coming to a halt on the edge of the pasture hard by. With a shaking hand Ashlynn dashed the tears from her cheek even as her mind struggled with the enormity of what had happened. With the knowledge came guilt. She should have been there. She should have stayed. Yet if she had, her blood would be staining the snow like theirs. What malign fate had chosen to spare her and destroy all she held dear?

Just then Steorra threw up her head and snorted. Instinctively Ashlynn looked up too, her gaze following that of the mare. The movement was followed by a sharp intake of breath and her heart lurched to see the mounted group not a quarter of a mile away across the fields. The cold light glinted on helmet and mail. Her jaw clenched. Normans! Had they seen her? All other thought fled before the knowledge that she couldn't stay to find out. If they caught her she would be as dead as the rest.

She urged the horse away and nothing loath the beast leapt forward, eager to be gone from the scene of carnage and blood. From somewhere behind her Ashlynn heard men shout. One glance over her shoulder assured her she had been seen. Spurring Steorra to a gallop she sped across the snowy fields towards the distant wood. If she could reach the trees it might be possible to throw her pursuers off the trail.

They retraced the route to the wood, hearing behind the muffled thunder of pursuit. Ashlynn estimated perhaps twenty armed men. Fear vied with rage in her heart and a determination not to meet her end here in the icy fields. Ahead she could see the wood and felt a small spark of hope for it covered a large area and she knew it well, having ridden over it since childhood. Soon enough she reached the edge of the trees and hurtled down the track, bent low on the horse's neck to avoid the overhanging branches that tore at her clothing and threatened to sweep her from the saddle. The snow was not so deep here but she saw with sinking heart that there was enough to leave a clear trail. The Normans couldn't fail to see it.

Ashlynn followed the path until it came to a fork and then branched off left. She knew the way would emerge from the trees close to the north road. After that she would be in the open for a while and the more vulnerable. However, her horse was swift and fresh and not carrying anything like the weight of her pursuers' mounts. It might give her the advantage and tip the balance.

At the edge of the trees she stopped briefly, scanning the open space before her. Her gaze lit on the copse hard by and seeing it the germ of an idea grew into being. Touching the mare with her heels once more she gave the horse its head. The game little beast flew along the road, her tracks mingling with those of other traffic, and then Ashlynn turned off into the trees again. The snow was sparser here and the dry leaves left no sign of their passage. Set back off the road and hidden among the trees was a rocky outcrop and she made for it now, knowing that on the far side was a shallow cave. She would stay there until her pursuers had gone past, then double back. If she made a circle through the fields she could rejoin the road further on. By the time the Normans realised what had happened she would be long gone.

She reached the outcrop in question and found the cave. There she dismounted and waited. In the distance thudding hoof beats announced the rapid approach of the Norman troops. Ashlynn put a hand over Steorra's muzzle, willing her to silence, holding her own breath as the riders drew nearer. The noise grew louder and louder still, drumming like the blood in her ears. Presently the thunder of hooves was so near it seemed she must see soldiers appear at any moment. In her imagination she could hear their triumphant shouts and see the grinning faces as they closed in for the kill. Then, just as quickly, the sound of hoof beats began to diminish. Ashlynn leaned against the mare's neck in undisguised relief. It had worked. They were gone.

She rode until the light failed and found an old barn by an abandoned homestead. The place had been deserted for years. Part of the roof was gone but the rest would provide some shelter for the night for her and for the horse. Exhausted and cold Ashlynn fought back tears. They would not help anything now. With an effort of will she unsaddled the mare and then set about finding something with which to make a fire. That part wasn't difficult for the fallen roof provided wood and there was enough old straw lying around to start it. With cold fingers she drew the flint and tinder from the pouch on her belt. It took a while and several false starts but at length a spark fell on the tinder and glowed into life. Blowing gently she coaxed the spark to flame and fed it the old straw. Then she added small pieces of wood and gradually built up the fire to a size where it would at least afford some warmth. She had no food but just then it didn't matter; she could not have eaten it anyway. Somewhere in the darkness an owl cried. An omen of death. Hers perhaps. Ashlynn trembled. At one stroke everything she had known and held dear was gone. Heslingfield was reduced to ashes and her kin were slain. She felt tears spring to her eyes anew as the memory of that terrible hour returned. As long as she lived she would see the flames, hear the dying screams of living creatures burning to death, see the bodies scattered on the bloody snow.

She was a homeless, penniless fugitive. Fleeing where and to what? If she eluded the Normans she might find herself prey to robbers on the road, or to cold and hunger. She had nothing beyond the clothes she stood up in and the horse she rode. Perhaps later Steorra could be sold—if they both survived the journey, if the weather and hunger didn't account for them first. Suddenly the balance of survival hung on an awful lot of ifs. In that moment it occurred to her that death might not be so very bad.

Pushing the thought away, Ashlynn considered her options. They were precious few. Her only recourse was to keep heading north. If she could somehow reach the Scottish court at Dunfermline she would throw herself on the Princess Margaret's mercy. Since that lady was about to become Malcolm's new queen and was known to be a pious and good woman, she might take her into service in the royal household. However, Dunfermline was a long way off and a vast tract of dangerous territory lay between her and it. The reputation of the local warlords was well deserved—men like Black Iain of Glengarron, ruthless and dangerous. She shuddered, thinking that cold and starvation might be the least of her worries. In comparison, sleep seemed to offer a tempting oblivion, albeit only a temporary one. Wrapping herself in her cloak she lay down on a pile of rotting straw and closed her eyes.

* * *

In spite of her weariness she only dozed intermittently and awoke just after dawn. For some time she lay quite still, trying to recall where she was. Then she saw the lightening sky through the jagged roof of the barn and memory returned with a sickening jolt. Shivering she glanced at the fire but it was now a pile of comfortless dark ash and she got to her feet, trying to ignore the aching stiffness in her muscles. For a second or two she thought about remaining where she was but just as quickly rejected the notion. It was too dangerous to linger. She must ride for the border. It would not be quick or easy but it was her only hope now.

In her mind's eye she could already see the long road stretching ahead and feel the aching cold of nights spent in the open, for how often would she be able to find shelter and food? As she saddled her horse she knew the poor brute was hungry too. Heaven only knew how she was to find fodder enough on the journey north, but without the horse her plight would be desperate indeed. Resolutely pushing such negative thoughts away she pulled the girth tight. She was alive and she had the mare. There was that much to be thankful for at least. Even so it was hard to dispel the leaden feeling in her stomach.

She led the horse from the barn but had not gone half a dozen paces before Steorra threw up her head and whinnied. Ashlynn looked up quickly and froze to see the circle of armed horsemen not a hundred yards away. In the pale light of the breaking dawn she could see their mail and helmets.

'Dear God,' she murmured.

How had they found her? What evil chance had led

them here? Were they the same men who had followed her before? Then she realised it didn't matter. They were Normans. If they caught her she was dead anyway. The thought awoke fierce resentment. If she was going to die she would at least give these scavengers a run for their money. Quickly she gathered the reins and mounted.

As she did so the riders began to advance at a walk, closing in on their quarry. Ashlynn took a deep breath and spurred the horse forward, moving from a standing start to a canter, heading for the gap between the nearest horsemen. Her only chance was to try and barge through them. However, they anticipated it, moving swiftly to intercept her, narrowing the space, cutting off the escape route. Ashlynn reined and the mare wheeled round. Then seeing another gap she drove forward again. For one brief moment she saw the open ground beyond their horses and thought she might reach it. Then they closed on her and a strong hand seized her reins and yanked hard, bringing her mount to a plunging halt. She could see the wolfish smiles on the faces all around her. For a moment she closed her eyes, fighting the threatening faintness. When she opened them it was to see a mounted Norman knight in front of her. The cold eyes raked her from head to toe and she saw him smile before turning to his nearest companion.

'A pretty wench, De Vardes.' The words were spoken in the Saxon tongue though heavily accented.

'Yes, my lord.'

'Well worth the chase, wouldn't you say?'

'Indeed, my lord.'

Ashlynn kicked her mount forward in one last futile attempt to break free. The animal plunged but the grip

on the bridle held firm. The Norman surveyed the proceedings with evident amusement.

'Whither away, wench? Surely you would not
deprive us of your company so soon?'

She looked around in mounting panic at the ring of
grinning faces.

'Get her off the horse.'

Men moved to obey. In spite of her resistance strong
hands dragged her from the saddle. With pounding heart
Ashlynn watched the knight dismount and move
towards her. All her instinct was to flee but the two
soldiers on either side held her fast. Then she was face
to face with her captor.

'Did you really think to escape?' A mocking smile
twisted his lips as he ran his gaze over her. 'Of course
you did. You couldn't know that Waldemar de Fitzurse
never loses his quarry.'

Ashlynn's eyes blazed with rage and hatred. 'Mur-
derers! Norman brutes!'

The words ended in a gasp for he hit her hard, a
stinging blow that brought the water to her eyes. Warm
blood trickled from her lip.

'These rebellious northern swine must be taught
better manners.' The words were quietly spoken but the
tone sent a chill through her.

'Shall I kill her now, my lord?' The man called De
Vardes stepped forward with a drawn dagger.

Ashlynn felt a hand in her hair yanking her head
back and then the icy point at her throat, but her eyes
never left Fitzurse. He would give the word now and all
this would end with one welcome thrust of the blade.

'Not yet,' he replied. 'I am minded to have her first.'

His hand casually brushed across the front of her gown. Ashlynn glared at him. The Norman's smile widened. 'I detect defiance here that would be humbled. The rest of you may take your turns when I'm done. If she's still alive after that then she's all yours, De Vardes.'

Ashlynn's stomach lurched. The swift death she had hoped for would not come. They intended to make her long for it instead. She saw Fitzurse glance over his shoulder towards the barn.

'Take her in there and strip her.'

Chapter Two

As they dragged her back towards the ruined building Ashlynn began to shout and fight like one possessed, her screams shattering the still morning air. It availed her nothing. If anything it seemed only to add to the enjoyment of the men who held her. They reached the barn and, kicking the door open, strode inside with Fitzurse following at leisure a few paces behind. Dry mouthed with horror Ashlynn struggled harder but in vain for they held her with ease. One man pinioned her arms while the other unfastened her cloak and let it fall, his hand moving across her breast with coarse and deliberate slowness. She shivered as he stepped in closer and gripped the neck of her gown. For one moment her gaze met his and saw the mocking smile before he ripped the cloth apart in one sharp downward jerk. Never taking his eyes off her face he did the like with the kirtle beneath pulling the material wide to reveal her breasts. Only then did he glance lower and the cold eyes glinted in evident appreciation. He was not alone.

'Well, now, a very pretty little chicken,' said Fitzurse. 'I would see more, Duchesne.'

His henchman grinned. 'As you wish, my lord.'

Ashlynn trembled as his hands reached for the fabric of her gown.

Outside among the trees at the top of the sloping pasture another group of horsemen drew rein in obedience to their leader's command. Mounted on a dapple grey stallion he held the powerful horse in check with one gauntleted hand while his keen gaze swept the scene taking in the barn and the group below. Then he glanced at the man beside him.

'It seems our information was correct, Dougal.'

'Aye,' replied his lieutenant. 'It has to be them.'

'It's them all right. That blue roan destrier down yonder belongs to De Vardes. The cur never strays far from Fitzurse's heel. In any case they've left a trail of devastation that a four-year-old child could follow.'

'Aye, Reedham, Welbourne, Heslingfield.' The other shook his head in disgust. 'The cowardly dogs attack women and children because they like the certainty of winning, my lord.'

'Let's shorten the odds and find out how they greet our Scottish steel. We'll hit them fast and hard. Pass the word back.'

As the latter hastened to do his bidding the rider on the grey horse never let his gaze shift from the scene in front of him. A few moments later he heard the soft scraping sound that accompanied the drawing of many swords. Then Dougal returned, blade at the ready, a gleam of anticipation in his eyes.

'Just say the word, my lord, and let us at them.'

His laird nodded. 'Kill as many as you can. We'll take no Norman prisoners. But remember…'

'Aye, I know. Fitzurse is yours.'

'That he is. The bastard little dreams this day is his last.'

Lifting his sword arm he touched the grey with his spurs and called the charge. Quivering with excitement the big horse leapt forward, hearing behind the echoing battle cry as fifty riders burst from cover and hurtled down the slope toward the foe.

Taken completely by surprise the Normans could at first only stare at the advancing tide of horsemen. Then, as they awakened to the impending danger, the instinct for self-preservation returned. Amid shouting and confusion they scrambled to remount, turning then to face the enemy with scant time to draw their swords before the Scottish vanguard was upon them in a deadly wave of steel.

The laird's blade cleaved its first skull and came back for a wicked lunge into the next opponent. He heard the death scream and was aware of the rider toppling sideways even as a third opponent closed in. Since both hands were engaged with sword and shield he used his seat and legs to guide the powerful horse beneath him. At the given signal the grey reared, striking out at the enemy with its iron-shod hooves. Thrown off balance by the attack the bay destrier screamed and staggered, its rider crying out in agony as half a ton of targeted power drove downward, cracking bone and driving steel links through leather and padding into the flesh beneath. Grey-faced and swaying in the saddle the rider swore at the pain in his ruined knee. Before he could regain his balance the Scottish sword slashed across his breast.

Saved by the mail hauberk he looked down, scrabbling
for the reins in an attempt to wheel the horse away from
the danger for the injured leg was useless. That
moment's inattention cost him dear and with a savage
thrust the Scot drove his blade into his enemy's ribs. The
man's face held a look of shocked disbelief. Then the
Norman's sword fell from nerveless fingers and he
toppled sideways from the saddle to lie still in the snow
amid a widening pool of red.

Reining in the grey, the Scottish warlord surveyed the
field. Everywhere the churned snow was stained red
and scattered with the fallen. The Norman numbers
were dwindling fast as he knew they must but his gaze
still sought one man. Rage burned anew as he discovered no sign of his quarry. Where the hell was Fitzurse?

Ashlynn heard from without the spine-prickling war
cry from fifty throats followed by a warning shout in
French and the sound of thudding hooves, then more
shouts and the clash of steel. Fitzurse frowned. For a
moment he was quite still, listening intently. The din
without intensified and his men released their hold on
her. Fitzurse's hand went to the sword at his side and in
cold terror Ashlynn saw him unsheathe the blade.
Seeing her expression he bared his teeth in a smile.

'Never fear, chicken, I'll be back and we shall
continue where we left off. Waiting will only make the
pleasure all the sweeter.'

With that he turned and strode to the door: then with
one last glance at his prisoner he was gone.

For some moments after Fitzurse left Ashlynn
remained where she was, weak with relief, her body trem-

bling with horror and revulsion, still unable to believe the
narrowness of her escape. Outside she could hear the unmistakable sounds of battle, the clash of arms and
neighing horses and shouting voices. Her heart leapt. She
had no idea who the new combatants were and cared
even less, but while men slaughtered each other she might
be able to make good her escape. If they saw her they
would kill her but it could not be worse than remaining.
Just a small taste of what Fitzurse had planned for her
made a swift end at the point of a sword seem infinitely
preferable. Even if the French did not survive the fighting
the victors might well decide to investigate the barn. If
they did they would find her and there was no guarantee
their behaviour would be any different. On top of that she
might just freeze to death for the cold was biting.

Shaking violently she pulled up the rent gown and
looked about for her cloak. It had been slung aside when
Fitzurse's men had begun to strip her. After a frantic
search she located it at last and threw it about her shoulders, holding it together over her torn clothing. Then she
crept towards the door.

Peeping through a crack in the woodwork Ashlynn
watched the pitched battle without. A large mounted
group of dark-clad and wild-looking warriors were
falling with evident enthusiasm upon the Norman mercenaries who were putting up a fierce resistance.
However, there appeared to be far more of the newcomers than there were of the French and several bodies
littered the ground already. It meant the fight would be
over all too soon. She must use the confusion to make
good her escape. Taking a deep breath she opened the
door a little way and slipped out, darting looks left and

right. An area of open ground surrounded the ancient barn but beyond it was a copse that might afford cover. Summoning all her remaining courage she edged along the wall to the rear of the barn until at length it was between her and any observers. Then she ran.

She was barely halfway to the trees when she heard the sound of muffled hoof beats behind and then a shout. A glance over her shoulder revealed the approaching Norman horseman, and her heart leapt towards her throat. Without staying to see more she fled. The sound of hoof falls grew louder and then Ashlynn was jerked off her feet. Suddenly vision became limited to galloping hooves and flung snow and a horse's shoulder, every bone in her body jarred by the swift pace. The saddle pommel pressed into her stomach making it harder to breathe.

After what seemed an eternity the horse slowed and she had a confused impression of trees and the sound of flowing water. A large gauntleted fist dragged her upright and a mailed arm closed about her waist. Chain mail links dug into her back. Chill air met bare flesh beneath her torn gown. Ashlynn glanced up and with sick horror saw that her captor was Fitzurse.

However, his attention was not on her just then but rather on the mounted figure who had reined in some thirty yards away. Automatically she followed his gaze and drew in a sharp breath as her startled mind registered a powerful dapple grey stallion almost seventeen hands at the shoulder. The beast was impressive enough but it was the rider who commanded every ounce of her attention. Flowing black hair framed a rugged, clean-shaven face that was arresting for the angular planes of cheek and jaw. It spoke of a man in his late twenties perhaps, but otherwise gave nothing away. Its very lack of expression sent a shiver to the core of her being. Boots, breeches, tunic and gauntlets were all of leather as dark as his hair and a great fur-lined cloak was thrown about a pair of powerful shoulders. He emanated an aura of dangerous strength, an impression enhanced by the wicked-looking dagger thrust in his belt and the great blood-stained sword casually held across the saddle bow.

For the space of several heartbeats neither man moved. Then her captor laughed softly.

'Well, well, I little thought to have the pleasure of meeting you again.'

'Everything comes to him who waits,' replied the other, 'and I have waited long for this moment.'

Fitzurse bared his teeth in a mocking smile. 'Ah, the aggrieved Scot. Not still smarting surely?'

''Tis you will smart, Fitzurse.'

'No, I shall have your head on a spear.'

The laird lifted his sword. 'This shall determine that.' Then the dark gaze flicked to Ashlynn. 'I see you're still in the habit of carrying off defenceless women.'

Fitzurse glanced down at his captive and his smile widened. 'Do you like her? I'll give her to you—by way of recompense.'

As he spoke his hand pulled aside the torn edge of her gown to reveal what lay beneath, ignoring her efforts to prevent it. The laird's dark gaze took in every intimate detail and lingered. In spite of the cold Ashlynn's flesh burned. Crimson-cheeked, she glared at the man on the grey but still that impassive face gave nothing away. Eventually his attention returned to her captor and when he spoke his voice was perfectly level.

'The only recompense I'll accept this day, Fitzurse, is your head.'

'Attack me and the girl dies.'

'Perhaps,' replied the other, 'but then so will you.'

Ashlynn watched as the stranger brandished the great sword aloft. The blade glinted in the cold light. With hammering heart she saw him nudge the grey stallion into a walk. She expected Fitzurse to advance and meet it, and could only pray that death would be swift when it came. However, instead of advancing, her captor reined back some ten yards and brought his horse parallel to the stream hard by. Swollen with rain and snow the stream was wide and twice its usual depth, the current swift and strong. Feeling his hold alter, Ashlynn's eyes widened as an unpleasant implication dawned. Surely he would not... The thought ended on a shriek as he lifted her clear of the saddle and flung her into the swirling water.

Fitzurse called to his opponent. 'If you want her, McAlpin, you'll have to pull her out.'

Stopped in his tracks for a moment the Scottish laird swore softly, his hand clenched round the hilt of the sword. The other held in the curvetting stallion. He glanced once toward the stream, saw the woman catch hold of an overhanging branch and smiled grimly. Then he spurred forward to meet his enemy.

Ashlynn surfaced with a choking gasp for the shock of the icy water drove all the breath from her body. Dragged along with the powerful current she fought in-

stinctively to keep her head above water. It was instinct
too that made her grab for the overhanging branch. It
arrested her progress but the water dragged relentlessly
at her clothing and with each passing moment the cold
sapped her strength. If she didn't get out and soon, she
was going to die. Somewhere in the background she
heard the clash of swords. A frantic glance took in the
fighting figures on the bank. Her clutching hands inched
along the branch. As she shifted her weight the wood
cracked like a whip. Ashlynn screamed and fell back
into the water. It swept her headlong on its course for
another hundred yards before slamming her against a
large rock. Her icy fingers clutched desperately at the
slippery surface for the force of the current threatened
to sweep her away again at any moment. Mentally she
wondered how long she could hold on. Another minute?
Two? A voice inside her head said it didn't matter. If she
did not drown the cold would kill her and then it would
all be over. She closed her eyes.

The exchange of blows was fierce and evenly matched
at first with neither man gaining the advantage until the
Scot's blade cracked against his enemy's head in a savage
back-handed slash. Had it not been for the helm the blow
would have severed the top of Fitzurse's skull. The
Norman reeled in the saddle, temporarily stunned. Iain
wheeled the grey round to go in for the kill. Then, from
somewhere behind him, he heard the woman scream. Involuntarily he glanced over his shoulder to where she had
been. The branch was gone and she too. He frowned.
That moment's diversion proved expensive for when he
looked back Fitzurse was bent low on his horse's neck,

spurring away through the trees. A hundred yards away three other riders in helmet and mail appeared. Seeing Fitzurse they reined in and waited. As soon as he had joined them, all four rode away at a gallop. The Scot glared after them then back at the stream. Just then the woman screamed again and, hearing it, he swore fluently.

Ashlynn could no longer feel her hands, only the drag of the water against her body. Soon she would have to let go and it would take her. Then, through the numbing cold, a voice penetrated her consciousness.

'Give me your hand, lass.'

She had a brief impression of a horse's neck and shoulder and a man's reaching arm. It towed her out and lowered her on to the bank. For a moment or two she lay there, gasping, unable to take it in, aware only of the cold, bitter, numbing and heart deep. Locked in its grip her body shook uncontrollably. Saddle leather creaked and then a pair of boots appeared in her line of vision. Her gaze followed them upward and came to rest on a face that was vaguely familiar. Memory began to return.

For a moment the Scottish laird was quite still, his gaze held by eyes the colour of cornflowers. They were the only colour in her face. The flesh on the delicate bones was deathly pale. He shuddered inwardly, reminded suddenly of another face and another time. This one would die too unless she got some warmth very soon.

'Come, stand up, lass.'

In response to that firm command Ashlynn struggled on to her knees. However, when she tried to rise, the sodden gown tangled itself round her legs and she staggered. Strong hands dragged her upright. She didn't see the swift appraising glance that took in every detail of her shivering form.

'I wager you'll live, but we need to get you out of those wet things.'

For a moment the words made no sense. Then, as the implication dawned, her hands clutched protectively at the torn edges of her gown.

'No.'

'Dinna be a fool. You'll catch your death.'

He reached for the front of her gown. Seeing his intent she turned to run but staggered again and almost fell, prevented only by the arm about her waist. Ashlynn shrieked, struggling to free herself from his hold but it was like doing battle with oak. The arm yielded not a whit. It swung her round instead bringing her eyes level with a broad chest. Panicking now she struck out with clenched fists. They might as well have been bird wings and, as they had relinquished their grip on her clothing, her garments fell open affording him an uninterrupted view of what lay beneath. He caught his breath. The reality close to only served to reinforce his earlier impression.

'Well now, not just a pretty face then.'

As soon as the words were spoken he regretted them, realising they were hardly calculated to reassure, but his temper just then was not of the best. Thanks to her his quarry was away and free. Just why he hadn't left the wench to drown was a mystery. Right now he half-wished he had.

'Be still, you little hellcat!'

'Let go of me!'

'I said be still,' he growled.

For answer Ashlynn kicked out and felt the blow connect. He gritted his teeth but his grip yielded not at all.

'All right, have it your way, you contrary little vixen.'

Without warning his hands closed on the edges of her gown and dragged it down over her shoulders. Ashlynn began to fight like a cornered wildcat. In her panic she saw only Fitzurse's men, felt their hands on her, restraining her while they did their will. It was all happening again. She wanted to scream but her throat was dry and suddenly it was harder to breathe for it was as though there was an iron band around her chest. The stranger's face loomed over hers. Then all colour drained from her cheeks and she was vaguely aware of him catching her before she fell into a dead faint.

She had no idea how long she was unconscious but when she came round it was to an awareness of voices, of men and horses. She was cold, her body shaking violently. Then something was supporting her shoulders and a hand was forcing a cup between her lips. She heard a man's voice.

'Drink this.'

The tone brooked no refusal. Hot sweet liquid carved a path down her throat and all the way to her stomach. Ashlynn gasped. He made her drink it all, but slowly, and by degrees the heat spread and began to warm the cold core within, enough for the shaking to subside a little. Becoming more aware she realised that she was swathed from head to foot in a huge fur-lined cloak.

Looking up for the first time she saw a black leather tunic. Above it was long dark hair and a face whose rugged good looks were only too familiar. Dark eyes met and held hers for a moment before turning their attention to someone opposite, out of her line of vision.

'We'll leave presently, Dougal. We've delayed long enough as it is and I want to reach Hexham tonight. Besides, the injured need tending.' He glanced up at the sky. 'We need to be back at Dark Mount before the weather closes in.'

'Aye, my lord.' Dougal paused. 'What about the lass?'

'We'll take her with us for the time being.'

'I can see your reasoning. For a drowned rat she's no so bad-looking. Dry, she'd be a welcome addition in any man's bed.'

Ashlynn's heart lurched. The man beside her glanced down briefly, his expression sour.

'This one would turn your bed to a couch of thorns.'

'Well then,' Dougal continued, 'sell her. She'd likely fetch a good price were ye minded to get one. Or ye could ransom her, did she have kin.'

He frowned. ' I'll decide later. In the meantime, where are the things I asked for? Where the devil is Archie?'

As if on cue another man hastened forward and handed over a bundle of cloth. 'Beg pardon, my lord. I'd a problem with the size.'

The laird looked down at Ashlynn again and then at the bundle he was holding.

'You'll be needing this.'

For a moment she stared at it and then back at him. Then, slowly, her dulled wits began to understand the significance of the great cloak around her and the immediacy of the soft fur against her skin. Her cheeks, so pale before, turned scarlet.

If she could have hit him she would have but both

hands were imprisoned beneath the folds of the heavy cloak. 'How dare you treat me like this!'

'Dare had nothing to do with it, you wee fool,' he replied. 'Your clothes were soaking and little better than rags anyway. If you'd kept them on you'd have gone down with a fatal ague for certain.'

'Is that your excuse?'

'It needed no excuse. 'Twas a matter of common sense.'

Bereft of speech she looked away. The man neither appeared nor sounded even remotely apologetic. Instead he drew her to her feet and taking a firm hold on her arm led her aside to a clump of bushes. Then he thrust the bundle of clothing at her.

'Put these on. They're not the most feminine of garments, but they're all that's available and they do at least have the advantage of being intact.'

Ashlynn glared at him. The dark eyes grew flinty.

'Perhaps you'd like my help, lass?'

'No.'

'Then dress and make haste or by heaven I'll finish the task myself.'

Her jaw clenched but she took the offering without further comment and retreated a few yards behind a small clump of bushes. Bare of leaves, they were not ideal to the task but provided a degree of privacy from prying eyes. A glance over her shoulder revealed that her large companion hadn't moved. Indignation surged: the brute had no shame at all! Then she reflected that it scarcely mattered; there was nothing for him to see now that he had not already seen before.

Giving her attention to the bundle she found it comprised a cloak in which were wrapped shirt, tunic, belt, trews and hose all clean and of strong and serviceable material. With them was a pair of leather boots. With no little relief she hurriedly pulled on the hose and trews and dragged the shirt over her head before divesting herself of the big cloak. Finally she pulled the tunic on. Like the shirt it was decidedly roomy but, she reasoned, it would allow for greater freedom of movement. It would be a lot warmer too. She fastened the belt but even on the last hole it still hung loose on her waist. The boots completed the outfit. Like everything else they were too big but better than going barefoot. Finally she threw the cloak round her shoulders and fastened it. Then, having retrieved the borrowed fur she rejoined her companion.

He watched her come, observing the transformation wrought in one comprehensive look. His expression gave nothing away but under that penetrating gaze she felt her anger mount again. With an effort she controlled it. The knowledge that she was beholden to the rogue didn't make things any better. Trying to gather a few protective shreds of dignity she drew in a deep breath.

'I suppose I should thank you for pulling me out of the water.'

'Aye, you should. If it hadn't been for you, Fitzurse would never have escaped.'

'I'm sorry he did.'

'So am I.'

'Why did you want to kill him?'

'That need not concern you.'

His wrath was almost palpable. That she should have been in part responsible only made matters worse. In a more diffident tone she said, 'I am grateful for what you did back there.'

The reply was a snort that might have been compounded of anger or disgust, or both. It brought her chin up at once.

'You could have left me to drown. Why didn't you?'

'Believe me, lass, I was tempted.'

With that quelling reply the conversation died, for Ashlynn could think of nothing to say and her taciturn companion clearly had no wish to pursue it further. Instead he took his cloak from her and put it on. Then, resuming his grip on her arm, he led her towards a shaggy bay gelding that stood among the waiting horses.

'Get on.'

There was nothing for it but to obey. He watched her gather the reins and swing into the saddle. Then he mounted his own horse and drew it alongside. A few moments later the whole cavalcade set off.

They rode in silence for some considerable time. The stranger made no attempt to break into her thoughts and in truth she had no inclination for speech either. In her mind she saw Heslingfield in flames and the bodies of the slain all around. Her jaw tightened. She would never see any of her loved ones again. There had not been a chance to bury them either or say a mass for their souls. They lay unshriven on the cold earth for the crows and the foxes to pick the flesh from their bones, or else their ashes lay in the blackened ruins of the hall. They were memories too bitter for tears. Once she had imagined that an arranged marriage was the worst fate possible. How naïve she had been to think so.

It wasn't until noon that the cavalcade stopped to rest. The landscape had changed as they progressed, wood

and pasture giving place to rolling hills and open heath
strewn with boulders and dead bracken. A few scrubby
trees leaned to the prevailing wind and, hard by, a brook
tumbled over a rocky bed. The riders turned off the road
and dismounted. Ashlynn watched the stranger step down.

'We'll stop here awhile,' he said. 'The horses need
a rest and the men too.'

Glancing around she realised with a start that there
were perhaps fifty of them all told, mostly long-haired
and bearded and variously dressed in stout leather tunics
and cloaked like their leader, and every one of them fully
armed. Remembering that they had defeated the
Norman mercenaries she shivered a little. Unaware of
her regard the men opened saddlebags and drew out
bread and cheese and pieces of dried meat. It was then
she remembered that she had eaten nothing since the
previous morning and precious little then. The stranger
threw her a shrewd glance.

'Come.'

He steered her to a boulder nearby that was a conve-
nient height to sit on. Then he opened his own saddlebag and drew out the food inside. When he offered her
a piece of bread she took it and fell to devouring it at
once. Observing this he passed over a chunk of cheese
as well before falling to himself. The solid fare was
coarse and plain enough but it lined the stomach and
took the edge off the clawing pains she had felt before.
They ate in silence and only when they had finished did
he bend his gaze on her again.

'Tell me, how did you fall foul of the Normans, lass?'

She looked away. It was a painful subject and she had
no wish to discuss it. He made no attempt to push her.

Instead he let the silence draw out and waited, though the quiet gaze never left her. Ashlynn forced herself to meet it and drew in a deep breath. He had saved her life after all so she supposed he was owed an explanation.

'They burned my home and slew my family. I was the only survivor.'

'How came you to escape?'

'I wasn't there. I'd gone out for a ride and when I returned…when I returned the rest were dead.'

'I see.' He paused. 'Where was your home?'

'At Heslingfield.'

'Heslingfield!'

'You know it?'

Recalling only too vividly what he had seen there, he could understand her earlier reticence. He would not revisit the nightmare now. 'I know *of* it. Lord Cyneric was its thane, I think.'

'Yes. He was my father.'

'I never met him but his reputation went before him: a brave fighter by all accounts. He had two sons I heard tell.'

She nodded and blinked back treacherous tears. 'They died trying to defend our home. Ethelred fell beside my father. I didn't see Ban's body and there was no time to look.'

'How did the Normans find you?'

'They had not gone far by the time I returned. When they saw me they gave chase. I thought they would kill me too at first but Fitzurse…Fitzurse had me taken to the barn and stripped. He meant to take his pleasure and afterwards let his men take theirs.' She drew in another ragged breath remembering every detail of the ordeal at the Norman's hands, the fear and the humiliation and the impending horror. The stranger was silent, waiting. Ashlynn's gaze was on the ground and she missed the expression of pity and anger in his eyes. 'Before he could do what he intended, your men arrived and launched their attack. In the confusion I tried to run away. The rest you know.'

'Where were you heading before the Normans found you?'

'North, over the border.'

'You have kin there perhaps?'

'No. I'd hoped to reach the court at Dunfermline and perhaps enter service there, but I didn't exactly have time to make a detailed plan.'

He did not miss the ironic edge to the tone but let it go.

'The border country is wild and dangerous; too dangerous by far for a woman alone.'

'There was no other choice.'

'No, I suppose not.' He paused. 'You never told me your name.'

'You never asked.'

One dark brow lifted. 'I'm asking now.'

'Ashlynn.'

'A pretty name and most apt, I find.'

As he spoke he knew the words for truth. Dougal was right: most men would find her a welcome addition to their bed. Unbidden his mind went back to the scene by the river and relived it with startling clarity. He indulged the memory for a moment and then pushed it away. That kind of distraction had no place in his scheme of things.

Unable to follow his thought and uneasy beneath that apparently dispassionate gaze Ashlynn forced herself to meet his eye.

'You still have all the advantage.'

'Aye, I believe I do.'

'Is your identity such a closely guarded secret that I may not know it?'

This time irony was underlain by a hint of impudence. Moreover, there was an expression in those blue eyes that was almost provocative as though she were testing the boundaries. It was tempting to show her just how close those were, but again he let it ride. His turn was coming.

'No secret, my lady,' he replied. 'I am Iain McAlpin.'

The name seemed strangely familiar somehow though it resisted precise identification. It niggled like a bad tooth. Earlier she had heard him say they would stay at Hexham that night. Where exactly? Surely no inn could cater for so large a party. Had he friends then who would give them shelter? His men called him lord. Lord of what? Where was Dark Mount? The missing pieces of the puzzle plagued her. Rather than labour over it she decided to ask. The answer was given readily enough.

'Dark Mount is a fortress at the head of Glengarron.'

'Glengarron!'

'Aye.'

She was suddenly very still as, in one moment of total comprehension, the last pieces of the puzzle fell into place.

'You are the Laird of Glengarron?'

'That's right.'

Ashlynn felt her stomach knot. In her relief at having escaped the hands of the Normans she had put herself into others every bit as dangerous, for who in the north of England had not heard of Glengarron or the man they dubbed Black Iain? It was small comfort to think she had no gold, nothing with which to trade for her freedom, in short nothing to tempt him at all. Then she remembered his earlier conversation with Dougal and her cheeks paled.

'What are you going to do with me?'

'I haven't decided yet, but you'll come with us as far as Jedborough at least.'

'Jedborough?'

'Aye, I've business there. When it's concluded I'll make my decision.'

She drew in a deep breath and tried to get her voice under control. 'You could leave me at Hexham.'

'I could, but I won't.'

'Why not?'

'It doesn't accord with my plans.'

Incredulous she glared at him but the gaze that met hers was unwavering and utterly disconcerting. Indignation swelled like a tide.

'Why should I co-operate with you?'

'Because you won't like the consequences if you don't.'

The threat was thinly veiled despite the mild tone with which it was delivered and, for a moment, it hung there between them. Given his previous experience of her, he was half expecting an outburst of rage. It never materialised, though her chin lifted at a defiant angle. In spite of himself he was amused and oddly touched. With somewhat grudging admiration he acknowledged that the lass had spirit as well as looks.

'Why are you doing this?' she demanded. 'My future can be of no interest or importance to you.'

'It isn't.'

'Then the only reason for holding me is concerned with profit.'

'Good enough reason, in my view.'

Ashlynn strove against rising panic. 'Leave me at Hexham.'

'I have just said I will not. The matter is closed.'

'I cannot…I will not go with you further.'

The dark gaze met and held hers but now there was no discernible trace of humour in it.

'You can, my lass, and you will.'

Chapter Three

The question of how to free herself from her captor exercised Ashlynn strongly now. What she would do after effecting an escape was uncertain; the important thing was to get away and find somewhere to hide. Somewhere he wouldn't think of looking. When he failed to find her he would perhaps give up for all his efforts seemed to be directed towards reaching Scotland. What was his business in Jedburgh? Who was he meeting there? *'After that I'll make my decision.'* Since she had no close kin who might ransom her, there was only one other way for her captor to profit. The Scots frequently seized prisoners on their raids across the border. Slaves were a valuable commodity. She shivered. Was this what the brute intended? The more she thought about it, the more likely it seemed. That being so, the more necessary it was to prevent it.

The first stars had appeared before they reached the outskirts of Hexham and already frost glittered in the blue twilight. The frozen breath of men and horses hung in the still air as the group drew rein and dismounted before an imposing walled manor. Ashlynn looked around her, taking in the house and the courtyard with its outbuildings and churned snow, while the men led the horses off towards a big barn. Then Iain took hold of her arm and guided her towards the house, a large rambling affair of timber and stone. A servant hastened to open the door and the laird strode into a large hall, drawing his captive with him. It was dimly lit and passages led off it. She was conducted down one of these and thence to a door off to the right which the servant opened. It gave on to a small bedchamber. The man set down the candle on the table and then withdrew.

Ashlynn cast a furtive glance around. The chamber was clean but sparsely furnished. There was a window, now shuttered fast, and a fire burning in the hearth. By its light she took in table and chair, a stand with a basin and ewer on it and, most prominently, a bed on the far side by the wall. With calmness she was far from feeling she turned to face Iain. The confines of the room served only to emphasise that powerful presence, and he was watching her now with an unnervingly penetrating gaze. Her chin tilted a little and, forcing herself to return that steady regard, she waited.

'You will sleep here this night,' he said then. 'I will have food sent to you shortly.'

'Whose house is this?'

'Does it matter?'

The tone brought a tinge of colour to her cheeks. 'No.'

'There are things it is better not to know.' He paused. 'You should try and get some rest. We have another long ride ahead of us tomorrow.' With that he turned to go.

At those words all her earlier desperation revived and she caught hold of his arm. 'Why will you not leave me here? Surely the price of one more slave matters little to you.'

'I told you that the matter is not open to further discussion.'

'I disagree.'

His hands closed on her shoulders, drawing her closer. The dark gaze bored into hers. 'Your opinion on the subject is irrelevant. I am the law here and you'll do as you're told.'

Ashlynn bit back the angry denial that sprang to her lips. He *was* the law here, every last arrogant inch of him. He was also very strong and much too close for comfort. She could feel the warmth of his hands through her clothing and the curbed anger behind his gaze. His face came much nearer to hers. Dangerously near. If he bent his head their lips would touch. The realisation both shocked and excited.

'Do you understand me?'

'I…yes.'.

'I hope for your sake that you do, lass.'

Unable to think of anything to say Ashlynn remained silent. He had half-expected her to argue further but when she did not the anger faded from his eyes and was replaced by something else entirely, something she could not name but which sent a shiver through her that had nothing to do with winter cold. Iain leaned closer, breathing the smell of wool and sweet air from her clothing and beneath it, the scent of the woman, subtle and arousing. The response caught him unawares and he drew a deep breath, mentally upbraiding himself. There could be no dalliance here, however tempting the thought might be. Slowly he pulled away from her.

'I must leave you now for I have other matters to attend to,' he said then. 'Get some rest, Ashlynn.'

His hands relinquished their hold and she was free. She remained quite still, watching him cross the room. He paused a moment on the threshold.

'If you require anything else let the servant know.'

As the door closed behind him she heard the sound of a key turning in the lock. She tried the latch anyway. The door didn't budge. For a moment she leaned against it, listening to the sound of his departing footsteps. When at length they died away she moved slowly back to the hearth and warmed herself before the fire, staring down into the flames, her thoughts in chaos.

Some time later the servant reappeared with a tray of food: good white bread and a large earthen pot of a fragrant meaty stew. She ate all of it for the long ride had sharpened her appetite. The food did a great deal to banish the chill and restore her spirits. By the time she had finished it was full dark and the edges of the room were blurred in shadow. She glanced at the bed. There seemed little else to do save sleep but at least it would be a welcome oblivion. Removing her cloak she undressed to her shirt and then curled up beneath the fur coverlets.

Having left Ashlynn's chamber Iain was heading for his own quarters when he met Dougal.

'Are the men settled?'

'Aye, my lord.'

'And the injured?'

'They too.'

'What of the lad we found at Heslingfield?'

'In poor case. If it hadn't been for the cold slowing the blood loss, he'd have died long before we found him.' Dougal paused. 'Have you told her?'

'No. She believes that all her kin were slain.'

'You really think he is kin? He might be just a servant.'

'They're related all right,' Iain replied. 'The likeness is too pronounced.'

'Well then, perhaps it is better she believes him dead like the others. Frankly, I doubt he'll survive and then she'd only have to go through it all again.'

Visualising the destruction he had witnessed at Heslingfield when they rode by, Iain nodded. 'She's been through enough just now. Let's wait on events. He might survive after all.'

'Aye, perhaps. If he does, it'll come as a happy surprise to her, won't it? Happy for us too were you inclined to sell him on later.'

'Keep me informed, Dougal, but say nothing to the lass. Tell the men to keep their mouths shut too. I'll tell her when the time is right.'

Having bidden the other goodnight Iain retired, but sleep did not come easily. On reflection, he wondered whether silence was the best course of action with regard to the injured Saxon youth. The resemblance to the girl was striking. It had been apparent at once. He could see Dougal's point and knew the advice was well intentioned, but at the same time was aware of a vague twinge of guilt. Was he right to keep her in ignorance? The lad's injuries were serious and there was a long way yet to travel. He was still unconscious which, given his other wounds, was probably just as well.

Then there was Ashlynn herself, spirited and rebellious too judging from her response to his plans. Recalling the scene that evening he frowned. Whether she liked it or not she was going along. There was no other viable alternative: to do anything else would take time. That would run counter to his plans and he couldn't afford to let it happen. Too much lay in the balance. Iain thumped the pillow hard: he was as far as ever from having his revenge, the work of months lost. By the time he completed his mission and was free to start hunting again the Norman might be anywhere.

The recollection of his enemy brought other related images: that first brief startling glimpse of the lass afforded him by Fitzurse *'Do you like her? I'll give her to you.'* That was swiftly followed by the memory of dragging her from the stream. In truth his sole intention in removing her clothing had been to restore some warmth to her body and quickly too. Yet when he'd stripped off the torn and sodden gown he had been unprepared for the beauty of what lay beneath or for the way the image would linger in his imagination. She had been understandably angry with him about that but, while he regretted the circumstances he could not for the life of him regret the memory of her naked body. Was that why he had been tempted this evening? His anger returned, this time directed at himself. Temptation was something he couldn't afford. In the years since Eloise there had been women, occasionally; women willing enough to satisfy his physical need. Those brief encounters were ideal: both parties bene-

fited in their different ways and then parted. There were
no complications, no entanglements, nothing to deflect
a man from his sworn purpose. He thumped the pillow
again. Once he was free of his obligations at Jedburgh
then he'd decide what to do with the girl.

The next thing Ashlynn knew it was dawn. With the
light returned all the detail of the strange room and the
consciousness of her current precarious situation. As she
recalled how it had come about her immediate dread was
submerged by much keener sensations of sorrow and
loss. For several minutes she didn't move until, with an
effort, she had forced back the negative emotions. They
wouldn't help her. She must help herself now.

Climbing from the bed she dressed quickly, trying to
marshal her thoughts. Whatever happened she would
not allow herself to be taken to Jedburgh or, God forbid,
Glengarron. Having made her feelings clear on that
score, she knew he would keep a close eye on her now
so it behoved her to be careful, to make it seem as
though she had bowed to his will. Having lulled him into
a sense of false security she would await her opportunity to escape.

Presently a servant appeared with a platter of food and
Ashlynn broke her fast. She had only just finished when
the door opened again. Her heart skipped a beat to see the
familiar figure standing there.

'In good time, lass. We need to move.' He glanced at
the bed across the room. 'I trust you slept well.'

'Thank you, yes.'

'Good. There's a long ride ahead.'

'You have no right to make me come along.'

'Right has nothing to do with it. You'll come along because it's expedient.'

'Not to me it isn't. I don't wish to go.'

'But then we're not discussing your wishes.'

If he was aware of her anger it was not evident, for his expression remained maddeningly unperturbed. Her fists clenched at her sides as she fought the urge to hit him.

'I won't go.'

'You'll go, lass—one way or another.'

The threat was plain and she knew it was not idle. He had the power to compel obedience. The expression in those dark eyes was deeply disquieting and she turned away from him, heart thumping, trying to think. Once across the border escape would become harder which meant she must get away before they reached it. In the meantime argument was futile and she would not bandy further words with him, but if Lord Bloody Iain thought she would tamely submit to his will he had another think coming.

Almost as if he heard the thought Iain's voice broke in. 'Dinna think of trying to run, Ashlynn. I'd find you again very quickly and then you might find my temper unpleasant.'

'What difference would that make? Your temper is always unpleasant.'

The words were out before she was aware and drew down on her a look that caused her heart to miss a beat.

'Put the matter to the test,' he replied, 'and you'll discover a great deal of difference, I promise you.'

With that he took hold of her wrist in a vice-like grip and led her out to the courtyard. The cold air hit her for there had been a hard frost in the night and everything was rimed with silver. Around them men were already mounting. Robbie approached leading his own horse and a pretty chestnut mare.

'Dougal told me to bring this for the lady,' he explained.

Ashlynn wasn't listening, her whole attention focused on the horse.

'Steorra!'

Hearing her name the mare turned her head and whinnied softly. With tears in her eyes Ashlynn went forward to greet her, stroking the furry neck, utterly relieved that the horse had taken no hurt from her recent adventures.

Iain regarded them keenly. 'I see you two know each other.'

For a moment all her resentment was forgotten. 'Where did you find her?'

'I didn't,' he replied. 'My men found her wandering loose after the battle and brought her along with the horses we took from the Normans.'

'I see.'

'Will you mount, Ashlynn, or do you need my help?'

The bland tone didn't deceive her for a minute, nor was the implication lost. Biting back the pithy retort that sprang to mind she lifted her chin.

'That won't be necessary.'

He watched her gather the reins and swing easily into the saddle. Then he mounted his own horse.

'Let's go.'

They rode at a steady pace and soon Hexham was far behind. To her relief Iain rode on ahead with Dougal and left her to the charge of the young man called Robbie. Though he cast sidelong glances at her from time to time, conversation was minimal. However, Ashlynn had no desire for it, her mind on other things. With every stride of the horse beneath her the feeling of desperation grew. Soon they would reach the border. Soon she would be lost. She could not allow herself to be sold into slavery or worse. Death would be preferable. Escape was a risk but a calculated one. All she needed was the opportunity.

It was a relief when the column stopped at noon and she could dismount and stretch her legs for already they felt stiff from the unwonted hours in the saddle. She wondered at these men that they showed no signs of the weariness she felt, or the cold either. As they led the horses to drink at the stream Ashlynn did the same, bending to scoop a handful of water. It was icy but it slaked her thirst. She was occupied thus when she heard a man shout. At once the cry was taken up and, straightening quickly, she looked round.

Half-a-dozen riders had just appeared round a bend in the road and almost ridden into the Scottish force. There followed a con-fused impression of helmets and mail and then startled voices and the clash of weapons. Moments later a small section of the Scottish vanguard was heavily engaged in combat and being cheered on by their companions who seemed to think it quite unnecessary to become involved. Recalling the fighting skill of the Scottish warriors, Ashlynn thought they were probably right. Far from showing any concern about the unexpected confrontation they appeared to be treating it as an amusing diversion. Certainly all their attention was focused on the scene. In that realisation she saw her chance. A furtive look around confirmed it. Ducking swiftly under the mare's neck she grabbed the reins and vaulted astride. Moments later the horse was across the stream and cantering up the slope on the far side.

The fight was fierce and intense. Taken by surprise, the Normans were immediately at a disadvantage and, although they fought for their lives, were no match for the skill of their opponents. It had been an easy victory but it also raised other questions. Dougal came over to join Iain who stood surveying the slain mercenaries.

'A small raiding party or scouts for a larger force?' he asked.

'Probably the latter,' Iain replied. 'The question is how large a force?'

Before the other could say any more, Robbie's voice broke in abruptly. 'My lord!'

Hearing the tone of alarm Iain turned quickly, his hand moving automatically to the hilt of his sword. Seeing no immediate threat he relaxed a little. Then his gaze went past Robbie and caught sight of Ashlynn's retreating figure. He swore softly. Crimson with embarrassment, the young man bit his lip.

'I'm sorry, my lord. I only turned my back for a moment.'

'Damn it, lad,' said Dougal, 'could ye no keep control over a wee slip of a lass?'

'I'll go after her.'

Iain shook his head. 'No, you stay with the rest. I'll fetch her back.'

'Aye, and give her a good hiding into the bargain,' growled Dougal. 'The wee fool deserves no less.'

'I'll deal with her,' said Iain. 'Meanwhile, get the men

away. There's no telling how big the rest of the Norman
force might be and I can't take a chance that would
jeopardise our mission. Make for Jedburgh as planned.
I'll catch up with you later.'

'Will you no take some men with you, my lord?' the
other replied. 'It'll be dark in another hour and there's no
telling how many more are out there, or where they are.'

'I'll be faster alone.'

'Aye, perhaps.'

'I'll take good care.'

'See you do.'

Iain turned and whistled for his mount. A few
moments after that, he had guided the stallion across the
stream and was heading the horse up the slope at a gallop.

Ashlynn reached the top of the hill and slowed a little,
glancing over her shoulder. For a moment or two she
could see no sign of pursuit. Then her heart missed a beat
to see the rider on the dapple grey heading in her direction. It needed no lengthy study to work out who he was.
Turning the mare's head she urged her on. The land above
the summit was open and dangerous for that reason: the
grey was bigger and faster and in this terrain would
overtake them soon enough. Looking swiftly round she
spied some trees in the distance and headed for them.

By the time she reached the wood the grey was
closing the gap rapidly. She needed somewhere to hide
and soon. The path through the trees was narrow but
though there was thicket on either side it was leafless
and afforded no concealing cover at this season. Even
as she took the information in the track forked. Forced
to choose she went left. A hundred yards further on she

realised it had been a serious error for the path ended
abruptly in a narrow defile bordered on three sides by
walls of rock.

Ashlynn turned Steorra and retraced her route but as
she neared the main track it was to see Iain's horse not
a hundred yards off and closing fast. In a last desperate
effort she urged her mount forward, conscious of the
hoof beats behind thudding like her own heartbeat.
However, though the mare was game her speed was no
match for the bigger horse. Worse, the trees ended
suddenly and the track came out into open land once
more. Two minutes later the grey drew level and a strong
hand grabbed the rein, drawing her horse to a gradual
halt. Before a word could be spoken Ashlynn kicked
free of the stirrups and leapt from the saddle. Then she
ran, heading back for the cover of the trees in a last desperate bid for freedom. She had covered only fifty yards
before a powerful arm swooped down. Moments later
it drew her up on to the front of the saddle and locked
around her. She fought the hold, struggling wildly.
Reining the horse to a halt, Iain glowered at her.

'Be still, you little hellion!' Then, as the words had
no effect. 'Stop this now, Ashlynn.'

'Let me go!'

'You know damned well I won't.'

Ashlynn twisted and slapped him hard. His jaw tightened and the dark eyes took on an expression that caused
her stomach to turn over. Too late she realised that some
unspecified line had been crossed and she was now in real
trouble. Without another word he dismounted, dragging
her off the horse after him. Ashlynn kicked and fought,
cursing him roundly, managing only to deliver another

ringing slap before she was thrown to the ground and pinned her there with a knee in her back. Iain glared down at his writhing captive.

'By God, I'll teach you to obey me, you little wildcat.'

'Get your hands off me, you Scottish bastard!'

'Scottish bastard is it?' Iain drew a length of cord from the leather pouch on his belt. 'Well then, I may as well live up to my reputation.'

Moments later she was bound hand and foot. Beside herself with fury, Ashlynn fought the rope even as she delivered a lengthy and blistering assessment of his character. Iain paused a moment and regarded his captive keenly.

'It seems to me that you're in no position to deliver insults, lass.'

'You deserve every one, you black-hearted villain.'

'Keep it up and I promise I'll warm your backside with my belt, you contrary little besom.'

It had been on the tip of her tongue to say he wouldn't dare but she choked the words off. The brute would not only do it but would enjoy it too. He had no sense of shame. Too late she was beginning to understand how he had earned his name. It was perhaps fortunate that she did not see the satisfied smirk that accompanied her sudden silence. A large hand hauled her upright. Then, adding insult to injury, he tucked her effortlessly under one arm and carried her to her horse. Moments later she was slung across the saddle like a sack of meal and tied there securely. After that he remounted and, having retrieved her horse's reins, set off again. Incandescent with rage now, Ashlynn tested her bonds, but to no avail. They weren't cruelly tight but they were fast. The brute had known exactly what he was about. The final humiliation would be returning thus to his waiting men. Almost she could hear their laughter.

However, Iain made no effort to retrace their earlier route but continued on his present course for another hour or so. To Ashlynn he spoke not at all, or she to him. For a while hot temper and a strong sense of grievance kept her from noticing the discomfort of her position. However, as the time wore on it made itself felt, and she began to repent of her earlier actions. Her bound limbs ached; the saddle pressed hard against her midriff and the chill was more apparent. More than anything she wanted to be freed from her bonds. If he would just cut her loose she would agree to ride anywhere he wished. Only pride kept her silent.

The light was going when at last the horses came to a halt before a small farmhouse. A man came out and, from his ready greeting, it was clear that Iain was no stranger to him. To Ashlynn he paid no heed at all. The two men exchanged a few words and, having directed his visitor to the barn, the farmer went indoors again. As Iain dismounted and led the horses toward the designated shelter, Ashlynn craned her neck to take a quick look around, now keenly aware of their isolated position and the fading light. Was this where he meant to rendezvous with his men? As yet she could see no sign of them and for the first time missed their presence. For all sorts of reasons she was aware of the old proverb about safety in numbers. Moreover, she was tired, sore and cold for with the approach of darkness the wintry bite in the air was pronounced.

When they reached the barn Iain led the horses to their stalls. Then he paused, surveying his captive. Ashlynn waited, silently willing him to cut her free, though still she could not bring herself to plead. He waited a moment more, then smiled faintly and untied the rope that held her to the saddle. Having done that, he untied her ankles and let her slide down. She stifled a gasp as her cold feet jarred on the hard ground and felt her legs buckle. Had it not been for his arm she would have fallen. It kept her upright while he dragged her across to some upturned barrels by the wall.

'Sit down there and don't stir.'

The tone implied that to do anything else would be a serious mistake. Ashlynn said nothing. In fact she had no intention of disobeying him, all thought of rebellion long gone. Apparently satisfied by her chastened demeanour he turned his attention to the horses. From her vantage point she watched as he unsaddled and rubbed them down, noting with reluctant approval the sure methodical way in which he performed each task. Having done what was necessary he fed them some grain and filled the hay racks. Only when the horses were settled and comfortable did he turn his attention back to his prisoner, surveying her with a cool speculative eye.

'If I untie your hands will you give me your word not to try and escape again?'

She nodded dumbly, too cold and tired to contemplate a further attempt now. He knelt beside her, his strong fingers working the knots until they slackened. Then, blessedly, the rope loosened and she was free. Flexing her wrists she began to massage the aching flesh.

'Where are we?' she asked then.

'Among friends. We'll stay here tonight.'

'But what of your men?'

'We'll catch up with them later. It's almost dark now and the countryside is crawling with Norman mercenaries. It's too dangerous to continue.'

Ashlynn shivered, knowing it was true. Along with that realisation came the first stirrings of guilt that it was she who had put them in this position. As the possible consequences dawned she began to see the extent of her folly and the reason for his anger. It occurred to her that, had he wished to, he could have followed his earlier inclination and thrashed her soundly. She swallowed hard. Knowing his strength she was devoutly thankful that he had restrained the urge. The only thing he'd bruised was her pride.

She was drawn from these thoughts by the return of the farmer. Again he glanced once at Ashlynn and then ignored her, speaking quietly with Iain before setting down a wooden tray on one of the barrels nearby. From under the cloth covering she could smell the savoury aroma of stew and realised suddenly that she was famished. Then she glanced at Iain. He had not beaten her but he could still punish her by withholding food. If he did it would be a long time before the next meal. She bit her lip, trying to ignore the growling in her stomach. Whatever happened she would not beg.

However, it seemed that such was not his plan for he handed her a bowl of the steaming concoction and a hunk of bread.

'Here. Eat.'

Rather shyly she took the bowl. As she did so her fingers brushed his. The touch sent an unexpected *frisson* along her skin. Avoiding his eye she focused her attention on the food and, unable to resist, fell to. The stew was thick with meat and vegetables and, after a day in the open air, quite delicious. For a moment Iain surveyed her in silence, then sat down and ate his own. They washed the food down with a beaker of ale.

By the time they had finished it was dark save for the small pool of light from the lamp. Ashlynn was beginning to feel better now for the food had restored some inner warmth and, even though the barn was chilly, it was better by far than being out in the bitter night air. She drew her cloak closer, keenly aware of the man beside her. She watched him gather the bowls and beakers and return them to the tray. Then he took the lamp from its hook.

'Come.'

She rose somewhat reluctantly from her makeshift seat. 'Where are we going?'

He guided her to the foot of a wooden ladder. 'Up there.'

'The hayloft?'

'Aye.'

Apprehension reawakened and she hesitated, looking from the ladder to him, more than ever aware of the darkness, the remote place and his physical proximity.

'Where are you going to sleep?'

'In the same place.'

'You will not!'

One dark brow arched a little. 'Are you going up that ladder, Ashlynn, or am I going to carry you?'

The mild tone didn't deceive her for a moment. He wouldn't hesitate. Glaring at him in impotent wrath she knew there was no choice but to obey and with thumping heart began to climb, conscious that he observed every step. He smiled sardonically; then followed her up and lifted the lantern, illuminating piles of sweet-smelling hay.

'It's likely not what you're used to, lass, but it's dry and a lot warmer than sleeping in the open.'

Ashlynn said nothing. It wasn't the thought of sleeping in a hay barn that disturbed her.

'We've a long ride ahead tomorrow,' he went on, 'so get some sleep while you can.'

The tone was gentler than the one he'd used earlier but still Ashlynn made no move to comply. She watched him hang the lantern on a nail by the ladder. Immediately the loft was plunged into shadow for most of the light fell below. Apparently unaware of her gaze, he divested himself of his sword belt and then he lay down beside it and stretched out, wrapping himself in the fur-lined cloak. Only then did he glance at his companion.

'Goodnight, lass. Sleep well.'

Seeing he made no move to touch her, Ashlynn felt slightly less anxious. Besides, after the rigours of the day, she was suddenly bone weary. Selecting a spot as far from him as possible, she too lay down and drew her cloak protectively around her. For a while she was quite still, ears straining to detect any movement from her companion, but none came. She could hear only the sound of the beasts munching hay in the stalls below. Outside in the distance a fox barked. She shivered and curled up beneath the cloak. The sense of loneliness intensified bringing tears welling behind her eyelids, and for a while she wept silently into the folds of the cloth.

Not for anything would she have let her sobs be heard
or given utterance to the grief that weighed upon her
heart like lead.

However, in the quiet of the loft even the smallest
sounds carried clearly. From where he lay, Iain heard the
pain and sorrow underlying those stifled sobs, and with
that all her aching vulnerability. All vestiges of his
earlier anger evaporated on the heel of that realisation
and he was unexpectedly touched, more so perhaps than
if she had wept openly. For a moment he was tempted
to go to her but then checked the impulse. Given all that
had passed between them she'd likely not welcome the
intrusion. Besides, what could he say that would in any
way diminish the loss she felt? Grief needed an outlet.
Better to let her have her cry out no matter how hard it
was to hear it.

Sleep came for her eventually but with it troubling
dreams of burning buildings and mounted men all in
chain mail with the light glinting on their helmets. Like
devils they rode through the flames striking down any
who tried to flee. The air rang with screams of pain and
terror. She could see her father and Ethelred locked in
a desperate fight against overwhelming odds. Then Ban
was there, shouting at her to flee. She tried to obey but
her horse's legs were moving too slowly and the
Normans closed in. She saw her brother fall, saw his
face as he went down beneath their swords. Then she
was being dragged from the saddle and the soldiers
closed round her, their leering faces filled with hideous
intent. Their hands reached out for her and she began to
fight. Somewhere she could hear a woman screaming…

She awoke wide-eyed and panting with terror, struggling against the strong hands that held her.

'Hush, lass, it's all right. It's all right.'

Through her tears Ashlynn became aware of lamp-
light and the man beside her. With a jolt she recognised
the face bending over hers and, involuntarily, her hands
clutched hold of him.

'But I saw them…Norman soldiers and Heslingfield
burning…the bodies in the snow…and blood, blood
everywhere.'

As he listened Iain's expression hardened, but his voice
was gentle. 'It was just a bad dream, lass. Nothing more.'

With that, some of the terror began to ebb though her
body was still shaking with reaction.

'It was so real.'

He drew her close, speaking softly, his hand
stroking her hair. 'The Normans canna hurt you any
more, Ashlynn.'

He continued to speak to her in the same gentle tone,
as he might have spoken to a child. Gradually she grew
calmer for his nearness was reassuring now, not threatening, and his strength comforting, like the smell of
wool and leather and wood smoke from his clothing,
smells that seemed familiar and soothing. Involuntarily
she relaxed a little, letting her head rest against his
breast. She could feel the steady thud of the heart within,
beating like the blood in her ears. His arms tightened
around her and she felt him drop a kiss on her hair. The
touch was light but it sent a flush of warmth through her
entire being. Ashlynn caught her breath and looked up,
meeting his gaze and seeing there an expression whose
intensity both excited and alarmed her. It aroused a

feeling unlike anything in her life before. She felt his lips brush her temple and cheek, kissing away the tears they found there. Then his mouth sought her lips. The pressure increased, gently, until her mouth opened beneath his, yielding to a more intimate embrace that awakened other pleasurable sensations that she had not known existed: sensations that thrilled and appalled sending a delicious shiver through her entire being.

Iain's heartbeat quickened as he felt that sudden tremor and with a sense of shock he felt his own hardening response, unanticipated and undeniable. The kiss grew more passionate as memory stripped her clothing away. The fire leapt and, unable to contain it, he crushed her closer, hungry now, wanting her, every particle of his being aroused by the taste and scent of her, the feel of her body in his arms again. He lowered her onto the hay and followed her down.

Unfastening her belt he pushed the tunic aside, sliding his hands beneath the fabric of her shirt, gently caressing, relearning with touch all the soft curves that his eyes had shown him before. The rediscovery sent a charge through the length of his body, a sensation of delight he had almost forgotten. Imagination outpaced him, turning his blood to flame.

He reached for the lacing of her trews. Seeing that hot devouring gaze Ashlynn felt her heart lurch and without warning she was suddenly transported back to the ruined barn and her mind filled with flooding panic. Instinctively she began to struggle, her hands pushing him away, her voice catching on a sob.

'No, no…please, I beg you, don't!'

The words acted on him like a bucket of cold water.

Looking into her face he saw fear and reluctance and with that sight desire ebbed. He rolled aside and drew a deep breath, trying to calm the wild thumping of his heart, trying to quell the riot of his thoughts. When he took her in his arms he had intended only to comfort her. He had not reckoned on that kiss. Innocent and sensual in equal measure, it aroused and disturbed, awakening memories he had thought safely buried. For all manner of reasons he could not afford the indulgence. How the hell had he let things get so far out of hand?

Aloud he said, 'It's all right, lass. I willna hurt you. There's nothing to be afraid of. Nothing's going to happen.'

'I shouldn't have…I didn't mean to…'

'Shhh.' He laid a finger gently on her lips. 'I think neither of us meant to.' He drew her cloak over her again and tucked it around her. 'Go back to sleep, Ashlynn, and sweeter dreams this time.'

With that he returned to his own side of the loft and flung himself down on his cloak. Those quiet words of reassurance might have satisfied her but he could no longer fool himself. Something had awoken inside him that he thought dead. The knowledge shook him to the core of his being and with it came a resurgence of anger for letting it happen. That was the first and last time. For both their sakes it mustn't happen again. He took another deep breath and let it out slowly. Then he wrapped the cloak around himself and shut his eyes. It was a long time before sleep came.

Chapter Four

Ashlynn was awoken by a hand shaking her shoulder.

'Time to move, lass.'

She came to with a start but, on recognising her companion, relaxed a little. Grey dawn light revealed the details of the hay loft and awoke the memory of the previous evening. With it came profound embarrassment and regret. What a fool she had been! What must he think of her? Yesterday it would not have mattered but now… A covert glance at her companion revealed nothing of his thoughts for he had moved away and was buckling on his sword belt. Ashlynn bit her lip.

'Iain, about what happened last night…'

His hands paused in their task and the dark eyes met hers. 'Nothing happened last night, lass.'

'I know.' She paused awkwardly. 'Thank you.'

Just for a second it took him aback. However, his tone was perfectly even when he spoke. 'I've never forced a woman yet, and I'm not about to start with you.' He finished buckling the sword belt and then moved to the ladder, pausing briefly to glance in her direction. 'Now we've established that, we'll get on our way.'

Having broken their fast on cheese and oatcakes they saddled the horses. Iain said nothing until they led the beasts from the barn. Then he paused, regarding her with a steady gaze.

'Will there be any need for me to tie you on your horse, lass?'

Under that piercing look she felt herself redden. 'No.'

'Do I have your word on that?'

'Yes.'

'Good. We'll be going then.'

With that he swung into the grey's saddle and waited for her to mount the mare. Then they set off. They rode in silence for some way, he seeming indisposed to talk and she not caring to intrude on his thought. From time to time she threw him a sideways glance but, as was habitual with him, his expression revealed nothing.

In fact his attention was on the countryside around them, looking for any sign of movement that might betoken a mounted force. Nothing stirred, save a few sheep grazing on the hillside. Detecting no immediate threat he relaxed a little, turning his attention to the girl at his side. She rode well, controlling the spirited little mare with ease. Once again he found himself curious.

'She's a fine horse,' he observed. 'A gift perhaps?'

'From my father.'

'He had a good eye for a mount.'

'Yes, he did.' The memory brought others that were unwelcome and she changed the subject. 'The grey is a fine animal too. What do you call him?'

'Stormwind.'

'It suits him. Did you train him yourself?'

He nodded. 'Aye, I did. A wild beast he was too when he was younger.'

Looking at the grey Ashlynn could believe it, and yet the rapport between horse and rider was pronounced. Having watched her father and brothers handling young stock she knew that such a sympathetic partnership had been forged out of skill and patience, not the use of the whip. Again it presented another facet of the man.

'I own to surprise,' he went on. 'About the mare, I mean.'

'Why so?'

'I expected to hear the word husband in connection with gift, not father.'

Ashlynn's gaze remained determinedly between the horse's ears. 'Did you?'

He paused, framing his next question with care but needing to know. 'Was your husband among those slain at Heslingfield, perhaps?'

'No.'

'Then…'

'I have no husband.'

'Why not?'

With an effort she kept her voice level. 'That is none of your business.'

'None at all,' he replied. 'I asked out of curiosity only. You are of age and you canna have lacked for suitors.'

Upon the word Athelstan flashed into her mind and, with his image, the knowledge that they would never marry now. The realisation brought both relief and guilt. And then, for no good reason, his face dissolved and Iain's took its place. Almost at once it raised a wry smile; he was the last man on earth her father would ever have chosen to be her husband. And yet, the thought persisted, what if he had? Would she have objected so strenuously to the match then? Would the thought of sharing his bed repel her? The answer was instant and shocking. Shocking because of who he was and shocking because, in spite of that, he was an attractive man. Worse, he engendered feelings that both disturbed and excited in equal measure.

Iain watched her closely, wondering at the thoughts behind that smooth brow. 'You make no reply.'

'There were suitors, only none I would marry.'

'Ah. You are hard to please.'

'Since marriage is for life should one not be careful about the choice of partner?'

'A fair point,' he conceded, 'but surely your father sought to guide your choice.'

'Yes, he did, but one cannot see through another's eyes.'

It was a partial truth only but it would have to suffice. As things stood she wasn't about to confide in him and, as she had said, it was none of his business anyway.

'True enough,' he replied. 'So tell me, what manner of man would you have then, lass?'

The directness of the question took her aback, but only for a moment.

'I'll know him when I see him.'

With that she touched the mare with her heels and cantered on ahead. Iain's lips twitched. Then he nudged the grey to a swifter pace, catching up a few moments later. Ashlynn spared him no more than a glance, keeping her attention resolutely on the way ahead. His question had unsettled her more than she cared to admit.

What matter if she did meet the man of her dreams? She had no kin, no land, no wealth; nothing to call her own save the horse she rode. It was hardly an attractive dowry. In tales of high romance the lover would care nothing for such mundane concerns as his lady's wealth: in real life things were different. Even if she had gone to Dunfermline and thrown herself on the queen's mercy, what then? She might have been given a lowly position of some sort, probably little more than a servant. Dunfermline seemed unlikely now. More probable was his disposing of her at Jedburgh. If not, would he take her to Glengarron instead? His power over her was total. He could do with her whatever she liked. She threw another swift glance at her companion and suddenly the possibility didn't seem so remote. She bit her lip. No matter how she regarded it, the future looked increasingly bleak and without hope of remedy.

They rode in silence again after that and Iain made no attempt to probe further. For the most part they held the horses to a steady pace putting more miles between them and the farm on the moors. It occurred to Ashlynn that the next night's accommodation might be very different from the relative comfort of a hay loft and, while it would not be the first time she had slept under the stars, it would certainly be the first in the depths of winter. It wasn't an enticing prospect. Now more than ever she pitied the plight of all those who had fled Durham.

At noon they stopped briefly to rest and eat before pressing on again. She noticed that Iain was keeping to tracks that skirted the hillsides, avoiding the open skyline where they would be visible for miles around.

Now, like her companion, she kept a watchful eye on the land ahead but still could see no sign of any living thing other than sheep and birds. Once again it was borne upon her that her actions the previous day had been foolish in the extreme and she would have given much to see the rest of the Scottish force once more.

She was jerked from these reflections by the sudden glint of light on metal among the rocks up ahead. Instinctively she shot a glance at Iain.

'Did you see that?'

His eyes never left the path. 'Aye, lass, I did.'

'Normans?'

'Doubtful. Robbers most likely.'

'Can we not—?'

Before she could finish, the rocks erupted with armed figures, four rough-looking men and all wielding wicked blades. Their expressions reminded her of nothing so much as a pack of hungry wolves.

Iain unsheathed his sword. 'Stay behind me, Ashlynn.'

With that the grey stallion leapt forward. She heard a scream as Iain's blade found its first victim. Almost simultaneously the big horse reared, striking out with iron-shod hoofs and a second man fell like a stone and lay still. Seeing the fate of their companions the others parted, closing in on either side so that Iain was forced to defend himself on two fronts. Ashlynn's heart leapt towards her throat. Another scream rent the air and a man fell, clutching his arm. A savage backhanded thrust opened his companion's throat.

Ashlynn exulted silently. Then exultation turned to fear as three more men emerged from concealment among the rocks behind him. She cried out a warning.

The grey wheeled in response but not quite fast enough. Hands reached up to drag the rider from the saddle. Instead of resisting Iain flung himself sideways, knocking his assailant off balance and the two men hit the ground. He rolled clear, coming to his feet in one fluid movement and leaving his attacker half-stunned in the dirt. The other two closed in.

Ashlynn glanced over her shoulder, half-expecting to see more assailants behind, but the way was empty. All she had to do was turn the mare and ride away to freedom. Even as the thought occurred, she saw the third man pick himself up and retrieve his sword, moving in on Iain's undefended back. She swallowed hard. Kicking her feet free of the stirrups she leapt from the saddle, dropping into a crouching run toward the nearest abandoned blade. As her fingers closed on the hilt she heard her brother's voice: *'Take your opponent by surprise if you can, and hurt him with the first blow. You may not get a second chance.'* As the robber raised his sword to strike, she swung at him. The edge bit deep. He cried out and staggered, clutching the wound, reeling round to face his unexpected assailant, his expression registering shock and rage. A second later it became malice and in one last deadly effort he lunged at her like a striking snake. Ashlynn leapt aside as the blade hissed past, bringing her guard up for the next assault. It never came. Her attacker collapsed in the dirt, blood pumping from the gash in his neck.

With pounding heart she threw a swift look over her shoulder; Iain was still hard pressed. Without stopping to think she launched herself at the nearest foe. He saw the movement just a second too late, crying out as the sword thrust through his ribs. For a moment he hung there, then slowly slumped and fell. She had a vague impression of the last man going down under Iain's blade a few moments later. Then it was over. Trembling with reaction, she drew in a deep breath, her gaze moving involuntarily toward her companion.

'Are you all right?'

He was breathing hard but standing yet, and now regarding her with an expression she had not seen before.

'Aye, lass, thanks to you.'

'It was thanks to me that this happened at all,' she replied.

'You couldn't have known yon scum would attack us.'

'No, but it *is* my fault we were separated from your men.' She swallowed hard. 'Iain, I'm so sorry.'

For the second time in five minutes he was completely taken aback for there was no mistaking the sincerity in her voice.

'Dinna fret yourself, lass. We'll meet up with them again soon enough.' She watched him wipe the blood from his sword and sheathe it again. 'In the meantime we need to get out of here.'

'You think there may be more of them?'

'No. If there were we'd know it by now, but there are plenty more like them hereabouts. Time is getting on and we've a way to ride before we reach shelter. I'd as soon do it in daylight.'

Ashlynn nodded. The thought of travelling through this country after dark had no appeal at all.

They retrieved the horses and for a while rode fast, putting distance between themselves and the scene of the recent ambush. However, they saw no one else.

* * *

It was dusk when they came to the farmhouse. Like the place they had stayed in before it was remote and again it seemed that Iain was known here for he was greeted with words of welcome before being directed to the stables. The latter was a long low building constructed of stone and thatch, but it was weatherproof and would afford shelter for the beasts and for themselves.

Ashlynn unsaddled Steorra and rubbed her down while Iain dealt with his own mount. Then she fetched grain from the nearby bin and fed the two horses while he filled the hay racks. When the animals were settled Iain removed the heavy cloak and sword belt and then eased off his tunic. Her startled gaze fell on the torn and bloody sleeve beneath.

'You're hurt!'

'A scratch only.'

'It needs tending. I'll go and beg some clean cloths. The farmer's wife may have some honey and woundwort salve too.'

Iain didn't argue. Nor did he follow her from the stable. A few minutes later she returned with the necessary items and a bowl of clean water. Seeing this he unfastened his belt and eased off his tunic. Ashlynn stepped closer and rolled back the sleeve of his shirt the better to inspect the wound. It was a long shallow gash, vivid against the paler flesh of his arm. It had bled profusely and she knew it must hurt. However, Iain made no complaint, merely observing her in silence. Keenly aware of that penetrating gaze and the proximity of the man, Ashlynn tried to concentrate on the task.

'I need to clean this but it may sting a little.'

He returned a non-committal grunt. She dipped a cloth and carefully wiped away the dried blood. For a moment or two he watched the deft movements of her hands before letting his gaze move higher. It lingered a little on the soft hollow of her throat before travelling to her face, a face whose delicate contours were as familiar to him now as his own hand. The ride and the cool air had brought fresh colour to her cheeks and loosened tendrils of hair from her braid. The effect was strangely beguiling.

'It would have been a lot worse if you hadn't been watching my back today,' he replied. 'Where did you learn to use a sword?'

As her eyes met his, the cornflower blue deepened with inner emotion. 'Ban…my brother…taught me a few basic skills.'

'He taught you well I'd say.'

She shook her head. 'I got away with it because I took my opponents by surprise. There wasn't much skill involved, believe me.'

'Skill enough for the task, lass,' he replied. 'It took courage too.'

Something in his tone and look caused her heart to skip a beat. To hide her confusion she bent more assidu-ously to her work.

'You had the chance to run back there,' he continued. 'Why didn't you?'

It was a good question, she thought, and hard to answer. Yet in that split second when the choice was offered she could not leave this man to die. 'Let's just say I owed you one.'

'Maybe so, but this doesna make us quits.'

Ashlynn's hands paused in their task. 'By that you mean Fitzurse.'

'Aye.'

'For what it's worth, I'm truly sorry he escaped.'

'Ach, well…I'll meet up with him again.'

'To settle that score you mentioned?'

'That's right.'

She hesitated a little. Then, 'May I ask what manner of score?'

'That need not concern you.'

The sudden coldness in his tone was jarring. 'I beg your pardon; I didn't mean to pry.'

Iain frowned, annoyed with himself for snapping like that but somehow the words had just come out. A verbal reflex, he thought ruefully. Even to his ears it had sounded boorish. He gritted his teeth. 'Forget it.'

It was as close to an apology as she was going to get. Ashlynn kept her face determinedly neutral while her hands spread salve on the wound. 'I cannot. It was thanks to me he escaped.'

He sighed and when he spoke this time the sharp edge was gone. 'It wasna your fault, lass. What happened that day was typical of the man.'

She laid a clean pad over the cut. 'I have never met anyone more evil.'

'Pray you never do.'

He watched as she began to bandage the arm. Once or twice her fingers touched his skin, a pleasing touch that was both gentle and unexpectedly sensual and sent his thoughts in forbidden directions. With an effort he brought them back.

When she finished tying the bandage he flexed the

arm experimentally. 'You've done a good job.' He glanced down at the pot of salve. 'Allow me to return the favour.'

Drawing nearer he reached out and brushed the stray wisps of hair from her face in a gesture that was both casual and oddly intimate, like the warm musky smell of his skin. In an instant it evoked the memory of the hayloft and that sudden startling kiss and her breathing quickened.

With great care he applied a little of the soothing balm to her bruised cheek, smoothing it lightly across the bone. Thence he moved to the cut on her lip, his touch as delicate as a butterfly wing. Having applied the balm he scrutinised his handiwork.

'That will suffice I think. In a few more days the marks will fade.'

Before she could reply their host appeared with a tray of food and Iain stepped away from her to greet him. Glad of the distraction she replaced the lid on the salve and tossed away the dirty water. When Iain turned back again she had herself under better control.

'Time to eat, lass.'

The food was simple fare, bread and vegetable pottage, but it lined the stomach and warmed the body. By the time they had done it was dark and the only thing to do was retire. Iain spread a thick layer of clean straw in the only empty stall and then turned to Ashlynn.

'Again, I regret the basic nature of the arrangements.'

She shook her head. 'It doesn't matter.'

True enough, she thought, it really didn't. One place was much like another now. Wrapping herself in her cloak she lay down. Iain retrieved his sword and unsheathed the blade. Then he too stretched out, laying the naked weapon beside him, the hilt by his hand. Having done that, he glanced across the intervening space and bade her goodnight.

He heard her reply and then the rustling of straw as she turned on her side. He had noticed that she always slept on her side. Drawing his cloak tighter he turned over too, taking care not to jar his injured arm. In truth he hardly felt it now. She had done a good job in tending him. More than that, he thought, but for her timely intervention today he'd likely have been food for the crows. No question but the lass had courage. She could have left him to die and seized the chance of freedom. Why hadn't she? After his treatment of her thus far he could hardly have blamed her. Then he'd almost bitten her head off when she asked about Fitzurse. His jaw tightened. He should have dealt with it better but her question had taken him unawares and he was not used to sharing his thoughts with a woman. In truth it was not a subject he wanted to discuss at all. The memories it evoked were too bitter.

In spite of her weariness Ashlynn found sleep elusive for her mind was crowded with thoughts. What was Iain's connection with Fitzurse? Some quarrel existed between them, but of what nature? Recalling his earlier response, she knew she wouldn't dare ask again. He kept his secrets close. For a while that day it had seemed as though the barrier between them had been lowered a little, but she was wrong. It was still firmly in place. Why that should have mattered was unclear, but somehow it did. Suddenly she wanted to know what drove this man. What events in his past had made him who he was? Had Fitzurse had a hand in that? Likely she would never know for their present relationship would be of short duration.

For the first time Ashlynn thought ruefully of her masculine attire. She could not recall the last time she had washed or combed her hair or looked in a mirror. Self-consciously she raised a hand to the bruise on her cheek. It was tender to the touch and no doubt an ugly colour into the bargain. Hardly a face or form to charm a man. Almost at once she smiled in self-mockery. If Iain had wanted her before it was merely because she was there, the only possible choice, and darkness hid all defects anyway. Men had different needs, she had been told, and would satisfy them where they could. The thought was sobering. More than ever now she was glad that she had not yielded in a moment of madness. To be considered by any man as an easy victory would have been anathema, but for this man to think so would have been even worse somehow.

Much to Ashlynn's relief the remainder of the journey passed uneventfully and they reached Jedburgh without further incident. At a fortified manor house about a mile from the town they made the rendezvous with Iain's men. As they rode through the gateway and into the courtyard Dougal hastened forward to greet the returning chief, his weather-beaten face creasing in a smile. Iain returned it, stepping down from the horse and handing the reins to a groom. Ashlynn followed suit, watching as the two men shook hands.

'It's good to see you back, my lord. We've been looking out for your return these last two days.'

His gaze flicked to Ashlynn and in that brief glance she saw contained anger and disapproval. The same expression was evident on the faces of the men nearby. She swallowed hard, knowing their anger was merited. Her actions might have caused her death and Iain's too, and while she could not suppose that hers would trouble them overmuch, their chief was a different matter.

If Iain was aware of the strained atmosphere he gave no sign of it.

'It's good to be back, Dougal.'

'Did you encounter any Normans on the road, my lord?'

'No, none.'

Ashlynn shot him a swift sideways glance. The answer was true as far as it went. Would he tell them of the encounter with the robber band? She dreaded to think how his men might react if they knew how close they had come to being leaderless. The knowledge of her folly returned with force. However, he made no reference to the incident and merely inquired of Dougal if all was well with the men. On receiving a reply in the affirmative he nodded.

'Well, then, shall we go in?'

He steered her towards the house, his hand warm and strong under her elbow. Not so long ago she would have considered that touch intrusive. Now it felt strangely reassuring. Once inside she was escorted to a chamber not unlike the one at Hexham. Her grateful glance around took in a cheerful fire and, blessedly, a bed. Tonight at least she would not have to sleep in a draughty stable. Iain paused on the threshold and for a short space they surveyed each other in silence.

'Is there anything you need, lass?'

Ashlynn glanced down at her clothes. Then, somewhat tentatively, she said, 'I'd like to wash. Perhaps borrow a comb.'

'I'll see what I can do.'

When he had gone she unfastened her cloak and laid it over a chair. The thought of being clean was suddenly very appealing. In the enclosed space she was keenly aware of the smell of horse and leather emanating from her clothing. Every part of her felt grubby. How much she would have given for an hour in the bath house at Heslingfield. Unbidden tears pricked her eyelids and she forced them back, swallowing hard. No use to think of it. Heslingfield was gone, part of a past life.

The arrival of the maid was a welcome distraction and in a short time Ashlynn was provided with a large basin, a jug of hot water, soap, comb and linen towels. She regarded them with real pleasure and in moments had stripped off. Washing had to be done in parts but she scrubbed herself as well as she was able, starting with her hair and working downwards. It took a while but eventually every inch of her was clean and glowing. Then, wrapping a dry towel round her, she sat down before the fire and combed out her hair, easing out the numerous small tangles until it slid freely through the comb. Then she let the heat of the fire dry it. That done, she combed it again. Restored now to its normal lustre it fell in soft waves down her back. Rather anxiously she lifted the polished metal mirror from the table and examined her appearance. The cut lip was healing but a dark bruise marred the left cheekbone. Then she reflected that it would fade, in time. The bruise would be gone at least, if not the memory.

* * *

While Ashlynn had been busy thus, Iain had been checking on the disposition of men and horses. Later he rejoined Dougal and received a more detailed report of what had passed in his absence. He listened without interruption, and then nodded.

'It is well. What of the injured?'

'Making good progress, most of them.'

'The Saxon youth?'

'Still with us,' said Dougal. 'He's a fighter, that's for sure.'

'Like sister like brother.'

'The wench is spirited, I grant you, but she's a head-strong troublesome little jade for all that. Did ye take your belt to her, 'twould be no more than her deserts.'

'Dinna think I wasna tempted, but that same trouble-some little jade saved my life two days since.'

Dougal stared at him. 'Saved your life? How so?'

Iain furnished him with a brief account of what had happened during the robbers' attack. The other heard him with mounting incredulity.

'Well, I'm damned. With a sword, ye say?'

'Aye, just so.'

The idea clearly appealed to the laird's companion and he permitted himself a grudging smile. 'A rare wench—for a Sassenach.'

'That she is.'

'Will she come with us to Glengarron?'

'It depends.'

'On what?'

'The king's will.'

'You'll discuss her case with Malcolm?'

'Aye. The lass originally intended to go to Dunfermline. If the king wills it, she may yet.'

Even as he spoke, the thought jarred though he could
not have said precisely why.

'You'll no sell her then?' said Dougal.

'No.'

'Ach, well, whatever you say.'

Iain left his lieutenant a few minutes later and made
his way back to the chamber where he had left Ashlynn.
There were things they needed to discuss.

Ashlynn heard the knock and, having assumed it was
the maid returning, bade the girl enter. It was a very different figure who stepped into the room. The sight
brought her to her feet with a sharp intake of breath.

Iain checked abruptly, his smile fading as he stared at
the figure standing by the hearth. Every vestige of boyish
appearance was gone, to be replaced by a feminine vision
that caused his heart to miss a beat. She was clad only in
a thin linen sheet. It stopped short at breast and knee and,
in between, the damp cloth had moulded itself to the
curves of her body. Unbidden his imagination stripped
it away and reminded him of what lay beneath, only
mantled now with tawny hair that hung in a soft curling
mass to her waist. Huge blue eyes met his.

'My lord?'

She had never called him by that title before and it
took him by surprise, not least because of the thoughts
it engendered. Involuntarily he glanced at the bed across
the room. Her lord? Hardly that, but, by God, if he
were... Recollecting himself he cleared his throat and
forced his thoughts back into line.

'I beg your pardon, lass. I came to discuss something with you but it can wait awhile.' He paused. 'Do you have all you require for now?'

'Thank you, yes.'

Ashlynn was aware that her face was glowing now with a lot more than the effects of soap and water; aware too of her present state of undress, and the disturbing nearness of the man. Nor could she fail to misinterpret the expression in the dark eyes. To her chagrin she saw him smile, a slow disconcerting smile that, though rare enough, did nothing to dispel her embarrassment. Clearly the rogue felt no such emotion. On the contrary, he seemed to be enjoying himself. With that realisation annoyance woke.

'Are you going to stand there all day?'

'It's a tempting prospect, lass. You clean up rather well if I may say so.'

Ashlynn glared at him. His enjoyment grew. Under other circumstances he'd have seen that unspoken challenge well met. He indulged the fantasy another moment or two, and then reluctantly retraced his steps to the door. When he reached it he paused a moment on the threshold.

'We dine in the hall with my men this evening. Until then, Ashlynn.'

With considerable relief she watched the door close behind him and then heard the sound of his retreating footsteps. With indignant haste she dressed again, heedless now whether her borrowed masculine attire smelled of horses or not. It occurred to her that it might be a good thing if it did. No man was likely to find that remotely attractive.

* * *

Iain made no mention of the incident when they met later, a fact for which she was grateful. However, when at length he had finished his meal and his cup was replenished, he leaned back in his chair and turned his attention towards her. Under that steady scrutiny the blood leapt in her veins.

'We need to talk, lass.'

Recalling his earlier words she took a shrewd guess. 'Business?'

'Just so.'

'Will yours keep you in Jedburgh long?'

'No, another day only.'

For some reason she had not been expecting that. Managing to keep her voice steady she said, 'And afterwards you will return to Glengarron.'

'Aye. The weather will close in soon and I want to be back before it does. Besides, my men are keen to see their wives and families again.'

'I see.'

'You spoke once of wishing to go to Dunfermline,' he said. 'Is that still the case?'

Ashlynn's heart beat a little faster. Now it was presented to her she was by no means certain it was what she wanted. However, to say so would make her sound indecisive and anyway there was no viable alternative plan.

'I must get my living somehow and can think of no other way,' she replied.

'Then I will speak to the king on the matter.'

'The king?'

'Aye. 'Tis he whom I've come to meet.'

Her surprise was unfeigned. 'When?'

'Tomorrow.'

She stared at him, her mind struggling to assimilate the information. If the king agreed to the request then tomorrow would bring a parting of the ways with Iain. In all likelihood she would not see him again. Once that thought would have gladdened her beyond measure. Now several different emotions vied for supremacy as she considered the ramifications. Underlying them all was something harder to identify. However, he was watching her closely now, waiting for her answer. Taking a deep breath she nodded.

'Very well.'

'So be it,' he replied. 'Of course, the king may refuse.'

'And if he does?'

'Then you'll come with us to Glengarron.'

'Oh.' It was a lame response and she knew it, but could think of no words that would have described her feeling just then. If Iain took her to Glengarron it could have only one ultimate outcome. To suppose anything else was naïve in the extreme. To think she had once regarded marriage as a problem!

Misinterpreting that reply entirely, he frowned. 'Whatever is meant to be will be, lass, whether you want it to happen or not.'

They left for the rendezvous at dawn accompanied by an escort of six men. The cold was biting and grey mist curled in wreaths above the fields. Every branch and blade of grass was furred with hoar frost. Ashlynn did not ask where they were going; that would become clear soon enough. She had slept ill the previous night, her mind in turmoil, no longer certain of anything.

Once or twice she glanced at the man beside her but his expression revealed nothing of his thought. Was he hoping that the king might grant her wish and take her to Dunfermline? Hoping that he might be rid of her for good? When she considered the trouble she had caused him already it would hardly be surprising. Once she would not have cared two straws for his opinion. Now, the thought of his disapproval was strangely discomforting.

The journey was short, little more than a mile, and ended outside a house hard by a small stone church. Half-a-dozen horses were tethered nearby, guarded by two armed men. Iain greeted the latter briefly, receiving a like greeting in return, and dismounted. Ashlynn followed suit. They went together into the house where a servant showed them into a small, sparsely furnished chamber. It was clean however, and a cheerful fire burned in the hearth. For a moment neither one said anything. As usual Iain's expression was unreadable.

'Wait for me here, lass.'

With that he left, closing the door after him. Ashlynn crossed the room and put her ear to the wood, listening intently. She heard a few murmured words beyond and knew then that there was a guard outside. The windows were high and barred with iron. Clearly she wasn't going anywhere. He fully intended that his parting instruction should be kept. An unnecessary precaution as she had no wish to leave just then anyway. She sighed and turned away to warm herself by the fire, trying to ignore the knot of apprehension in her stomach and wishing she could hear the conversation taking place elsewhere.

* * *

Malcolm listened carefully while Iain delivered his report on the military situation in England. As ever it was clear and precise. Moreover, it favoured his plans entirely.

'This falls out better than I had hoped.'

'William's forces are divided in dealing with several different rebellions, my liege; not only in Northumbria but also along the Welsh Marches and in the east, in the Fen country.'

'Then he'll be too busy to deal with Scottish incursions across the border,' Malcolm replied. Clapping his companion on the shoulder he poured two cups of whisky from the jug on the table. 'Let us drink to his confusion.'

Recalling the destruction he had witnessed on his journey north, Iain nodded. 'Right gladly.'

When the toast was drunk they fell into companionable silence. Iain gathered himself to broach the next subject. The king eyed his companion shrewdly.

'There is something else on your mind, I think.'

'Your Majesty reads my thoughts.'

'We've known each other a long time you and I. We've hunted and caroused together and fought side by side in battle. You have watched my back and risked your life to save mine, my friend. So, if it pleases you, will you not tell me?'

Iain explained then about Ashlynn, or at least related the essential facts. Malcolm listened with close attention, his penetrating gaze never leaving the other man's face. He had not lied when he spoke about friendship. Iain McAlpin was one of the few men he liked and trusted. That liking was mutual and, in consequence, Malcolm had learned something of his friend's past, a confidence he had never broken. Moreover, kingship had taught him early about the need to read men accurately, and what he saw here surprised him greatly. Had his companion known how much this spare account was revealing to his listener, he might have been much surprised in his turn.

'A bad business,' Malcolm commented when the tale ended. 'The maid is lucky to be alive. She has no kin who could take her in?'

'None, my liege.'

'Had she been a commoner I'd have suggested you sell her to the highest bidder. I suppose you still could as she has no kin to pay a ransom for her.'

Iain's brow drew together. Now that the matter was so baldly stated it seemed strangely unwelcome.

'Is she fair?' the king went on.

'Aye, she is.'

'Well, that's something. Of what temperament is she?'

'Spirited, my liege.'

'Unfortunate, but it would soon be beaten out of her I have no doubt.'

Iain frowned. That had not occurred to him before but now he admitted the truth of it. The life of a slave was one of drudgery and unquestioning obedience. For a woman it had other connotations too, especially if she was attractive. He remembered the first time he had set eyes on Ashlynn, remembered her torn dress and Fitzurse's mailed fist pulling the cloth apart. The memory was accompanied by a surge of anger, for it was but a short step to imagining what else would have

happened had the brute been allowed to follow his inclination. Could he be responsible for selling the girl
into such a fate? It took but a second to know the answer.

'I'll not sell her, my liege.' He hesitated. 'I wondered
if some place might be found for her at court.'

Malcolm shook his head. 'The court is no place for a
girl alone. Nor has she any dowry that would attract a
suitor. 'Twould only be a matter of time before she attracted the attentions of a very different kind of protector.'

Again Iain was forced to recognise the truth of that
statement and with it a fresh twinge of guilt. Perhaps he
should have left the girl in Hexham after all. Yet if he
had, what would she have done? Her fate there might
have been no different.

'Since you will not sell her and she cannot go to Dunfermline, there is only one other honourable solution,'
Malcolm continued. 'You must take her to wife.'

Iain's cup paused halfway to his lips as the ramifications dawned. Mentally recoiling, he was shocked into
temporary silence. Then he shook his head.

'I have no mind to marry again, my liege.'

'Your loyalty to your wife's memory does you much
credit, but you cannot live in the past.'

'I know it. Eloise is gone and there's naught can
change it.'

'Yet you are a man for all that, and you have a
man's needs.'

'When I want female company I can find it.'

'Of course. Nothing wrong with that, but you cannot
get heirs thus.'

It was an aspect of the matter that Iain had not chosen
to dwell on, but now that the topic had been raised he

confronted it. 'I'll marry again and breed sons, but not until I have destroyed Fitzurse.'

'I understand your desire for revenge and know you have good cause, but this quest has dominated your life these last eight years,' the king replied. 'A man needs more than hatred to sustain him. He needs the healing touch of a woman. You have been a widower long enough, my friend. 'Tis time to put the past behind you and move on.'

'I cannot move on knowing that my enemy lives and thrives, and a woman cannot help me there.'

'Marriage will show you the way as it has shown me.'

The king's regard for his newly affianced bride was well known and Iain forced a smile. 'Fortune has favoured your Majesty.'

'I would that all men might be so blessed.'

'It is a state to be hoped for rather than attained, by the majority at least.'

'Perhaps, and yet having attained it once do you not seek it again?'

'There seems little point in seeking what may not be found, my liege.'

'And yet I sense you are not entirely indifferent to this girl.'

It was a shrewd shot. Recalling what had happened in the hayloft Iain knew he could not deny it. However, wanting a woman was one thing, marriage quite another. Seeing his companion made no reply, Malcolm seized the initiative.

'If it is God's will, you may yet meet Fitzurse in combat. In the meantime you must look to those areas of your life that you have neglected. You must get sons to carry on your line.' The king eyed him with a level gaze. 'Besides, you have in some sort become the maid's protector already. Make it permanent.'

Nothing could have been more genial than his expression or his tone but Iain knew better than to think the words a suggestion only. His heart turned over as he saw the precipice looming. The king intended to be rid of the problem and with the least possible inconvenience to himself. Belatedly Iain realised he should have foreseen this and mentally cursed his own stupidity. Malcolm was nothing if not cunning.

'You must take her to wife,' he repeated. 'It is the only logical step.'

'My liege, I—'

'You must take the girl in marriage and there's an end.' The words were quietly spoken but the tone was as inflexible as steel.

Iain took a deep breath and gave the only possible answer. He wished now that he'd kept his mouth shut and never mentioned the subject at all. This was a damnable complication, one he didn't need or want. Nor did he imagine for an instant that Ashlynn would welcome it either. However, to disregard a royal command was out of the question. He had to get her consent. God knew it was going to take all his powers of persuasion. Then he reflected that once he had her safe at Glengarron there would be time to spare; time for them both to get used to the idea. Malcolm's next words undeceived him.

'Excellent. You shall wed the girl this day and I myself shall stand witness.' He gave his companion a beaming smile. 'Go, fetch the bride, and bring her to the kirk. Let the matter be settled once and for all.'

The interview was over. For a moment Iain was rooted to the spot before he recollected himself enough to make obeisance to the king and withdraw. Once outside the door he swore softly, needing that temporary vent for his feelings even though, just then, he wasn't quite sure what they were.

Ashlynn stared at him, dumbfounded. He had to be joking. Yet nothing about his expression suggested that he was anything other than deadly serious. With that look came the first stirrings of unease. Mingled with it was another feeling she didn't want to examine too closely.

'Malcolm has no right to do this.'

'He is the king, Ashlynn.'

'Not my king. I owe him no obedience.'

'But I do, and may not disregard a royal command.'

'Then let the fault in this be mine, not yours.'

'It's no use, lass. Face the facts. Even if the king were to take you to Dunfermline it would be to place you in a position of lowly servitude. It would only be a matter of time before some swaggering young buck took you to his bed.'

'I would not so demean myself.'

'Do you really think you'd be given any choice?'

She swallowed hard, having the unpleasant suspicion that he was right. He read her silence correctly and nodded.

'The only option left you now is marriage.'

An inexorable tide was sweeping her further and further out of her depth but Ashlynn fought the current anyway.

'I will not let your king treat me like a chattel.'

'We are in Scotland now. My king may do as he wills.'

It was the truth and she knew it though it did nothing

to lessen her present consternation. Nominally at least marriage did afford an honourable alternative to her predicament, but it was also irrevocable. The idea had been bad enough when it involved an unattractive man. Now it was infinitely worse.

'And what is your will in all of this?' she asked then.

'In this matter my will is the king's.'

'Damn your will and his too!'

She would have turned away but he prevented it, taking her shoulders in a firm grip.

'You will bend to it, lass, I promise you.' His gaze locked with hers. 'You can do nothing else.'

That also was the unpalatable truth, a fact acknowledged in strained silence. Unable to bear that intense scrutiny she lowered her gaze. It was capitulation and they both knew it.

'Better the devil you know, lass.' His hand closed round her arm. 'Come.'

'Where are we going?'

'To the kirk.'

'The kirk! Now?'

'There's no time like the present. Besides, the king is waiting.'

He drew her with him to the door. Ashlynn hung back, fighting panic. The hold tightened.

'It's no use, my sweet. There's no escape now—for either of us.'

Chapter Five

The church was freezing and empty at this hour, save for the waiting priest and the figure beside him. Malcolm was a physically impressive man with the powerful build of the warrior. Ashlynn had an impression of brown hair and a weathered face with shrewd appraising eyes. She could imagine that in battle they would look without pity on the enemy. They took in every detail of her unorthodox appearance but gave no clue as to the thoughts it engendered. No doubt all the circumstances had been explained anyway. The priest, however, was regarding her with cold disfavour. Women were not welcome in churches here, never mind a woman so outrageously clad. If he said nothing it was due to the exalted nature of the company.

The king glanced towards him and nodded. 'Let's get on with it.'

Ashlynn drew in a sharp breath. Then Iain's hand pulled her on to her knees beside him. In that moment she knew only a desperate and irrational urge to flee.

She knew it was irrational because there was nowhere to run. In any case half-a-dozen of Malcolm's men stood by the door. Her fate had been decided. Tears and pleas would avail her nothing, even if pride had not forbidden their utterance. Through the chaos of her thoughts she was aware of the priest intoning the words of the marriage ceremony. The whole scene was like something from a bad dream, except it wasn't a dream and she would not wake to find it all untrue.

As one in a daze she heard Iain repeat all the requisite words. And then it was her turn. When it came to the key question she hesitated, wanting to shout her defiance at the Scottish king, to say no, and to consign him and Iain McAlpin both to a place of great heat. The temptation was almost overwhelming. Almost. The silence drew out and grew louder. Though the man beside her didn't move she sensed the sudden tension in every line of him as he waited. Ashlynn swallowed hard, then made her answer, hearing the softly exhaled breath when she uttered the words.

Why had she? Certainly not from fear of his king, though she could hardly have forgotten the power of the silent royal presence just behind them, but rather what Iain had said before: *'Better the devil you know.'* The choice was stark: take him or accept a fate that would likely be much worse. No choice at all. She knew it and so did he. Yet there was more to it than that, as she now admitted. What she resented here was the method not the man. Toward him what she felt was not indifference and she could no longer pretend to herself that it was, and that made everything so much more complicated.

Since there had been no time to provide a ring Iain

improvised with the one he wore on his thumb. It was ludicrously big but served its turn. When the words were all spoken and the ring on her finger he kissed her, a gentle kiss on the mouth which burned none the less and set her pulse racing. Understated and subtle it was underlain with a deeper promise whose implications quickened every fibre of her being.

Then the king moved forward to offer his congratulations, bowing over her hand. Ashlynn lowered her eyes, her face an expressionless mask. Malcolm regarded her keenly for a moment and then looked at Iain.

'You spoke true, Glengarron. Your lady is most fair. Guard her well.'

'I intend to, my liege.'

Iain took her hand then and raised it to his lips. For an instant their eyes met but, as so often, his face gave little away. Did he share the resentment she felt? This marriage had been forced upon him too. Given the choice he would never have entered into this bargain. From the outset he had regarded her as an encumbrance. What possible argument could have persuaded him to agree to this? She lowered her gaze quickly, this time to hide her confusion. Then she handed him back the thumb ring.

'For safe keeping,' she said. 'It would be too easily lost.'

He returned her a wry smile and slipped it back on his hand. 'I promise you a proper wedding ring, lass, as soon as occasion permits.'

They went out to the horses and Iain took leave of his king. As the royal party rode away, he turned back to Ashlynn.

'Come, my wife.'

The use of that title and all it implied sent another wave of heat the length of her body. Not so long ago the notion of a forced match with Burford had filled her with anger and abhorrence. Now a very different husband claimed her. Soon enough he would take her to his bed and make his possession complete. Power-lessness kept her anger very much alive. Yet in the entire chaotic pantheon of emotions at that moment, abhor-rence was conspicuously absent. With an effort she kept her voice level. 'Where are we going?'

'Home—to Glengarron.'

The journey that day was long and cold, but Ashlynn was scarcely aware of physical discomfort. Her thoughts had turned inward, trying to come to terms with what had happened, trying not to contemplate the future too closely. For the most part they rode in silence, the swift pace not being conducive to conversation. However, when they did stop to rest the horses at noon it quickly became apparent that news of the laird's marriage had spread. Dougal took it upon himself to issue each man with a dram of whisky from the keg on the wagon, and proposed the toast to the newly married couple. A loud cheer rent the air.

Iain looked down at his bride and smiled wryly. 'It seems they approve, my lady.'

Ashlynn shot him a swift glance but remained silent, not knowing what to say. In truth the press of grinning faces was a little daunting, though oddly she could see none of their former antipathy now. Rather than show any apprehension she forced herself to an outward display of calm.

'Will ye no kiss the bride, my lord?' called a wag from the crowd.

A roar of approval greeted this, followed by the chant of *'Kiss! Kiss! Kiss!'* Iain handed his cup to Dougal. Then he took Ashlynn in his arms, crushing her against him and bringing his mouth down on hers in a searing embrace. Another roar erupted around them. Ashlynn scarcely heard it, aware only of a rush of warmth deep within, like the sudden rekindling of a flame. The flame leapt and became fire. Unable to help herself she yielded to it, her body melting against him, her mouth opening to his.

In that moment of unexpected surrender he felt his own desire quicken and imagination tantalised, offering another glimpse of something he had thought was lost. If they had been alone… The thought stopped him in his tracks: this was a union undertaken out of duress, not love, and they had an audience besides. Ashlynn only kissed him now because she could do no other. Reluctantly he drew back a little, letting the general noise wash over them, his gaze burning into hers.

'By God, lass,' he murmured, 'you play the game well.'

Her cheeks turned pink, much to the delight of the spectators for though they had not heard the words they thought they could guess the import. She took refuge in their noisy enthusiasm, trying to calm her thumping heart, overwhelmed by the sudden knowledge within it. She darted another glance at Iain but the look in his eyes did nothing to restore a tranquil mind. Did he really think this was some game to her?

It was no small relief when the column mounted up again and set off. The pace was steadier now but the cold no less for that. As they rode, the hills closed in around them, a barren snow-clad waste of rock and heath and dead bracken that vanished into mist above. Ashlynn shifted her weight in the saddle, aching with the chill and the long hours spent on horseback and longing for nothing so much as a warm fire and hot food, wherever they might be found. However, not for anything would she have uttered a word of complaint. These men already regarded her as a liability and, although their manner appeared to have softened a little today, she would not give them any cause to despise her further. Nor would she have them think the less of their chief for wedding a soft Sassenach wench. Pride kept her chin up and her tongue silent but, as the afternoon wore on, the effort became greater.

Iain, riding alongside, saw her pallor with concern and could well understand the cause. The journey was hard enough, never mind all that had gone before. Had it been any other woman he would have expected tears at least by this, but then, he acknowledged, Ashlynn wasn't just any woman. Experience had shown him her courage; he could only guess at the will-power that kept her going when others would have cracked. By rights she should have after all that she had endured of late. Her silence touched him more than any words could have done and seeing her composure now he felt the first stirrings of pride.

The afternoon was wearing on when they came at last to the head of a narrow valley. Seeing the sudden lightening of spirit in the faces of the men nearby, Ashlynn glanced at Iain. Interpreting that look aright he nodded.

'This is Glengarron.'

She should have felt relief to hear those words but now her stomach knotted instead. This was the lion's den, the place from which there was no escape. The cavalcade rode into the misty glen in single file for the way was narrow with trees on one side and the peaty waters of a racing burn on the other. On either side the hills rose into the low cloud and marked their passing with the muffled echo of the horses' hooves. After about half a mile the glen widened out and through the snow the muted outlines of houses were just visible in the distance. However, it was not the houses that held Ashlynn's attention for there, dead ahead, a great granite outcrop thrust up from the ground and, brooding over the whole scene, a fortress that might have grown from the rock itself.

The horsemen made straight for it and then she discerned a huge wooden gate, studded and banded with iron and seeming to lead straight into the hillside. Someone called a cheery greeting which was returned and the gate swung open to reveal a narrow defile between sheer walls of rock. Wide enough to take two horsemen abreast, it wound upwards to another gate. This too swung open and they emerged into a large walled courtyard with various buildings along its sides, all overshadowed by a great tower of wood and stone. Iain glanced at his wife.

'Welcome to Dark Mount, lass.'

Ashlynn said nothing, being temporarily incapable of speech and fighting to control a rising sense of dread. Iain dismounted. Seeing there was nothing else to be done, Ashlynn slid reluctantly from Steorra's saddle. Standing there among the throng of horses and men she

h

felt suddenly very small, and the feeling of isolation and vulnerability increased. Then she became aware that Iain was watching her. Not for a bag of gold would she have displayed the fear that gripped her now and so she lifted her chin and forced herself to meet his gaze. His expression was unreadable.

'Come.'

He guided her towards a great iron-clamped door. The space beyond was subdivided and, as her eyes adjusted to the relative dimness she had an impression of store-rooms and pantries. The smell of food suggested the presence of kitchens. They bore left towards a stout oaken staircase. It led up to the great hall. Glancing round apprehensively she had an impression of a large, stone-walled chamber with high and narrow windows. However, most of the light came from the wall brackets and the candles set on huge circular iron chandeliers. Greasy trestle tables, littered with the stale remains of a meal, ran along three sides of the room. Its wooden floor was begrimed with mud and strewn with old straw whose musty smell mingled with ancient food odours and burning tallow. Shields and weapons adorned the walls along with huge and dusty racks of antlers. Wolf and fox masks snarled from among thick cobwebs. One wall was dominated by a great stone hearth where several big logs blazed, the sole source of comfort in the place.

As Ashlynn surveyed the scene cold dread settled like a lump in her stomach. Was this gloomy lair to be her home from now on? It hardly deserved to be dignified with the word home. Prison seemed more accurate somehow. Unwilling to contemplate it longer she turned away towards the fire.

Though she had spoken no word her expression was more eloquent and Iain frowned. As a stronghold Dark Mount had served him well but, he admitted, it could not pretend to cosiness or comfort. It had lacked a ruling female presence for too long. His mother was the last woman to leave her stamp upon the place, a stamp that time and absence had almost obliterated. He shot a sideways glance at Ashlynn. Her courage was not in doubt, but whether she had the skills to follow in his mother's footsteps remained to be seen. The memory brought back others far more bitter, memories better left buried. To banish them he summoned a servant and rattled off a string of orders. The man hurried off and presently several others could be seen scurrying about. One brought food and hot possets. Others hastened to the stairs carrying brooms and logs and other items less obvious to the casual glance.

'The servants will prepare a chamber, lass. In the meantime come and take some food.'

She followed him to the table and sat in the chair he indicated though in truth nerves had driven her appetite away. Unwilling to let him see it she forced herself to eat some bread and a little salted beef and then drank the posset. Its fragrant spicy warmth put some heart into her. Iain leaned back in his chair, surveying her shrewdly, sensing the tension and the fear beneath that outward calm. The thought recurred that most women in her situation would have gone to pieces by now. The lass had courage all right.

A little later the servant returned to say that the room was prepared. She saw her husband rise and hold out a hand to her. For a second she hesitated but common sense decreed there was no other choice than to go with him. Reluctantly she accompanied him to the stairs. There proved to be another two floors above the hall, variously divided into living quarters. On the topmost of these he stopped before a stout wooden door and, pushing it open, stood aside for her to pass. Beyond it was a moderate-sized room. Its stone walls were stark and free of ornament but the bare floor was clean enough. The sole furnishings were a small table and two chairs and, on the far side, a bed strewn with furs. A fire burned in the hearth but, being only recently lit, had not yet taken the chill off the air or dispelled the faint odour of mustiness and damp. On the table an oil lamp was burning for the window was shuttered fast against the cold. Ashlynn shivered inwardly.

'If you need anything Morag here will attend you,' he said.

The serving woman, buxom in thick homespun, might have been any age between forty and sixty. Her grey eyes regarded Ashlynn with frank curiosity. However, their expression was not unkind and when Ashlynn smiled it was returned. Iain glanced at the servant and jerked his head towards the door.

'Wait outside.'

The woman bobbed a curtsy and withdrew. For a moment husband and wife faced each other. In spite of the chill Ashlynn felt sweat start on her palms for she was keenly aware that the servant's restraining presence was gone and there was a large bed just across the room. Not only that, her husband was a head and shoulders taller than she, weighed roughly eighty pounds more,

and was much too close for comfort. The dark eyes held
a disquieting expression and were focused on her face.
In confusion she looked away. In fact he guessed her
thoughts with shrewd accuracy but just then had no intention of following up his advantage.

'The accommodation is rough and ready at present,'
he observed, 'but no doubt you'll amend it to your liking
in due course.'

Not knowing quite what to say Ashlynn remained
silent.

'Is there anything more you require just now?'

She shook her head. 'Nothing more.'

He moved towards the door. 'Until later then, Ashlynn.'

Weak-kneed with relief she watched the door close
behind him, then sank down on one of the chairs. It took
her a moment or two to recover her self-possession.
She was recalled by Morag's return.

'Do you require anything, my lady?'

'Yes. I would wash after my journey. I would also like
a change of clothes if that can somehow be arranged.'

'I'll see what I can do.'

When Morag had left, Ashlynn took another glance
round the room and shivered, instinctively moving
closer to the fire, seeking some comfort from its
warmth. However, it did little to dispel the sensation of
sick dread that sat like lead in the pit of her stomach.

Some time later the woman returned with a jug of hot
water, soap, towels and a comb. Over her arm she
carried a clean shift and a gown of brown woollen cloth.
With them were woollen stockings and a pair of sturdy
leather shoes.

'These are as near to your size as I could guess, my lady.'

Ashlynn thanked her. Then, as the servant poured water into the basin and laid the towels ready, she unfastened her cloak and tossed it on to the bed before divesting herself of belt and tunic. Since the cold did not encourage her to strip off she contented herself with bathing her hands and face. With Morag's help she combed and braided her hair and then pulled on the clean shift, stockings and gown. The latter was too big but not unduly so, and they contrived to disguise the fact with the aid of a girdle. Ashlynn glanced down at herself, smoothing the skirt with her hand. The cloth was warm and serviceable, the colour practical, but the garments had no pretensions to beauty or elegance. They could hardly have been more different from the ones she had worn hitherto. However, beggars couldn't be choosers. Morag handed her the cloak and she put it on, glad of the additional layer.

'Will there be anything else, my lady?'

'No. I thank you.'

The servant withdrew then and Ashlynn was left alone. Once more her sombre gaze took in the details of the room and for the first time noticed the door, partially concealed by shadow, in the side wall. When she tried the handle it didn't budge. She wondered what lay on the far side—a store room perhaps. It was of no importance and there would be time enough to find out later. In the meantime she needed to get away from this chamber. She let herself out but, instead of retracing her steps along the way she had originally come, set off in the other direction. It brought her at length to another narrow wooden door. This one was unlocked and yielded quite easily when tried. It led out on to a short flight of steps and thence up to a flat roof area at the top of the tower. Dusk was drawing in. In a little while it would be full dark.

The knowledge did nothing to lighten her mood. Wrapping the cloak closer around her Ashlynn moved to the crenellated wall and peered out between the stone merlons, but there was little to be seen save snow and swirling white mist. She recalled what Iain had said about the weather closing in. Soon they would all be its prisoners. She felt as one standing at the edge of the world in some uncharted waste, a place where different rules obtained and where, just out of view, lurked unspecified dangers. It was very cold out on this exposed place and far from an ideal refuge, but she didn't want to return to her chamber and certainly had no intention of going down to that filthy, cheerless hall where there was a better-than-even chance of meeting her husband.

Now that he had intruded on her thoughts again she found him harder to dismiss than she would have liked. He had told her that he had never forced a woman, but she wasn't naïve enough to think that would hold good for marriage too. It was a husband's right to take his wife whenever it pleased him. She knew full well that it would please him. Involuntarily her mind returned to the great fur-strewn bed. How would it be to lie with him, to yield completely to his will? The memory of the hayloft returned with all its startling intimacy: the warmth of his body against hers, his kisses hot along her throat, the touch of his hands on her naked flesh…

Ashlynn forced the thoughts away even as her mind

reiterated the truth. She was not indifferent to him. That was the worst of it. For men the marriage bed was not about emotion, only a necessity for the getting of heirs. For a woman it was different. Where there was any kind of initial attraction, such intimacy would invariably lead to stronger feelings; in this case, feelings that were not reciprocated. Iain had married her at the king's command, but the human heart could not be commanded. She would be the means by which he sired his heirs, nothing more. Her wishes had counted for nothing in the face of the king's will. She was effectively Glengarron's prisoner but, unlike other prisoners of rank, no ransom would ever buy her freedom. She was tied to this man and to this God-forsaken place for good. In any case, even if she did have her freedom, there was nothing to go back to. Whichever way she looked at it the future seemed every bit as bleak as the landscape around.

Just then the subject of her thoughts was checking on the comfort and condition of his injured men. Iain had made it a rule never to leave an injured man behind to die of cold or wounds, or to fall victim to scum like William's mercenaries. A long and bumpy journey in the back of a wagon was painful and undesirable, but not as bad as the alternative, and all the injured had received good tending at Jedburgh. Iain guessed that if they had survived so far they'd likely live to tell the tale. He stood now looking down at the face of the young man on the pallet before him. For all the waxen pallor of cheeks and brow the Saxon was a good-looking youth and well made too.

'How is he?'

The old woman, who had been examining her patient carefully glanced up for a moment, regarding the laird with cool grey eyes.

'He's lucky to be alive with those wounds and such a bad knock on the head withal. 'Tis small wonder he has a fever.'

'Will he pull through it?'

'He's young, and clearly of a strong constitution or he'd not have lived thus long. God willing, he may yet survive.'

'Tend him well.'

'Depend on it, my lord.'

He nodded. If anyone was going to save the youth it was she. None in Glengarron knew more about healing than Meg. He just had to hope his faith in her would be justified now as it had been so many times before. He continued his round of the injured, stopping here and there to have a quiet word or to put a reassuring hand on a shoulder.

By the time he finished it was dark and the courtyard covered in glittering rime. In a day or two the snow would come in earnest. They had returned to Glengarron just in time. Fitzurse was lost to him for the moment, but there were compensations: a less arduous regime, hot food, roaring fires and a comfortable bed.

That last turned his thoughts in another direction and he sighed. The immediate future was hardly calculated to fill him with unalloyed delight. His new bride was angry and resentful and, behind that brave front she wore, more than a little afraid. He could well understand the reason for it. However, he was her protector now whether she liked it or not. God knew she needed one.

As he recalled the bruises on her face his anger resurfaced. He had no time for the kind of brutality that entailed. No man worthy of the name indulged his strength in such a way against a woman. If nothing else their marriage had put an end to that. No man would ever touch her again, save he.

He had arranged for them to dine alone together in a private chamber prepared for the purpose. It was much warmer than the hall and permitted of greater intimacy. Besides, he knew that his wife wasn't ready to run the public gauntlet just yet and there would be time enough to let the inhabitants of Glengarron see their new lady. Stories would be circulating like wildfire as it was for many of his men had wives and families all too eager for the latest gossip, and the laird's unexpected marriage was the juiciest morsel in years.

For a while he warmed himself by the fire in the hall holding his hands to the blaze. The light shone on the gold thumb ring, giving the metal a reddish lustre: the colour of passion. He grimaced. A forced match was hardly likely to be the precursor to passion and yet twice, briefly, there had been a spark between them. For a moment the memory of the hayloft returned to tease him. He could not deny the attraction he had felt. Could the spark be rekindled? In a little while he would know the answer.

It had been in Ashlynn's mind to refuse when a manservant came to announce that the evening meal was served. However, a moment's reflection was sufficient to let her see the lack of wisdom in this, for though she had only known him a short time it was long enough to be sure that Iain would fetch her himself if she denied him her presence. Accordingly she followed the servant obediently, expecting that he would lead her to the hall. Instead she found herself in the chamber next to her own. Her husband was waiting for her.

For the space of several heartbeats they faced each other. Ashlynn saw that he had changed his clothes and now wore dark hose and a tunic of crimson wool, belted at the waist and richly embroidered at neck and sleeves, the colour a perfect foil for his dark hair and eyes. Those eyes were now fixed on her, and she was forcibly reminded of the shortcomings of her current attire. However, he seemed to find nothing amiss for he smiled faintly and bowed low over her hand.

'Come and sit down, Ashlynn.'

In fact, Iain had temporarily forgotten that his wife had no other garments besides the borrowed ones she had been wearing. He guessed that Morag had attempted to remedy the matter for the brown woollen gown was clearly a servant's garb. It was also too big and tended to conceal her figure rather than emphasise it. He eyed it with quiet disfavour, realising it was a matter he was going to have to address in due course.

Unable to follow his thought, she felt herself redden, feeling unwontedly self-conscious. The recollection of her bruised cheek and cut lip only intensified the feeling. Rarely had she appeared to such disadvantage and certainly never before a man. Not just any man either. She was more than ever aware of that handsome charismatic presence and it made her feel awkward. He on the other hand seemed quite at ease and led her now to the table.

Although she still had little appetite she was glad of

the business of dining for it kept him at a safe distance. She had no real idea of what she ate that evening but she took her time, dreading the moment when the meal would be over and the atmosphere of cosiness would become intimacy. Covertly she looked around at the appointments of the chamber. It was comfortable enough but practical too, a man's room. She could see a doorway leading off it and guessed with a feeling of mounting dread that beyond it lay his bedchamber. It was then she realised where the locked door in her own room led to.

Iain settled himself back in his chair, his hand toying with his wine goblet. He had taken several of these with the meal but the wine appeared to have touched him not at all. He surveyed her keenly now, the dark eyes shrewd. Ashlynn bridled instantly.

'Must you stare at me like that?' she asked.

'Does it displease you then that a man should look at you?'

To answer yes or no would have been equally ridiculous and she said nothing.

'Besides,' he continued, 'I know it isn't the first time. You told me yourself that you'd had admirers.'

Admirers yes, she thought, but none with the power to unsettle her so thoroughly. Besides, back then she had always been the one in control of the situation.

'I would wager there were many. Yet you never met one who pleased you?'

'No.' She paused and threw him a speaking look. 'I still haven't.'

The dark eyes gleamed. 'That's better. I feared for a moment that you'd lost the fighting spirit.'

'If you did you were much mistaken.'

The challenge was there and unequivocal too. In spite of himself his enjoyment grew. 'I'm glad to hear it, truly. I once thought that a marriage of convenience was like to be dull. Now I am reassured that it will not be.'

Ashlynn listened in disbelief and then returned a faint ironic smile. 'Dull? With you?'

'You flatter me, lass.'

'Not in the least.'

'Of course not,' he conceded. 'I should have known better.'

'Do you want flattery?'

'No, but I doubt you'd deal in it anyway. Your tongue is too sharp for that, and backed up at need with tooth and claw.'

The allusion brought a deeper colour to her cheeks. 'I regret that I can offer you no dowry in mitigation of these faults.'

'I can live with that,' he replied.

'Perhaps you should have chosen a rich wife while you had the chance.'

'I would not have married again, any more than you would have taken a husband.'

For a moment Ashlynn was very still, her eyes fixed on his face. 'This marriage is not your first?'

Iain met and held her gaze. He didn't know why he had said it. It had not been his intention but perhaps it was just as well. Better she should learn it from him than servants' gossip.

'No, it isn't. However, my first wife died some years ago.'

'I'm sorry.' She hesitated but couldn't help herself. 'What was her name?'

His fingers tightened round the cup. 'Eloise.'

'Eloise? That is French is it not?'

'That's right.'

'How came you to meet and wed a Frenchwoman?'

'I spent six years in France completing my military training.'

'I see.' Ashlynn digested this in silence and summoned all her courage to ask the next question. 'Was it a love match?'

'Aye,' he replied, 'it was. But, as I told you, it was long ago.'

Her heart sank. His words might relegate his former wife to the past but he had not been able to disguise the feelings that lay beneath. Clearly the memories were powerful still. The knowledge caused a strange pang. Eloise must have been quite something. *I would not have married again...*

'And now the king has forced you to take me.'

The bleakness in her tone caused the dark gaze to soften a little. 'We neither of us had any choice, lass.' He paused. 'Nor can we change the past.'

For a moment she saw Heslingfield in flames and forced the image back. With an effort she managed to keep her voice level. 'As you say.'

'Your life is here now, Ashlynn. It may not have been the one you would have chosen but I promise you it will be safe.'

She watched him rise from his chair and, with thumping heart, followed suit. He halted a few feet away.

'So what now, my lady?' He glanced over his shoulder

at the door she had noticed earlier. 'Yonder lies my bed-chamber. If it pleases you to join me, I would be most happy and most honoured. If not, over there is the way out.'

Her surprise was total and for a moment or two she could only stare at him, torn between reluctance and something harder to identify. He saw her hesitation and moved in closer. She felt the warmth of his hands on her shoulders. She knew she should pull away now while she could and despised her own weakness for not doing so. His arms slid round her shoulders and waist, drawing her against him. His mouth closed over hers. A familiar flicker of warmth ignited deep within, her pulses racing for that seductive nearness, for the scent and the taste of him. Sensing that reawakening fire, he tightened his hold and the kiss grew more intimate, more knowing, the kiss of a man completely familiar with women and completely confident of his power. Ashlynn tensed. The wife he loved was dead. This meant nothing to him beyond the consummation of a bargain. She could not risk her heart in such an enterprise for her heart was all she had left. That knowledge increased the sense of inner desolation and she shivered.

Iain felt that tremor and drew back a little, looking down into her face. In it he saw reluctance and his eyes narrowed a little. Almost immediately she found herself free.

'You need have no fear that I'll force more on you than my name, Ashlynn,' he said. 'I'll have you willing or not at all.'

'Then you don't mean to…you won't—' She broke off, floundering.

'No, I don't mean to. There's time enough, lass.'

The words, delivered with such quiet assurance, served only to reinforce the truth. He did have time, but underneath that statement was a colder reality. While he had sufficient honour not to force her, the fact that he chose not to prosecute his right was further indication of how deeply he resented this marriage. How could this compare to what had gone before? How far she must fall short in his eyes—an unwilling bride and an unattractive one to boot! Ashlynn lifted her chin and gathered about her what dignity she could muster.

'I think time will make little difference,' she replied, 'since we are together only at the king's command, not personal inclination.'

The barb went deeper than anticipated but his tone remained calm. 'As you say, and yet the situation carries its own inevitability.'

'You may believe that, but it's not a view I share.'

'Maybe not, but if you think about it you'll see that I'm right.'

'I have no wish to think about you at all.'

'None the less, you will abide here from now on and you will see me every day of your life whether you want to or not. In the meantime you may return to your room if you will.'

Ashlynn's jaw tightened as she clamped the lid on anger. 'Gladly, my lord.' She moved towards the outer door and paused a moment. 'I bid you a goodnight.'

Taken by surprise Iain could only watch her retreating figure until the door closed behind her. Then he sighed and turned away toward the hearth, staring down into the flames, his fist clenched above the lintel.

Ashlynn regained the relative sanctuary of her own

room. Now that she was alone, anger quickly cooled leaving her feeling only weary and disconsolate. She should not have let him provoke her but somehow she had been unable to help herself. He was so confoundedly arrogant! Her response had been as much a defensive reflex as anything. Of all the possible beginnings to marriage this surely must rank as one of the most disastrous.

She shivered. In her absence the fire had burned down in the hearth and the room was growing chill for the servants had understandably assumed she would be spending the night elsewhere. Stripping to her chemise she climbed quickly into bed, burrowing under the furs for warmth. Lying there alone in the darkness she could hear the wind against the shutters, a lonely, desolate sound—as desolate as her own heart. In spite of fatigue it was a long time before sleep eventually claimed her.

Chapter Six

When she awoke next day it was to see bars of grey light through the shutters. By their pale illumination the details of the strange room came slowly into focus and with them the recollection of her predicament. She shivered. Raising herself on one elbow she glanced across at the hearth but the fire was reduced to a heap of ash. The room was freezing now.

Ashlynn slipped from the bed and struggled into her clothes as fast as possible. Then she splashed water on her face and dragged a comb through her hair. She had just finished when Morag appeared with a platter of food which she set down on the table. Her glance went to the bed across the room and though she made no comment her expression was curious. However, nothing could have been more courteous than her tone.

'Lord Iain sends his compliments, my lady, and says he will attend you presently.'

Ashlynn felt her heart sink. Now what? She had no desire to see him at all but in truth no way to prevent it.

'Very well. In the meantime, please remake the fire and see that it remains lit. This room is like a tomb. It will take several days to take the chill off the air.'

As Morag bustled about Ashlynn turned her attention to the food, wondering how to comport herself in the forthcoming interview. Though neither of them had sought it they were both trapped in this marriage. Anger and resentment were pointless now. Somehow this must be faced. Besides, she knew from experience that it was worse than useless to get angry with him, and she had need of every ounce of composure she could summon.

However, when Iain appeared a short time later he made no allusion to what had passed before. Nor did he comment on her pallor or the shadows beneath her eyes even though he missed none of it. In truth it touched him more than he expected. He also seemed to recall that his words last evening had scarcely been calculated to win her over. With hindsight they seemed at best to suggest indifference, something he had not intended at all. Ashlynn's wit was quick and sharp and she was becoming adept at finding the chinks in his armour. Even so, he shouldn't have retaliated in that way. Adopting a rather gentler tone he bade her a good morning.

'If you wish it, Ashlynn, I will show you Dark Mount. It is your home now and you should become acquainted with it.'

She forced back the immediate urge to refuse, acknowledging the truth of his words. This was her home now, whether she wanted it or not. It would have been foolish to reject the offer. In any case curiosity overrode apprehension.

She nodded acquiescence. 'As you wish.'

'Come then, lass.'

They spent the next hour on a leisurely tour. Dark Mount was bigger than she had first thought and complete with storehouses, stables, smithy and workshops. From time to time they stopped so that he could introduce her to some of his people. She made a point too of remembering names and speaking to those whom she encountered, if only briefly. It was too soon to know if she would ever be fully accepted here but clearly it would be as well to get off on the right foot.

She was also conscious of having angered his men by her earlier misguided attempt to escape en route to Jedburgh. It had been foolish in the extreme and she greatly regretted the matter now. No doubt the story had been related round many firesides already. She would not cause his people to hold an even poorer opinion of her behaviour. They were courteous enough and eyed her with frank curiosity, but she knew they were reserving judgement until they should know her better. She could not find it in herself to blame them. Perhaps in their place she'd have done the same. In the meantime she took care to behave to everyone with becoming courtesy and a pleasant word or smile at least. Iain, observing, said nothing, but her manner towards his people pleased him and he saw the guarded approval in their eyes.

Although she was quiet at first Ashlynn began to relax a little as time went on, and, as they walked and explored, he realised he had an attentive companion. She asked intelligent questions and listened to the answers.

She was quick of apprehension and he had but to tell her something once for her to remember it. It reaffirmed his view that the pretty face concealed a sharp mind.

'It is a thriving community,' she said when at length they paused on the threshold of the barn. 'You seem to have everything here you are likely to need.'

'Almost,' he agreed, 'but 'tis as well to be prepared for every eventuality.'

'And are you?'

'Mostly.'

She looked around, her comprehensive gaze taking in the neat stacks of sacks and barrels, the harness and coiled ropes. Then, seeing the items in the far corner, she raised an eyebrow.

'Sledges?'

'Very useful for transporting supplies in the snow.'

'Ah, yes, of course.'

He smiled faintly. 'I try not to be caught napping.'

'I have no doubt of that. Has Dark Mount ever come under attack?'

'Aye, in the past. But no enemy has ever prevailed.'

'Do you have enemies?'

'Few living, and only one of any consequence.'

'Fitzurse,' she replied.

'Aye, he. And one day I'll find him.'

The words had been spoken casually enough but a great deal more lay behind. However, remembering his earlier response Ashlynn didn't dare to question him further. He was not a man to cross lightly. His earlier treatment of her had demonstrated as much, though with hindsight it had also shown considerable restraint. While he was not given to fits of fury she knew instinctively that his anger once roused would be doubly dangerous. Throwing a covert glance at her husband now it was hard to imagine the battle rage on that calm face, and yet she knew it concealed passions that ran deep: a passion for war and a passion for revenge. The ghosts of the past haunted the living. Recalling that snowy field littered with corpses she shivered inwardly.

That evening she ventured down to the hall, knowing that the intimate arrangement of the previous evening would not be repeated. Part of her was glad and another part daunted. From what she had seen of the place, it was clear that dining in the hall was unlikely to be a comfortable experience. Besides, it was a masculine domain and she had not been bidden there. Iain had issued no positive invitation to join him, nor had he said that she should not. Their encounter earlier had been amicable enough but would he welcome her presence in an all-male preserve? If he rejected her how would she deal with the humiliation? For some time she hesitated. Then summoning all her courage she went down.

When she arrived Iain was already there along with many of his men. Ashlynn paused in the doorway surveying the scene, her heart beating a little faster, conscious of being the only woman present. On the other hand was she not the lady of the house now? At that recollection her chin lifted and she crossed the floor to join her husband.

As the men became aware of her presence their conversation died and all eyes followed her progress. Under their keen regard her discomfort increased. Iain looked round and for a moment he seemed surprised to see her there. Her heartbeat accelerated. Was he annoyed? Would he see this as an intrusion and send her away?

However, it seemed that was not his intent. He rose and taking her hand, conducted her to the chair next to his. She sank into it thankfully. Around them the conversation started up again.

'This is an unexpected honour,' he said.

She inclined her head in acknowledgement while he gestured to a servant to fill her cup.

'I thought you might prefer your room.'

'Hardly,' she replied.

Recalling the somewhat austere nature of that chamber he winced inwardly.

'In any case,' she went on, 'is it not fitting that we should dine together?'

'Aye, I suppose it is.'

Ashlynn took a sip of wine, very much alive to that steady regard. What was he thinking when he looked at her? Was he remembering that other marriage, the one he had entered into for love? At least he had not humiliated her before his men and that was something. Iain made no further remark on the matter and then the food arrived, diverting his attention and apparently obviating the need for conversation. Taking her cue from him she addressed herself to the meal.

The other men ignored her for the most part, though she was aware that one or two covert glances came her way. Ashlynn looked ruefully at her humble makeshift attire. It was hardly the dress of a noblewoman. However, by accepting her presence here this evening and seating her beside him, Iain had tacitly established her position. She was not Eloise but she was his lady now and they would accept her as such. It was a small step but a significant one. Her back straightened. She might not look the part but she could at least act it.

It was not until they had finished eating that Iain turned his attention towards her again. She had begun to wonder if he had forgotten about her. Being used to conversation and friendly banter at table she found this silence awkward and a little unnerving. When he picked up the wine flagon and gestured to her cup she nodded, conscious of surprise. He wasn't dismissing her just yet then. Perhaps they might talk a little. Their earlier conversations had whetted her curiosity and so much about this man was still a mystery. Summoning her courage again she put a toe in the water.

'How long have you been Laird of Glengarron?'

'Five years.'

'I thought it longer, coinciding with your return from France.'

'I did not go back to Glengarron then.' He paused. 'I hired out my sword instead.'

'But what of your wife? Was she not with you?'

'Eloise died in France. I returned alone.'

Ashlynn heard the edge in his voice. Most like his wife had died in childbed or from fever. They were common enough occurrences after all. However, she sensed that this was not the time to delve further and dropped the subject, fearing to alienate him. Instead she shifted the focus of the discussion. 'You hired out your sword to the king?'

'Aye, Malcolm was ever one for recruiting able fighters and there was plenty to be done in his service,' he went on. 'It kept me occupied, until my father's last illness. Then there was no choice but to return.'

'You speak as though you were reluctant to do so.'

'I was. My father and I were never close and, after my mother's death, things got much worse. She had always smoothed things over between us but when she was gone...' He made a vague gesture with his hand. 'Dark Mount was not a congenial place to be. I was only too glad to get away in the end.'

Though the words were quietly spoken Ashlynn heard the bitter note beneath. Heard it and identified with it in part.

'Were you reconciled at last?'

'No. He did not favour my support of Malcolm and it deepened the estrangement between us. I was with him at the end but by then he was too ill to speak. Yet I sensed he wanted to.'

'That is something at least. Would that I might say the same.'

He regarded her curiously. 'You quarrelled with your father?'

'Not in that way.'

Iain waited, suddenly wanting to know.

Ashlynn smiled sadly. 'My mother caught a fatal fever shortly after I was born. Her death was a terrible blow to him.'

'I can understand that, but not that he should blame you for it.'

'He tried hard not to, but never quite succeeded in hiding his thoughts. It was always there between us.' She sighed. 'I think it was why he wanted me to marry Ath—' She broke off, conscious of having almost said too much. 'Wanted me to marry,' she amended. 'In that way I'd be out of his sight for good.'

He noted the correction and wondered what she had been going to say. However, he knew better than to push her. A confidence could not be forced. He didn't know why he had spoken to her of his father. It hadn't been his intention, but somehow the words had come out anyway. Perhaps it was no bad thing. Certainly the tension of the previous evening was conspicuous by its absence.

Ashlynn retired a little later leaving the men to drink. Having returned to her room she undressed, laying her garments carefully aside. Once again their ugliness impressed itself on her mind. It was not a problem that would be easily solved since she had no money to buy cloth and thread, even if she knew where these things might be procured locally. The thought of asking Iain for money was anathema. Self-respect forbade it. Clearly he saw nothing amiss with the present arrangement and if he did not, she would not raise the subject. If anyone else found it a matter for remark, that was just too bad. Fine clothes were only a form of vanity when all was said and done, and yet she missed them all the same. They were something else she had taken for granted, like looking attractive. It shouldn't matter, but somehow it did, especially now. Iain's face drifted into her mind. Even if she were appropriately gowned would it make any difference there? Would he ever look at her in the way he had once looked on Eloise? Would she ever be able to influence his thoughts? Somehow she couldn't see it happening any time soon. The knowledge of her powerlessness was oddly lowering. With a sigh she climbed into bed and burrowed under the furs for warmth.

However, sleep would not come and for a long time she lay awake listening to the sound of the wind in the chimney. She shivered, thinking how different it was from her chamber at Heslingfield. Thoughts of home revived the faces of her family and suddenly a lump formed in her throat. The last time she felt like this she had been in a hayloft and Iain had comforted her. The memory of his arms around her then only served to enhance her loneliness now. She tried to check it, to force the lump back again but it resisted every attempt and grew bigger, swelling in size until it threatened to choke her. Turning her face into the pelts she began to sob as though her heart would break.

Iain left his men carousing and made his way up the stairs. Truth to tell he was in no mood to drink for his mind was elsewhere. Ashlynn's appearance at table that evening had served as a sharp reminder that his life had changed. While he had no quarrel with her presence, he had not lied when he had said it was unexpected—unexpected and oddly impressive in its quiet dignity. It could not have been easy for her. Nor could it be easy adjusting to her new life at Dark Mount. Though she never spoke of it he sensed her homesickness. Worse, it was something that he could do nothing to change. Heslingfield was gone for good. Only one small hope remained in that direction.

Having reached his room he took himself off to his bedchamber. He was in the process of undressing when he caught a faint sound from the next room. His brows drew together and he stepped closer to the connecting door, listening intently. The sound of sobbing was unmistakeable, great heart-wrenching sobs that pierced him to the core. For a moment he remained where he was, torn by indecision. His hand went to the handle, hovered briefly, then slowly withdrew. He retreated and, with a sigh, continued undressing.

For a long time after that he lay awake in the darkness, listening to the sounds from the other side of the door. He wanted to go to her and speak what words of comfort he could, but knew he must not. Not yet. This outpouring of grief was long overdue. In its shuddering sobs he heard all the fear and pain and loss that she had kept hidden behind the brave mask she showed to the world. He always knew it must erupt at some time, but he had not anticipated its depth and force. Nor could he ever have guessed how much it would grieve him to hear it.

Ashlynn woke late feeling heavy-headed, her eyelids swollen and pink-rimmed. Reluctantly she slipped from the bed and struggled into her clothes. Then she bathed her eyes in cold water. She had just finished when Morag appeared with a platter of food. She set it down on the table. Her glance went briefly to Ashlynn's face and her expression registered concern.

'Are you quite well, my lady?'

'A slight headache,' Ashlynn replied. 'I slept ill last night.'

'Can I fetch you anything?'

'No, thank you. I shall be recovered soon enough.'

Morag seemed not entirely convinced but did not pursue it. When the servant had gone Ashlynn turned her attention to the food but, after a mouthful, abandoned the attempt. Her appetite had gone and everything tasted like ashes. Pushing it away she went to the hearth and stood for a time, staring down into the flames.

Eventually her attention was drawn by a knock on the door. She took a deep breath, mentally composing herself.

'Come in.'

Iain opened the door and paused on the threshold. For a moment he surveyed her in silence, but if he noticed anything amiss he did not remark on it.

'Good morrow, Ashlynn.'

She returned the greeting and waited, part of her wishing he would go and leave her alone and part curious as to why he was there. Then he stepped into the room.

'I would like you to join me, lass. There is something I would show you.'

'What is it?'

'You'll see.'

It was on the tip of her tongue to refuse and he saw it.

'Please,' he said.

'Is it a mystery then?'

'If you come with me, all will be made clear.'

She hesitated another moment and then rose to join him. To her surprise he led her back to the staircase and down to the next floor. After following the passageway for a little space, he stopped outside one of the chambers. Ashlynn eyed him quizzically and waited, wondering what it meant. He vouchsafed no explanation but merely opened the door and stood back to let her enter.

The room was smaller than hers and even more sparsely furnished, but it was clean and warm with a cheerful fire burning in the hearth. On the far side an old woman was sitting at the edge of a bed. She looked up on hearing the visitors arrive and inclined her head in acknowledgement of their presence. Iain spoke a few words in Gaelic to which the woman responded briefly. However, Ashlynn paid no heed. Her attention had moved on to the bed which was occupied, apparently by one of the injured men who had been brought back to Dark Mount following the battle with the Normans. Then she became aware that her husband was speaking, and in English this time.

'How is the patient today, Meg?'

'A little better, my lord. Conscious anyway, though still very weak.'

Ashlynn looked from one to the other in puzzlement but Iain's hand was under her elbow, drawing her further into the room. When they reached the bedside she looked down at the injured man lying there. He was very pale and his face was stubbled with many days' growth of beard, the same tawny shade as the hair visible beneath the bandage. The eyes regarding her now were deep blue and staring as though they had seen an apparition. For a moment she stood transfixed and the colour drained from her face.

'Ban?'

'Ashlynn?' The voice was weak but familiar for all that. 'Is it really you?'

'Ban!' Then she was beside him, her trembling hands brushing his face, his breast, his hands. All were real and warm. 'I thought you were dead. I thought I'd never see you again in this world.'

'I almost was dead. Fortunately the Normans thought so otherwise they'd have finished me off.'

Her incredulous gaze took in the bandages swathing his ribs and shoulder and the other round his head. For a moment she said nothing, and then suddenly burst into tears. The old woman put a comforting hand on her arm.

'It's been a shock for ye, lass. But the right sort of shock, I ken.'

Ashlynn was beyond speech and only sobbed the more.

'You're supposed to be glad,' said Ban. 'Now you're like to drown me and finish what the Normans started.'

It drew a ragged laugh and she tried to dash away the tears with her hand. With the other she was holding one of his tightly as though, if she did not, he might vanish before her eyes. He eyed her critically a moment and then looked up at the man beside her.

'I think I have you to thank for my life.'

'Others must take the credit for that.'

'May I know who you are and how my sister comes to be here?'

'I am Iain MacAlpin of Glengarron.' As he spoke the name he saw instant recognition in the young man's face. 'I met your sister by chance when she was fleeing from the Normans. She has since done me the honour of becoming my wife.'

'Your wife?' Ban stared at him thunderstruck for a moment before his gaze went swiftly to his sister's face. For the first time he noticed the fading bruises there and his eyes narrowed. 'Ashlynn, he hasn't hurt you?'

'No, certainly not!' The words came out more forcefully than she'd intended but she would not have Ban under any kind of misapprehension on that point. 'These came courtesy of a certain Norman lord.'

'But how came you to be married? And to *him* of all men?'

She saw the anxiety in his face and the pain around his eyes. 'It's a long story, Ban, and it will keep for now.'

At this point Meg intervened. 'Aye, it will. You'll have time enough to catch up on all your news. Meantime, the laddie needs rest if he's to recover his strength.'

It was a hint and Ashlynn made to rise but Ban detained her. 'You'll come back?'

'Of course, I'll come back.' She smiled. 'Do you think I'd leave you so soon?'

Only then did he release her hand. Reluctantly and with several backward looks she allowed herself to be led away. However, once the door closed behind them Ashlynn turned to face Iain, her face pale with contained emotion.

'All this time you knew he was alive and yet you said nothing.' Her voice caught on a sob. 'How could you do that?'

'Ashlynn, I…'

'I thought everyone I'd ever loved was dead and you let me go on thinking it when a word from you would have made all the difference.'

'It wasn't like that, I swear it.'

'What kind of man are you, Iain, that you could even consider such a deed?'

'Will you at least let me speak before you judge me?'

Ashlynn bit her lip. He looked at her pale tear-stained face and waited. Then at length she nodded.

'Very well. Say what you want to say.'

'My men and I passed through Heslingfield not long after the Normans had left.' Seeing her expression he nodded. 'It was on our way north. Fergus and Dougal found your brother among the injured. He was unconscious but just breathing. We had no idea who he was, only that he was nigh unto death and certainly not one of the Normans. We tended him as best we could and put him in the wagon. I didn't put two and two together until I heard you speak of your brother. Even then I said nothing because I thought the lad was going to die, and you had already lost him once. I didn't want you to have to go through it again. You had already been through so much.' He paused. 'If I was wrong, I'm sorry. Please believe that, if you believe nothing else.'

For a long moment she said nothing, her eyes missing no detail of his expression. It spoke of remorse and sincerity. He saw her draw in a long shuddering breath.

'I believe you did what you thought was best,' she said at last, 'but it was a decision you had no right to make.' The blue eyes filled with tears anew.

'If I've hurt you, lass, I'm truly sorry for it.'

The tone also sounded sincere and she wanted to believe that it really was but the tears spilled over anyway. Completely overwrought she had no way to stop them. Then she felt his arms around her holding her close.

'Shh, lass, don't cry. It's all right.'

Suddenly he felt all the tension go out of her but her body shook as she wept on his shoulder. For some time they remained thus while he let her have her cry out. Eventually the tears subsided a little and she lifted her head to find him regarding her with deep concern.

'I've been a fool. Forgive me, Ashlynn.'

Even as he spoke he realised that fool was an understatement; he should have listened to his inner doubts and told her long since. By seeking to spare her pain he had caused her far more. What he had never anticipated was how much her tears would hurt him.

She drew in another shaky breath, searching for the words, but emotion locked her voice in her throat as reaction set in. Her head swam. A strong arm caught her by the waist as she slumped, and another went under her knees, lifting her effortlessly. Then he carried her back upstairs and set her down gently in a chair by the fire. Frowning to see her pallor he put his own cloak around her and then poured some spiced wine, heating it with an iron from the fire, before handing her the cup.

'Drink this.'

Obediently she took it. He watched her sip the hot liquid and with no small relief saw some of the colour return to her cheeks.

'That's better.' Satisfied that she was recovering a little, he poured some wine for himself and pulled up a chair beside her.

Becoming properly aware of her surroundings for the first time Ashlynn realised with a start that they were in his room, the chamber where they had dined together on their first evening at Dark Mount. It aroused some mixed feelings. Iain, watching her closely, guessed at it. Her nerves were raw enough already before this morning's nerve-shattering discovery.

'I'd hoped to cheer you with the news but I see now the shock was too sudden. I should have prepared you for it first,' he said.

'It was a shock,' she agreed, 'but, as Meg said, the right kind at least. It was just a little overwhelming coming so soon after…after everything else.'

Iain's jaw tightened, thinking that the 'everything else' to which she referred had been a fearful load for anyone to bear, let alone a fragile girl.

'I had no wish to be the cause of further tears in you, Ashlynn.'

'I know that now. It was just the discovery that I hadn't lost everyone after all.' She paused. 'Ban and I were always close. He is only a year older than I am.'

'He has the look of you too.'

'The hair and the eyes,' she agreed. 'A family trait.'

'He's a good-looking youth, and a brave one I'm thinking.'

'He was always thus. Nothing would ever stop Ban when he had it in mind to do something, no matter how reckless or how dangerous.'

'And you were right beside him or I miss my guess.'

It drew a faint smile and he saw the blue eyes soften as she looked into the fire. He wondered what she was remembering. There was so much he wanted to know but still he would not try and force her confidence. She was wary of him and with good reason. Accordingly he kept silent and waited.

'We had so many adventures as children, often to our father's grave displeasure. It didn't stop us though. The risk seemed worth the thrashing somehow. We had our share of those for though our father was not a cruel man he was strict. There were limits to what he would tolerate.'

'And you pushed those limits.'

'Often. And many times we got away with it. My father said I was a hoyden and that I needed—' She broke off and her cheeks reddened a little.

'Needed what?'

Ashlynn shook her head.

He wondered what she had been about to say but let it go, being unwilling to stop her in this expansive mood. He poured more wine into her cup.

She drank it down and felt its pleasing warmth spread through her. Once she glanced covertly at the man beside her for she recalled all too well what her father had once said in a fit of exasperation: *'You need breaking to bridle, my girl, and somewhere is the man to do it. You need a husband and one with a firm hand too.'* Would he be amused to know that the prediction had come true, in part at least? Perhaps so, but never would he have dreamed to see her wed to the Laird of Glengarron.

'My father and older brother fought at Hastings,' she went on. 'When the battle was lost they managed to escape and return home. Both my brothers dreamed that one day the Norman tyrant would be overthrown but my father called it a foolish dream. He said they were there to stay. He would not permit Ethelred or Ban to have any part in the rising against de Comyn's men.' She paused. 'Perhaps he should have. At least then Heslingfield would have burned for a reason.'

Iain caught the note of unwonted bitterness in her voice but he could not blame her.

'Innocence or guilt matter not to the Normans,' he replied. 'What happened at Heslingfield is being repeated all across the land 'twixt York and Durham. The Conqueror means to crush Northumbria into the dust.'

'To what end? So that he can be king of a graveyard?'

'To make it absolutely clear that he will suffer no challenge to his power or to his authority.'

'It serves but to make him a more hated tyrant.'

'Hated, aye. But feared more.'

'Must a man be feared in order to govern?'

'Aye, he must, but he has no need of the kind of brutality the Normans rejoice in.'

Ashlynn fell into reflective silence. He saw that she had stopped shaking now and the warmth of the fire and the drink had made her more relaxed. The fur cloak had slid back off her shoulders revealing the mane of tawny hair beneath. In the light of the fire it was shot with red and took on a resinous sheen that served to enhance its beauty. Seeing it, Iain found himself wanting to touch it, to run his fingers through it. He wanted to put his arms around her, to hold her close and kiss away her pain. However, he did none of those things. A fragile bond was being established in this room and he would do nothing to destroy it.

She looked up and surveyed him with curiosity. 'Do your men fear you?'

'They have nothing to fear from me.'

'But they do not cross you.'

'That is why they have nothing to fear.'

It drew a smile from her. 'And those men who do cross you?'

'Only do it once.'

The words were lightly spoken but their import was not and she shivered inwardly. However, it was not totally due to fear. It was a feeling akin to one she had known before, when she and Ban were about to embark on another reckless adventure. It was not totally divorced from apprehension but underlying it was something else, something concerned with excitement and danger and the allure of the forbidden. Regarding him now, it occurred to her that the face she had earlier considered merely arresting was very much more than that, like the dark eyes burning into hers now. The expression there was familiar and disturbing. Shaken by the direction of her thoughts Ashlynn decided it was the wine talking and sought safer ground.

'When can I see Ban again?'

'You will see him tomorrow. As he grows stronger you will be able to visit him for longer periods.'

'How long was he unconscious?'

'Several days. Then he was delirious with fever. For a while even Meg thought he might not live.'

Ashlynn felt only relief and thankfulness. She had been hurt by his failure to tell her but that had been a misjudgement on his part, not done out of malice. She saw that now. In the immediate shock after finding Ban alive she had been overwrought and that, on top of the existing concerns, had caused her to overreact. The knowledge brought a sharp twinge of guilt. The reality was that he had given her back her brother, an unlooked-for gift of inestimable price.

'I did not thank you for saving Ban but I do so now, and unreservedly.'

The tone was gentle and tender, different from any she had used hitherto, and the look that accompanied it likewise. It was also sincere, a realisation that warmed his blood more thoroughly than the wine. With an effort he controlled it.

'You should rather thank Fergus and Dougal. 'Twas they who found him.'

'But I think it was you who made it a rule never to

leave injured men behind,' she replied. 'And you who had him brought here and tended. Were it not so he would never have survived.'

'I'm right glad he has, lass.'

'You have shown him much kindness. More than I could ever have supposed.'

'You find it hard to believe then that simple kindness exists among the Scottish savages?'

She reddened a little. 'The tales about you paint a different picture.'

'Ah, and which particular tales would they be?'

'Tales of murder and kidnap, of rape and theft.'

'It is true I have killed many men but they had just as much chance of survival as I did. Every warrior knows the realities of combat,' he replied. 'I have kidnapped, but 'twas a man as it happened. His father tried to renege on a business agreement and I had to find another means to get what I was owed. I have known different women but never raped one. As to the rest I confess it freely, but I have only ever taken from those who had plenty to give.'

'I'm glad to learn that you live by such a strong moral code.'

'I live by a different code from the one you may be used to, lass, but it is not entirely without honour.'

'No, I think it is not.' She stood on tiptoe and kissed his cheek. 'And I thank you from the bottom of my heart for saving Ban.'

The dark eyes met and held her own. 'No thanks are necessary and I do not want your gratitude, Ashlynn. If you would kiss me let it be for myself.'

Chapter Seven

In the days that followed Ashlynn spent as much time as she could with Ban, though mindful not to tire him. He was still very weak but the terrifying pallor was gone and a healthier colour returned to his cheeks. Moreover, he could take nourishment now and, by the end of a week, was propped up on cushions and looking about him with interest. In the first days of their reunion they had not talked much, being content to know merely that the other was there. Later, as he regained a little strength, they spoke more, of different things, trivial enough in their way, each glad just to hear the other's voice. Sometimes, when he was asleep, she would sit and watch him, willing strength to return and restore him to full health.

She had been sitting thus rapt in thought one afternoon when he awoke. She saw him smile.

'Still here?'

'Where else?'

'I thought I would never see you again.'

'Nor I you.'

For several moments the emotion was too great for words. Ban's sombre gaze was fixed on her face for there was yet a shadow over the joy of reunion. He chose his next words with care. 'There are still many things I would know, Ashlynn.'

'I will tell you whatever you wish.'

'Then tell me what happened after the Normans left. Everything that I have missed.'

'Very well. But I warn you, it's a long story.'

'I'm not going anywhere.'

Taking a deep breath she began to speak, relating the story as she knew it, of her treatment at Fitzurse's hands, of her flight from the barn and her meeting with Iain. How he had saved her from the icy river and brought her along with him, and how she had discovered only later who he was. She spoke of the journey north and of her marriage, leaving out nothing, or almost nothing. His face darkened as he listened and she saw his hand clench on the coverlet.

'He forced you to wed him?'

'He married me at the king's command. For Malcolm it was the obvious solution and the one to cause him least trouble.' She sighed. 'There could be no place at Dunfermline for a penniless, friendless girl and a Saxon to boot.'

'You had me.'

'I did not know that and Iain did not tell me because he did not think you would live. I genuinely believe that now.'

'He has not hurt you?'

'No. On the contrary, he has kept me from hurt, even at the risk of his own life.'

Ban relaxed a little. 'I cannot say I like it, Ashlynn. The man has a reputation of the blackest kind. However, I owe him much.'

'We both do.'

'So it seems.' He paused. 'And if, as you say, he saved your life and has since treated you well then I have no cause to feel animosity towards him.'

'He has treated me well. I have no grounds for complaint on that score.'

Ban shook his head as he tried to assimilate what he had heard. 'It is most strange to hear such welcome and unwelcome things at once. Perhaps his reputation has become exaggerated.'

'I think perhaps it has, but I can only speak as I find.'

'And what do you find?'

'A man of his word, a leader, a fighter, one whom other men follow.' Even as she said it her mind added, *a man unlike any other*. 'He lives by his own rules but he is not dishonourable.'

He shot her a penetrating look. 'Do you love him?'

Ashlynn's cheeks grew pink. What was love exactly? She had heard it described as all encompassing, unchanging in the face of time and adversity, a passion so strong that death could not conquer it. A passion she had only dreamed of. The kind of passion that Iain had felt for Eloise.

'I…I respect him.'

'I see. Well, respect is a good enough basis for marriage. 'Tis said the rest comes with time.'

Ashlynn bit her lip. She would not tell him that respect was as far as it was ever going to go, or could ever go. Unwilling to linger in such dangerous waters she turned the conversation to other things. However, her brother's words stayed with her a long time afterwards. They might have comforted her had she not already known that her husband's abiding passion now was for revenge.

Unbeknown to Ashlynn, Iain paid her brother a visit of his own. He had long meditated it but wanted to give her space and time on her own with Ban, and the young man a chance to recover from his wounds. However, he also knew that the lad did not view the marriage with favour. Ordinarily Iain would not have cared a fig for any man's opinion on the matter but things now were not quite so simple. He could not live in such proximity to his wife's brother and be at odds with him. The nettle must be grasped. Accordingly he chose his moment when he knew Ashlynn was not by and presented himself at the bedside.

While Ban did not greet him with open hostility his expression was carefully neutral. Iain concealed a smile knowing the lad was reserving judgement.

'You are making good progress I see.'

'Yes, I thank you.' The tone was courteous but stiff.

Iain gestured to the stool that Ashlynn had not long since vacated. 'May I?'

'As you wish.'

For a moment they regarded each other in silent mutual appraisal like two combatants weighing each other up.

'I think that there are things you must want to know,' said Iain. 'If you wish it you may ask what you will now and I will answer truthfully.'

For a moment he saw surprise in the blue eyes, then it

was gone and the neutral expression returned. The lad was evidently better at hiding his thoughts than his sister was.

Ban nodded, his gaze never leaving the other man's face. 'It is true that I have questions to ask. Ashlynn has told me much but...'

'But?'

'There are things she did not say.'

Iain was quite sure of it. He waited.

'I cannot pretend that I was overjoyed when I learned of your marriage.'

'I had gathered as much.'

'But she speaks well of you.'

Iain only just managed to hide his surprise. 'Better perhaps than you think I deserve.'

'You do have a certain reputation.'

'True.'

'However that may be, my lord, she has told me how you saved her life and how you took on the role of her protector.' Ban paused. 'For that I must thank you.'

'Believe me, it is an honour.'

Ban searched that handsome face for any sign of mockery but he found none. The tone had been earnest too. Was it mere smooth courtesy or could it be that the man cared rather more than he let on?

'My sister and I are very close. Her well being and her happiness are important to me.'

'To me too. I promise you to look to the first, and that I'll strive by every means for the second.'

Ban unbent a little. 'She tells me that you have treated her well.'

For the second time Iain concealed surprise, feeling strangely pleased. His wife had demonstrated a degree of loyalty he had not expected. Did that stem from mere gratitude or could it be that she had warmed towards him of late? The notion produced an answering heat within, the kind he had not expected to feel again.

'Did she so?'

'Yes.' Ban hesitated. 'I must confess that when I first saw those bruises on her face I thought…'

'That I had put them there?'

The young man reddened. 'Yes. I'm sorry.'

'It was a reasonable suspicion, under the circumstances.'

'She told me what really happened and that you slew most of the bastards responsible.'

'Aye. Now that really was a pleasure.'

The tone was perfectly even but Ban did not miss the glint in the dark eyes. It confirmed him in the opinion that his new brother-in-law was not a man to cross with impunity. Not that he had any intention of doing so. On the contrary, he was beginning to warm to him rather more than he had thought he would. For all the man's dire reputation there was a directness about his manner and speech that Ban liked. Of his prowess in battle there was not the least doubt. However, the Laird of Glengarron had one more surprise in store. Crossing to the door he summoned the servant who had been waiting without. The man entered bearing a sheathed sword which he handed his master before withdrawing once more.

'I believe this is yours.' Iain reversed the weapon, offering it hilt first.

For a moment Ban was speechless. With a trembling hand he reached out and took it. One glance sufficed for the rest. Then blue eyes met brown. It was several more moments before he felt able to control his voice.

'I never thought to see this again. Where did you get it? How did you know it was mine?'

'It was found beside you after the battle. It bears the device of a falcon on its pommel, the crest of the Thanes of Heslingfield, I believe.'

'Yes.' Ban's hand clenched round the hilt. For the first time it occurred to him that he was now the thane, albeit fugitive and dispossessed. The sword suddenly became a most poignant symbol of all that was lost, and his throat tightened.

Seeing the powerful play of emotions on his face Iain made a shrewd guess at the thoughts behind. From the moment he saw it he had recognised the quality and craftsmanship of the weapon but, looking at Ban's expression now, knew it had significance far beyond its own intrinsic beauty.

'It is a fine weapon. I thought you would be loath to lose it.'

With an effort Ban got his voice under control. 'Indeed I would, my lord. It was a gift from my father. I thank you for its return.' He paused. 'It would seem that now I am doubly in your debt, and in truth I know not how I can repay it.'

'If you wish to repay me then you will get well and make your sister much happier.'

Ban found nothing to say for he could not put into words what was in his heart. The dark gaze met his and held it for a moment.

'Get well, Ban.' Iain moved to the door and paused just long enough to bestow one last smile. Then he was gone.

* * *

Ashlynn closed the storeroom door and took a leisurely look around. When Iain had first shown her around Dark Mount it had been one of many chambers they had visited. This was the first time she had been back. Her gaze passed over a stack of empty wicker baskets and a pile of old sacks and moved on, coming to rest on several large chests. Initially they had rated no more than a casual glance but curiosity was roused now and there was time to indulge it.

The chests were heavy and banded with iron, the bolts stiff with disuse, but with perseverance she managed to slide them back and lift the dusty lids. A pleasant scent drifted out to greet her and she realised then that the box was lined with cedar. The reason quickly became apparent. Inside were heavy folds of thick-woven cloth. She ran her hand over the surface, tracing the outline of a colourful embroidered bird. It was beautiful and in spite of herself she gave a gasp of delight. Two other chests revealed similar tapestries, all perfectly preserved by the cedar lining.

Ashlynn's appetite was whetted now. A further search revealed a large and slightly moth-eaten bearskin rug, a mirror of polished metal with an ornate frame, a wooden screen finely carved in the likeness of fruit and leaves and an elegant silver flagon with half-a-dozen matching goblets. Open-mouthed with delight she ran her fingers over the curved handle, marvelling at the workmanship and wondering where they had come from. Such things were made to be enjoyed, not hidden away and forgotten. Her own spartan chamber would benefit greatly by the addition of some attractive furnishings. That would involve asking Iain, of course. She bit her lip and closed the chest lid carefully.

* * *

For two days she had hesitated over the matter
before deciding that cowardice was never going to
solve the problem. Having made up her mind she went
in search of Iain. Knowing he was unlikely to be in
his chamber she tried the hall but it was empty of all
save servants so she made her way downstairs. She
was only halfway down when she heard the din of
what sounded like fighting. For one dreadful second
her mind was filled with Normans in helmets and
chain mail. Then common sense returned. A swift
glance out of the lower door revealed the truth: the
courtyard was full of men locked in close physical
combat or paired off for sword practice. The air rang
with the sound of clashing steel and shouts of derision
or encouragement. Her startled gaze moved quickly
from the wrestlers to the swordsmen, seeking her
husband out. Then she saw him and her breath caught
in her throat.

Like the rest of the men he had stripped to the
waist, apparently unconcerned by the cold air, but the
rest were an irrelevance now. Her attention was
riveted on Iain. She had not thought before that a
man's body could be beautiful, but that had been quite
wrong. His arms and torso might have been sculpted
so clearly delineated was the heavy musculature
beneath his skin. Dark hair tapered from the broad
chest and led the eye to a narrow waist and hips and
thence to long, muscled legs.

Even though she already knew something of his
ability, Ashlynn was still drawn to watch, held by the
lithe power of the man and the skill and control with

which he fought. He moved tirelessly, testing his opponent's ability, looking for a weakness and when he found it exploiting it ruthlessly. Recalling her lessons with Ban she smiled ruefully. Against such skills, her own were puny. All at once the incident with the robbers returned and she knew without a doubt that she had been lucky. But for the element of surprise she would have been skewered. Given a fair fight she had no doubt Iain could have accounted for his attackers single handed. Even Ban, whose skill she respected, would have been hard pressed to hold his own against him. With that knowledge came the first stirring of pride, as unexpected as it was genuine.

At the end of the bout Iain sheathed the sword and donned his shirt and tunic again. She watched Dougal stroll across to join him. They exchanged a few words and then were joined in turn by one or two others. In a short time the group was engaged in animated discussion. From the accompanying gestures it seemed to be about the finer points of sword play. Once she saw Iain look round, his eyes scanning the spectators. They saw her at once and she felt again the power of that casual regard. Would he disapprove of her presence here? His expression gave no hint of annoyance but then it was often hard to tell what he was thinking. Her pulse quickened. Would he come over now? She hoped he might. His men already had a low opinion of her and, if she went to join him, they might take such an interruption ill.

However, Iain remained where he was, apparently seeing no reason to leave the present company. Around them the exercise continued, drawing his attention that way. He must have made some quip for she saw his companions laugh. The conversation resumed. Ashlynn bit her lip and turned away. The message was clear enough. He was busy and she was unwanted here. She should go.

'The wrestling bouts are fun to watch are they not, my lady?' said a voice beside her.

Ashlynn started and, looking round, recognised Robbie. For a moment she felt awkward for it was he whom she had given the slip when she ran away, but his expression now was genial. If he bore her a grudge it wasn't apparent. From the question she realised that she must have been staring at the wrestlers, though in truth had seen nothing of them.

'Er, yes,' she said. 'Who do you think will win?'

'Fergus,' he replied without hesitation. 'There isn't a man in Glengarron who can match him for strength or skill.'

Looking at the individual in question Ashlynn could see the truth of that remark. Fergus was massively muscled and looked to be roughly the size of a barn door, but for all that he was fast and agile.

She nodded. 'I can well believe it.'

'I'm just thankful he fights on our side.'

Ashlynn took the point as Fergus raised a big and brawny opponent over his head and tossed him into the banked snow at the edge of the courtyard, much to the rowdy enjoyment of the onlookers.

'I think I would not like to meet him on a field of battle.'

'Or in an alley on a dark night,' returned Robbie with a grin.

'Heaven forbid.'

They laughed, each visualising the possibility.

'But then all Glengarron's men are able fighters, are they not?' she continued.

'Aye, my lady, they are. Lord Iain trains them well.'

'So I see.' She eyed him with curiosity. 'Have you ridden with him long?'

'Going on four years now.'

'Four years? A long time.'

'Not so long. There's many have been with him longer.'

'A man to inspire loyalty then.'

'Indeed he is, my lady. He looks after his men and all who depend on him. There's not a braver laird in the whole border country, or one more cunning.'

'I can believe that.'

'You'd be right to, my lady. A man would have to get up very early to catch Iain of Glengarron.'

They lapsed into companionable silence for a while, but the conversation had given Ashlynn plenty to think about. Almost from the first she had recognised in Iain the qualities of strong leadership. It had been evident in the quiet assurance with which he moved among his men and the way in which he spoke to them. He called each one by name. She never heard him raise his voice but his slightest word was obeyed to the letter. Having seen their skill in battle she knew they were a formidable force. If their opinion of their leader was so high then that respect had been earned. Such men did not give their loyalty or their regard easily.

Robbie eyed her curiously. 'I've heard it said you're no so bad with a sword yourself, my lady.'

'Who told you that?'

'Dougal. He said that when you and Black Iain were attacked by robbers you killed six of them single handed.'

She gave a gurgle of incredulous laughter. 'Dougal overrates my skill. It was only two and I took them by surprise.'

Robbie grinned. 'I wish I'd been there to see it all the same.'

Across the courtyard Iain was apparently still engaged in easy conversation. However, he was also keenly aware of the scene opposite. It was too far to catch the words but he heard the pair laugh. His jaw tightened. When she was with him Ashlynn rarely laughed yet somehow, in mere minutes, Robbie had overcome her reserve, God rot him! Iain had always acknowledged his wife to be a pretty woman, but since the bruises had faded from her face it had become obvious that she was more than just pretty. When she appeared in the hall his men followed her with their eyes. Hitherto she had never given the least sign that she was aware of the attention but now she seemed to find pleasure in Robbie's company, apparently hanging on every word. Moreover, the young man was near Ashlynn's age and well favoured withal. Even her clothing blended with his, damn it. In this throng she might, to the casual eye, have passed for a local lass—a local lass or a servant. His brows drew together.

'What does the lady here? This is no fit place for a woman to be.'

The voice had come from the fringes of the group around Iain but the words were clearly meant to be overheard. They recalled him at once and he turned, giving the speaker a long and level stare. Recognising that look the rest fell into awkward silence.

'Well, Archie,' he replied, 'some might say it's not a

woman's place to fight off a gang of armed robbers either, but she did it all the same.'

Beneath the weight of that cool gaze the speaker coloured faintly. 'Beg pardon, my lord. I meant no disrespect.'

'I'm glad to hear it,' said Iain. 'Lady Ashlynn may do as she pleases without reference to you.'

The other lowered his gaze. 'As you say, my lord.'

The words fell into the surrounding silence and rippled outwards. Iain remained quite still, waiting. However, no further comment was forthcoming from any quarter and a few moments later the men turned away and resumed their earlier conversation as though nothing had happened. A remark from Dougal about one of the nearby swordsmen reclaimed Iain's attention and he made some reply, forcing his attention back to what his companion was saying. However, in spite of his best efforts his gaze was repeatedly drawn to the pair on the fringes of the wrestling. Ashlynn's attention was seemingly absorbed by the spectacle and she never looked his way. Then Robbie spoke to her again and she glanced up, smiling. Iain's gaze smouldered.

It was perhaps half an hour later when the combatants stopped to recover their breath and take a mug of ale. The gathering broke up into little groups, all talking and laughing together. Ashlynn excused herself and moved away then. It had been entertaining to watch the proceedings but, even with a cloak on, she was beginning to feel the cold. She was halfway to the door of the tower when a hand on her arm arrested her progress. She looked round quickly and felt her heart miss a beat.

'Iain.'

'I take it you enjoyed the practices,' he said. The words were quietly spoken but carried a nuance of something harder to define.

'Yes, very much, although that was not the reason I came out here.'

'Oh? And what was the reason?'

'I was looking for you.'

'I'm flattered. For a while I thought it might have been someone else.'

His gaze flicked toward Robbie. Ashlynn stared at him in genuine astonishment. Surely he couldn't have thought… For a second she felt a strong urge to laugh, then looked at his expression and decided she had better not. All the same he could not possibly be jealous. That was ridiculous. Before she could say more he took her arm and led her back indoors. Only when they reached the hall did he stop and draw her round to face him.

'What was it you wanted to speak to me about, lass?'

She took a deep breath and seized her chance, explaining about her discoveries in the store room. Listening, Iain was taken aback and, in spite of himself, faintly amused. Whatever else he had been expecting it wasn't that.

'So I wanted to ask…may I put those things to use?'

She waited, wondering if he would be angry. However, his expression did not suggest it and his tone when he spoke was perfectly level.

'You need not ask my permission, Ashlynn. This is your home now. Arrange it as you please.'

Footsteps on the stairs announced the arrival of some of his men and with that he favoured her with a bow and left. For a moment she watched him go, feeling strangely bereft. Clearly he had no further interest in the matter or in her either. Turning away, she summoned a servant and bade him find Morag.

Some hours later Ashlynn surveyed her chamber with something approaching real pleasure. The cold stone walls were concealed now by the glorious tapestries, hanging there in many-coloured splendour. By her bed the bearskin rug covered a large section of floor. The bed itself and the chairs were adorned with colourful cushions. In one corner was the carved screen. The mirror lay on the table with the flagon and cups. Now that the fire had at last taken the chill off the air the overall effect was of cheerful cosiness.

'It looks fine, my lady,' said Morag, surveying it critically.

'Yes, it does,' she agreed. 'Much less like a convent cell.'

They both laughed. Then Morag turned to go. Ashlynn saw her check slightly and turned to see Iain in the doorway. He stepped aside to let the servant pass and then came in, looking casually around. She experienced a moment of misgiving, wondering what his reaction might be. However, she needn't have worried.

'You've done a good job, lass.'

'Thank you. I think so too.'

He glanced down at her and smiled faintly. All at once the room seemed a lot smaller and a lot warmer. The bed on the other hand seemed to have grown much larger. Her heartbeat quickened and in the name of self-preservation Ashlynn took a step away.

'The tapestries are finer even than I expected. Where did they come from?'

'France,' he replied.

Her heart sank as an unwelcome possibility suddenly dawned. Had these things belonged to Eloise? Suddenly she was mortified. Why hadn't such a possibility occurred to her before now?

'They belonged to my mother,' he continued. 'After she died they were put away. I'd almost forgotten about them, but it seems fitting now that they should return to their rightful place.'

She let out the breath she had been holding, feeling almost weak-kneed with relief.

'Did she die long ago?'

'Aye, when I was four and ten. My father packed away everything connected with her, including me.' He smiled wryly. 'Although I was sent to France rather than the storeroom.'

'That must have been hard.'

'Not really. It was a relief in many ways. As I told you, my father and I were never close. He had a quick temper and frequently exercised it on me, whether it was merited or not.'

Although there was nothing remotely self-pitying about the tone of voice Ashlynn sensed the hurt beneath. Sensed it and identified with it.

'Well, families are strange things, are they not?'

'Aye, lass, they are.'

'Children are vulnerable enough without having to contend with the enmity of a parent.'

The tone was even but he caught the wistful expression in her eyes.

'We play as the dice fall,' he replied, 'and perhaps it makes us stronger.'

'Perhaps.'

'You are strong in spite of your father,' he said. 'Strong and brave.'

There was no hint of mockery in the quiet tone and Ashlynn looked up in surprise. Then she shook her head.

'My father's word was reckless.'

'Then he didn't know you very well, did he?'

Disconcerted by the unforeseen direction of the conversation, Ashlynn changed tack. 'Did you have no brothers or sisters?'

'Three other siblings died in infancy but I have a sister living.'

'A sister? What is her name?'

'Jeannie.'

'Shall I meet her soon?'

'I doubt it,' he replied.

'Oh, she lives some distance away then.'

'Not so far, but in recent years we have become—estranged.'

Ashlynn took a deep breath. 'May I ask why?'

'We quarrelled.'

'I'm sorry to hear that.' She paused. 'Could you not make it up again?'

'No.' He sighed. 'This disagreement admits of no remedy.' Then seeing her puzzled expression he went on, 'It concerns Fitzurse.'

'Fitzurse!' Ashlynn was genuinely astonished. 'How so?'

'Jeannie thinks I should give up my quest to find him.'

'I see.'

'No, you don't. You have no idea.'

The tone was unwontedly harsh. She could hear anger

and, beneath it, something that sounded more like pain. The expression in his eyes was glacial. One part of her mind quailed, telling her to back off and leave it alone. Yet the stronger part knew she could not. This must be faced. She needed to know, to understand. Instinctively she reached out and laid a gentle hand on his arm.

'Then will you not tell me?'

For a moment she thought he was going to snub her as he had before, and tell her it was none of her concern. She saw him draw a deep breath as though to steady himself.

'If anyone has a right to know I suppose it is you,' he replied.

Her heartbeat quickened and she waited, unwilling to do anything that might break the mood now.

'I told you that I was married before and that my wife had died,' he continued. 'Fitzurse was the man responsible for that.'

Ashlynn stared at him, stunned and appalled together.

'My father had sent me to France in order to complete my military training. His sister was… is…married to a French nobleman, the Comte de Vaucourt, a man renowned for skill at arms. It was in their house that I met Eloise. She was…most beautiful. I believe I fell in love with her at first sight.'

As she listened Ashlynn kept her face determinedly neutral, hiding the turmoil of thoughts behind.

'My feelings were reciprocated and, since there were no objections to the match from either of our families, we married. For a while we were very happy. However, I had a jealous rival.'

Ashlynn's gaze met his for a moment. 'Fitzurse.'

'Aye. He had had designs on Eloise himself and took

it much amiss that her hand should be granted to one he
saw as a foreign interloper. That it was so clearly a love
match piqued his pride even further. So, believing
himself slighted, he planned his revenge.'

'What did he do?'

'The Comte de Vaucourt arranged a boar hunt and a
large party rode out that day, including Eloise and
myself. Somehow, in the course of the chase, she
became separated from the rest. Fitzurse's men were
waiting and, seeing their chance, carried her off to his
castle some few miles distant.'

Ashlynn paled, remembering her own encounter with
Fitzurse and knowing too well what the man was
capable of. Iain took a deep breath.

'He raped her repeatedly and then, when he had
done, gave her to his men. When they had had their sport
they released her. We eventually found her in the fields
not far from Vaucourt. Somehow she must have made
her way back there. She was in such a state that only
the greatest effort of will could have kept her going.
Above all else she wanted to see Fitzurse punished, to
be avenged. Having gained that holy assurance she
seized the dagger from my belt and ended her life.'

'Dear God.'

'The shame was not hers but she could not live with it.'

'What did you do?'

'I sought redress through the law. Like a fool I
thought that having right on my side must result in
justice. However, when the matter was brought before
Duke Richard, Fitzurse swore that Eloise had gone with
him of her own volition, that it had been only the two
of them involved. He had powerful friends who bore

false witness to that effect. And since those same men had provided the gold to fund his wars, the Duke inclined to their part. I would have killed Fitzurse anyway and to hell with the consequences but, knowing that, my uncle had me forcibly returned to Scotland for my own safety.'

'How did he do that?'

'He drugged the wine one evening. I woke up on board a merchant ship bound for the Firth of Forth. I cursed my uncle's name at first but, with the wisdom of hindsight, I saw that he was right. I'd live to fight another day. In the years that followed he sent me regular intelligence from France. In that way I learned Fitzurse had taken service with Duke William and was bound for England. Then I knew my turn was coming.' He paused. 'My one fear was that my enemy might have perished at Hastings along with all those others. Happily he did not.'

'And you have sought him ever since.'

'Aye, and one day we will meet.'

There could be no mistaking the cold purpose in his tone and Ashlynn shivered.

'That day may be far distant,' she replied.

'One year or ten, it makes no difference. I shall keep my vow.'

As the ramifications became clear, Ashlynn knew a moment of deep sadness. Would the evils of the past never be exorcised? If they were ever to build a life together its foundations could not be those of hatred and revenge. And if they did build a future could he ever feel for her what he felt for Eloise?

Mistaking the cause of her silence he eyed her

ruefully. 'It's not a pretty story. Perhaps I should not have told you.'

'No, it isn't pretty,' she replied, 'but I'm glad you did all the same. It makes so many things clear.'

'Does it?'

'Yes, among them why your sister should have asked you to give up your quest.'

He frowned. 'Jeannie doesn't know what she asks.'

'I think she does. She wants you to move on.'

'That is not possible.'

'Isn't it?'

'Not until I have rid this earth of Fitzurse.'

'I know as well as anyone why you hate this man, but we cannot alter what is past, Iain.' She squeezed his arm. 'Let it go. Look to the future instead.'

Her touch, though gentle, was warm. He could feel it beneath his sleeve. The effect was both soothing and sensual. He forced himself to ignore it along with the haunting expression in her eyes. 'There can be no future until this is settled. My vow was made in blood and it will be met in blood. I will not be forsworn.'

'Will you sacrifice everything to that end?'

'If needs be.'

'Does that include me?'

'This has nothing to do with you, Ashlynn.'

'How can you say so? How can you even think it?' she replied. 'I too have cause to hate Fitzurse, but if I let hatred govern my life he will have won. Don't you see?'

Iain's jaw tightened. He could not doubt the sincerity of the words or mistake the plea in her tone, but nor could he cede the point. 'You will deal with him in your way and I in mine.'

With that he turned and left her. She knew then beyond doubt that she was one of the things that would be sacrificed to this cause. Iain had married her only because he must. He wouldn't let that get in the way of his ambition. Nor, she reflected sadly, could she hope to win his heart. Quite clearly, Eloise had it still.

Chapter Eight

In the meantime, Ban was recovering well from his wounds and Ashlynn observed his physical progress with satisfaction. Of more concern was his state of mind. He never spoke of Heslingfield or what had occurred there but the events had inevitably cast their shadow over him. Although he had not entirely lost his former cheerful demeanour he was subject now to long periods of silent introspection. She had no need to ask what he was thinking about; the expression in his eyes was more eloquent.

Typically, he wanted to get back on his feet and left his sick bed at the first opportunity. Ashlynn went to visit him one morning to find him up and dressed.

'Ban, what on earth are you about? You're not strong enough yet.'

'I cannot lie there any longer, Ash. It has been weeks.'

'Three weeks. If you're not careful you'll tear those wounds open.'

''Tis but the shoulder I need to favour for a while. The rest are almost healed.'

'I'd say the one to your head has addled your brain.'

'Not so, sister mine. You fuss over nothing.'

'True enough, I suppose. A blow there could never do serious damage.'

Ban grinned. 'If I were not wearing this sling I'd make you pay for that impertinence.'

'I'm trembling at the narrowness of my escape.'

Suddenly she became aware that he was looking past her towards the doorway, and turned to see Iain there. To judge from his amused expression he had overheard much of their exchange. Ashlynn appealed to him now.

'My lord, tell him he should not be abroad so soon.'

'Alas, I fear my words would fall on deaf ears for I detect a strong streak of stubbornness in your family.' He came into the room and surveyed Ban keenly. 'Besides, I think lying abed has but a finite charm.'

'You speak truth, my lord.' Ban regarded his sister in triumph.

'This is a conspiracy,' she replied.

Iain smiled. 'Not at all, though I fear you are outvoted on this occasion.'

'All right. I know when I'm beaten.' Ashlynn fixed Ban with a speaking look. 'Just don't do anything foolish for a while, I beg.'

'You know me.'

'Yes, quite.'

In fact Ban showed remarkably good sense for several days, taking things slowly at first and contenting himself with gentle exercise within doors. However, he, like Ashlynn, loved to be outside, and before too long proposed a turn about the courtyard for some fresh air. It was with some misgivings that she agreed to accompany him, but she knew that even if she refused he would go anyway.

When Iain had said her brother was stubborn it had been no more than the truth.

In fact, her worries were unfounded. Ban showed no signs of a relapse and, as the days passed, the fresh air restored his colour and his appetite. Gradually he increased the time he spent out there and when the men were practising with swords he would linger to watch and gradually, through her husband's agency, was drawn into their conversation. Finding him interested and knowledgeable the men accepted his presence among them and Ashlynn, observing from the sidelines, was grateful for it. He needed their company and with it a chance to think about something other than the past.

'Your brother looks much better,' Iain observed, coming to join her one morning.

'Yes, he does.'

'He seems much more animated of late.'

'Male companionship is proving beneficial. He has been shut up for too long with mine.'

'I think no man would object too strenuously to that,' he replied.

The words were casually spoken but the look that accompanied them was not. For many reasons it was disturbing, not least for its lingering warmth. Moreover, she could detect no sign of tension in his manner now; their former conversation might not have happened.

'All the same fresh conversation is always welcome,' she replied. 'It is not good to be too long alone with sombre thoughts.'

'No, it isn't.' He paused. 'Perhaps you too might find new company stimulating.'

'New company?'

'Yule is almost upon us. It is the custom here to hold a feast.'

'Yule,' she murmured. 'I had forgotten.'

Ordinarily she would have looked forward to it. This year she had been dreading it but since the destruction of Heslingfield it had become an irrelevance and she hadn't given it a thought. It was as though her mind had deliberately blotted it out. Guessing at some of her thoughts Iain laid a gentle hand on her shoulder.

'I'm thinking it will not be an easy time for you, lass, or for your brother either. Do you wish me to abandon the feast this year?'

She regarded him with real surprise and for a moment found it hard to speak, not least for the warmth of his touch and his look. Then she shook her head. 'Thank you, but no. It will not be easy, as you say, but it must be faced. Besides, I would not put a damper on other people's enjoyment and neither would Ban.'

'Neither would I…what?' inquired a voice behind them.

Ashlynn turned to see her brother. 'Iain was asking whether we wished the Yuletide feast to be abandoned this year on account of what happened to Heslingfield.'

Ban met his sister's gaze and held it. Then he turned to look at Iain. 'No, my lord, not for the world would I have you do so. Rather, let the occasion be held as it always was at Heslingfield. In that way all the right memories may be kept alive.'

He reached for his sister's hand and squeezed it. Ashlynn managed to return his smile. The sight of it pierced Iain to the heart.

The following day the fine weather broke and the grey sky grew leaden, threatening snow. The wind was bitter. One brief exposure to that icy blast on the roof terrace sent Ashlynn hurrying back to the warmth of her room. She had not been there very long before someone knocked on the door. Feeling sure it would be Ban she bade the caller enter. However, it was a very different figure that appeared on the threshold.

'Good morning, Ashlynn.' Iain surveyed her in silence for a moment and then smiled faintly. 'May I come in?'

Gathering her wits she answered in the affirmative and watched him step into the room. Then he turned and beckoned to someone without. To her astonishment four women entered, all total strangers and all of them carrying a variety of large bags and bundles. They smiled as they made their duty to her. In bemusement Ashlynn looked from them to him.

'Madame and her assistants have just arrived from Dunfermline. They'll be staying with us for a few days.'

'Will they?'

For the first time she realised he carried under his arm several bolts of cloth which he laid on the bed. His companions bore several more. Soon the fur coverlet was transformed into a riot of colour.

'What's this?' she asked.

'Your new wardrobe, my lady,' he said, 'or the basis for it, at least.'

'New wardrobe?'

'Aye, and not before time.' He eyed her homespun gown with disfavour. 'Since the day I first saw it I've wanted to get that ghastly dress off you. I'd have done it a lot sooner but the ladies here had commitments at the royal court and could not be spared.'

'They've come from the royal court?'

'That's right.'

Incredulous and speechless Ashlynn watched him cross to the door again. He paused on the threshold.

'I'll leave you to it then.'

With that he was gone. Ashlynn tried to gather her scattered wits and turned to look at the rolls of cloth on the bed. The elder seamstress hastened to fetch the azure silk. Drawing out a length she held it against Ashlynn.

'The colour looks well on you, my lady.'

'It's beautiful,' she replied, running her fingers over the surface of the material. 'I never saw anything so fine.' It was no more than the truth. Never would she have dreamed of owning such a gown.

However, before she had finished admiring the blue, Madame gestured to an assistant to fetch a bolt of red velvet, considering it intently, letting her gaze rest on Ashlynn's face and hair a moment and thence to the slender form below, taking in the whole picture.

'This will also look well,' she said. Seeing Ashlynn remain silent, the seamstress regarded her keenly. 'Does the cloth displease you, my lady?'

'No, it's beautiful. It's just that I find it hard to choose between the two.'

'No need, my lady,' replied the other, 'since we are to make half-a-dozen new gowns.'

For a moment Ashlynn was rooted to the spot. Half-a-dozen new gowns! Never in her life had she been permitted more than one new dress at a time and, even then, not in fabrics like these. Madame smiled.

'So we keep the red I think.'

'I, er…yes.'

The red bolt joined the blue.

Half an hour later those two had been joined by four others in gold, cerise, forest green and mauve. Then she found herself being measured by the giggling assistants. From time to time Madame spoke to them in the French tongue, apparently giving detailed instructions. Ashlynn looked on in awed silence. She dreaded to think what all this must be costing. Never could she have envisaged so generous a gift. These cloths were sumptuous, fit for the royal court indeed. Apart from the dress material there were also lighter, finer fabrics of the type suitable for chemises and stockings. These too came under close scrutiny as Madame picked out the shades that would complement the rest. Then, when she had taken her client's measurements, the dress patterns emerged from a leather bag. Ashlynn regarded them with concern.

'Aren't they a little revealing?'

'These are the latest styles, my lady. Let me show you.' She gestured for the younger woman to come closer. 'Notice the wider sleeves. They allow the colour of the chemise to show to advantage. The bodice fits close to the body.' She let her gaze rest on her client a moment. 'A figure like yours should also be shown off to best advantage, my lady.'

Ashlynn wondered what on earth Iain was going to

say about that. The proposed style was so far removed from the modest drape of a Saxon gown that it was vaguely shocking, but the woman in her found it hard to resist. The thought occurred that such a fashion might also be pleasing to a man, if for rather different reasons. Would it please Iain? Would he truly *see* her then? With almost uncanny prescience Madame interjected.

'My lord was most insistent on this point.'

'He was?'

'Oh, yes, my lady. Gowns in the French style. Those were his instructions.'

Ashlynn made no more demur. There was little time to dwell on the matter because the seamstress's assistants wanted to measure her feet. Having done so, they traced out the size on soft leather prior to cutting out shoes which would later be sewn to fit her.

'It will take a few days to complete the work,' said Madame, 'but I hope it will meet with my lady's approval.'

Ashlynn was quite sure of that. She could hardly wait to see the results. Iain's face imposed itself on her mind. Would her choice meet with *his* approval? She hoped so. He had made her a most generous gift and one she had certainly not been expecting. It behoved her to thank him at least.

When the session ended she sought him out and found him in the hall.

Iain heard her in silence and then replied, 'As the wife of a laird it is fitting that you should dress as one. Do not feel obliged to thank me.'

'I did not thank you from a sense of obligation, my lord, but because I meant it.'

There followed another short silence before he inclined his head in acknowledgement. 'Then I accept your thanks in the spirit they were meant.'

After he had left Ashlynn took herself off to the roof terrace needing space to try and order the riot of her thoughts. She was tempted to pinch herself to find out if she woke or slept. It would not have surprised her in the least to discover the last couple of hours had been a dream. Never in a thousand years would she have expected him to think of this, but she was woman enough to appreciate it and to look forward to seeing the finished gowns. It would be good to wear truly flattering feminine garments again. Would he find her attractive then? She glanced down at the homespun dress and sighed. He obviously considered her a perfect fright at present. Almost at once she was ashamed of the notion; she ought to be beyond this sort of foolishness. They would have company over Yuletide and he wished her to look the part she played, that was all. Had he not made it clear enough? She could have no hopes of him.

Quite deliberately she turned her mind away from Iain to the matter of Yule. If they were to have a feast then arrangements needed to be made for that and for the guests. Rooms must be cleaned and beds prepared. Then there was the hall. The very thought of it was enough to bring a grimace to the face. After years of neglect and solely masculine influence it was more like a temple to barbarism than the heart of the house. However, that was about to change. Ashlynn lifted her chin. Like it or not, she was mistress here now. Had she not been told to arrange matters as she pleased? Having made up her mind she returned within doors and summoned Morag.

'Gather all the household servants in the hall. I want to talk to them.'

Some time later a disgruntled steward waylaid Iain below stairs with a string of queries. Did his lordship really mean for the hall trestles to be taken down and scrubbed? Was the straw to be changed when it had barely been down six months, and the floor swept at that time too? Since when had dust and cobwebs ever hurt anyone? Had his lordship really intended that the majority of the servants should be taken from their regular duties to carry out such work, or that two of them should go out for a whole morning to collect greenery and leave him, Davy Kerr, shorthanded as a result?

Iain listened with concealed surprise but said nothing at first, waiting till the man ran out of breath.

'Who ordered this?' he asked then.

'Lady Ashlynn, my lord.'

'Did she so?'

Davy Kerr's pigeon breast swelled with virtuous indignation. 'Aye, my lord.'

Iain eyed him steadily. 'Then you'd best get to it, man.'

For a moment the steward could only stare at him in disbelief. 'Beg pardon, my lord?'

'You heard me. Get to it.'

'Very well, my lord.' Kerr threw him a fierce stare and then bowed stiffly before turning to go.

'Oh, and Kerr…'

'My lord?'

'Don't ever question Lady Ashlynn's orders again.'

The tone was soft but the look in the laird's eyes was not. Kerr swallowed hard and nodded, then scuttled away as fast as he could.

Iain continued on up the stairs and came to the hall. He stopped in his tracks on the threshold. The room was a hive of frenetic activity with servants bustling about in every direction, armed with brooms and pails and scrubbing brushes. Ashlynn's slender regal figure stood in their midst directing operations. Homespun gown or not she had an air of natural authority about her and no one questioned the instructions she delivered with such cool and firm assurance. The men looked slightly bemused but the women's expressions approximated more to triumph. For a while Iain stood and watched in silent amusement and considerable enjoyment. If he'd ever entertained any doubts about her ability to run his household they had just been removed. He'd seen military commanders with less skill.

'What the devil's going on?' asked a voice beside him.

Iain glanced over his shoulder to see Ban. 'I believe your sister is readying the hall for the Yuletide celebrations.'

'Ah.'

'I take it you've seen this before.'

'Oh, yes.'

'She looks to be very thorough.'

'You have no idea.'

Iain grinned. 'So what would you advise?'

The younger man surveyed the scene for a few moments longer. 'That we make ourselves scarce.'

'My thought exactly. How about a jug of ale and a game of chess?'

'A most excellent suggestion, my lord.'

* * *

It took most of the day and a small army of servants to clean the hall to Ashlynn's exacting standards. By then the men she had sent out earlier returned with a cart full of fragrant greenery to decorate it. When it was carried indoors it filled the air with sweet fresh scent. Ashlynn drafted all available hands to help and by the time they had done she surveyed the result with real satisfaction. Beside her Morag nodded approval.

'The place looks like it used to in the old days, when Lady Alice was alive.'

'Lady Alice?'

'Lord Iain's mother, God rest her soul.' Morag shook her head. 'She always had the hall decked thus for the feast. After she died things were never the same. But then men have no sense of these things.'

'Some might say they have so sense at all,' replied Ashlynn.

Morag chuckled. 'You're not wrong there, my lady.'

Ashlynn gathered all the servants together. 'You've done a magnificent job. Now go and get something to eat and drink. You've earned it.' Having dismissed them she went to sit down by the fire feeling weary now herself.

Ban and Iain found her there a little later. Both men stood looking round the room in open-mouthed amazement.

'God's bones,' murmured Ban, 'it looks like a different place.'

Iain mentally agreed. It did. Apart from the obvious cleanliness it smelled wonderful, a mingling of green foliage and fresh straw and scrubbed wood. The old tallow lights had been replaced with fine beeswax candles which threw a sweet soft-scented glow over the whole room. In an instant he was transported back to his childhood when his mother had been alive, and he felt his throat tighten. Then he became aware that Ashlynn was watching him.

'Do you like it?' she asked.

'I think it's perfect, lass. Just perfect.' He took her hand and carried it to his lips. 'Thank you.'

He had never used quite that tone before. It was gentle and tender and it took her unawares, like the warm touch of his fingers on hers and the imprint of his kiss on her skin. She made no attempt to withdraw her hand from his and he seemed in no hurry to relinquish it. Only when a servant appeared with a query for Ashlynn about the serving of the evening meal did he reluctantly let her go.

The atmosphere in the hall was different that evening, for once the men had recovered from their initial astonishment their mood lifted to match the cheerfulness of the surroundings. There was more laughter and good-humoured banter. Ashlynn too relaxed in the lighter atmosphere, and she was gladdened to see Ban smile. However, as time wore on the exertions of the day began to take their toll and eventually she excused herself from the gathering. This time Iain rose with her and escorted her as far as the door. For a moment the dark gaze surveyed her in concern.

'You look tired, lass.'

'I am,' she admitted.

''Tis not to be wondered at.' He paused. 'Thank you for your efforts today. It has been a long time since Dark Mount looked like a home.'

There could be no mistaking the sincerity of the words or the expression in his eyes as he raised her hand to his lips. Not knowing quite what to say she remained silent, every fibre of her being alive to him. Would he take her in arms now? If he did, what then? Recalling the power of his kiss and how it had set her aflame it took but a second to know the answer to that. He surveyed her just a moment longer and relinquished her hand.

'Goodnight. Sleep well, lass.'

In silent confusion she acknowledged that what she felt was not relief but something akin to disappointment. She bade him goodnight and turned away. He watched her until she was out of sight.

Two days later the weather changed and it snowed again overnight. By morning all the landscape was transformed. Ashlynn surveyed it for a while from the roof terrace before making her way down to the hall. Finding no sign of Iain or her brother she went outside.

The courtyard had been cleared and the snow banked high against the walls. It was bitterly cold but the wind had dropped and the ice crystals courted the sunlight like flung diamonds. Ashlynn smiled and breathed deeply, enjoying the moment. She would take a turn or two before starting work. In spite of what had gone before there was plenty to be done. Her mind moved ahead, thinking of food for the feast. She would consult the cook about that in due course...

Her thoughts were rudely interrupted by a large ball of snow which caught her squarely in the chest. Looking up indignantly she saw her brother some yards off regarding her with a speculative smile. In that moment he was so much the old Ban again that her heart swelled. The feeling was short-lived as another snowball caught her shoulder. Ashlynn's eyes narrowed.

'Just you wait!' With a speed born of expertise she fashioned a missile and lobbed it back. Ban ducked and it skimmed his cloak but, when he turned round again, the next one hit him in the face. Spluttering, he heard her laugh.

'My aim is still good, brother.'

'Too good, you minx.'

Several more men had emerged from the hall and other bystanders watched with interest, among them Iain who had just emerged from the smithy hard by. Ban fired off several more shots with varying success for he was still using his left hand to avoid straining the recovering shoulder. However, he kept up the pressure. Ashlynn found herself trying to dodge Ban's missiles while throwing her own, and her usually accurate aim became less so. A large snowball, intended for Ban's chest, flew past and hit Iain instead. She heard several sharp intakes of breath from the onlookers and then muffled snorts of laughter. Ban guffawed. For a moment Ashlynn was still, but remorse was short-lived and mischief reasserted itself in a wide grin.

Seeing it, Iain lifted an eyebrow and strolled casually towards her. Undeceived by this apparent nonchalance, Ashlynn turned to flee. He caught her in six strides and lifted her off her feet with no more difficulty than he would have lifted a wisp of straw. Her shriek of protest went unheeded. Then he glanced down at his struggling burden with a glint in his eye that boded no good at all.

'Throw snowballs at me, would you, lass?'

'You don't understand…'

'Oh, I think I do.'

He carried her to the edge of the courtyard where the cleared snow was banked in great heaps. As she saw him grin an unwelcome suspicion dawned.

'Iain, no!'

'No?'

Ashlynn struggled harder. 'Don't you dare!'

'You know better than that, lass.'

'You wouldn't…'

The sentence ended on a shriek of outrage as he dropped her into the huge white drift. Roars of laughter erupted from the spectators. Then, almost as though at a signal, other missiles began to fly amid yells and curses and laughter and soon the air was thick with them. For a moment Iain surveyed the scene, grinning. Then he glanced down at Ashlynn who, almost completely engulfed, was trying unsuccessfully to extricate herself.

'Help me out, you villain!'

'Villain is it now?' He shook his head. 'Not content with an unprovoked attack you insult me into the bargain.'

Torn between laughter and frustration she moderated her tone. 'I beg your pardon, my lord. Won't you please help me up?'

His grin widened and he surveyed her a moment longer. Then, reaching down a hand, he caught hers and hauled her out of the white mound. Covered from head to foot she was grinning herself now. He shook out her cloak and then began to brush some of the snow from her hair. As he did so a stray missile caught him round the ear. Unable to help herself Ashlynn laughed out loud. His expression was eloquent but far from stopping her amusement served only to fuel it.

'It seems to me, wife, that you do not demonstrate the proper respect due to your lord and master. I am minded to show you the error of your ways.' He crooked a finger. 'Come here.'

Ashlynn backed away. 'I shall not.'

'Is that right?' He advanced slowly. 'And I thought I'd cured you of disobedience.'

The tone was decidedly ambiguous. Withal there was an expression in his eyes that she hadn't seen before but it was definitely not to be trusted.

'Iain?'

She backed up a few more steps but still he came on. Then, without warning, his hand shot out and grabbed her wrist. Ashlynn gasped and tried to resist but in a matter of seconds was thrown over a broad shoulder. Ignoring the accompanying yells of protest he carried her across the courtyard and back to the tower. When eventually he set her down again they were in the great hall.

For a moment they faced each other, she half-laughing and half-panting as she tried to draw her breath, he drinking in every detail of her. Much dishevelled now, with snow still clinging to her cloak and melted drops in her hair, she seemed to glow for the cold had brought the colour to her cheeks and her eyes sparkled with mischief yet. There was withal a most provocative smile on her lips. He drew her closer, looking down into her face with an expression that was both alarming and exciting together. Then his mouth was on hers and excitement superseded alarm and banished it as Ashlynn swayed against him, surrender-

ing to the moment, knowing this was what she had
wanted him to do. Her mouth opened beneath his and
the kiss grew deeper and more intimate. Involuntarily
her arms stole around his neck, her hand stroking the
warm curve at the nape of his neck beneath the dark
mane of hair.

The touch sent a thrill to the core of his being re-
awakening the hunger he had felt before, a hunger he
once thought he could not know again. His hold tightened about her, lifting her off her feet, crushing her
closer. He felt her mouth respond to his and tasted again
its sweetness on his tongue, breathing the fresh clean
scent of snow on her hair and clothes and beneath it the
subtle erotic scent of the woman. He wanted her, here,
now, wanted to lose himself in her completely...

A discreet cough alerted them to other presences and
they surfaced, looking round to see Fergus and Dougal.
Ashlynn's cheeks turned a much deeper shade of pink.
With a wry smile Iain relinquished his hold on his wife
and watched her turn away toward the hearth. As the
men approached Ashlynn drew in a deep breath to try
and compose herself, to still the dangerous thumping of
her heart. A covert glance at Iain revealed nothing of his
inner thought and certainly none of the powerful
emotion that gripped her now. His voice when he spoke
to his men was calm, unforced. It recalled her to reality.
What had occurred had begun as a bit of harmless fun
and somehow gone further than either of them had
intended. She smiled ruefully. It was certainly no more
than that to him. Yet she had seen a side of him today
that she had never dreamed existed, a side that was mischievous and playful and, she admitted, doubly attrac-

tive. When he laughed it lit his whole face and brought a warm gleam to his eyes. She realised then it was the first time she had ever seen him laugh like that.

'If it pleases you, my lady, the new gowns are ready for your inspection.'

Ashlynn looked round to see Morag. 'I beg your pardon?'

'Your gowns, my lady?'

'Of course, I'll come directly.'

Throwing a swift glance at the men she left them to talk, and moved quietly to the stairs. She never saw the dark gaze that followed her every step of the way.

The finished gowns exceeded her expectations in every way. They had been beautifully made and she looked at them with delight. Morag was open-mouthed to see the array of garments: chemises, bliauts, shoes, even a cloak made of good wool cloth and lined with marten fur. It was far warmer than the old one and Ashlynn knew she would be glad of it as the winter tightened its grip. She spent the next hour trying each of the garments in turn under the critical eyes of the seamstress and her assistants. Ashlynn had no fault to find. Madame's instinct for colour and style had been unerring. The gowns fitted her figure to perfection and she could see from the women's expressions that they became her well. Would Iain approve? She hoped he would for in truth it had been a most generous gift—generous and unexpected. The timing couldn't have been better either. Now she would have no cause to feel ashamed before the Yuletide guests.

In the meantime she gave orders for one of the big cedar-lined chests to be brought to her chambers. It would be ideal for the safe storage of the new gowns. Having organised that, she helped Morag lay the dresses within. The servant eyed her quizzically.

'Will you not change your gown now, my lady?'

'Not now. Tomorrow.'

'Ah, for the feast.'

'Just so.'

'I think you'll break hearts, my lady.'

Ashlynn smiled wistfully knowing there was one heart at least that would remain for ever out of reach.

Chapter Nine

The Yuletide feast saw the arrival of many guests. Ashlynn had dressed with care for the occasion, donning the forest green bliaut. It was simple and elegant, set off by the soft cream chemise beneath, the combination enhancing the tawny sheen of her hair. With Morag's help this was now neatly braided down her back with matching green ribbons. A girdle embroidered with brown and gold flowers rode her waist.

Ban, calling in a little later, surveyed her critically. Ashlynn smiled and gave him a twirl. 'Do you like it?'

'It's stunning,' he replied. Then, glancing over his shoulder, 'What say you, my lord?'

Iain, who had just appeared in the doorway, stopped in his tracks. For a long moment he surveyed his wife in silence, his gaze missing no detail. In fact he found it hard to tear his eyes away. Ban had not overstated the case; she really was stunning. The new gowns might have cost a small fortune but, looking at the result, it had been worth every penny.

'I think the assessment quite correct,' he replied.

There could be no mistaking the expression of warm approval in his eyes or the way they lingered on her figure. For the first time since she had left Heslingfield Ashlynn felt as though some lost part of her had just been restored and it lifted her spirits in an instant. She laughed and swept a low curtsy.

'I thank you, my lords.'

Ban grinned. 'Are you ready, Ash? The guests are approaching.'

'Yes, I just need my cloak.'

She retrieved it from the chair nearby but Iain stepped forward and relieved her of it.

'Allow me.'

He settled the garment on her shoulders and then fastened the brooch at the front. His hand brushed the neck of her gown, a casual and lightly caressing touch that set her flesh tingling in response. Then he held out his hand.

'Shall we?'

They descended the stairs and reached the bottom in time to see the riders clatter into the courtyard. Now that they were closer Ashlynn scanned the faces with interest. Counting the servants there were a dozen all told, ranging in age from four to forty. It took her by surprise to see the children among them but it was a pleasant discovery. How long it must have been since Dark Mount had heard children's voices.

Before she could pursue the thought she became aware that Iain's attention was not on them but rather on the accompanying adults, and suddenly there was tension in every line of his body. Following his gaze she saw it was fixed on a pretty dark-haired woman. The woman returned his stare for a moment or two and then allowed her male companion to help her from the saddle. Ashlynn had an impression of a burly bearded individual clad in a great fur cloak. For a moment he and Iain faced each other in silence. All around them the others were silent too, as though waiting for something. The tension was almost palpable. Then the newcomer held out his right hand. Iain stepped forward and took it in a firm clasp.

'It has been a long time, Duncan.'

At this the others relaxed visibly. Ashlynn's curiosity mounted. She exchanged glances with Ban and saw him raise an eyebrow. Evidently he too was at a loss. Then she turned her attention back to the little scene before them.

'Aye, it has,' Duncan replied. 'Too long, I'm thinking.' He glanced down at the woman beside him. For a moment she didn't move, her eyes fixed on Iain's face. In it Ashlynn saw both wariness and longing. Iain returned her gaze and held it.

'This is an unexpected pleasure,' he said.

'Unexpected I have no doubt,' she replied. 'As to the last, I wonder.'

'Then be in no doubt. You are welcome here, Jeannie.'

Ashlynn's heart missed a beat. This had to be the mysterious sister he had mentioned before.

'It is good of you to make the journey in such weather,' Iain continued.

Duncan snorted. 'It wouldn't have mattered if the drifts were five feet deep. Jeannie was determined to come.'

'I'm flattered.'

'Aye, you are, you rogue,' retorted the lady.

Undisturbed by this mode of address, Iain regarded her keenly. 'Can it be that you have missed me, sweet sister?'

She ignored the gibe. 'I wanted to know for myself if the rumour I've been hearing is true.'

'Oh, and what particular rumour would that be?' he replied.

'The one about you carrying off a beautiful woman and then marrying her. Duncan wouldn't have it, and I must admit I thought it ridiculous at first, but when I had the story from more than one source I became curious.' She fixed him with a sharp eye. 'What have you been up to, brother?'

Iain's lips twitched. 'I carried off a beautiful woman and then married her.'

Her jaw dropped for a moment but she recovered quickly. 'If you are trifling with me, Iain MacAlpin, I warn you now...'

'I wouldn't dream of it.' He turned toward the two figures behind him and smiled. 'Come. Allow me to present my wife, Lady Ashlynn, and her brother, Lord Ban. Ashlynn, this is my sister, Jeannie, and her husband, Duncan McCrae of Ardnashiel.'

For a second there was a pregnant silence. Duncan's blue eyes sparkled and he laughed softly in utter disbelief.

'Well, in the name of all that's wonderful.' As he ran his eye over Ashlynn his smile grew. 'I am truly delighted, my lady, although where this ugly brute found anything so beautiful I'll never know.'

Ashlynn curtseyed and returned the smile. 'The pleasure is mine, my lord.'

Duncan turned then to Ban and held out his hand. 'I'm

glad to make your acquaintance, sir. Did he carry you off too by any chance?'

Ban grinned. 'Aye, my lord, he did—in a manner of speaking.'

'Is that so? Well, by heaven, there's a good story here or I miss my guess, and I would fain hear it.'

'I also,' replied his wife.

The two women faced each other and Ashlynn found herself looking into an arresting face framed with curling dark hair. Jeannie was perhaps five or six years her senior. She was taller too and her figure fuller, but it was the eyes that one remembered for they were dark and piercing like her brother's. They missed no detail in their frank appraisal.

'I once thought that nothing my brother could do would ever surprise me again, but I see I was wrong.' She softened the words with a smile. 'For once it feels good to be wrong.'

With relief Ashlynn saw the smile reach the dark eyes and with it came the first glimmer of hope that she might now find a woman friend. Jeannie indicated the three children who stood nearby.

'My sons, Jamie and Andrew, and my daughter, Fiona.'

As the children made their duty to her Iain surveyed them with frank astonishment. 'Good God, but they've grown. I hardly recognise them.'

'How should you?' replied Jeanne. 'You haven't set eyes on them in nigh on three years.'

The tension was back and Ban interjected quickly. 'Children always grow fast, do they not?'

'So it would seem,' replied Iain.

His young relatives looked up at him with wide-eyed

apprehension for the tallest of them came no higher than his belt. The little girl's lip trembled. Ashlynn smiled.

'You are all welcome here,' she said. 'Now you are come I see that we shall have great fun this Yuletide.'

The gentleness of her tone seemed to offer reassurance and they began to look a little less anxious.

'We shall have feasting and music and, if you wish, we shall play some games. Would you like that?' she asked.

They nodded solemnly.

'Good. In a little while we shall go in together and you shall tell me what games you like best.' She held out her hand and after a moment's hesitation the little girl took it.

Iain watched the scene in fascination. He would never have suspected that she might like children or have such an easy way with them. They seemed to like her too and pressed round her now, clearly sensing safety. Him they continued to regard warily. He supposed it was scarcely to be wondered at. They must have forgotten his existence. Almost three years! The realisation caused an unexpected twinge of guilt. To cover it he introduced his wife and brother-in-law to the various cousins who made up the remainder of the party. When at length that duty was performed he gestured to the door.

'Shall we go in then?'

Jeannie smiled at Ashlynn. 'Aye, let's do that. Then we'll find a quiet corner somewhere and you can tell me how you had the misfortune to be married to my brother.'

Iain threw his sister a speaking glance which she ignored. Ashlynn began to like her more and more. She caught Ban's eye and saw him grin. Then they all went in together. After their guests had taken refreshment and been shown to their various quarters, Ashlynn went to inquire if Jeannie had everything she needed.

'I shall do very well. In truth I had not expected to find such comfort here,' she replied, looking round. 'You have made your mark already.'

In fact Ashlynn had raided all the upper storerooms for rugs and hangings and with the aid of Morag and the other servants had put them to use. She had also commanded that fires be lit in the guest chambers some days before, in order to take the damp chill off the air. In consequence the rooms looked and felt much more cheerful. It was pleasing to discover that her efforts were appreciated.

Her sister-in-law gestured to the chair opposite. 'Will you not sit awhile? Then you can tell me your story for I long to hear it.'

Ashlynn related the main events, leaving out only what was too personal to be shared. As she listened, Jeannie's face registered horror and sympathy but when it came to the part about the wedding her dark eyes narrowed.

'Did my brother force you to wed him?'

'He could not do other than marry me, my lady, since the king commanded it.'

'Malcolm disposes as he sees fit and always to suit himself,' replied Jeannie. She eyed Ashlynn closely for a moment. 'Has my brother treated you well since?'

'Yes, very well. He has been most generous.'

'Has he indeed? I'm relieved to hear it.'

'I have no cause for complaint.'

'You must be the first person ever to say so.' Jeannie smiled. 'But that's enough of him for the moment. Tell me about *your* brother.'

Ashlynn explained how she and Ban had been reunited. When she finished there were tears in her listener's eyes.

'It is a strange fate indeed that brought you here, but I am so glad it did.' She paused. 'Iain and I have been at odds for some time, and I began to fear that our estrangement might never end. It is in part due to you that it has a chance of doing so.'

'Then I am glad of it. Families should be united.'

'Aye, they should.' Jeannie eyes her quizzically. 'Did my brother tell you the nature of our quarrel?'

'He said that it concerned Fitzurse.'

'It is true. What Fitzurse did was cruel beyond believing.' The older woman sighed. 'Yet I could not bear to see Iain so consumed by rage and hatred.'

'I can understand that.'

'He and I were very close at one time. He was the person I looked up to most. Our childhood was not an easy one and he stood up for me many a time against our father.'

Ashlynn remained silent, listening avidly. She wanted so much to know more about the man she had married.

'He took some beatings on account of it,' Jeannie went on, 'but I never saw him cry. It was as though it had become a point of pride with him not to. When our mother died the situation got much worse. Iain said it was our father's unkindness that caused her death. Perhaps in part he was right.'

'I'm sorry to hear it.'

'He and Father had a terrible row and came to blows as a result. A short time later Iain was sent to France.'

'But what of you?'

'I was rescued by an aunt, one of my mother's sisters. She was ever a kindly soul and her house seemed like heaven to me. The three years I spent with her were among the happiest of my life. It was there I met Duncan. He came courting after that and when I turned sixteen we married.'

'Did you ever hear from Iain?'

'He would send word from time to time. It was clear that France agreed with him.'

'He married there, did he not?'

'That's right.' Jeannie paused. 'Did he tell you what happened to his wife?'

'Yes.'

'It almost destroyed him. I never saw a person so changed. For a while I thought he might run mad. However, he channelled his energies into fighting instead.'

'That was when he joined Malcolm.'

'Aye, and began to carve out a reputation for himself into the bargain. He always was a good swordsman and he honed his skill. Those who saw him in battle said he was fearless. As time went on he became involved in a lot of other wild exploits and his reputation grew.'

'I had heard of it long before I met him,' replied Ashlynn.

Jeannie nodded. 'He had learned the value of being feared.'

'But you did not fear him?'

'No, I feared *for* him. I dreaded what hatred and rage might turn him into and begged him to give up the quest for Fitzurse, but he would not and so we quarrelled.' She sighed. 'Heaven knows how often I have regretted it.'

'You did what you thought you had to do.'

'Yet it got me nowhere and earned his enmity into the bargain.'

'But surely that is at an end now,' said Ashlynn.

'I hope so, for this quarrel has resulted only in tears and bitterness and we have seen enough of that.' Jeannie regarded her keenly. 'Perhaps now that he has you my brother will put aside the thought of revenge.'

Ashlynn smiled sadly, knowing she possessed no such influence. Iain was set on a course that could only end in bloodshed and death—for him or for Fitzurse, or both. Nothing she could say would ever change his mind.

Further friends and relations appeared later that day, braving the weather to make the ride to Glengarron. All were warmly welcomed and, Iain having performed the necessary introductions, all received the news of the laird's marriage with frank astonishment. Suddenly Ashlynn found herself the centre of attention.

'She's a bonny lass and no mistake,' said Duncan who was standing next to Iain by the fireplace, watching as Ashlynn and her brother talked with Jeannie and some cousins across the room. 'You've done well for yourself there.'

'I know it,' replied Iain.

'I like the brother too. He's a brave lad if what you say is true.'

'That he is.'

'They've had a bad time, the pair of them.'

'Aye, they have.'

'The rumours are true then. William really is laying waste to Northumbria.'

'It's true all right. Heslingfield was only one of many manors to fall victim to his revenge.'

Duncan shook his head in disgust. 'It's indefensible to punish the innocent. The man's a monster.' He darted a glance across the room to Ban. 'What is the lad going to do once he's fully fit again?'

'I don't know. We've not discussed the matter as yet.'

'Well, there's time enough.'

'So there is.' Iain held out his cup to be refilled by a servant. 'No doubt he'll tell me his mind when he's ready.'

His gaze returned to the group across the room, though in truth the only one he saw was Ashlynn. He was glad to see her developing friendship with his sister and gladder still to see her smile and laugh. Today she looked every inch the lady she was. As his eyes lingered on the curves of her slender figure now so enticingly revealed by the new gown, his mind dwelt tantalisingly on what lay beneath. He knew he wasn't alone in his admiration; he had seen the way the eyes of other men were continually drawn back to her. It did not displease him. Let them look. None would dare to touch: she was his. The knowledge did nothing to diminish his pride.

The feast that evening was a splendid and sumptuous affair and the hall was filled with conversation and laughter. Iain, watching the succession of dishes appearing from the kitchen could not but be impressed. Once again Ashlynn's ability to plan and organise surprised him. It was a facet of her personality he had not suspected. Watching her smiling and talking to their guests she looked every inch the lady of the manor. There was no trace now of the boyish imp or the wildcat and yet he knew both were still there. This unpredictability was, he reflected, part of her considerable charm. He never knew what facet might be revealed next and it both intrigued and fascinated him, arousing his curiosity and making him want to discover more.

Keenly aware of that apparently casual regard Ashlynn turned to meet his gaze and saw him smile.

'An excellent feast,' he said. 'You have surpassed yourself.'

His words brought a glow of pleasure and she returned the smile. 'You must thank the cook for it, not I.'

'Had it not been for you I doubt we'd have seen anything like this. His imagination seemed not to run much beyond a haunch of venison or a side of mutton before this.'

'I added a few ideas of my own.'

'So I see, and I'm glad of it. This board would not disgrace a king.' He paused. 'Where did you learn all this?'

'Even Sassenach girls are brought up to know about the managing of a household, my lord.'

'Who'd have thought it?'

She shook her head. 'It's no use. I shall not allow myself to be provoked.'

'What a pity.'

'I think you enjoy provoking people.'

'Only where there's such a strong element of unpredictability.'

Ashlynn laughed. 'I hardly think that applies in this case for you know full well that I have a temper and one too easily roused.'

'Not so. You were ever unpredictable, lass, but as to the rest, you never lost your temper without good cause.'

The quiet tone held no trace of levity and it caught her off balance for, while she felt perfectly capable of holding her own with him in any amount of verbal sparring, it was harder to know how to deal with this.

In the event she was saved the trouble because the musicians struck up and heralded the start of the dancing. Iain rose and held out his hand.

'Will you honour me, my lady?'

Once again she was caught unawares. However, after a moment she gave him her hand and allowed him to lead her out. Soon the other couples formed around them. Dancing was not an activity she would have associated with him, but it soon became apparent that, for so tall a man, he moved with considerable grace.

'Where did you learn to dance?' she asked as the figure brought them together.

'In France. In my aunt's house it was *de rigueur*, just as it was for every page and squire to learn how to comport himself in company.' He grinned. 'Six months under her tutelage was enough to knock off the rough edges.'

'I thought you went there for military training.'

'So I did, but the two things went hand in hand. Sometimes it was hard to tell the difference.'

Ashlynn laughed. Then the dance separated them again but his words had given her much to think about. The wider reputation of the man they dubbed Black Iain concealed a personality far more complex, and it intrigued her.

When the measure ended her hand was claimed by other partners and he as host invited other ladies on to the floor. She noted that, without exception, they never took their eyes off him, looking up into his face and smiling, clearly hanging on his every word. It was borne upon her yet again that her husband was a very attractive man.

Later, when the musicians took a break, the company demanded the appointment of a Lord of Misrule to lead the future festivities. After some lively banter a youth called Hamish was duly elected. Ashlynn recalled that he was one of Iain's many cousins. Lord of Misrule was a role he stepped into with ease. His first act was to call for a game of blind man's buff, a suggestion received with much favour, especially by the younger members of the gathering. Accordingly a blindfold was produced. Then Hamish turned to Ashlynn.

'As Lord of Misrule I decree that you shall wear the blindfold first, my lady.'

Taken totally by surprise Ashlynn held up her hands in protest but the company would have none of it and in the end she yielded, laughing. The guests cheered. As Hamish fastened the blindfold over her eyes, Iain handed his cup to Duncan.

'It has been a while since I've played this. Let's see if I remember how.'

To his brother-in-law's amused surprise he joined the others in the centre of the hall to the general approbation. Ashlynn heard the increased laughter but knew not the cause. Then Hamish spun her round and let go. Swaying a little she regained her balance, edging forward with outstretched hands. She heard rustlings in the straw underfoot as people skipped out of the way, and heard giggling and laughter all about her. For a while she stumbled around and then, unexpectedly, her hands met the woollen fabric of a tunic. Exploring further they discovered a man's arms and then a pair of broad shoulders. The laughter grew. Suddenly the arms closed round her waist and shoulders and crushed her against a lean hard body. Then a man's mouth was over hers in a kiss that had nothing of gentleness in it but something quite other.

Taken by surprise Ashlynn had no time to struggle and the hands that had moved instinctively to push him away suddenly lacked the will or power to do so for deep within a treacherous spark awakened and then flamed, spreading like fire through her veins. It was a kiss so blatantly passionate that it drew shocked gasps from the delighted spectators. When eventually he released her there was a moment of complete silence. Then roars of approval shook the rafters of the hall. Breathless and astonished Ashlynn removed the blindfold and stared into her husband's face. His eyes were alight with amusement. He was also very clearly enjoying her evident confusion. Speechless, Ashlynn relinquished the blindfold to Hamish and, since there was no help for it, allowed Iain to lead her aside. When they were a safe distance from the others she confronted him.

'You did that on purpose, didn't you?'

'That's right. It's the point of the game you see.'

The words took her straight back to their wedding day. He had kissed her then for the benefit of others. She hadn't been able to help her response then either. *'By God, lass, you play the game well.'* Was this part and parcel of the same thing? Indignation was replaced by hurt and uncertainty.

'This is all a game to you, isn't it?'

Amusement faded. 'A game? What are we talking about here, Ashlynn?'

'You know full well.'

'I don't think I do. Explain it to me.'

'This…this whole situation.'

'You're angry because I kissed you in public?'

'No.'

'Then why?'

Even as she sought the words to tell him, Duncan appeared beside them.

'Forgive me, but I need to borrow your husband, my lady.' He grinned and jerked his head towards the far side of the room. 'There's an argument over yonder that would be settled.'

Her heart sank but there was only one possible answer. 'By all means.'

Iain gritted his teeth knowing there was nothing for it save graceful compliance. However, before he left he fixed Ashlynn with a penetrating look.

'I'll be back, my lady, and this discussion will be resumed.'

Sick at heart she watched him walk away. Just when everything seemed to be going well she had alienated him. What had possessed her to say it? Of course it was a game! Why couldn't she have left it at that? She knew perfectly well where his feelings lay.

When Iain left her he fully intended to return as promised and have the matter out. However, that was easier said than done. By the time he had settled the argument amongst Duncan's circle the dancing had started again and Ashlynn's hand was claimed for every measure. He noticed too that she made no attempt to seek him out or even look in his direction. What had happened to anger her so much? Surely a kiss could not be the cause, no matter how public.

From his vantage point Iain watched his wife laughing and talking with the other guests. To anyone else she would have seemed quite at ease. Iain, looking more closely, was undeceived. He could sense the tension in her. It occurred to him then that what had happened earlier might be due to reasons other than he had initially supposed. She must be missing her home and her family. With her emotions in this fragile state it would not take much to upset her. What was it? How he wished she would tell him. He was so preoccupied with the thought that at first he failed to notice the woman who had come to stand beside him.

'She's very beautiful, Iain.'

He looked round and saw Jeannie. 'Aye, she is.'

'And charming too,' his sister went on. 'She has but to smile to have men eating out of her hand. Women as well it seems.'

'She has charm and to spare.'

'I had not realised your taste was so good.'

'I'll take that as a compliment.'

'I can quite see why you wanted her to wife.' She paused. 'What is much less clear is why she agreed.'

'Don't flatter me, Jeannie, whatever you do.'

'You forced her to wed you, did you not?'

'When the king commands it is unwise to do anything other than comply. I had no more choice in the matter than Ashlynn. Malcolm solved the problem with as little inconvenience to himself as possible.'

'And yet you have not done so badly by the bargain.' She shook her head. 'In truth it is Ashlynn I feel for. A woman has no chance when pitted against the will of powerful men.'

'She has an honourable position here. The alternative would have been a lot worse.'

'So you were the lesser of two evils then?'

'If you choose to put it like that.'

'Oh, I do. As I said, I know you well, brother. All the same, I'm fascinated to see you in the role of protector to a lovely woman.'

'I can assure you it is a role I take most seriously.'

'I'm glad to hear it. The lass has had a bad time of it by all accounts.'

'Aye, she has, but that is over now at least. Nothing shall hurt her again if I have the power to prevent it.'

The words were quietly spoken but Jeannie heard the resolution that underlay them and looked up in surprise, yet there was no mistaking the ingenuous tone. Recalling the cold and bitter man he had been before, she realised that something fundamental had changed and her heart knew a glimmer of hope.

Iain tossed off the remainder of his wine and cast another look across the room. Seeing his wife surrounded by a crowd of admirers all vying for her attention, he experienced a re-awakening of the feeling he'd had when he saw her with Robbie that day in the courtyard. Annoyance turned in on itself. He had no grounds for jealousy. Ashlynn was beautiful and men admired her, wanted her. Yet for all her banter and smiles she knew how to hold them at arm's length. That of course just had the effect of making them try harder. He should know. He too was fully alive to his wife's physical charms. At night he lay awake knowing there was but a door between them and that he had the key, knowing how easy it would be to use force. However, he wanted more than mere bodily submission. She must come to him or it meant nothing. And so he waited…and waited. Just when he thought he was making progress he found himself back where he'd started.

Watching her now he saw her excuse herself from the group and move to speak to her brother who was standing nearby. She put an arm about him, a casual and loving gesture that meant nothing and everything. His jaw tightened as jealousy resurfaced for the second time. What on earth was the matter with him that he should lose his customary sense of perspective over something so trivial? Ban was her brother and she loved him. Why should she not? The lad was handsome and brave and good company withal. In his presence she opened like a flower in the sun. With him her smile was unforced, her laughter from the heart. Ban too played his part well. It was a testament to their spirit that they would not inflict their sorrows on others even though the wounds were still raw.

His admiration grew, along with his frustration for, while he knew that Ashlynn wasn't totally indifferent to him, she never looked at him as she looked at Ban, never smiled in quite that way. He had once told Ashlynn that she would see him every day of her life whether she wanted to or not. How ironic then that it was he who now suffered the torment of seeing her every day, of speaking to her, of being close enough to touch her and yet knowing himself as far away as ever. Be that as it might, he would know the cause of her displeasure before this evening was over.

* * *

Ashlynn felt only relief when the female members of the company started to drift away. Soon she too could escape and seek the sanctuary of her chamber. Out of the corner of her eye she could see Iain talking to Duncan and Jeannie. She saw him take his sister's hand and smiled to herself, glad to see that some degree of amity had been restored. The two of them strolled towards the door to be joined by several other ladies. There they paused while he bade them all a courteous goodnight. When they had disappeared from view he turned back to the room at large, his gaze searching. It found Ashlynn at once and held her. If she had been expecting him to return and mingle she was mistaken; he remained exactly where he was, waiting. The message was plain. To leave the hall she must pass him first and he wasn't about to let that happen.

Knowing there was no point in delaying the inevitable Ashlynn excused herself from the company. Iain watched her come. For a moment they surveyed each other in silence. Then he took hold of her arm. The grip didn't hurt but it would not be resisted either. He drew her with him into the corridor. Ashlynn glanced up, expecting him to stop but he didn't. Instead, and much to her consternation, she was conducted up two flights of stairs and along the corridor to his room. He pulled her in with him and closed the door behind them. Then he leaned upon it, surveying her keenly.

'Now that we are quite private, you and I going to talk, lass.'

'There is nothing to say.'

She took a step towards the door but he did not move.

'I think there is, and you're not leaving until this matter is resolved.' He paused. 'Now, tell me what it was so offended you that you must avoid me all the rest of the evening. I cannot believe it was just a kiss.'

Ashlynn shook her head sadly. Just a kiss. That really was all it meant to him. 'It doesn't matter.'

'It does matter. If my memory serves me aright, you spoke of playing games. It carries an imputation I don't much care for.'

'Did it strike a nerve, Iain?'

His eyes narrowed a little. 'You think that my kissing you was some kind of game?'

'Wasn't it?' she replied. 'Wasn't it just a charade for the benefit of your guests? You did it very well too I may say. I think they were convinced.'

He gave a hollow laugh. 'Is that what you think?'

'What else is there to think?'

'That I might have kissed you because I really wanted to, that the passion wasn't feigned, that you're so beautiful I don't know how to keep my hands off you.'

'Because you want me in your bed you mean.'

'Aye, I do, in case it's not already clear. What's wrong with that?'

She swallowed hard. 'Everything, when you love someone else.'

'What!' His brows drew together. 'Who is it that you think I love, Ashlynn?'

'Eloise!' She flung the name at him. 'You told me as much yourself. She's the reason you never remarried, would never have remarried until the king commanded it. I believe you only agreed because you needed heirs to continue your line.'

For a moment he was quite still, regarding her intently, his face white. Then, when he was sure he could keep his voice under control, 'Do you so?'

'It's the truth.'

'I think you and I need to get a few things straight.' He took a deep breath. 'Since you've raised the subject we'll start with Eloise.'

'I don't want to hear it.'

'You're going to hear it,' he replied. 'You'll not make such statements without giving me the right of reply.' He fixed her with a gimlet stare. 'You accuse me of loving Eloise still and so I do, but not in the way you seem to think. What I cherish is not a hopeless, pointless passion but the memory of a brief happiness; happiness I never thought to have until I met her and which, for a long time after her death, I believed was lost for ever. Then you came into my life.' He made a vague gesture with his hands. 'I'll not pretend I fell in love with you at first sight; it wasn't until the first time I kissed you that I realised there was an attraction. Even then I tried to deny it, but the longer I was with you the more difficult it became.'

'Very difficult,' she agreed. 'So much so, that it was the king who ordered our marriage.'

'Malcolm had his own reasons. Whatever they were he was several moves ahead of me at that point. But, when he compelled us to marry, it made me think about what I really wanted.'

'Oh, and what did you decide?'

'That I want to build a future with you. That I want a family, children who will grow up knowing a father's care. If all I wanted was to sire heirs I'd have done it long since. The reason I haven't is that I never met the woman I wanted to share that with. After what I had with Eloise I could never settle for anything less. I thought I could never have that again, until I met you.'

Ashlynn's gaze searched his face, her heart thumping painfully hard. The words had sounded sincere. 'Is that the truth?'

'On everything I hold sacred.'

Ashlynn turned away, trying to make sense of her chaotic thoughts. They both wanted the same things—almost. He had not spoken of his desire for revenge but the word hung there between them. She knew it hadn't gone away; that it was still an issue; that they needed to confront it. But if she spoke its name the spell would be broken, the moment lost. She had alienated him once tonight already through ill-considered words. Now he was trying to put things right. How could she destroy what had been so hard won?

Iain didn't move, made no attempt to touch her, but his voice was calmer now, steadier. 'I know as well as anyone can what you've been through, lass, and no one could have faced it with greater courage. When you took my name I swore to protect you, and if I had the ordering of the world nothing should ever harm you more.' He paused. 'With you I have found what I never thought to have again with any woman. I hoped that you had begun to care a little for me. Was I wrong?'

She shook her head. 'No, you weren't wrong. It's just…'

'Just…?'

'That I was afraid.'

'Of me?'

She turned to face him again. 'Of being hurt.'

'I would never deliberately do anything to hurt you.'

In spite of all attempts to blink them back the tears welled in her eyes and spilled over. Very gently he drew her against his breast and let her rest there, safe in the circle of his arms, and for the first time all the tension went out of her and she knew only the rightness of being there.

He dropped a kiss on her hair and then, as she looked up, another on her mouth. Ashlynn returned it, a slow and lingering embrace that turned his blood to fire. For a moment the dark gaze burned into hers and saw there what he had hardly dared to hope for.

'I want to kiss you again, lass, but I'm afraid if I do it'll not stop there.'

'Who said I wanted it to?'

His heart performed a sudden and dangerous manoeuvre and for a moment or two he didn't move, being entirely unsure he had just heard her aright. Then she reached up and drew his face down towards hers. This time it was she who kissed him, a passionate affirmation of the feelings she could no longer conceal.

He lifted her in his arms and carried her into his bedchamber and undressed her there, laying aside her garments before removing his own. Ashlynn caught her breath, taking in all the lithe and sculptured beauty of the hard-muscled body. Then he was beside her, drawing the furs over them, his mouth on hers, his hands exploring the curves of her flesh, subtle, arousing. And the world became a fusion of sense impressions, the coarse linen sheet and the soft wolf pelts, flickering light from the fire, the faint smell of wood smoke and the warmth of his flesh against hers, the erotic scent of musk on his skin, the taste of wine on his lips. His mouth moved lower, caressing neck and throat and breasts, sending a delicious shiver the length of her body. Ashlynn yielded herself up to it, wanting this, wanting him, no longer able to deny what she felt. Now there was no fear or doubt, only the sweetness of belonging, as though something long sought had been found.

He took his time, restraining desire, controlling passion, fighting the predatory urge that would make possession an act of violation. She would be his, finally and absolutely. He knew now he had wanted this from the first, a knowledge he had tried to deny, just as she had. And so he relearned the beauty of her body whose perfection his eyes had ascertained long before, his hands moving across waist and hip and thigh, and thence to the secret place between, gently stroking, teasing, rousing, feeling the answering rush of hot warmth, feeling the first shudder in her body's core. A body made for this. His knee parted her thighs and he entered her, gently, encountering resistance, moving past it and then deeper into her, moving in slow rhythm, holding back, feeding the fire and bringing her with him.

Ashlynn gasped, feeling him thrust deeper into her, moving with him now, her body arching into his, each rhythmic stroke sending pleasure coursing through every fibre of her being. The cry caught in her throat. And then restraint was gone and there was a final fierce possession before release and the hot sweet rush of a mutual shuddering climax.

For a little while he remained inside her, breathing hard, looking into her face, seeing there an echo of his own wonder. He had expected to enjoy this; what he had not anticipated was the sheer soul-filling delight of it. Gently he withdrew and collapsed beside her, deliciously sated. He had given her pleasure in order to leave her wanting more; he had not realised that the effect might rebound on him with such force.

Beside him Ashlynn drowsed, exhausted. He smiled and drew the pelts over her again, dropping a kiss on her shoulder. Then he curled his body round hers and held her close, listening to her soft breathing until he too fell asleep.

Chapter Ten

Ashlynn stirred and then stretched luxuriously, her body filled with a sense of well being. Opening her eyes slowly to the new day she became aware of a strange room and for a moment or two couldn't remember how she had got there. Then memory began to wake and she smiled to herself. Turning her head she let her gaze drink in the details of the sleeping face beside her. While the realities of the marriage bed had come as no surprise, she could never have imagined they would be anything like what had happened last night. The recollection sent a flood of warmth through her loins. The only cloud on her horizon was that he had not actually said he loved her. Not in so many words anyway. *Cared for* was not quite the same thing. Perhaps he found the words too hard to say.

In the meantime, she was aware of the advancing hour and that they had a house full of guests. Casting a furtive glance upon the sleeping figure she turned away, looking around for her clothes and finally spied them across the room. She began to ease herself from the

bed. An arm closed about her waist, pulling her backwards. A moment later she was looking up at Iain's
face. He smiled.

'Where did you think you were going, wife?'

'We have social obligations, my lord.'

'Let them wait.'

'But it's broad day. Too late to be lying abed.'

He grinned widened. 'I assure you, 'tis early yet, my
sweet, and in truth last night did but whet my appetite.'

'You are quite shameless.'

'You're not the first person to say so.'

'I can believe it. Whoever dubbed you Black Iain
knew you well.'

The dark eyes gleamed appreciatively. 'Well then,
perhaps I should live up to my name.'

As the implication dawned Ashlynn's inner demon
woke. It might have been entirely seduced last night but
that didn't mean it was tamed. Without warning she
twisted, trying to escape the restraining arm but it held
her with consummate ease. Iain laughed softly. The
sound caused her to redouble her efforts. She twisted
again but instead of pulling away threw herself forward,
landing across his chest, hands forcing his shoulders
back against the bed. She smiled triumphantly. A
moment later triumph turned to a gasp of dismay as he
rolled, pinning her beneath his weight and cutting off
all protest with a kiss. Pleasurable warmth spread the
length of her body. Moreover, it was clear her efforts had
done nothing to diminish his desire either. Ashlynn
writhed, testing his hold. It yielded not an inch.

'Let me go, villain.'

'Not a chance, lass.'

* * *

The sun was considerably higher before they emerged
to face the world. However, no one seemed to find it amiss
and their arrival in the hall was greeted with amused
smiles. As they broke their fast Ashlynn kept her attention
on the food, feigning nonchalance and trying not to dwell
on recent events in the bedchamber. Even now her flesh
seemed to burn with the recollection. When at length she
had finished her meal she glanced up to meet Iain's eye
and saw him smile.

'What shall we do today?' he asked.

'Since the snow is here we might as well make the
most of it.'

At these words the children who had been playing
nearby fell silent, their eyes on her face. Seeing all those
hopeful expressions Iain was intrigued.

'What exactly did you have in mind?'

'Well, there are some sledges in the barn,' she replied.
'Perhaps we could take them out on to the hill.'

A babble of excited chatter erupted and was promptly
shushed by the older ones. All eyes turned to Iain and
they waited, hanging on his reply with painful longing.
He let the silence drag out for a few seconds more and
then grinned.

'Why not?' he said.

A cheer rent the air. He beckoned them closer. They
obeyed, though still keeping to a respectful distance.

'The older boys can fetch the sledges from the barn.'

At the word sledges other ears pricked up.

'We'll go with them, my lord,' said Hamish, throwing
an eloquent look at Donald.

'Absolutely,' his friend replied. 'Just to be sure they come to no harm, my lord.'

Ban got to his feet. 'I think I'd better go along too. There are lots of children to take care of after all.'

'Indeed there are,' Iain replied. Then he looked at Ashlynn. 'I think some responsible adults should go accompany them, don't you?'

She laughed. 'You just read my mind.'

'Can I come too, Aunt Ashlynn?' said a timid voice beside her.

She glanced down and saw Fiona. 'Of course you can come.' Smiling she took the child's hand in hers. 'You shall walk with me.'

Iain grinned. 'It looks like we have a full complement then.'

Five minutes later they went to join the excited little crowd in the courtyard. When the boys re-appeared with the sledges they all set off. The older children soon drew ahead, some of the lads engaged in a running snowball fight on the way. Ashlynn's pace was of necessity slower to accommodate Fiona's shorter strides. Iain paused to let them catch up. He could hear Ashlynn speaking to the child, her tone gentle and patient, drawing her companion out and making her laugh. Clearly she had a way with children.

'I never thought of you in this role,' he said when they had rejoined him. 'It suits you.'

'Does it?'

'Very much so.'

The words were quietly spoken but they contained a nuance she had not heard before. It turned her thoughts in another direction entirely and sent a flush of warmth through her entire being.

They walked on for a while but, as they drew nearer their goal the snow became deeper. Fiona stumbled over the skirt of her gown. Ashlynn's hand prevented her from falling but it was clear that progress was going to be slow.

'You go on ahead,' she told Iain.

'I have a better idea.' He bent and lifted the child up on to his shoulders. 'Hold on tight now.'

Fiona was quick to obey, torn between anxiety at being so far from the ground and the thrill of having so exalted a position. However, as they walked on she began to relax and enjoy herself, exchanging occasional shy smiles with Ashlynn. In fact Ashlynn was amused and oddly touched. She had never imagined Iain unbending this far and yet he did it so lightly and withal so naturally. He would make a good father. The ramifications to that sent another flush of warmth through her. She shot him a sidelong glance and saw him smile.

By the time they reached the slope the older members of the party were already organising themselves. Iain lifted Fiona down and gave her into the safe keeping of two older girl cousins and then watched as Hamish and Donald embarked on their first run. However, their balance was awry and the sled went hurtling off course towards the burn. With yells of dismay they tried to take evasive action, only to lurch sideways into a hidden boulder just below the surface of the snow. The collision pitched them headfirst down the hill, to the huge enjoyment of the onlookers. Undeterred the other participants climbed aboard their own sledges and went speeding away. The air rang with shrieks and laughter.

Having seen the others underway Iain turned to his wife. 'Will you adventure with me, Ashlynn?'

The tone was casual enough but there was a mischievous expression in his eye that gave her pause. Seeing her hesitation Iain seized the advantage and went straight in for the kill.

'What's the matter, lass? Are you afraid?'

He saw her chin come up and grinned, knowing his faith hadn't been misplaced. Taking her hand he led her away from the main group to a much steeper part of the hill. Ashlynn looked at it with trepidation. The lower slope had produced speeds that were hair-raising enough. This was something else again. At the base of the slope the ground curved out and then ended abruptly in a sharp drop to the burn, dark and deep and swift-flowing at this season.

'Are you sure about this, Iain?'

'Of course. Jeannie and I came here often as children. It's an exhilarating run I promise you.'

Unwilling to back down from the unspoken challenge she seated herself gingerly on the sledge and he climbed on behind, locking his arms around her.

'Can you swim by the way?' he asked.

'Swim!'

'Aye, for when we end up in the burn, ye ken.'

Before she could reply he pushed off and heard her shriek as the sled gathered speed, hurtling down the hillside at a dizzying rate. Ashlynn gasped as the wind stung her face and brought the water to her eyes, seeing through blurred vision the burn approaching with horrifying rapidity. Uttering a wail of dismay she closed her eyes. However, what she hadn't known was that the view from above was foreshortened and where the land flattened out at the bottom of the slope there was in fact a considerable distance to the stream, easily enough space for the sled to come to a safe stop well short of the water. Speechless she sat for some moments in stunned disbelief, her heart in her throat. Iain too was unusually quiet. When she looked round it was to see him shaking with silent laughter. Ashlynn glared at him.

'You horror! You frightened the life out of me.'

Rather than expressing any kind of remorse Iain's merriment seemed to increase. Incredulous she could only stare at him, her body still trembling with reaction. Then, as the initial shock subsided, the humour of it struck her and somewhat ruefully she began to laugh too.

'Truly you are well named!' she said.

'Admit that you enjoyed it.'

'If terror can be said to be enjoyable then, yes, I admit it.'

'Is it not such moments of terror that make us feel most alive?'

'Don't try to philosophise, villain. What you enjoyed was scaring the daylights out of me.'

'I canna deny it.'

Ashlynn grabbed a handful of snow and pushed it in his face. 'Take that!'

The words were succeeded by a gasp as, without warning, he tipped her backwards into the snow and then followed her down, pinning her beneath him. Worse, there was a gleam in those dark eyes that she recognised all too well.

'Have you not learned that there are fearful penalties attached to that kind of thing?'

Then his hands were round her, tickling her ribs unmercifully. Ashlynn shrieked, trying in vain to escape.

'Now then, beg for mercy, wife.'

'I will not.'

'Say you so?'

His efforts intensified. Helpless with laughter she had at last to cry quarter. 'Enough, Iain, I yield.'

'Then I claim the right as victor to name the terms of surrender.'

'Which are?'

For answer he took a leisurely kiss. Powerless to prevent it she had perforce to submit. However, the experience was enjoyable to a most disquieting degree. Furthermore the expression in his eyes did nothing to detract from that. For a long moment they remained thus, until other voices broke the spell. They looked round to see Hamish and Donald approaching along the path at the top of the crest followed closely by Ban with James and Andrew.

'Such perfect timing,' murmured Iain between gritted teeth. 'I swear Hamish does it on purpose.'

Ashlynn laughed and he threw her a speaking glance. Then she felt his weight shift as he got to his feet. A moment later he reached down and took her hand, pulling her up after, and together they toiled their way back up the hill.

As the oncoming quintet drew nigh Ashlynn saw her brother's speculative grin as he took in her dishevelled appearance. However, before he could comment Hamish spoke up.

'We're following your example, my lord. This looks like much more fun.'

'Indeed it is,' replied Iain. Then in an aside to his wife, 'The slope's quite exciting too.'

Ashlynn gave a snort of laughter and then hurriedly turned it into a cough. Donald regarded her with hopeful eyes.

'Will you come with me, my lady?' he asked.

'Thank you no. Once was enough.'

In evident disappointment he joined Hamish on the sled. Beside them Ban followed suit with James and Andrew. Then all five set off down the hill again.

For a moment Iain followed their progress and smiled. However, when he turned to his wife his expression was quite serious.

'Was once really enough or will you adventure with me again, Ashlynn?'

His eyes met and held her own and she recognised in his face the invitation that was both challenge and promise. Her spirit leapt, remembering the heart-thumping excitement of the first dizzy rush down the icy slope. She knew now that she had never been in danger, that he would not have let anything happen to her. It had been exhilarating and not just because of the purported risk. Being with him was the real exhilaration. She saw him smile and hold out his hand to her. For the briefest moment she hesitated, then smiled in return.

'Yes, I will.'

Iain's fingers closed around hers. 'Come then, my sweet.'

This time there was the thrill with none of the terror and they reached the bottom of the hill in gales of laughter.

* * *

At the end of that afternoon when they walked back through the snow to Dark Mount, Ashlynn's cloak was soaked along with the hem of her gown and her shoes, and her fingers tingled inside her gloves, but there was a glow inside her that rendered such details irrelevant. In truth she had not thought two months ago ever to feel so alive again. For the first time she began to glimpse a future that was not filled with fear, a possibility that she might, after all, find happiness here in this remote and wild land.

Ashlynn returned to her chamber and changed out of her wet garments. The task had not long been completed when there was a knock at the door. Her heart leapt as she bade the caller enter. As the door opened she saw her brother on the threshold.

'Oh, Ban.'

He smiled faintly. 'Were you expecting someone else?'

'I thought it might have been Morag.'

'Ah.' He glanced round, taking in the pile of discarded garments. 'Am I interrupting?'

'No, of course not. Come in.'

'I need to talk to you, Ash.'

Seeing that he looked unusually preoccupied she gestured to a chair. 'Well then, won't you sit down?'

However, he ignored her invitation and moved closer to the hearth, looking down into the fire. Ashlynn waited, puzzled, feeling the first stirring of unease.

'I have been thinking,' he said at last.

'About what?'

'The future.' He turned to face her, regarding her with a steady gaze. 'Your husband has been a most generous host, but I cannot stay here indefinitely. I must make my way in the world. Since the best chance of doing that is to go to Dunfermline and seek military service, that is what I mean to do.'

'But your shoulder is not completely healed yet.'

'No, but it grows stronger with every day. In the New Year I shall get back into training and by the spring I shall be fit again.'

Ashlynn bit her lip, fighting the rising sense of dread. 'I don't want you to go, Ban.'

'I know but I must. Surely you see that?'

'Yes, but…'

'But what?'

'You are all I have left of family. I will miss you dreadfully.'

'And I you,' he replied, 'but we will see each other as time and occasion permit. Besides, you will be too busy to miss me for long.'

Ashlynn turned away to hide the tears that threatened. Frowning, Ban took her by the shoulders.

'No need to be despondent. I'm not leaving yet. There's plenty of time for you to get used to the idea.'

'I think I will never get used to the idea.'

'You must, Ash. Our ways lie along different paths now.'

'Does Iain know about this?'

'Not yet, but I shall speak to him soon.'

She turned and regarded him with imploring eyes. 'Must you really go?'

He gave her a gentle smile. 'You have found your place, Ash. Now I must seek mine.'

He left shortly after this and Ashlynn paced the floor

in mounting distress. In a matter of weeks Ban would be gone. He was an able swordsman and she had no doubt of his finding the situation he desired. And after Dunfermline what then? He had spoken of their meeting again from time to time but she was realist enough to know it could not be often. What if something were to happen to him? Life was precarious; doubly so for one who earned a living by the sword. He was the last remaining tie with everything she had held dear. If she lost him… Suddenly, all her former fears rose like a tide and she sank trembling on to a chair.

That evening she was quieter than usual and despite the music and laughter all around the feeling of heaviness persisted. Involuntarily her thoughts turned from the present to the last Yuletide celebrations at Heslingfield, to the hall and the great log burning in the hearth and all the walls festooned with winter greenery. She could see her family and hear again their laughter and merry banter as they moved among their guests. Almost she could hear music and song and smell the rich fare issuing from the kitchen for Lord Cyneric was renowned for keeping a fine table. Not only was he a good host, no one was ever turned away from his door no matter how humble. Remembering it, she felt the tears start. Yule would never be celebrated more in Heslingfield. A great Saxon house was gone, along with all its tradition of hospitality and good fellowship.

'Ashlynn?'

Jeannie's voice recalled her and she looked up with a start to find both her sister-in-law and husband regarding her closely. 'Forgive me.'

'Are you all right?'

'Yes, perfectly.'

With an effort she dragged her attention back to the room and the company.

'Duncan and I want to invite you to Ardnashiel in the spring,' said Jeannie. 'You will come, won't you? I would not lose you so soon.'

'I would be delighted.' Ashlynn looked up at Iain. 'That is, if…'

He smiled and then turned to his sister. 'I will bring her, I promise.'

'I shall hold you to it.'

'I wouldn't dare disobey,' he confided to his wife. 'My sister has a fearsome tongue on her.'

Ashlynn smiled. 'Then I'll look forward to the spring weather.'

'It will come soon enough.' Jeannie threw her brother a shrewd glance. 'And you will be off adventuring again no doubt.'

'That depends on the adventure,' he replied.

Neither of them had spoken the word revenge but it was tacitly understood and Ashlynn felt a sudden sense of foreboding. When all the festivities were over and the guests were gone would his thoughts turn that way? Would the thaw see him gone too? He was a man of action, a man driven by a blood oath. Once the fine weather came he would be drawn from Dark Mount to ride with his men once more, and her brother too would leave for Dunfermline to sell his skills. This magic winter world that held them was only a dream, an illusion that would vanish with the snow. She knew it now and a strange feeling of dread entered her heart.

The two people she loved most would be gone and she would be alone again. She also knew that what she felt for Iain was much more than physical attraction. Somehow she had come to care for him more deeply than she would ever have thought possible. It was a very different emotion from the one she felt for Ban, and it could not be denied.

Iain, alive to every nuance, sensed that something was wrong and determined to know the reason for it. However, the demands of the guests were many and the laws of hospitality required that their needs came first.

It was therefore much later when they had retired that he found his moment. Ashlynn had gone ahead of him and when he entered the room he was surprised to see her still up. She was sitting by the fire and had evidently been deep in thought for she started on hearing him enter. He saw her smile and crossed the intervening space to take her in his arms. Then he sat down and drew her on to his knee.

'Something is amiss, Ashlynn, and has been all evening. What is it?'

'How did you know?'

'Your face speaks before you do, my sweet. It always has.' He smiled. 'So tell me.'

'It's what Jeannie said earlier.'

'About what?'

'About you leaving in the spring.'

He surveyed her in surprise. 'When the warmer weather comes I'll ride again with my men. But do you really think I would stay away from you for very long?' He kissed her lightly on the brow. 'It couldn't be done.'

'But you will still seek out Fitzurse.'

'You know I must.'

'Yes, and if you find him he may kill you and if he does what shall I do then?'

'Hush, lass. There's no need for you to be afraid of that.'

'How can I not be?'

'Fitzurse likes to win by treachery. In a fair fight he has little chance and he knows it.'

'Can there ever be such a thing as a fair fight with such a man?'

'Aye, there can, and one day he'll have to meet me.'

Ashlynn sighed and looked away. Very gently he turned her face to his.

'The ghosts of the past must be exorcised, Ashlynn, or haunt us ever more.' He paused, surveying her closely. 'But this is not just about Fitzurse, is it?'

She shook her head. 'Ban is going to leave.'

'Ah.'

'He plans to go to Dunfermline and seek service there.'

'I'd say he'd every chance of success.'

For a long moment she was silent and the blue eyes were veiled beneath sooty lashes. Then he saw a glistening tear slide down her cheek.

'Ach, lass, don't cry.'

Unfortunately this had the opposite effect to the one he had intended and more tears followed. He regarded her in concern. Ashlynn took a deep breath and tried to recover herself.

'Forgive me. I know that you must go and Ban too, but I cannot bear the thought of anything happening to either of you, of losing you.'

His arms tightened about her. 'You'll never lose me, lass, no matter how hard you try, or Ban either if

I know aught about him. Not at odds of less than twenty to one anyway.'

It drew a reluctant laugh. 'I never used to be insecure—until the Normans came.'

'You need never feel insecure. Nothing shall hurt you if I can prevent it.'

He took her face in his hands then, brushing her tears away, kissed her very gently on the mouth.

'You mean a great deal to me, lass, and I would never wish to be the cause of tears in you.' He smiled. 'As for that brother of yours I will speak with him as occasion permits. If his mind is set on going to Dunfermline, then I might be able to help him; I have certain acquaintance there who could be useful.'

'Thank you.'

'Now, my dove, the hour grows late and you should be abed.' He got to his feet bringing her with him. 'I mean to see to it that you are—right soon.'

In a very short time he had unfastened and removed her gown, tossing it over the chair. Then he led her to the bed and watched her climb in, burrowing down beneath the pelts. Without taking his eyes off her he removed his own clothing and came to join her. Then he made gentle and tender love to her, afterwards holding her close until she slept.

The following day dawned with leaden skies and rain. Mist shrouded the hills and the air was bitter. It was no weather to tempt the guests out of doors so the men amused themselves with chess and dice while the women talked. Hamish took the younger members of the company aside and devised pastimes for their amusement.

At his suggestion that chill afternoon they gathered for a game of foxes and hounds. Hamish carefully established the physical parameters within which it could be played.

'The foxes may hide anywhere in the tower, but not beyond. The hounds will give them the count of one hundred to get away. Then they'll come looking. Whoever is found last wins the game.' He paused. 'However, first found must pay a forfeit.'

The youngsters clapped delightedly. Hamish looked around to where his host was standing with several older members of the gathering.

'Will any of you ladies and gentlemen join in? Can I prevail upon you?'

They laughed and shook their heads. Hamish shrugged and looked at Ashlynn.

'How about you, my lady?'

She laughed. 'Why not?' She glanced at her brother. 'Ban?'

He returned the grin and nodded. 'Why not indeed?'

A cheer went up as they crossed the room to join the children. Hamish turned to Iain.

'And you, my lord?'

Iain grinned. 'How could I refuse?'

His words were greeted first with looks of surprise and then an even louder cheer. Ashlynn watched as he quit the group of adults and came over.

Hamish called the group to order. 'Very well. Lady Ashlynn, Lord Ban, you are the foxes in this first round. You have till the count of a hundred to find somewhere to hide. One…two…'

They exchanged startled looks and departed for the stairs with alacrity. Once out in the corridor they paused.

'We need to split up,' he said. 'I'm making for the storerooms. You?'

'Upstairs,' she replied.

'Good luck.'

With that he took off, heading swiftly down the staircase. Ashlynn grinned and then fled for her own chosen sanctuary.

Back in the hall Iain waited through the count. When at last it was complete he left with the others, watching as the children scattered. It was in his mind that none but he should find his wife. He moved into the passageway and up the first flight of stairs, feigning to look in different places on the way, but ever heading away from the rest, moving towards the top of the tower for he knew with near certainty where she would be.

Ashlynn smiled to herself, well satisfied with her hiding place. Although the roof terrace itself offered no hiding place the recess in the adjoining wall of the tower served the purpose. Located behind the door it was out of the line of vision and anyone taking a cursory glance at the terrace would easily miss it. She wrapped her cloak more closely about her though in truth she was not cold for the marten fur was snug and the chill air against her face was invigorating. Luckily it had stopped raining for the time though the clouds held promise of more.

Suddenly she caught the sound of voices in the near distance and she drew in a sharp breath, shrinking back against the stonework. A few moments later she heard someone open the door that gave on the roof. Then she heard Donald's voice.

'No, there's no one here. Let us try below.'

Another male replied in the affirmative and the door closed. Ashlynn grinned. The chances were good now that she would not be caught at all. That was something of a relief for Hamish would certainly think of some dastardly forfeit. At times that young man's imagination took a distinctly wicked turn. She was recalling some of the more recent examples when she heard the door open again. This time there were no voices, only the sound of footsteps, unhurried and deliberate and heading in her direction. Her heart leapt, knowing before she saw him who it would be. A moment later she was face to face with her husband.

'My lady.'

He smiled then, a mischievous expression that told more clearly than words his discovery of her had been no mere chance. Ashlynn returned the smile, eyeing him speculatively.

'You knew from the first where to find me, didn't you?'

'Let's just say I had a pretty good idea.'

'I had not thought to be so transparent.'

'It's usually a mistake,' he agreed. 'It gives your opponent the advantage.'

The expression in those dark eyes was enough to stir deep misgivings and she stayed where she was. He surveyed her with amusement.

'You cannot escape, Ashlynn. Besides, it's very unsporting to try.'

She grinned. 'It's very unsporting to cheat, villain.'

'No cheating; just a thorough knowledge of the ground and the quarry.' He nodded towards the recess. 'Ordinarily that's a very good hiding place. I have used it myself before now.'

The easy conversational tone didn't deceive her for a minute. However, she was powerless to escape her fate and mentally resigned herself.

'Come, my lady.'

Iain took hold of her wrist in a grip that, though it caused no discomfort, was as inflexible as steel. Then he drew her back inside and shut the door.

'Did you and Hamish collude over this?' she demanded.

'Hamish is completely innocent.'

'That's unusual for him. Even so I dread to think what forfeit he will dream up.'

'Hamish is not exacting this forfeit. I am.'

For a moment she could only stare at him. 'You?'

'That's right.'

As the implications dawned Ashlynn glanced around. The passageway was quite deserted and, in spite of the torches, dimly lit for the afternoon light was fading. Her heart began to beat a little faster.

'You can't do that.'

His expression was suggestive of polite interest. She tried another tack.

'It's against the rules.'

'I don't play to the rules, lass. You should know that.' Without relinquishing his hold he retraced his steps along the passage as far as his chamber and drew her inside. She heard the key turn in the lock. In no doubt now as to what he intended Ashlynn felt her heartbeat accelerate dangerously. She saw him smile and advance. Undeceived by the smile she backed away.

'There's no escape, Ashlynn.'

'Is that so, villain?'

'Aye, it is.'

Ashlynn hid a smile of her own, remembering the interconnecting door that led to her own room. If he thought he'd trap her so easily he was mistaken. Enjoying the thought of his forthcoming chagrin she turned and fled, darting through the open doorway into his bedchamber, heading for the exit. Iain watched her go and his grin widened. Then he strolled after her towards his room arriving in time to see Ashlynn reach the connecting door. Her hand closed on the handle and tugged hard. It yielded not at all. Automatically her gaze went to the lock and found it empty.

'Is this what you're looking for?' he asked.

She whirled round and saw him on the further threshold. In his hand was a large iron key. Speechless she watched as he closed the bedroom door behind him and locked that in turn, the full extent of his plan now apparent. She was exactly where he had intended her to be.

'You devious rogue.' Her voice was low and the tone indicative of grudging admiration as she watched him advance. 'You had it all worked out, didn't you?'

'In any campaign one must have a plan.'

Then his hands were on her shoulders and suddenly his face was much closer, the dark eyes burning into hers.

'Kiss me, Ashlynn.'

Annoyed with herself for falling so neatly into the trap and even more annoyed for enjoying it, she made a token attempt to resist. His hold tightened. He took the kiss at leisure, a knowing and insistent embrace that ignored resistance until resistance was abandoned. Then he carried her to the bed.

* * *

Later as they lay together beneath the furs Ashlynn glanced up at his face and seeing him smile returned it.

'That was quite a forfeit, my lord.'

'No,' he replied. 'The forfeit was only a kiss.'

'A kiss!' She pushed herself up on one elbow. 'Why you utter…' Words failed her in the face of that blatantly unrepentant grin. Then she launched herself at him. Iain guffawed. There followed a short unequal struggle before he grabbed her wrists and pinned them to the bed.

'All's fair in love and war, lass.' He was still holding her lightly enough, but still leaving no possibility of escape for the blue eyes held a militant light. 'And now I have you captive I'm not about to let you go.'

Reluctantly she laughed. 'We can't stay here, Iain. What about the game?'

He bent and kissed her again. 'Do you know, lass, I have a feeling you're going to be the undisputed winner.'

Chapter Eleven

After two days of rain the sky cleared and, as the snow had melted away from the lower lying areas of ground, Hamish suggested that the men might go out for a ride. It was an idea that met with instant favour. Ashlynn looked at her brother.

'Will you join them?'

He shook his head. 'I'd love to, but I'm not sure if my shoulder would stand the pace just yet. I need to put the matter to the test—on my terms.'

'Let's go out by ourselves then, and we can set the pace to suit.'

'I'm game if you are,' he said, 'and it has been a while after all. If I don't get back on a horse soon I'll forget how.'

She laughed. 'Very well, but I think we should not go too far at first. You are like to be sore else.'

Iain, who had followed the exchange, surveyed them with a smile. 'I'll have a groom go with you since you're not familiar with the country hereabouts.'

They went down to the courtyard together and mounted up. For a little way their paths lay together and Iain rode beside them to the fork in the trail where he and his men were to leave them. He bade farewell to Ban and then leaned down to drop a kiss on his wife's cheek.

'Until later, Ashlynn.'

He smiled and turned his horse's head. For a moment or two her gaze followed the dark-clad figure on the grey stallion. She was regretting his absence already. Telling herself not to be so foolish she brought her mount alongside her brother's.

They kept the pace steady but Ashlynn could see that Ban was enjoying the excursion and it pleased her to see him smile in the old way. Their guide led them through the length of Glengarron, intending to ride a wide loop round the valley. While it was good to get some fresh air again, the damp cold was penetrating and Ashlynn wasn't at all sorry that they'd opted for a shorter excursion this time around.

They had reached the end of the valley when the groom reined in, staring at the distant hillside. Ban frowned.

'What is it, Callum?'

'I'm no sure, my lord. I thought I saw movement up yonder.'

All three remained still, their eyes straining to see, but the hillside seemed deserted.

'It might have been a deer,' said Ban.

'Perhaps,' Callum replied. The tone suggested he was unconvinced.

'What else? Surely no one would ride into Glengarron uninvited?'

'They'd be wiser not to, my lord.'

Ashlynn's gaze searched the scattered rocks and clumps of rain-darkened heather but could detect no sign of movement. She decided it must have been an animal of some kind which, startled by their approach, had made off through the undergrowth. All the same the stillness felt suddenly eerie.

'I think we should go back now,' she said.

Callum nodded. 'A good idea, my lady.'

Ban eyed them both thoughtfully and then glanced once more at the silent hillside. 'Just as you wish.'

They turned the horses' heads and began to ride for home, picking up the pace a little. Once Ashlynn glanced over her shoulder, but there was nothing to be seen save the hill and the shrouding mist above.

The others returned some time later, all mud spattered and all in high good humour after the fresh air and the exercise. Iain rejoined his wife by the hearth and sliding an arm about her waist, kissed her soundly. Ashlynn smiled.

'I take it you enjoyed your ride, my lord.'

'Indeed I did, though I missed your company.'

'Liar. You were far too busy talking about horses and hunting if I know anything about it.'

He grinned. 'Not so busy as to put all thoughts of you out of my head.'

'What thoughts?'

He bent and whispered in her ear. Ashlynn blushed scarlet.

'You are incorrigible.'

'So I've been told.' He paused. 'All the same, your guess about hunting wasn't so far wrong. The next suitable day we get, we'll take the hounds for an outing. Will you come?'

Her eyes brightened. 'Can you doubt it?'

He looked at Ban. 'How did your excursion go today?'

'Well enough, my lord,' he replied. 'The shoulder is mending apace. It won't be long before I'm fully fit again.'

He made no mention of what had passed earlier and Ashlynn decided he was right. What was there to say after all? It was suspicion only. They had seen nothing.

'I'm glad to hear it,' Iain went on. 'The rain will clear soon enough. Then we'll see some action. In the meantime a little sword practice wouldn't come amiss. What say you to a short bout?'

'I'd be honoured.'

Ashlynn darted a glance at her brother. 'Are you sure about this?'

'Why not?' he replied. 'I won't overdo it, but I need to start some time.'

She looked from one to the other in disbelief. 'In this weather?'

Iain grinned. 'I'm not such a martyr to the art. We'll use the barn.' Then, seeing his wife's anxious expression, he continued, 'Have no fear, my lady, I will return him safe and sound.'

She sighed and watched them go. In a few weeks Ban would indeed be fit again. After that he would leave. It was time to face the unpleasant truth. Her brother had his own life to lead and she had no right to expect him to remain at Dark Mount if it was his inclination to go. Their destinies lay along different paths for a while at least but perhaps, if the fates were kind, they might overlap from time to time. Besides, she too had duties and responsibilities now and must face up to them.

Out in the barn the two men moved through the warm-up routine and Ban was cautiously optimistic. As he had said, some of the strength was returning to his shoulder. Daily exercise would re-educate the muscles and help him build up the stamina he had lost erewhile. From time to time he glanced at his brother-in-law but if Iain noticed he gave no sign, his concentration entirely on what he was doing. It was habitual with him. Whatever he undertook he did with commitment and attention to detail. It occurred to Ban then that he could learn a great deal from a man like that. When he remembered his initial doubts he felt foolish. Iain MacAlpin might have his faults but he was also a man to respect. Would he find another such among the lords at Dunfermline? He hoped it might be so. All the same he knew he was going to miss Dark Mount for in the few weeks he had been there it had become like a home to him, a home he had never thought to have again. Leaving Ashlynn would be hardest of all, like losing her anew. It was comforting to know at least that she would always be safe, safe and loved.

Ban was startled out of his thoughts by Iain's voice.

'Shall we try a little practice now?'

'Why not?'

The blades engaged and they moved through the regular drills. Ban, tense at first, began to settle into the familiar rhythms. Though he had already seen Iain fight he was once again awed by the lithe power of the man, of the tireless repetitions and the grace of the movements in which the blade became an extension of his arm. Ban was a capable swordsman but all at once he knew he was seeing the standard to aim at. However, it soon became evident that it was going to take a while to achieve his goal for after a short spell of more vigorous use his shoulder began to ache and the weight of the weapon to increase dramatically. Seeing it shake in the young man's grasp Iain lowered his own blade.

'That's enough for today, I think.'

Ban smiled apologetically. 'I fear it is.'

'Even so that shoulder has made remarkable progress.' Iain sheathed his sword. 'It will not be long before it's as good as it ever was.'

'I pray you are right for I hope to make my living thus.' Ban brushed beads of moisture from his forehead, noting as he did so that his brother-in-law hadn't even broken into a sweat as yet. With a rueful smile he sheathed his own blade. 'I imagine my sister has told you as much.'

'Aye, she did.' Iain bent to retrieve his tunic. 'She said you were thinking of going to Dunfermline.'

'That's right.'

'Well, if you still wish to do so then I'll gladly furnish you with an introduction.'

'That is most generous, my lord. Particularly when I consider how much I already owe you.'

'You owe me nothing.'

'I think you understate the matter.'

'Not so.' Iain shrugged himself into the tunic and belted it. 'Family must stick together.'

Hearing those words Ban felt a surge of pride and pleasure for in that one brief and casual comment he was brought into the fold, given a place and a sense of belonging.

'You speak true, lord.'

'That being the case I have a proposition to put to you.'

Ban stopped in the act of reaching for his own tunic. 'A proposition?'

'Aye. Stay here at Dark Mount. I can always use a good man.'

For a moment there was silence. Iain smiled faintly.

'You don't have to make up your mind now. Take your time. Think it over.'

The younger man reddened but recovered himself quickly. 'You mistake, my lord. My silence was not due to hesitation but surprise. Do you really mean it?'

The dark eyes met and held his. 'I should not have said it else. Besides, I would be loath to see you go.'

'I would be loath to go, my lord.'

'That's settled then.' The easy smile appeared again. 'Now I need to speak to Dougal. In the meantime perhaps you should go and tell your sister.'

Ban found Ashlynn in the hall by the hearth. She looked up and smiled as he entered.

'How was the practice?'

'Well enough, but there's a long way to go yet.' He flexed the shoulder and winced a little. 'It still lacks much of its original power.'

'It is like to take some weeks, but there's no hurry. You can't leave anyway until the warmer weather comes.'

'I'm not leaving at all.'

'I don't understand.'

'Iain has asked me to stay. To join him.'

'What…what did you say?'

'I said yes of course.'

For a moment she was speechless for the feeling of joy and relief was so intense that her throat was too tight for words. Then she was out of her chair and hugging him tightly.

'I'm so glad.'

'To tell you the truth I'm glad too.'

'Are you really?' She held him at arm's length for a moment and her blue gaze met his. 'You're not just saying that? It's not just because of me?'

'No. When Iain made the offer to ride with him I was more than happy to accept. He's a man I respect, a man I could follow.'

Ashlynn nodded. She had seen his growing admiration for his brother-in-law and had been glad to see the friendship between the two. However, she knew that Iain had not just made the offer because he saw potential in her brother. It had been done to please her. The knowledge warmed her to the core of her being. With that simple gesture he had made her happier than he could ever know.

Even as she was thinking about him he arrived with Dougal, and the two of them came over to the hearth where she and Ban were standing. Dougal beamed to see them and held out his hand to her brother.

'Lord Iain's just told me the good news. I'm delighted.'

Ban reddened a little as he took the proffered hand. 'It is an honour, believe me, sir.'

'Let us drink to it.'

Iain called for wine and presently proposed a toast. 'To friendship and brotherhood.'

Ban raised his cup solemnly as he repeated the words, a brief and informal version of the oath of fealty he would swear later before his lord and in the sight of his men. Once he looked at Ashlynn and saw her answering smile. When the toast was done the conversation fell into more general topics and she let the men talk, allowing the words to wash over her, having eyes only for Iain. He had done this for her. With a full heart she met her husband's glance and saw him smile, the familiar easy smile that made her heart leap.

Seeing Dougal and Ban deep in conversation he came to join Ashlynn. She looked up at him with shining eyes.

'How can I thank you?'

'No thanks are necessary. It was a logical step to take. Ban needs to make his way in the world and I need good men. Two birds with one stone, you see.'

'Three,' she replied, 'for you have also made me very happy.'

'If you are happy then I am content.'

'I am happy, Iain, more than I ever dreamed of being again. After Heslingfield was destroyed I could see no future. You made me look beyond that.'

His throat tightened for he had never thought to hear such words from her. Yet they were heartfelt, of that there could be no doubt.

'We will build a good future, you and I,' he replied.

'Will we?'

'Can you doubt it?'

'I want so much to believe, Iain, to let go of the past but it lours over us yet.' Her eyes met his and he saw the quiet anguish there.

'What is it, lass?'

'Fitzurse.'

For a moment or two the name hung between them. Ashlynn laid a hand on his arm.

'If you really want to build a future let go of your hatred, Iain.' She paused. 'Such ancient grudges cast a long shadow and they are corrosive. I do not want our life together to be tainted with the evils of the past.'

His expression grew sombre. 'You do not know what you ask, Ashlynn.'

'Yes, I do know—more than anyone.'

'I made a sacred promise. Would you have me break it?'

'I demand nothing. I ask only that you think about it.'

'This is not fair, Ashlynn.'

'It was not fair that Fitzurse destroyed Heslingfield and murdered my kin,' she replied, 'and I have thought often of revenge. But it will not restore my home or make my family live again. They are gone and nothing will change it.' She paused. 'The only way now is forward, to make the most of what we have.'

'With you I have found what I never thought to have again, but I cannot know true peace until Fitzurse is dead.'

'Will you allow him to taint the future as well as the past, Iain? If so, then he really will have won.'

She turned sadly away, leaving him alone. He sighed, watching her go, torn between wanting and frustration. Did she expect him to break his oath? To be forsworn? Time might have made his memories easier to bear but it did not change the instinct for revenge. His hand tightened around his cup. What Ashlynn asked was impossible. How could he have the kind of future he wanted and know all the time that somewhere his enemy lived and prospered?

* * *

Ashlynn did not return to her room but instead left the tower and took a turn about the courtyard, needing the air and the space to clear her mind. At least it had stopped raining now though everything smelled of damp. She glanced up, watching rags of cloud scudding across the sky above the water-darkened stones of the tower, and shivered, drawing her cloak closer. It wasn't the weather to be out of doors and yet she had no wish to return to the hall just yet. Seeing the stable door just a few yards away she made for it. It was dry within and warmer too, the air sweet and pungent with hay and horses. Letting her eyes adjust to the dimmer light she walked along the stalls until she came to the one that housed Steorra.

The mare heard her step and turned, whickering softly. Ashlynn smiled, and slipped into the stall, rubbing the horse's nose affectionately. When the bad weather let up it would be good to get out for a ride. Iain had mentioned a hunt. The prospect was alluring.

The thought of Iain brought their recent conversation to the fore again and she sighed. She had hoped her arguments might prevail with him but in retrospect wondered if she had done right to raise the topic again. A blood oath could never lightly be forsworn and he had every right to want revenge. Considered dispassionately it was understandable, and yet how hard it was to be dispassionate when considering the possible price of such revenge. Would it take him from her? Was this new-found happiness to be so soon destroyed? She understood then that her request had been in part about her own insecurities. The knowledge did not make her feel any better.

A footstep behind her made her turn, expecting to see one of the grooms. However, it was a very different figure that stood there. For the space of a dozen heartbeats they faced each other in silence.

'I thought I might find you here,' he said.

Ashlynn gave Steorra a final pat and came to join him at the entrance to the stall. 'Iain, what I said before...I'm sorry. I had no right to ask it.'

For a moment the dark eyes registered surprise. Then he sighed. 'You had the right, lass.'

'No, an oath like that is sacred. I see it now and I apologise.'

'Ach, lass, you've nothing to apologise for. Besides, there was much truth in what you said.'

Now it was her turn to feel surprise but before she could say anything he went on. 'I have carried the desire for revenge in my heart for so long it has become part of me. Not one of the better parts, I fear. Even now, I'm not sure I can let it go.'

'Iain, I—'

'No, hear me out, I beg.' He took a deep breath. 'If ever our paths cross, I will slay Fitzurse, but I'll not deliberately seek him out any longer.'

Her heart began to beat a little faster. 'Do you mean it?'

'I would not have said it otherwise, lass.' He eyed her keenly. 'Will that content you?'

It was so much more than she had ever expected that for a moment it was hard to speak. Then she nodded. 'Yes.'

Iain knew that a week ago, a day even, he could not have made that promise, but for the first time he had glimpsed something he wanted more than revenge. At some deep level he understood that a fundamental change had taken place and that it was due to his feelings for Ashlynn. He should have felt angry or resentful but he didn't. The feeling was liberating, as though a burden had been lifted.

'Then let the matter rest there,' he said.

'Thank you. In truth I did not expect so much.'

'I want that future we spoke of.'

'And I also. I want your children, Iain, and I want them to grow up knowing their father, not hearing about him at second hand.'

He smiled wryly. 'They'll come to know me well enough. More perhaps than they'll like.'

'I doubt that. It's my belief you'll make an excellent father.'

'Is it so? And what put that thought in your head?'

'Watching you with your little niece. You have a talent there.'

'Well, I've been practising, ye ken, for the real thing.'

'God willing, you'll have the real thing soon enough.'

She stepped closer and reaching up drew his face down to hers for a lingering kiss. When at length they came up for air he saw her gaze move beyond him towards the far end of the building. Instinctively his own turned to follow it and came to rest at the rear on the ladder that led up to the hayloft. Then he gave her a quizzical look.

'When first I came here you took me on a tour of Dark Mount,' she said.

'So I did, lass.'

'But you never did show me what lies up there, my lord.'

Iain felt his heart miss a beat. Then he grinned. 'That can soon be rectified.'

They made the ascent and he drew the ladder up after them, before leading her deeper into the loft space. There he spread his cloak on the hay under the eaves. For a moment they faced each other. Then he knelt, drawing her down with him, closing his arms around her. He felt her mouth open to his letting him taste the sweetness beyond while her body moulded itself to his. He withdrew just long enough to unfasten his belt and tunic and discard them. Then he rejoined her, his lips grazing her cheek, moving thence to her neck and throat while his hands raised the skirts of her gown. Ashlynn moved to accommodate him and felt him lift the fabric clear and then the warmth of his hands on her skin. Her flesh tingled in response. She slid her arms around him, running her tongue along his throat, tasting its salt warmth, breathing in the erotic musky scent of the man, letting her hands explore and caress the hard muscled flesh of his back beneath the shirt. The kiss grew deeper. Her hands slid to the fastenings of his breeches and loosened them, stroking the flesh beneath, feeling the hardening response. She heard him draw in a sharp breath, then pushed him back on the cloak and sat astride him, feeling him slide into her, taking the full length of him.

Iain had fantasised about making love to her in different ways and places but the reality far exceeded the dream. Moreover, there was an expression in her eyes that he had not seen before. It was both teasing and mischievous and it sent a wave of heat through his loins. He wanted her, reached for her hips, drawing her down on him, arching into her, thrusting deeper, desperate to answer that mounting fire. Ashlynn smiled, refusing to be hurried, making him wait.

'Ashlynn, I beg you...'

'All in good time, my lord.'

Bending forward she brought her mouth down on his, taking the kiss at leisure before resuming where she'd left off before, moving against him with deliberate and teasing slowness, fanning the flames. Iain's breath caught in his throat as another wave of pleasure hit him.

'Have mercy, lass.'

She heard him groan and smiled again, a very wicked and provocative smile that did not go unnoticed. Iain gritted his teeth.

'I warn you, my sweet, I intend to have my own back for this.'

'Revenge again, my lord?'

'Don't be in any doubt about it.'

He moved deeper into her and this time she made no reply save for a long and shuddering intake of breath. Then she was moving with him, building the tempo until it ended a little later in a mutual protracted climax.

Afterwards, they lay together beneath her cloak, sharing their warmth. Ashlynn snuggled close drowsing, her head against his shoulder. He bent to kiss her forehead and tightened his arms about her, still finding it hard to believe what had passed or the extent of the pleasure he had experienced. In truth he had not thought to find this again with any woman; had not thought to feel this way again about any woman. Yet somehow it had happened and he could no longer deny it. Nor could he deny the fascination she held for him. Each time he thought he was nearer to knowing her she surprised him anew. If this was a foretaste of what was to come... It led his mind along new and delightful paths and he felt his groin grow warm again.

Ashlynn was roused from her doze a short time later by a kiss, gentle and lingering at first but becoming deeper as she roused to consciousness. His hands drew her skirt and shift upwards. Ashlynn opened her eyes, regarding him quizzically.

'My lord?'

The dark eyes gleamed and he smiled, a deeply disturbing smile that sent a thrill of excitement the length of her body.

'I did warn you, lass.'

'About what?'

'That I intended to get my own back.'

By the time they returned to the tower it was dark and the smells from the kitchen indicated that the evening meal was about to be served.

'Now that was good timing,' he observed with a grin.

'Is food all you men think of?' she replied.

'Not all.' He drew her hard against him for another kiss.

'No more, my lord. I must go and change. Anyone seeing me now would think I'd been for a tryst in a hayloft.'

He shook his head. 'Shocking how people always think the worst. Heaven knows where they get such scandalous ideas.'

She smiled. 'I cannot imagine.'

They made their way up the stairs and, by sheer good fortune, reached the top floor unnoticed. There she left him and went to her own chamber to bathe and change her attire. Her body still burned with his love-making and every limb ached from that delicious and protracted revenge. Recalling the details she smiled to herself. Then, having hastily stripped off her clothing, she washed and donned a fresh shift and gown. With Morag's help she combed and braided her hair with matching gold ribbons. By the time she had finished no vestige remained of the tousled wanton and in her place was the elegant and gracious hostess.

Iain noted the change and grinned as she took her place beside him at table. For a moment or two he let his gaze linger on the curvy figure beneath the golden gown, letting his memory dwell on what lay beneath. It also recalled what had passed that afternoon. When in the early days of their marriage he had dreamed of her surrender he could never have guessed that her passion would equal his own, or that she would have the power to arouse him so far.

Aware of that penetrating gaze Ashlynn kept her attention first on the food and then on her guests lest with one glance she revealed the thoughts going through her mind. However, much of the talk that evening was about hunting and, since it had actually stopped raining outside, the tone was optimistic.

'If the cloud breaks up we might get a day yet,' said Duncan.

'Aye, we might.' Iain looked at Ashlynn. 'Do you still wish to come?'

'I wouldn't miss it,' she replied. 'Besides, I think some fresh venison would be most welcome among our guests.'

He turned to his brother-in-law. 'What say you to some hunting, Ban?'

'I'd like nothing better, my lord.'

'That's settled then.' Iain smiled. 'We're due for some sport.'

'A hart of ten?'

'With any luck. If the weather holds up we'll send Sim out early with his lymer and see what it can find for us. There's not a dog with a keener nose for miles around.'

Knowing the risk now of an endless male discussion about the minutiae of hunting, Ashlynn caught Jeannie's eye and saw an answering sympathy.

'I am sure we all look forward to some good sport tomorrow, brother. However, for now shall we have some music?'

Ashlynn recognised her cue. 'What an excellent idea.'

At her speaking look the suggestion was picked up and endorsed by several other ladies.

Iain smiled and submitted graciously. 'Very well. What would you have?'

Some called for music and others a song. Much to her surprise Ashlynn saw a servant hand her husband a lute and she watched him move to a stool nearby. Then he began to tune the instrument. She had not known he possessed any musical skill. Others evidently did for his acquiescence drew applause. Then he turned to Duncan.

'Will you favour us with a song, brother?'

Another chorus of approval greeted this, intensifying as Duncan got to his feet. It seemed the audience had a song in mind for they called out their choice most emphatically. With a laugh he inclined his head in consent. Listening attentively Ashlynn discovered that he had a good voice and he sang well to general acclaim. Then Jeannie was called upon for a rendition. Her protests availed her naught and at last she capitulated. The song

was a ballad as near as Ashlynn could tell for the words
were in Gaelic. The voice was strangely beautiful and
arresting with an elusive quality that tugged at the heart
for it seemed to her to be filled with heartache and loss.
Unbidden and unheeded tears sprang to her eyes. The
tune held her to the end and she joined in the thunderous applause. Glancing at Ban she could see that he too
had been moved.

She had been expecting Jeannie to sit down after this
but Iain said something to her and, having gained her
agreement, he began to play again. However, when she
sang this time he joined with her. His voice was fine and
strong, a perfect complement to hers and again in the
sweet Gaelic tongue. Ashlynn listened in complete
amazement wondering how many more unknown facets
there might be to this man she had married. When they
finished the applause was tumultuous. This time
Jeannie did sit down and presently her brother began
another tune.

On the opening bars the conversation faded and the
listeners fell silent. Iain fixed his gaze on Ashlynn and
began to sing, a soft and beautiful melody that was un-
mistakably a love song. It wasn't necessary to understand the words to know it. In stunned surprise she
listened, held by the expression in those dark eyes that
spoke more than the words. She could not have looked
away even if she had wanted to. With the swift thumping
of her heart came the knowledge that this was much
more than a song: it was a public declaration. That
understanding was followed by a moment of exquisite
pain in which everything around them vanished until the
room contained only the two of them and the only

sounds were the lute and the voice fused in that haunting expression of love and longing. Her heart acknowledged it and in that instant understood what it had tried so hard to deny.

When eventually the song ended the silence stretched out for several heartbeats before the room erupted. With one part of her consciousness Ashlynn heard the applause wash around them, but her eyes never left his. Then she saw him smile and her breath caught in her throat. Iain handed the lute to Hamish and returned to reclaim his place beside her.

'That was beautiful,' she said. It was the truth, like the emotion overpowering her now. 'I did not know you could sing.'

'Another example of my good aunt's training,' he replied. 'She was ever fond of music and encouraged the pursuit in others.'

'Did she teach you that song?'

'No, I knew it long before I went to France. It was one of my mother's favourites.'

'I see.'

He took her hand and pressed it to his lips. 'Indeed I hope you do, lass.'

Across the room Hamish strummed a few opening chords and launched into a rollicking tune whose chorus demanded loud audience participation, and the ensuing noise precluded further conversation.

It was much later before the singing ended and some of the guests began to take their leave.

Ashlynn expected Iain to linger as was his wont but to her surprise he accompanied her up the stairs. They strolled together along the passageway until they reached his chamber. Drawing her gently inside, he shut the door. Then he turned to face her, for a moment or two regarding her in silence.

'There is something I would give you, Ashlynn. I've been waiting for the right moment.' He reached into a pocket and drew out a small square of folded cloth. 'This is long overdue but I hope you'll think the wait worthwhile.'

He took her hand and placed the little package in her palm. She returned him a swift glance but his face revealed nothing. Curious now, she unwrapped the gift carefully, and then drew in a sharp breath. Inside was a ring. It was made of gold and exquisitely fashioned in an intricate pattern of love knots. For a moment she stared at it in silent wonder and then looked up at him.

'Where ever did you get this?'

'I had the smith make it. He does subtle work from time to time, in between his regular tasks.'

'He is highly skilled.'

'I'm sorry it's taken so long. I'd meant you to have it long since but Ewan will not be hurried.'

'Quite rightly,' she replied. 'He's a true craftsman.'

'You like it then?'

'It's beautiful, Iain.' She extended her hand. 'Will you do the honours?'

He took the ring and slid it on to her finger. Then he smiled faintly. 'It fits a lot better than the last one.'

'It's perfect. Thank you.'

He led her to the adjoining chamber and undressed her there, before removing his own clothing. Then he followed her to bed. Mindful of the demands he had made earlier he made none now, being content just to hold her close. She felt his body curl protectively around hers and smiled, sharing his warmth until they both slept.

Chapter Twelve

The following morning the chief huntsman went out at dawn. He returned from the quest with the intelligence that the lymer had found red deer in the wooded depths of a neighbouring glen. Among them was the coveted prize of a hart with a ten-tined rack of antlers.

Thus it was that a large party of riders, male and female, met in the courtyard. Spirits were high and the air filled with laughter and good-humoured banter. Ashlynn, mounted on Steorra, went to join her brother. Together they cast a critical gaze over the hunting dogs, part mastiff, part alaunt, huge lean beasts with wicked fangs.

'They look to have the strength and tenacity of the one breed and the reckless courage of the other,' he observed. 'If anything is going to bring a wild animal to bay, I think they will.'

'You're right,' said Iain who had reined his horse in alongside. 'Once they get the scent they don't give up.'

Soon the company set off, riding at a steady pace, reserving the stamina of the horses and dogs until they would be required. Ashlynn could feel Steorra's excitement. The mare longed to be off and made no secret of the fact with prancing steps and pricked ears. Like her the bigger animals were champing at the bit too. Stormwind essayed a half-rear and received a sharp word of warning from his rider in return. The big horse dropped his head and snorted in disgust. Ashlynn shot a sidelong glance at Iain and saw him slap the dappled neck good-humouredly.

'Behave yourself, you great lummox!' he told the horse. 'You'll get your chance soon enough.'

She laughed. 'He is impatient, my lord.'

'Aye, you'd think he'd never heard a hunting horn or seen dogs before.'

'All horses love the chase.'

'That they do.'

'They are not alone in that.'

His smile faded and for a moment his face grew serious. 'Stay with the other women, Ashlynn. This is wild country, and you're a stranger to it just now. It would be easy to get lost.'

'I'll do as you advise, my lord.'

He nodded. 'The border lands can be dangerous. This is not a good place to be alone.'

Recalling their encounters on the way north she could see the reason for his caution. 'Do you suppose there may be any danger?'

'Not for a party this size,' he replied.

'That's good to know.' She threw him a mischievous grin. 'I have no sword to hand this day.'

He returned the smile. 'That's as well for any robbers hereabouts. Not that I think there will be many of those. Your reputation will have frightened them off for sure.'

Ashlynn laughed. 'Not *my* reputation, I think.'

Iain turned to Ban. 'Did you know that your coaching had been so successful?'

'How so, my lord?'

'Did your sister not tell you that she single-handedly accounted for some very desperate villains?'

His brows drew together. 'Ashlynn never mentioned anything of the sort.'

'No? Well, she's very modest, ye ken.'

'So it would appear,' said Ban. 'Will you not bring me up to date on the subject, my lord?'

'I'd be delighted.'

Ashlynn threw her husband an eloquent look which he noted with enjoyment and promptly ignored. Then he favoured his brother-in-law with a colourful account of what had happened on the way to Jedburgh. Ban listened with mounting shock and incredulity but underneath it all was pride.

'You're a dark horse, Ash,' he said when the account was done at last.

Iain nodded solemnly. 'That's just what I said.'

'I was lucky,' she replied.

'Even so.' Ban grinned. 'Remind me not to make you angry.'

'She's a terror when her dander's up,' Iain informed him.

'You don't have to tell me, my lord. I grew up with her.'

'So you did. Was she always like it then?'

'You wouldn't believe the half of it.'

'Really. You must fill me in on some of the detail I've missed.'

'This is outrageous!' Ashlynn stared at them in disbelief. 'A conspiracy in fact.'

Iain's enjoyment mounted. 'Aye, lass, that's right.'

'In truth I don't know which of you is worse. I think I shan't stay to find out.'

With that she turned Steorra and rode back a way to join Jeannie, leaving the two men to their conversation.

It took about an hour to reach the glen where the lymer had found the deer. There the hunters deployed relays of hounds along the known tracks of the quarry. Ashlynn studied the wild and rugged terrain and understood why Iain had counselled caution. It would indeed be easy to lose oneself in this countryside. However, she had no intention of doing anything so foolish.

The lymer had done its work well and the other hounds picked up the scent very quickly and streamed away in full cry. Hearing the huntsman's horn the riders followed as fast as the terrain would permit. The men on their bigger, more powerful mounts soon drew ahead. Knowing that the chase could be lengthy Ashlynn made no attempt to push the mare too hard at this stage. Her stamina might be needed later when they came to more open ground. With care they would both have strength enough to last the day. Mindful also of what Iain had said, Ashlynn kept close to the other women riders. Most of them would have ridden here before and some like Jeannie probably knew the ground well. It was only common sense to be guided by their knowledge and experience.

The trail led along the glen for some way, threading through heath and rock before turning off up the wooded hillside. For a while the pace was reasonably swift for the trees were big and widely spaced. However, as the quarry made for the denser thickets the pursuit became more challenging because the rider's concentration was on the avoidance of low branches and slashing twigs. The pace slowed somewhat of necessity and Ashlynn took a swift look around. Just then the horn sounded some way off to the left and all the riders turned in that direction.

The hounds flushed the deer from the covert and made for open country. Here the relays would come into their own since, over distance, the hounds lacked the hart's stamina. With fresh reinforcements however, the chances of catching up with the quarry were greatly increased.

The ride was exhilarating as Ashlynn had known it would be and she gave the horse a little more rein, revelling in the speed and the clean cold air on her face. Up ahead she could see Iain's grey with the other leading horses and once she caught sight of Ban before his mount was swallowed up among the bays and chestnuts around him. She smiled to herself. Her brother was certainly fitter. The hunt would do him good in other ways too. Her thoughts were interrupted a few moments later as the foremost huntsmen disappeared into the cover of some trees.

It was at that point when, out of the corner of her eye, she became aware of other riders. A cursory glance revealed a group of about a dozen horsemen, approaching fast at an oblique angle. Curious, she took another, closer look. It seemed likely they were more of Iain's men and certainly there was nothing to tell them apart, being clad in the same leather hunting costumes. However, something about them gave her pause. She frowned, knowing something wasn't right but being unsure what. As the horsemen came on she realised it wasn't their appearance that was amiss but their course, for it became increasingly clear that they weren't following the main hunt; they were heading for the group in the rear. Now the leading body of huntsmen were in the trees the women riders were caught in the open and ripe to be cut off from the rest. Ashlynn felt the skin prickle on the back of her neck. A glance at her sister-in-law revealed she'd seen the horsemen too.

'Who are they, Jeannie?'

'I don't know,' she called back, 'but I don't like the look of them.'

'Nor I.'

Some of the other ladies had noticed the oncoming riders now and were looking distinctly nervous. Jeannie shouted across to them, 'Spread out and ride for the trees! Go!'

They needed no second bidding. Ashlynn bent low over Steorra's neck and gave the mare her head. The chestnut leapt forward in response. Now more than ever she was glad she hadn't pushed the horse before. Nearer and nearer came the thundering sound of pursuit. Another horrified glance revealed how much closer they were; she could see the riders' faces set in lines of grim determination. In that second Ashlynn knew she wasn't going to reach the shelter of the trees. It was too far. Their mounts were bigger and more powerful and, at each stride, closing the gap between. In desperation she shouted to Steorra, urging her on, but the little mare was already running flat out.

In helpless anger Ashlynn could only watch as a horseman swept alongside and seized her reins. She heard shouts and then both horses were pulled to a plunging halt. Moments later she was surrounded. Only then did she realise what it was that been eluding her: the costumes might have disguised their identity from a distance but the cropped hair marked them immediately as Normans. Wild-eyed she looked around and saw with rising horror that Jeannie had been taken too. The other women were unmolested and fast disappearing into the distance. Then a man's voice broke into her consciousness and her stomach lurched as she recognised the speaker. De Vardes! For a second he favoured her with a gloating smile before turning his attention to her companion.

'Tell McAlpin that if he wants his wife back he must win her in single combat.'

Jeannie's face was pale but her dark eyes flashed fury. 'Against whom?'

'He'll know.'

'Where?'

'The circle of standing stones beyond Glengarron. Tomorrow at dawn. He's to come alone.'

'No! Don't do it!' Ashlynn broke in. 'Tell him to stay away!'

'You'd better pray he doesn't, my lady,' replied De Vardes. 'Otherwise we'll return you to him a piece at a time.' He looked back at Jeannie. 'Just deliver the message.'

'I'll deliver it,' she replied. 'I'll tell you something too:

if you harm Lady Ashlynn there won't be a corner of hell for you to hide in after.'

'The lady will not be harmed, so long as McAlpin does as he's told. However, any attempt to follow us now will result in me cutting her throat the moment we sight pursuit.'

With that he jerked his head at the man holding the reins of her palfrey. He relinquished his hold. Jeannie threw Ashlynn an eloquent anguished look and then reluctantly turned her horse and rode away towards the wood. For a moment De Vardes watched her go. Then he brought his mount alongside Ashlynn's. Without a word he pulled the reins from her grasp and drew them over Steorra's head. Then, he led her away.

Iain heard his sister in expressionless silence, his eyes like iced flint in the pallor of his face. Beside him Ban turned white. All around them the others fell silent too as they listened to the message, every countenance registering anger and disbelief.

'He said you'd know your opponent,' Jeannie went on. 'What did he mean? Who is it, Iain?'

'Fitzurse.'

'Dear God, not he.'

'The same.'

Ban shot him a piercing look. 'Fitzurse! Was not he the man responsible for the destruction of Heslingfield?'

'Aye, he was.'

'You know him by more than repute, I think.'

'Aye, I do, and but for circumstances I'd have slain him long since. But he'll not escape again. This time I'll rid this earth of him once and for all.'

'What are you going to do?' asked Dougal.

'Meet him. What else?'

With that he turned his horse for home. For a moment they watched him go, then gathered their wits and set off in his wake, silent and grim-faced.

Iain rode mechanically, his mind elsewhere and his gut knotted with cold rage. Eight years rolled away, to another day and another hunt. Two women he had loved; two women taken from him by the same man. This time however, there was going to be a different outcome. He had once thought that he could never love again, a mistaken belief if ever there was one. It was a love hard earned but all he could see now was Ashlynn's face. Eloise had been the glorious passion of his youth, a wonderful romantic dream whose beauty would remain with him always. This was different again, a love found in maturity, slower to grow but engendering a deep and lasting need, an emotion that engaged mind, body and spirit. His love for Ashlynn had made him whole again. With her image came the knowledge that this wasn't just about settling an old score now, it was about his reason for living and his hopes of a future.

The swift pace brought them back to Glengarron an hour later. Within a very short time of their return everyone at Dark Mount knew what had happened and the atmosphere so cheerful before became brooding and angry. The insult to the laird was an insult to them all. However, it was Ban whom Jeanne watched now, not her brother. The young man's face was so white it looked bloodless. Guessing only too well at the thoughts behind, she laid a gentle hand on his arm.

'Have no fear,' she said, 'we'll get her back.'

'Aye, but alive or dead, my lady?' he replied.

'Fitzurse will not harm her,' said Iain. 'She's too valuable to him alive. He means to use her to get to me.'

'You canna believe he'll meet you in single combat?' said Dougal. 'It's a trap for sure.'

'Of course it is, and yet I mean to make the bastard face me.'

'How? You ride in alone and you're dead.'

Iain shot him a piercing look. 'Who said anything about going in alone?'

His lieutenant returned the look and held it. 'You've got a plan.'

'Aye. Have all the men come here to the hall. I need to talk to them.'

As Dougal hastened to obey, Ban stepped in. 'I mean to do my part in this, my lord, whatever you decide upon.'

Iain nodded grimly. 'You shall, good brother. I swear it.'

Ashlynn had no idea how long they travelled or of where they went, her mind being too full of dread for Iain. Recalling the day she and Ban had ridden out with Callum she guessed that it had been no deer on the hillside. Glengarron had been watched. Moreover, for the enemy to get so close argued that they had help, somewhere local to use as a base. A man like Iain had enemies. Had the Norman been able to exploit that? The more she thought about it the likelier it seemed.

Her captors rode until they came to a lonely grange. It was an imposing building and clearly the property of a man of some substance, but the grey stone walls

and high arrow slit windows gave it a dour and forbidding aspect. The cavalcade clattered through an
arched gateway and into the courtyard beyond. There
Ashlynn was pulled off the horse and taken into the
building. Thence she was led up a spiral stone staircase to the topmost floor and thrust into a small turret
room. Then the door was slammed shut behind her and
locked. Footsteps retreated down the stairs.

Trembling she massaged her bruised wrist and
looked around. The room was cold and gloomy, the
only light filtering in through one small window set
high in the wall, and was devoid of all furnishing save
for a thin straw pallet and, in one corner, a slop bucket.
The narrow door was iron bound oak and had no handle
on her side. There was to be no escape from her prison.
For some time she paced the floor in helpless rage but
eventually gave it up to sink disconsolately on to the
straw pallet.

Some time later she heard more footsteps on the
stairs and then the sound of a key in the lock. Ashlynn
sprang to her feet and moved away toward the far wall.
The door opened and then a man stepped into the room.
Her heart leapt towards her throat. Fitzurse!

He surveyed her for a moment and then smiled
faintly. 'We meet again, my lady.'

He advanced a step or two and a second man
followed him in. He was younger than Fitzurse by about
ten years or so and shorter by a head. She had an impression of a stocky and slightly corpulent frame clad
in a stained tunic. Lank and greasy brown hair hung
about a stubbled face whose pale blue gaze was now

fixed on their prisoner. Then he smiled, revealing stained teeth.

'So this is McAlpin's woman.'

Fitzurse shot him a sideways glance. 'That's right.'

'I'd heard tell she was fair but the tales didna do her justice.'

Ashlynn swallowed, clutching the edges of her cloak, and her gaze returned to Fitzurse.

'Allow me to introduce our host, Sir Robert Fraser. He's been looking forward to meeting you.'

'That I have,' replied the other.

Fighting down a sense of foreboding she forced herself to remain calm.

'Why have you brought me here? What do you want?'

'I want Iain McAlpin,' Fitzurse replied. 'With your help I'm going to have him too.'

'You have no right to pursue him here. This land is not under your king's jurisdiction.'

'A minor point, and one that need not trouble us.'

'Where is this place?'

'Dungavan,' replied Fraser. 'Does the name mean anything to you, my lady?'

'No, should it?'

'Perhaps not,' he returned, 'though you'll be hearing a lot more of it in due course.'

'You speak in riddles.'

'Like my lord Fitzurse, I have a bone to pick with your husband too.' He gave her another nasty smile. 'It's concerned with kidnapping and extortion.'

Warning bells went off in her mind as the words revived a memory, but before she could identify it precisely he went on.

'I've waited a long time to even the score but, as the saying goes, everything comes to him who waits.'

'What do you mean to do?'

'Tomorrow my enemy will die, but before he does he'll know I take his wife.'

Ashlynn's stomach knotted and only with a supreme effort of will did she force herself to meet his gaze.

'You will never take his wife.'

He laughed softly, a sound that chilled her to the core. 'Your loyalty does you credit, my lady, but after a night in my bed you might change your mind.'

'I doubt that.'

The pale eyes hardened. 'You are haughty, but that will soon change, I promise you—if my lord Fitzurse doesn't humble your pride first.'

Ashlynn's heart hammered in her breast and she darted a swift look at the Norman. He saw it and nodded.

'Ah, yes. We have unfinished business you and I.'

'We have no business of any kind.'

'You're wrong. We were interrupted as I recall, but I always finish what I start.'

'Finish it now if you like,' said Fraser. 'It makes no odds to me. I'll have her later after all.'

The icy knot in her stomach grew larger as the walls of the room began to close in. There was only one door and they were between it and her.

'No,' replied Fitzurse. 'I'll finish it tomorrow when I take her in front of McAlpin. He can watch—before I cut his throat.'

'I think it will be you who dies tomorrow,' said Ashlynn. 'You are no match for him in single combat.'

'Single combat? How naïve. Say rather a ring of steel.'

'I might have guessed you'd resort to treachery,' she replied. 'But Iain won't fall easily into a trap.'

He moved towards the door, pausing on the threshold. 'He will.'

'You seem very sure of that.'

'I am sure. After all, you are the bait.'

They left her then, locking the door behind them. Ashlynn leaned back against the wall, trembling in every limb. The tears she had controlled before welled behind her eyelids. Iain would ride to meet his old enemy tomorrow but he would not ride away. This time he would die. She knew then that if he did she would die too and by her own hand. Rather a swift death with him than a lifetime without him, or dishonour at the hands of his enemies. In that moment she understood why Eloise had ended her life. The knowledge gave her courage. If it came to the choice she knew she would do no less.

No one else came to her prison after that and she was offered neither food nor water, though in truth she could not have eaten anything. Gradually the light faded and the cold intensified. Ashlynn wrapped her cloak closer about her and curled up on the straw pallet. As evening turned to night she began to doze intermittently but every time she closed her eyes she saw Iain's face and the feeling of sick dread increased. Miserable and shivering she waited for the dawn.

Having gone over the plan in detail Iain dismissed his men and repaired to the roof terrace, needing some time alone. He stood by the stone parapet, looking out over the darkening glen but in truth it was not the hills that

he saw. Somewhere out there was Ashlynn. The thought
of her fear and despair tormented him, but it wasn't that
alone. For all his calm words to Ban and the rest his
heart was riven by doubt. Had they hurt her? Had
Fitzurse sought to finish what he had begun before?
Would he do to Ashlynn what he had done to Eloise?
Iain's fists clenched and he drew in a deep breath of cold
air to combat the nausea that knotted his stomach. The
Norman was ruthless and cruel and he knew there was
no surer way to hurt his foe than this.

'Dear God, let her be unharmed,' he murmured. 'It
took so long for me to find her. Let me not lose her now.
Let me not lose the hope she brings.'

With a bitter sense of irony he remembered his
promise to forswear all thought of revenge. *'Unless our
paths cross.'* And now their paths had crossed. Was
Fitzurse always to be his evil nemesis? Was it part of
some divine plan? Well then, he would not seek to cir-
cumvent it. Tomorrow he would ride to meet his enemy,
and his destiny.

Chapter Thirteen

The circle of stones stood on the hill beyond Glengarron. Higher than a man and twice as wide, the silent monoliths remained unchanged by the vagaries of time or weather though the race that built them had long since vanished. Their brooding presence commanded the hill top. All around in every direction open moor land stretched away beneath a louring sky, the sere heath dark and sombre beneath a chill wind. The only other sounds were of creaking saddle leather and muffled hoof falls on peaty soil. As they drew nigh the place, Ashlynn saw with sick despair that Fitzurse and Fraser had chosen well. Here their enemy would be completely alone, isolated from any form of help. They, on the other hand, had with them a dozen armed men, murderous odds by any standard. The party reined in and came to a halt some yards outside the ring of stone.

Fraser looked around at the empty heath. 'He's not here.'

'Then we wait,' replied Fitzurse.

'He will not come. It would be madness and he knows it.'

The Norman glanced at Ashlynn. 'He'll come.'

She forced herself to meet his eye, regarding him with cold contempt. 'He will not be so easy to kill.'

'On the contrary, I expect it will be very easy, in the end.' Seeing Ashlynn's cheeks turn a shade paler, Fitzurse smiled appreciatively. His cold gaze stripped her, bringing back other memories. 'I'll say one thing for McAlpin. He always had good taste in women. It's the one thing we share.'

Fraser returned the smile. 'The one thing we're all going to share.'

Sickened with disgust she turned away, refusing to dignify the gibe with a reply. As she did so her gaze fell on the lone horseman approaching out of the east. Her heart began to thump painfully hard. Even from a distance there could be no mistaking the dark-clad figure on the dapple grey stallion.

'Iain,' she murmured.

In that second she knew that she loved him, unconditionally and beyond all reason. He was her lord. There could be no other as long as she lived. In that moment of awful clarity she knew the sublime terror, the awful vulnerability of loving and all its aching need.

Following her gaze Fitzurse saw the advancing figure and his smile widened as he glanced at Fraser.

'There we are. I told you he'd come.'

He turned then to his men and ordered them to dismount. Two of them dragged Ashlynn off her horse and hands like iron closed round her arms as they flanked her, dragging her forward to stand in clear view, while the rest ranged themselves in a semi-circle behind their leader who alone remained mounted. All eyes watched the oncoming rider.

Fitzurse spoke quietly, never turning his head. 'Let him get closer before you shoot. There must be no mistakes. I want him alive.'

De Vardes nodded. 'There will be no mistake, my lord.'

For the first time Ashlynn noticed the crossbow he held at his side and her throat dried as she realised the intent. When the quarry was close enough for a clear shot De Vardes would use it to cripple and bring him down. Once Iain was injured and unable to defend himself, they would take him prisoner. Then they would exact their final revenge. Panic stricken she tried to break free but the restraining grip on her arms only tightened in response, holding her still. Seeing it, Fraser laughed.

'It's no use, my lady. Nothing can save Glengarron now. Two hours hence his head will adorn my gates.'

Sick at heart she could only wait and watch as the man she loved rode towards his death.

Iain approached at a leisurely pace, his gaze taking in every detail of the scene ahead, undeceived by the apparently quiet demeanour of the waiting men. He mentally numbered fourteen, including Fitzurse. Three stood off to the side, holding the horses, the rest were arrayed in a semi-circle, watching him come. All their attention was focused on him. It was what he had counted on.

As he drew nearer his gaze never left the waiting Normans. He knew full well Fitzurse had no intention of meeting him in single combat; most likely the plan would be to bring him down and capture him alive. Everything depended on what happened in the next couple of minutes. Even as the thought formed itself he saw with silent satisfaction the several dark-clad figures that rose like wraiths from the heather behind the Norman force. Seconds later the three men who had been holding the horses fell silently with their throats cut, never knowing what hit them. Iain smiled grimly. Unaware of what was taking place behind, Fitzurse kept his eye fixed on the approaching horseman.

'Get ready, De Vardes.'

The Norman raised the crossbow and took careful aim. Ashlynn screamed a warning. The bolt flew and seconds later the horseman lurched in the saddle and then slipped sideways. Fighting deadly faintness she could only stare at the spot and the riderless grey stallion now standing with trailing reins.

'Got him.' De Vardes was quietly exultant.

'Excellent,' said Fitzurse. 'Now bring him in.'

'Aye, my lord.'

De Vardes cast aside the bow and drew his sword. 'You three men, come with me.'

Ashlynn watched in helpless horror. In a short time now Iain would be their prisoner and they would kill him, but not quickly, dear God not quickly.

In torment she saw De Vardes and his companions advance, but they had taken no more than half-a-dozen paces before they checked, frozen in mid-stride. Then they dropped like stones. Only then did she see the crossbow quarrels embedded between their shoulder blades. Before her brain could take it in she heard a warning cry. More thuds followed and the hold on her arms slackened as the two men on either side of her fell away with cries of pain, bolts sunk deep in their ribs. Seconds later the heath all around erupted with living forms, dark clad, their faces stained with peat as though the womb of earth had just delivered them. Taken totally by surprise the Normans had not even time to draw their weapons before the Scots were upon them with sword and dirk. What followed was brief, bloody and brutal. Ashlynn gasped, looking around in shocked bewilderment. Before her frightened eyes a savage figure seized Fraser by the hair and yanked his head back. He had time for one strangled cry before the naked dagger slit his throat from ear to ear.

Hard by Fitzurse fought to control his plunging horse, realising too late how he had been tricked, even as his furious gaze took in the scale of the disaster. Then, seeing the day was lost, he turned and spurred away. Off to the left of the fleeing figure Ban lifted his bow and took aim. The quarrel flew. A moment later the horse screamed and fell, crashing on to its side in the heather and pinning its rider to the ground.

'Good shot,' said Dougal. 'For a Sassenach, that is.'

Ban returned him a cool smile, never taking his eyes off the struggling figure on the ground. His hand went to the hilt of the blade at his side. 'Say the word and I'll finish him.'

'No.' The Scot turned to the men beside them. 'Bring him here—alive!'

Trembling with reaction, Ashlynn looked around in stunned disbelief, her mind unable to accept what her eyes were telling her. Somehow, in a matter of minutes, the Norman force had been annihilated. Her gaze came to rest again on the riderless stallion standing some hundred yards off, and her cheeks paled.

'Iain!'

Then she was running, her heart sick with dread, knowing what she must find. But before she got halfway there another dark-clad figure rose out of the concealing heather and caught hold of her. Ashlynn shrieked, kicking and struggling, fighting furiously. It took several moments before she recognised the voice speaking her name. Then she froze and looked up, seeing his face for the first time.

'Iain?'

Half-fainting with relief she felt him draw her close, crushing her close to his breast as though he could never let her go, and for a moment neither of them spoke. Then he looked down into her face.

'I thought I'd lost you. I thought...' He took a deep breath, summoning the courage to ask the question uppermost in his mind. 'Are you all right, lass? Did he hurt you? Did he...?'

'No.' She shook her head. 'I'm not hurt.'

He experienced the sensation of heartfelt relief. 'Thank God. Every moment since he took you from me I've lived in dread of what he might do.'

'He was saving his revenge for today. He and Fraser both.'

'Fraser! So that's who was helping them.'

'He spoke of a long-standing grudge.'

'I'm sure he did. 'Twas he I kidnapped once when his father reneged on an agreement.'

'But what of you, my lord? Are you not hurt?' She

held him at arm's length, her anxious gaze searching for signs of injury. 'De Vardes shot you.'

'I let them think he had.'

He smiled down at her and then his mouth was on hers in a passionate and lingering kiss. When he eventually drew away it was to see tears on her face.

'They meant to kill you, Iain. They meant to make me watch…' Her voice caught on a sob.

'Ach, lass, I'm sorry.' He drew her to his breast until her sobs quieted a little. 'You should not have had to suffer for my fault.'

'It doesn't matter now. His plan failed. It's over.'

Iain glanced towards the waiting men. 'No, lass. Not yet.'

She looked up quickly. 'What do you mean?'

'There's one more thing I have to do.'

Her heart beat a little faster and with a sense of dread she followed his gaze to where his men stood. Then she recognised their prisoner.

'Iain, you promised…'

'I promised not to seek him out and I have kept my word. He has sought me.'

'That is true, but even so I beg you…'

'This must be settled, Ashlynn, and I mean to see that it is,' he replied.

The tone was implacable and she knew that no words of hers would change his mind. They walked back to where Dougal and the others waited. In their midst stood Fitzurse, his hands bound. Seeing his sister, Ban hastened to greet her with a glad smile, folding her in his arms. Then, as he glanced down and saw her tear-stained face, his joy faded a little.

'Dear God, are you all right, Ash? Did this scum hurt you?'

'No, he did nothing, beyond holding me prisoner.'

'I thank heaven for it.' Ban threw a cold glance at the captive. 'But this vermin will pay for his crimes in due course.'

'Aye, he will,' replied Iain.

'It is your right, my lord,' said Ban, 'for yours is the prior claim. I acknowledge it and yield in obedience to the duty I owe you. But let his payment take into account the destruction of Heslingfield and the slaying of our kin.'

'It will, good brother, I swear it.' Iain looked at Fitzurse and then at Dougal, nodding toward the ring of stones. 'Take him in there.'

His men moved into the ancient monument and formed up in a large inner circle leaving Fitzurse at its centre. Then each one drew his sword. The Norman darted swift looks around him but could find no way out. Moreover, the faces that met him there were cold and hard, entirely without pity or remorse. He licked dry lips. The Scottish laird strolled into the circle, a naked sword in his hand. He halted a few yards away.

'Cut his bonds.'

When Dougal had obliged, Iain thrust the sword into the earth and left it quivering there. Then he drew his own blade and looked at Fitzurse.

'Defend yourself.'

The tone was soft but there could be no mistaking the intention behind. Fitzurse edged forward, his gaze darting between the sword and his waiting opponent, half-expecting some trick. It never came; the other man made no move towards him. Then his hand closed on the hilt and the weapon was his.

The two men circled each other and Ashlynn caught her breath as Fitzurse rushed forward. Iain side-stepped, parrying the thrust easily. The blades engaged again as the Norman attacked with a rain of fierce blows. Each time his sword was met and turned aside. Then, without warning, Iain lunged. Too fast for the eye to see, his blade caught his opponent across the upper arm. The only sign of its passing was the sudden red stain that bloomed through the rent sleeve of the leather tunic. Fitzurse glared at it and then retaliated with another series of savage cuts. Again they were turned aside. Another swift lunge and Iain's sword drew a deeper gash along the other arm. Biting back the cry of pain the Norman gave a little ground, circling once more, warier now as he looked for an opening. Then he darted in again. This time Iain gave ground. Fitzurse smiled and went after him. Too late he saw the feint. The Scottish sword opened a gash along his ribs. Fitzurse snarled, clapping a hand to his side, feeling there the sticky warmth of blood. In fury and desperation he laid on anew, succeeding in driving the other man back by the sheer ferocity of the attack. Sparks leapt from the edges of the blades.

However, no matter how hard he tried he could not penetrate his enemy's defence and his sword met only steel or empty air. Another cut appeared on his left arm. He realised then that the Scot was playing with him, meaning to weaken him gradually, until he could step in and deliver the *coup de grâce*. Fitzurse knew a moment of panic. The wounds he had sustained were bleeding freely and the pain increasing. Sweat broke out on his forehead. He had fought many opponents but never one as fast or as skilled.

'Why do you not end it?' he demanded.

'I'm not ready to end it yet,' the Scot replied.

Fitzurse reeled away towards the edge of the circle, seeking blindly for some means of escape but was met with a ring of steel. Seeing there was nothing else for it, he turned and stumbled back towards his enemy. Iain let him come. The Norman laid on again, but his blows were wilder now and careless costing him a slash to the leg. He cried out as blood poured from the wound, staining the grass at his feet.

Ashlynn drew in a sharp breath, her gaze fixed on Iain's face. It was utterly remorseless, the face of a warrior whose hand wielded death, a face that fascinated and appalled. Beside her Ban never moved, riveted by the spectacle before them, understanding now exactly what he was watching.

It went on for some time until Fitzurse, bleeding from a dozen cuts, sank to his knees, exhausted, his expression filled with loathing.

'End it then, damn you.'

Ashlynn trembled, waiting for Iain to deal the death blow. It did not come. Instead he lowered his sword, regarding his enemy with contempt.

'I'll not take your worthless life,' he said then. 'I'll leave your fate to a higher authority.'

'What do you mean?'

'My king is well acquainted with your evil deeds already, and his views on those who violate the peace of his realm are well known. You're going to Dunfermline.' He turned away and gestured to Dougal and Fergus. 'Get him on a horse.'

Fitzurse paled, knowing the swift death he'd looked for would not be forthcoming. In its place was something far worse. The realisation of how much worse filled him with desperate fury. He struggled to his feet and lifting the sword rushed at his enemy's unguarded back.

Ashlynn screamed a warning. Iain spun round, sword raised to block the coming blow. As he did so Fitzurse's injured leg gave way, throwing him off balance and on to the thrusting point. The Norman froze in his tracks, hanging there, an expression of shock on his face, before both legs buckled and he fell.

Ashlynn looked on in shuddering disbelief. Then she ran towards her husband and a moment later was in his arms. He held her close and for the space of several heartbeats neither one spoke.

'I'll not pretend to be sorry that he's dead,' he said at last, 'but I truly intended to let Malcolm deal with him finally.'

'It wasn't your fault. Fitzurse was treacherous to the end.' Her voice caught on a sob. 'I thought he'd killed you.'

'But for your warning he might have done. I thank you, lass.'

'I can scarcely believe he's dead, that it's over now.'

'It's over. Today the ghosts of the past have been laid.' Even as he spoke the words he knew them for truth. The burden of hatred had been lifted along with all its corrosive power. Eloise could rest in peace for his promise to her was fulfilled, and he could move on. 'Fitzurse can harm us no more. Or anyone else for that matter.'

'I thank God for it, and for keeping you safe.'

'I thank Him too, lass.'

'If you had been slain today I would have died afterwards. If you were gone there would be no point in living, for without you I could never be truly alive.'

For a moment he was quite still, his heart full. The dark gaze burned into her own, intent, seeking the answer to an unspoken question. Ashlynn knew immediately what it was.

'I love you, Iain. More than my own life.'

'And I you, lass. When you were taken from me I finally understood how much. I have lived in dread since then lest history should repeat itself.' He drew a shuddering breath. 'But God was merciful this time.'

'Yes, He was.'

'It's a gift I value above all else. You are most precious to me, Ashlynn.'

'As you are to me, my lord.'

'My love and my wife,' he replied. Then he drew her close in a much more intimate embrace making further speech impossible.

Epilogue

Ashlynn sat on a sun-warmed rock by the side of the
burn and turned her face to the blue vault of the sky
where a lark was singing. The liquid notes spilled joy
on to the receiving earth and seeped into the soul like a
healing benediction. For a while she followed the
progress of the bird until it was no more than a dark dot
on the edge of heaven. She smiled and brought her gaze
back to earth, letting it range along the wooded slope
of the glen, taking in the new green on every branch and
twig, breathing the scent of grass and loam where
splashes of yellow and white announced clumps of
celandine and anemone. In the distant fields cattle
grazed and new lambs frolicked. The land had thrown
off the icy shackles of winter and everything around
seemed to rejoice in the knowledge.

She was so engrossed in the scene that she failed to
hear the soft hoof falls on the turf behind her, only
becoming aware of the approaching horseman when
his mount snorted. Startled from her reverie she looked

round quickly and then smiled, getting to her feet. The dapple grey stallion stopped a few yards away, its rider surveying her keenly. Then he returned the smile.

'This is a most pleasant surprise.'

'Indeed it is. I did not expect you back from the village so soon, my lord.'

'My business there did not take as long as I feared it might.'

He brought his leg over the front of the saddle and dismounted, letting the rein fall so that the horse might graze. Then he came to join his wife, sliding an arm about her waist. 'I swear you get more beautiful each time I see you.'

'This is blatant flattery.'

'Not so.' He bent and kissed her soft mouth. ''Tis fully two hours since last I set eyes on you and I can avouch that your beauty has grown.'

Ashlynn laughed. 'My beauty, or your lust, my lord?'

'All right, my lust.' He seized hold of her with a teasing growl and, ignoring her startled shriek, took a much longer and more intimate kiss that sent the blood coursing through her veins. 'But what are you doing here, lass? Don't you know how dangerous it is to walk out alone?'

'It is too fine a day to be shut up indoors. Besides, there is no danger in walking alone in Glengarron. It is most strongly guarded.'

'Glengarron is especially dangerous,' he replied. 'Have you not heard about the reputation of its lord?'

'I have heard some rumours about that. Should I be worried?'

'At this moment you should be very worried.' He

swept her up and then took another lusty kiss. Breathless and laughing Ashlynn struggled in vain. The dark eyes gleamed. 'It's no use to try and escape, lass. You're in my power now and I'm minded to have my way with you.'

'Alas, the rumours are true then.'

His lips brushed her cheek and neck and throat sending a delightful shiver along her skin. 'Aye, they are, as you're about to discover.'

Ashlynn giggled. 'I beg you will be gentle, my lord.'

'Gentle? Why so?'

'Because I'm going to have a baby.'

The words stopped him in his tracks and all amusement faded. For a moment he stared at her, thunderstruck. 'A baby? When?'

'Next winter.'

'Ashlynn, are you sure?'

'Quite sure.'

A slow grin lit his face. 'That's wonderful!' Then another thought occurred to him and he regarded her with concern. 'But you should have told me before, lass. I wouldn't have been so rough. Have I hurt you?'

'No, you haven't hurt me.'

Feeling somewhat relieved he set her down gently, letting his gaze travel the length of her but could detect no sign of the child beneath the smooth surface of her gown. 'How long before it shows?'

'Not long. Another month perhaps.'

'How long have you known?'

'I have suspected for a while, but I wanted to be sure before I told you.'

He took her hand and raised it to his lips. Ashlynn regarded him askance.

'Nothing terrible will happen if you kiss me again, Iain.'

Nothing loath he accepted the invitation. Immediately he felt the familiar spark leap between them but he controlled it now, unwilling to do anything that might harm her or their child. And so the kiss was gentle and tender, conveying without words the thoughts of his heart. Then they sat together on the rock, enjoying the solitude and the sunshine and the secret knowledge they now shared.

'If our child is a son I would have him grow up to be a warrior like his father,' she said. 'If a daughter, then fair and wise.'

'Aye,' he replied, 'and with her mother's spirit.'

'I'm not sure that's such a good idea.'

'Not so. I would not have a milk-and-water maid in her place.'

'Whatever this child grows up to be, it will know its parents' love.'

His face grew serious and he nodded. 'Aye, lass, so it will.'

Having spent his youth finding out what fatherhood was not, he had a more than fair idea of what it should be. It was a role that, hitherto, he had only considered from a distance. Now it was about to become reality. The notion both scared and delighted him.

Unable to follow his thought Ashlynn eyed him quizzically.

'Will you mind very much if the child is a girl?'

Drawn back to the present he returned her gaze. 'No, lass. I won't mind as long as you and she are well.' He grinned. 'Besides, there is time aplenty to sire sons.'

She laughed. 'You sound very certain of that, my lord.'

'I am.' He bent and brushed her mouth with his. 'For I could never long resist the enchantment you have cast. I think the spell will not be broken while I live.'

The sun was past its zenith when they strolled back to the quietly grazing horse. Having lifted her on to the saddle he mounted and turned for home, keeping the grey to a gentle easy walk. Ashlynn relaxed against him, enjoying the warmth of his chest against her back, secure in the protective circle of his arm. Here, with him, in the glory of the spring sunlight the shadows of the past receded. All around them new life quickened like the child in her womb giving promise and hope for the future, a future that, not so long ago, she could never have dreamed would be hers.

Unable to follow her thoughts Iain bent and kissed her cheek. 'Happy?'

'Very happy. And you, my lord?'

'More than I could ever have hoped,' he said. And meant it.

* * * * *

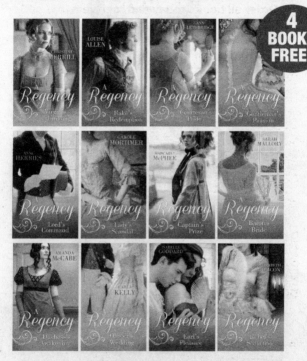